DYING
for the
Christmas Rose

CAROLE OTTESEN

Also by Carole Ottesen:

The New American Garden

Gardening with Style

Ornamental Grasses, the Amber Wave

The Native Plant Primer

The Herbal Epicure

A Guide to Smithsonian Gardens

Murder House, a Cape Breton Mystery

Translations from the German:

Berry Gardening

Bonsai

Orchids

Heartfelt thanks to Jan Gibson, Ruth Snyder, Nancy Flinn, and Judith Tyler for editorial suggestions, to Andrea Ottesen for assistance with design, and to Richard Tyler of Pine Knot Farms for the spectacular photos of hellebores on the cover and in this book.

"Plant hunting rarely involves serious climbing; mostly it is marching and scrambling. But the risk of losing one's way, or being injured by falling rocks, or tumbling over a cliff, or getting into a fix, is an ever-present menace. Of course, such risks become a part of your life; you do not think of them, though common prudence makes you careful. Your aim is to be bold, but not rash; cautious, but not fearful."

F. Kingdon Ward *Plant Hunting on the Edge of the World*.

PROLOGUE

If he had lived, Ted Adkins might have gone on to join the grand tradition of plant hunters. Of course, most people—even most gardeners—have never heard of the great plant hunters. Names like F. Kingdom Ward or David Douglas, let alone Tate Adkins, are not exactly household words. It's only in this rarified little world of the really hard-core horticulturists and gardeners that plant hunters are venerated.

And in this little world of plant people—hort heads, hortisexuals, plant nerds, whatever you want to call them—Tate Adkins was a big shot. Horticultural societies and botanic gardens clamored to hear him speak. He was always flying off somewhere—England, Germany, New Zealand—to talk about his work.

Exactly how he got to be the king frog in this little pond is something to which I have given a great deal of thought. Because, basically, he got a degree in horticulture. Then, he started breeding plants–just like lots of horticulturists do. He specialized in hellebores and he does have some good ones, but nothing truly amazing. Of course, he was smart, but so are most people in his field. And I am certainly more intelligent than he was.

At first I couldn't figure it. I even paid for one of those internet searches on him. I got a few nuggets out of that, but for the longest time I didn't get it.

And then one night, at an after hours gathering during a Hardy Perennial Association meeting, it hit me. Tate's noisy little clique gathered after the day's events in a bar a few doors down from the hotel where our meeting was being held.

I was there, too. Not that anybody invited me to come along, or, once I was there, asked me to join them. Or waved me over. Or so much as glanced at me.

Even though I had been a member of Hardy Perennials for two years, nobody paid me the slightest bit of attention. It was like I was invisible. So I watched them. Openly. I just sat there, sipping my white wine and watching them. I actually wanted someone to notice me staring at them. They never did.

Mostly, I watched Tate. I found him very attractive. He wasn't handsome in the usual way, but he made the absolute most of what he had. He kept himself trim. His skin was tanned from working out of doors. He had good eyes—clear Irish blue and he had a great hair cut. I swear he had his hair cut so that a lock of black hair would slip down over his forehead.

He dressed well. Not in traditional business style with a coat and tie. No, he always wore jeans. Nice, clean, tight-fitting jeans. But he wore them with bright blue shirts that matched his eyes. They were obviously expensive and always professionally laundered.

It struck me that everything about him was the best he could make it. And then it came to me. It was so simple and obvious. The thing that took him a good part of the distance was smart packaging. That, and his air of supreme confidence. He presented himself as he wished to be seen. Attractive. Smart. Knowledgeable. And, yes, superior. With a memorable name. Tate Adkins is a distinctive name.

Not many people know that his real first name is Ronald. Ronnie Adkins just doesn't have the same cachet, does it?

Packaging and appearance. It made him stand out and that made all the difference. That's what I've learned from him.

When Backenbrook Arboretum organized a trip to Slovenia to collect hellebores, I signed on. I had to pay my own way, of course. Backenbrook sent Tate free of charge. Okay, I know, I know. He works there and collecting species hellebores in the mountains of Slovenia was tailor made for him. Backenbrook needed new blood for a series of hellebores they were going to launch for the popular garden market. Tate was going to develop them.

So, yes, it was logical for Tate to go on that particular expedition. But of the seven horticulturists who work at Backenbrook, it seems like it was always Tate Adkins chosen for the plum trips—with all expenses paid by the Arboretum.

On that expedition to Slovenia, I got to observe Tate Adkins a bit more. I'll say this for him. He had balls. When we were looking for hellebores in those mountains, you really did have to be careful. It's not like there were guard rails along the trails or a rescue squad ready to save you if you slipped off the path. You were on your own on those trails and some of them were pretty dicey.

Mostly, it was just difficult walking because there were loose rocks and it wouldn't have taken much to sprain an ankle. But every now and then the trails would narrow way down until there was not a lot between you and eternity. In those places, it was such a long way down that whenever I looked over an edge, I got dizzy.

"The Christmas rose, *Helleborus niger*, with its pure white flower and poisonous black root, has an aura of good and evil. The meaning of the name is lost in time, but it is thought to be "food to kill."

Elizabeth Lawrence *A Southern Garden*

1

Mim Fitz showered, washed and blew her hair dry, and changed into the soft white kimono Tate had brought her from Japan. Now she leaned back against the bank of pillows on the Chinese daybed. Of dark, ornately carved rosewood, the daybed was an antique she'd spotted at Terry's Treasure Trove, a great warehouse full of antiques and collectable junk on Maryland's Eastern Shore. Terry, a skinny man with a carrot-colored goatee, said it was an opium bed. Perhaps because of that, she fell in love with it and bought it on the spot. And luck was with her. Although it was a good eight inches longer than a regular twin bed, it had fitted with only a hairsbreadth to spare against the back wall of what was once the sleeping porch of her hundred-year-old house.

It really wasn't a sleeping porch anymore. A few years ago, the installation of floor to ceiling, energy efficient windows had not only winterized the space, it turned the old porch into a sitting room with a million dollar view over the wildflowers, ferns and hellebores in her shade garden.

That view was what gave her the inspiration to install floor to ceiling mirrors on the back wall to reflect the garden and the wide spreading branches of a mature bigleaf magnolia tree. When the magnolia bloomed in early summer, the effect was magical. Lounging on the Chinese bed made her feel like she was in a tree house, up and away from everything.

The sleeping porch was well used. Ensconced on the daybed, she read and talked on the phone. With the advent of Tate in her life, the room became the place where they hung out.

In September, just over two months ago, they had U-Hauled his furniture here. Now this was his house as well as hers.

With a kind of amazed gratitude, she realized that ever since she met Tate, she felt like she had awakened in a romance novel—no, not a romance novel–a bodice ripper—and she was its lusty heroine. How had this happened? For the decade of her marriage, sex had been so dull and mechanical, she would rather have ironed shirts. Now she could hardly wait for Tate to return and the evening to begin.

He was due back any minute. He had spent the week at a conference at Stanford. Right now, he should be on his way home from the airport.

Downstairs in the dining room, the table was set. Four tall white tapers waited to be lit. Dinner, *coq au vin*, was warming in the oven. A tossed salad waited in the fridge. And here, next to the Chinese daybed, were two wine glasses. An uncorked bottle of Sauvignon Blanc sat ready in a cooler on a small table.

She heard what sounded like the crunch of gravel in the driveway. She listened. If it were Tate, after the clunk of a car door shutting, there would be a pause and then she would hear the click of the front door opening. She waited for the familiar sounds.

Yes! The key turned in the lock with a click. The door opened with just the smallest squeak and then there was a gentle thud as it closed. He was home!

"Tate?" she called as she imagined him hanging up his coat in the front closet, setting down his suitcase on the foyer floor. He probably hadn't heard her. She pictured him rifling through the mail on the hall table.

She waited. Perhaps he didn't know she was upstairs. She called out again. Maybe he couldn't hear her. But then, finally, she thought she heard a footfall on the stair.

"Tate?" There was no answer. Another footfall. And another. He still didn't answer. Surely he could hear her now.

Why didn't he answer? Something was wrong.

At the sound of steps ascending the staircase, an oddly familiar chill settled over her. Why? She couldn't remember why, but she knew this had happened before. There was a reason for it, but she couldn't remember why. If he would just answer her! She thought about calling out to him again, but something stopped her.

She knew somehow that the thing that was happening had happened before. Something bad. She couldn't quite remember, but she knew she didn't want it to happen and there was no way to stop it.

She listened, mesmerized as the sound of footsteps on the stair became heavier, closer. She hoped it was Tate. No. The footsteps were much too heavy for Tate. It was not Tate. It couldn't be Tate.

Now she remembered. She went rigid with fear. It couldn't be Tate!

She sat very still, not wanting to see, but unable to close her eyes. She backed into the far corner of the Chinese daybed and tried to make herself very small. Now she knew what was coming.

The steps sounded in the hall, measured and heavy. They crossed the threshold into the bedroom and paused. Blood pounded in her ears. Terror washed over her.

Very slowly now, the heavy footsteps continued across the bedroom floor. They were heading toward the sleeping porch. She backed into the wall, hugging a pillow to her chest. She held her breath. She didn't want to look, but her eyes were riveted on the doorway. She felt powerless to avert her gaze.

She knew exactly what she would see, but it always shocked her. And then it was there and she couldn't take her eyes away from it. The dark figure halted in the doorway and raised a hand, dangling a single bloody glove. Its face was featureless except for a pair of glittering, eyes that bore into her, as if beseeching her…to do what? She didn't want to know.

2

Mim Fitz woke up in a cold sweat, sobbing. She'd dreamed the dream again—the one that began in warm memory and ended as a nightmare. After her sobs subsided, she lay quietly for a very long time, staring at the gray rectangle of doorway that led from her bedroom to the sleeping porch. It was starting to get light. She could just make out the leafless branches of the magnolia.

In the year after his death, she had dreamt of Tate almost nightly. Now, it had been months since the last time she'd had the nightmare. She knew very well what had brought this on.

She rolled over and made it out in the dim light. There it was, her red suitcase. It had been an extravagant purchase she'd made on the press trip to Helsinki. She loved the red suitcase for the memories it brought, and liked using it because it was chic and unique. But today the sight of it, packed full, zipped up and ready to roll, started butterflies whirling in her stomach.

Today, the first dark morning of December, she was to leave for the Horticultural Writers conference in Philadelphia. If she weren't going to the conference, she could roll over and go back to sleep. But she had to go. Because one evening, she had sat at the computer very late into the night and made reservations.

An email had announced a Horticultural Writers conference. The focus of the conference was on hellebores or *Helleborus*, the botanical name for the evergreen Lenten and Christmas roses that bloom in winter.

Her first reaction had been shock. This conference would bring together the people who bred and worked with hellebores. All of the eastern growers would be there, if not speaking, then in their booths at the trade show. The only one missing would be Tate Adkins.

Mim had begun seeing Tate a little over two years ago. They met at a Rock Garden Society meeting. She had been researching an article on shooting stars for her column in *Washington Home* magazine. She was the garden editor. He was speaking on "Small Bulbs for the Rock Garden." He had been so knowledgeable, she had been amazed to learn his real specialty was hellebores.

Just over two months before his accident, they had begun combining households. She looked back on the time they had been together as a rosy, glowing interval wedged between periods of dull loneliness. Now, after almost two years, it was always startling to consider how little time they had actually spent together. If you counted it in days, their being together had been so painfully short, it was astonishing how immense, how world changing it had been. Not even a hundred days! It had been a golden period that dominated her consciousness. and, sometimes, defied reason. A ringing phone could still elicit a momentary thrill of anticipation before it was doused by cold reality.

"Tate is dead," she said out loud. When they found his body, he was still clutching a hellebore and a glove.

The image of that glove and the phantom's pierceing eyes haunted her.

Tate's death was still difficult to grasp. At the time, it had been unbelievable. After the first shock wore off, she had walked around in a rage, furious at a man who could risk his life for plants. She cursed him and she cursed his hellebores.

After the rage, she had simply avoided the whole subject of hellebores—until the very night she got the email announcing the conference. Mim was not at all a superstitious person. Yet the confluence of the timing and subject of the conference and her particular mindset that night—a sense that there was something she had to do—decided it.

She went to the Horticultural Writers' site and registered for the conference—and not just the conference. She also signed on for the extra day of workshops. It was a way of honoring Tate and what might have been.

That's what she told herself when she charged the conference to her credit card and reserved a hotel room. That's what she thought every time she saw four days blocked out in her appointment book.

Mostly, she pushed the whole reeling ambivalence of attending the conference to the darkest back corner of her mind. She had awakened the next morning and every morning thereafter and hadn't changed a thing until she knew that it was too late to back out.

Despite being in her cups the night she signed up, she had been logical enough to anticipate cold feet. To make it impossible to back out, she had prepaid everything. She knew herself well enough to understand that her frugal nature wouldn't let her back out of anything that didn't offer full refunds.

In addition to the conference and the workshops having been prepaid for two months, as of today, it was too late to cancel her hotel room. What's more, she had already bought an Amtrak ticket to Philadelphia online.

When she told her friend Sally that she was going to attend this conference on hellebores, Sally congratulated her on "moving on."

Why was everyone so fixated on "moving on"? All she wanted was her life back. To do that, she had to re-enter the world of horticulture which encompassed Tate's world and the people in it as well. If she could just get that over with! She had to jump this first big obstacle.

Doing it at a Horticultural Writers conference would make it a little easier. She would be with old friends in a very structured environment. The coming meeting seemed custom-tailored for the task. Virtually anybody who had anything to do with hellebores would be there.

Because seeing Tate's colleagues without him at her side would be painful, she made it as easy on herself as possible. Instead of driving from Washington to Philadelphia on I-95, she would take the train, a little luxury. It might only be a three hour drive, but taking the train would certainly be more relaxing.

On a practical note, the train would save the parking fees at the hotel and she could bring her laptop and write as she rode. Not only did it make the whole trip less of an ordeal, she would arrive at 30th Street Station fresh and relaxed having finished her next article.

That was the plan. In the end, that isn't exactly what happened.

Trench coat on, purse over her shoulder, red suitcase ready to roll, Mim was about to leave the house, when the phone rang. She shouldn't have answered, but she did. It was Phyllis Butner, the new managing editor and the publisher's latest squeeze.

"Aren't you supposed to be leaving for someplace right about now?" Phyllis asked.

"I'm just about to go out the door," Mim answered and instantly realized her error. If ever there were an Olympic competition for personality disorders, Phyllis would take the gold for passive aggression.

"Good thing I caught you," Phyllis exhaled with audible satisfaction. "Well, this won't take too long." Mim heard the triumph in her voice. .

"My dear, I know how rushed you are, so...I've talked to Susan," Phyllis began. Her tone was all sugary concern. "And Susan has offered to help you! She said she would write the garden article for the January issue." Phyllis said it as if Mim had begged for help and Susan was generously coming through. Susan was Phyllis's sister, "an English teacher. She teaches creative writing."

The hell she will, Mim thought but refrained from saying anything inflammatory. Phyllis liked nothing better than a fight.

Phyllis had brought on her sister Susan as a copy editor, but as she continually reminded Mim, sister Susan was not only a creative writing teacher, she was an outstanding gardener. Phyllis tirelessly offered "to lighten Mim's load" by having her sister help Mim out by writing her garden articles.

Mim steadfastly refused to be "helped," but the need for constant vigilance brought stress into a job that had been a delight under the former editor.

"That's thoughtful of you, Phyllis," Mim said, "but I've already started the January article and will have it done with plenty of time to spare," Mim crisply responded.

"John thinks it's a good idea, too." Phyllis said as if Mim had not spoken. John was the publisher. God knows what she had said to him.

"Well, I'm on top of the article for the January issue and *I* plan to finish it," Mim pronounced. With Phyllis, it was important to be concrete and not leave anything open to interpretation. "And I'll email John today to let him know that I am almost done with it and I do plan to finish it."

"Well, Susan has cancelled an appointment to make time to help you out." Phyllis's tone held umbrage, as if Mim had asked for help and was now turning it down.

"I would never ask her or want her to do that. Please tell her thanks, but no thanks. And sorry for her misunderstanding." Mim looked at the clock. She should have been at the bus stop by now.

"Are you absolutely sure?" Phyllis demanded shrilly. The sugar was gone. "Because I have to have it first thing Monday morning."

Bull shit. That was a week ahead of deadline.

"No problem Phyllis. Consider it done! Gotta run. Bye!" Mim hung up.

Phyllis's telephone call caused Mim to miss the Ride-On to Metro which ran only hourly after ten in the morning. She could see the blue and white bus getting smaller and smaller in the distance as it continued down Tuckerman Lane toward Grosvenor Metro. As she watched it disappear, she remembered that Pixie Macklin, the only neighbor at home during the day, was visiting her son and grandchildren in Connecticut.

She debated whether she should call a cab, but decided it would be quicker to drive. There was nothing for it but to go back for her car, drive to the Grosvenor station, and park in the Metro garage. So she'd alternately rolled and dragged the chic red suitcase the two blocks back home. She unlocked the door, reentered the house, searched for the car keys, and finally found them under newspapers in the kitchen.

The drive to the Metro garage took just thirteen minutes, but she had to circle for another ten before she found a parking place on the fourth level. She checked her phone. The time allotted for a calm, unhurried beginning to this trip was ticking away.

She ran down the concrete stairs, grabbed the suitcase and hauled it thumping behind her. In less than a minute, she was out of the garage and running across the parking lot toward Grosvenor Station.

The ride on Metro's red line seemed interminable. Before the train finally reached Union Station, she was already standing at the doors waiting for the train to stop. She exited the car, wove her way through the crowd, wrenching the suitcase upright every time it tipped over. She charged up the escalator, pounded across Union Station's marble floor, passing the café with its tantalizing aroma of fresh coffee. She sped by the smart shops, all squeaky clean windows and polished brass, before arriving at the automatic ticket machines. There her progress ground to a halt.

Two people waited ahead of her at the machine with the shorter line. The first one, a man in a camel hair blazer, expertly inserted his credit card and obtained his paper tickets. But the woman directly ahead of her dug her wallet out of a dark green leather purse the size and shape of a waste can. Next, she fumbled getting her credit card out of the wallet. Then, credit card in hand, the woman stood for a minute reading the directions. It was all Mim could do, not to grab the woman's credit card and insert it into the machine for her.

Finally, finally, it was Mim's turn. She inserted her credit card and watched two paper tickets emerge from the slot. She grabbed them and ran to Gate D where she caught up with the tail end of the small gaggle as it passed through the gate en route to the platforms.

With four minutes to spare, Mim entered a coach car. It was nearly empty. She chose a window seat in the center of the car.

After she hoisted the suitcase into the overhead compartment, took off her trench coat, and collapsed onto the seat, she knew that this morning's lavender-scented bath had worn off. She was glowing from exertion. From the roots of her blonde-rinsed hair to her polished pink toenails, she felt coated with a slick film of sweat. It might be December, but the temperature in Washington had risen to an unseasonal, but not unprecedented 64 balmy degrees Fahrenheit.

Because her bulging suitcase couldn't accommodate anything with more bulk than a thong, she'd been forced to wear the coat. It would probably come in handy in Philadelphia.

Now, she folded the coat neatly and put it on the seat next to her. In light of the few travelers today, it could probably stay there all the way to Philadelphia's 30th Street Station. In the event the car started to fill up, the coat might deter potential chatty seat mates. There was work to do.

She reached into the big, black, and very heavy shoulder bag that held her laptop and paperwork. Her fingers skimmed the contents, identifying each by touch. Two paperback mysteries. Now, these would have to wait until she finished the article.

Her fingers sifted through a folder that held less substantial material—including the sketches of a garden she was planning for the Kiblers, her newest clients. Somewhere among the sketches would be the narrow, rectangular conference brochure. She had avoided reading it in the frantic weeks leading up to her departure. In part, it was because she had been super busy.

In addition to enticing roses to bloom all over Washington, the weeks of warm weather had brought more work. Several clients had asked her to design gardens, something she did to supplement her writing income, but usually only in spring when the days stayed bright into the evening. Taking on the extra work seemed so much more onerous when days darkened at five o'clock.

Her work days were long enough already. Every morning, she dragged herself out of bed at five. In her pajamas, wrapped in a woolen poncho, she drank sweet, hot coffee while working on the garden designs. Then, as in ordinary days with normal working hours, she showered, dressed, and sat down at the computer in her tiny office promptly at nine. She ate lunch at her desk, or, for the last few warm days, on a bench in the garden. Evenings when she could, she met with clients.

The last two weeks had been an exhausting blur. But that wasn't the whole reason she had not read the conference brochure. She couldn't blame the new design work, or the always hectic approach of Christmas, or even the dreadful Phyllis. She had put off examining the brochure because of the volcano of emotions this conference evoked.

The speakers would the friends and colleagues Tate had talked about. She would meet them, he had promised. They would travel to the Jersey Shore in the early spring area to see Danny Cullen's fabled garden. They would drive to Maryland's Eastern Shore to see the Taylors who bred outstanding hellebores at Locust hill Nursery. This had been his world. Had he lived, he, too, would be en route to this conference.

She was traveling alone now, carrying on for Tate in her own small way. Had that been her reason for signing on to the conference? Those intentions, crysal clear under the influence of wine on a dark, lonely evening, floated amorphous, out of her reach in the sober light of day.

3

As the train chugged northward, Mim experienced a curious sense of moving toward an unfulfilled but unidentified duty. Being in motion also had the paradoxical effect of ratcheting down her anxiety about attending the conference a notch or two. And, after the hard work of the past month–to say nothing of the new managing editor, it would be great to get away.

Okay, she would have to face the people who made up Tate's world without him, but she would also enjoy hearing what they had to say. It would be so good to meet and catch up with her fellow horticultural writers, too. And she was looking forward to spending time with Sally Flinn. They planned to collaborate on a book about designing with herbs.

This morning in the haste of departure, she'd been too frazzled to make sense of a last-minute email from Sally. She had printed it out while she finished dressing and stuffed it into her bag. Now she found the printout and began to read.

"Hi Mim,

I submitted the proposal to Foresters last week. I have a call in to them, but probably won't hear anything until next week. Like you, I have to have a project to think about in the winter – keeps me from getting "barn sour", as our old riding instructor used to say about the horses cooped up in their stalls all winter. What a nutty winter it's turning out to be. It's been in the high 60's here!

Until tomorrow, Sally"

Mim and Sally hoped that Foresters, the foremost publisher of things horticultural, would take it. She replaced the email in her brimming black bag. Her hand slid over a new paperback mystery, but obediently, it kept going until it located her laptop. To finish the article by Monday– a totally unnecessary demand from Phyllis–she would have to work on the train.

Her next assignment for the magazine was an article about hellebores which she had suggested to Phyllis as "Christmas roses." "Lenten Roses" would have been more accurate, but it was the recognition factor of the familiar words "Christmas" and "roses" that worked with Phyllis. It had worked so well that, uncharacteristically, Phyllis had okayed it with only a "Good. Roses are good." Then she added, "Could you try to make it understandable to regular gardeners? Oh well, Susan can go over it." Susan, the high school teacher who gardened.

Mim could feel a familiar irritation rising. She shook it off. Dwelling on Phyllis was self-destructive. She had to keep out of the mire. Phyllis would self destruct soon enough.

Mim took a deep breath to clear her mind. She looked out the window. On this trip up the eastern seaboard from Washington, DC to New York, you never lost sight of human development. They were still in Maryland, but all the way to New York, you could see little beyond variations of the same developed landscape. It struck her as tired and dirty and used up. Even in the wild places, the grasses and vines were what horticulturists called "opportunistic aliens," plants from other places that took over.

Slowly, calm returned. Mim began thinking about how to start the article by asking why anyone should grow these plants. Why indeed? She felt a flood of inspiration.

Because hellebores do a lot of things right. Christmas roses bear their white flowers in the darkest part of the winter, often peeking through a blanket of snow. The Lenten roses, also shade-tolerant perennials, bloomed later—in February or March. And, after they bloomed, the seed heads were attractive for another two months. They were evergreen and grew into broad, low, mounds, a great shape for edging shrub borders. Furthermore, they were exceptionally long-lived. And deer wouldn't touch them!

Were there any drawbacks? The only one Mim could think of was that around bloom time, the old leaves that had turned brown needed cutting back to set off the flowers and give the garden a neat look. That was a small enough price to pay for all of the positive attributes.

There was a great argument for hellebores as perfect plants. She had never really thought about them in this way before. She typed "Christmas and Lenten roses do a lot of things right." That was too awkward. And Phyllis would jump on the "Lenten roses" if she saw it right off the bat. She would insert the Lenten bit later in the text. Mim erased "Lenten roses" and "a lot of things" and wrote "everything." "Christmas roses do everything right."

Mim caught herself looking out of the train window and daydreaming. She turned her attention back to the computer screen and read what she had written. She paused at the thought of the many species in the hellebore genus beyond the more popular Lenten and Christmas roses. She wished she could at least *mention* other species within the genus.

She comforted herself with the thought that her readers would be lucky if they could find the more common ones—the Christmas and Lenten roses–at local garden centers. Forget about the less common kinds.

She was about to begin typing why it was that hellebores did everything right when she was startled by a tap on her shoulder.

"Mim Fitz!" A tall, trim man in elegantly understated black was standing in the aisle, swaying with the movement of the train. He looked at once strange and familiar—someone out of context. She stared at him for a moment before she returned his greeting.

"Kevin Minnahan!"

He bent to take the seat beside her. In one smooth movement, he picked up her trench coat and folded it before placing it on his lap.

"Hello Beautiful," he said and bussed her cheek.

"Kevin? What are you doing here?" she asked, instantly sorry to have sounded ungracious. She began again. "It's great to see you." She smiled at him and then looked back down at the computer screen, hit the save option, and closed the file.

"Are you on your way to New York?"

"Philadelphia! To …" he said, pulling out a brochure from his pocket. "To the Horticultural Writers District II Meeting," he read. "Whew! That's a mouthful." Then he folded the brochure neatly in two and replaced it. "Mind if I put this in the overhead compartment?" he asked, holding her coat in two hands like an offering. Without waiting for an answer, he stood up to stash her coat while Mim digested his words.

"Why are you going to the meeting?" she asked incredulously. "You're not a member are you?" Stupid question, she thought instantly. "Last I heard, you were a travel writer!" Kevin specialized in conveying very exact and complete pictures of the places he wrote about, even if they were not always flattering.

He knew nothing—absolutely nothing–about gardening. He found her work amusing. He enjoyed teasing her and entitled every email he sent with a headline like 'Slugs on the Rampage!' or 'Beetle Army Marches on Washington.'

"Well," he grinned. "I haven't committed fully just yet. It's only another twenty bucks if you don't belong…*to the horticultural writers of district two,*" he added, waggling his eyebrows. He looked at her hard.

"I thought you might be on this train. But I almost didn't recognize you. When did you go blonde?"

"I didn't. But I've been using a blonde rinse on my hair to cover the… Oh for heavens sakes, Kevin!" Mim sat up and adjusted her sweater.

"I *meant* you look great. Nice sweater," said Kevin.

"Thanks! Best purchase I ever made," she said. The long, elegant sweater jacket had become her uniform.

"Well, it looks good on you. You look great." Kevin settled himself comfortably into his seat. "I called the magazine and talked to, who's your editor?"

"Phyllis Butner," Mim sighed.

"Guess she hasn't self-destructed yet," Kevin smiled broadly, showing his perfect, blazing white teeth.

"Nope. But I don't think she'll last long. They're already taking bets on how many more weeks she'll be there."

"You called the magazine? I'm surprised Phyllis even talked to you. What did you say?" Mim asked. Before he could answer she threw out two more questions. "And how did you know about the hort writers conference? It's not exactly your bailiwick, is it? Come on Kevin, what's up? "

"In answer to your first question, I told her we were rooming together."

"Oh Kevin, you didn't!"

"No, I didn't." Kevin smiled and adjusted his horn rimmed glasses. "Actually, I told her that Beate Pappenheim, who is on the awards committee, had suffered a hemorrhage and would not be able to make the conference and we needed you to fill in for her and I would have to prep you en route."

Mim groaned.

"In answer to question number two, I found out about the conference on the internet," Kevin continued. "I was researching hellebores. I'm writing a story on them."

"You! Kevin, you're a travel writer—an *investigative* travel writer. What do you know about hellebores?"

"Actually, I don't know a damn thing about them. Anyway, the plants themselves are not my focus. They'll be peripheral to my story. I write about people and what happens to them and why."

In his efforts to capture the soul of each place he visited, rather than discuss the typical tourist destinations, Kevin honed in on people. Always ruthlessly honest, he had a genius for capturing the spirit of a people and the beauty of their homeland without shying away from its unpleasant truths. He had written lyrically about the grandeur of Newfoundland, but also about how the moratorium on cod fishing had reduced fishermen there to poverty. He had celebrated the proud and generous spirit of the mountain people of Nepal, but wrote about how trekkers, bringing in much needed capital, were littering the foothills of the Himalayas and contributing to the destruction of the native flora.

The story Mim remembered best was one that Kevin had written about Sita Bai, an Indian girl from Bangalore, a progressive Indian city, whose unprogressive parents had sold her into prostitution at age twelve. A Devadasi, a prostitute devotee of the goddess Yellamma, she died at sixteen of the complications of AIDS.

"I'm going to call the story 'curse of the hellebores.' Don't you love the way that sounds?" Kevin grinned. "Now tell me, what is a hellebore anyway? I was hoping you would fill me in on the way up."

"*You* want to know about hellebores?" She smiled. Kevin had never gardened in his life. He lived in a penthouse apartment on Connecticut Avenue just over the District line. He was absurdly proud of his only house plant, an iron plant that probably owed its life to his frequent trips away. As a travel writer, he was gone as much as he was at home.

"And why the curse of the hellebores? Isn't that a wee bit melodramatic? Not like Kevin Minnahan's signature no-nonsense, utterly un-sentimental approach."

"I'm serious about the 'curse of the hellebores'. Surely, you as a member of the Horticultural Writers Society must have heard of the bad luck that follows people who breed them? That's the story I want to tell." Kevin wasn't smiling now. He was looking at her cautiously.

"You're talking about those two English breeders who were killed, aren't you?" Mim said carefully, skirting the thought of Tate that came immediately to mind. She frowned, remembering. "Marion Petersfield was a famous hybridizer and the other one– a man, I don't remember his name–died in an automobile accident." Mim looked out the window as if something out there might jog her memory.

"Wilson McCoy," said Kevin.

"Yes, that's right. Wow! You have done your research! Wilson McCoy— he died not long after Marion Petersfield." Then she remembered.

"Wait! Wait a minute! Petersfield and McCoy were lovers! That's the reason the curse idea first got started. Because they were lovers. They split over something to do with hellebores. Hellebores were supposed to put the kibosh on relationships," she said, smarting internally as the words came out. It had certainly worked for Tate and her.

"They both died. And, their deaths were close together. No, wait! Marion Petersfield was murdered!" It all came back to her. Marion Petersfield had been brutally murdered. Years ago.

"Kevin, that's sensational, but not exactly breaking news. It was maybe six or eight years ago or more. I'm not sure I see enough in it for a story," Mim said thoughtfully.

"Mim, Petersfield and McCoy aren't the only ones," Kevin said gently. His eyes were wide behind his glasses.

"I was on a press trip in the Balkans with Walkingtours when Tate Adkins was killed."

4

After JP got the inn keeper to take a photo of our group, it started to rain. After that, probably half of the members of our expedition decided to pack it in and lounge around the inn or go back to bed. I wish I had. But I didn't. No. Instead, Tate and I started out. I guess I ought to say Tate left the inn and I followed him.

The trail was wet— even a little slushy in parts. There was still snow on the mountain tops. I got wetter and colder by the minute. Tate didn't seem to notice the weather. He never did. But on that morning, I remember, it was like he was more out of it than usual, almost like he was in some kind of trance. I mean, he was hatless and gloveless, and there was water dripping off his nose and he just kept on going and looking for those plants.

I knew exactly what he was looking for. The day before, the entire expedition— all eighteen of us— were hiking together, strung out along a trail. We were looking for Christmas roses. All of a sudden, I happened to look back and off to one side and I saw this big colony of pink Christmas roses. Pink, not white! They were amazing! Beautiful! In the right breeder's hands those pink Christmas roses could bring a fortune! I saw them first. Then, I noticed that Tate saw them, too.

He already had his trowel in hand and he was fishing around in his backpack for collection bags. He was always so obvious! At the time, I was afraid everyone was going to see them.

But luckily, just as he was about to collect some of those plants, Katie Hiscock stumbled. She tripped on a rock in what happened to be a very high, narrow place. She almost fell off the mountain. Jenny and Olga grabbed her. One hung onto her backpack and the other got a hold of a leg. They literally kept her from rolling over the edge. That's how close it was.

So Tate couldn't very well go about his business cold-bloodedly digging out those Christmas roses, could he? I'm sure he wanted to. I know I did. But we had to call it a day. And we just about had to carry Katie and her gear back to the inn. She was undone, shaking and so white, her freckles stood out like polka dots.

In the commotion, nobody else noticed those pink Christmas roses. I watched Tate look over at them and fix their location in his mind. So the next morning, I knew he was planning to go back and get them. I knew it and I waited. And, when he left the inn, I followed him. We walked for about an hour and every time the trail narrowed at a high place, he slowed down. He was cautious, even if he was completely oblivious to the weather.

More than I wanted those Christmas roses, I wanted to be alone with Tate. That was the main reason I followed him. Yes, I knew that he lived with someone, but from the moment our party arrived in Slovenia, I felt his eyes on me. I can always tell what people are thinking. I knew that Tate had been sending me secret messages from the moment we got there.

There were always so many other people around, it was hard for us to be alone. JP Chiasson and the rest of that little clique followed Tate everywhere. And Tate and JP– I couldn't stand JP—went off by themselves every morning. Except for the last day when JP stayed behind to take his pictures.

So I snatched at the opportunity to be alone with Tate. For one solid week before that, every time—the minute we were alone– JP or one of the others would interrupt. They were doing it on purpose. I could tell. So, on that last morning, while JP was occupied with his pictures, I went with Tate to give him a chance to be alone with me.

We walked for over an hour. Now that I had him alone, I knew he felt a little awkward, so, to put him at ease, I just kept talking about whatever came into my head. I told him what I was working on. I told him all about my breeding program. After a while, we both felt a little easier so I talked about other things. To make a long story short, I opened up about everything! And I hinted that I returned the feelings he had for me.

That's when he turned around and looked like he wanted to check who I was. His eyes went from wide and kind of unfocused to narrow like he couldn't understand what I said. Then, his face changed. I saw it. I saw the look that passed over his face the way the headlights of a car light up trees along a road. It was pity and... disgust.

5

When Kevin told Mim he had been in Slovenia at the same time as Tate, Mim was shocked into silence. The train rattled across the Susquehanna River Bridge. She looked out at wide water as she digested the information.

"I didn't know you were there—in the Balkans. How did I miss that?" She turned to him and said with a hint of accusation, "You never said anything about it."

"We were trekking from place to place and the group he was with was out doing the same thing–only they were looking for plants," Kevin continued. "Our group crossed paths with theirs on a couple of occasions. For a couple of nights, we stayed at the same inn. I should say the *only* inn—outside of Otric."

Mim sat motionless as stone. She felt Kevin examining her face. She answered his unspoken question.

"Yes, Kevin. I knew Tate."

"I thought you might. I thought he was probably in your little group—one of your Washington plant mafia types. Did you know him well?"

"Yes."

She looked up and met eyes that held sympathy. Kevin could be scarily perspicacious sometimes. She didn't have to add what he now probably sensed from her tone of voice, from her facial expressions, using his uncanny sixth sense, that she and Tate were more than just friends.

"I didn't know that you had gone to the Balkans," she repeated, still stunned by this information.

"That's because, right after that trip, I didn't see you for a long time. I had piggy-backed another trip—to Dubrovnik and the Croatian islands—and then," he breathed out a long sigh, "I spent a week in Palermo."

Palermo. Yes. She remembered a postcard. That would be...what was her name? Luisa? The Italian photographer. Kevin had a way of charming and acquiring admirers on his travels.

"I was gone for a long time." Kevin was saying. "Immediately after Palermo, I went to Nepal. And when I got back, you were gone."

"Yes. I spent a month in France," Mim said automatically, wincing at the memory of a precipitous and ill-considered liaison she had entered into there. Kevin glanced at her inquisitively. He guessed.

"A sweet young man. A stupid mistake," she said. "I was so, so tired of feeling sad."

Then, several months after Tate's death, they both attended the painter Brodie Stapleton's eightieth birthday party. A huge crowd and a circus theme. Kevin had come as the bearded lady. She had come as herself and left early.

Kevin reached over and stroked Mim's cheek.

"It was serious, wasn't it? " Mim nodded.

"Just before...the accident," she let out a long sigh. "Just a few weeks before, we began combining our households. I've got a bigger yard. More room for plants," she gave him a wry smile. "He was going to move all his plants over when he got back..."

"You loved him." It was a statement, but Kevin's pale eyebrows were raised. His expression was a question. Mim shrugged.

"You know what? Right after it happened, I hated him. I lived in a constant stage of rage. How could a grown man throw away his life for plants! I was so angry I was going to kill every hellebore in the garden."

"But you didn't?" Kevin's blue eyes were big and round and smiling. Mim returned the smile.

"No. But I wanted to. I actually worked myself up into a fit of, of..." She searched for the right word. "I guess it was really just self pity. I was actually going to whack them all to death with a spade. Tate had already planted some of his seedlings for me in my back garden. I was going to start with those."

"What happened?" Kevin smiled. Mim rolled her eyes.

"Well, I found the seedlings Tate had planted for me. They were these sweet little cushions. They were small and perfect! To this day, they still haven't bloomed. How could I kill them? It would be like committing infanticide!" Mim looked out the window. "I felt ridiculous!"

"I just went back into the house and cleaned the bathroom." Kevin grinned. Mim smiled.

Kevin took her hand. Lord! She was glad Kevin would be attending the conference!

They had first met on a press trip to Scotland and hit it off immediately. Ever since, they were pals, sidekicks who listened to each other's tales of romantic escapades. Because, in the time they knew each other, one or both of them had always been romantically involved with someone else, their relationship had grown to be comfortably platonic. They emailed with some regularity. They spoke by phone now and then and, when Kevin was in town—which was rare–they got together for dinner. Though they saw each other very infrequently, when they did, they always fell into the same comfortable camaraderie as if they'd been childhood friends. They were both writers with specialties. Mim wrote about plants and gardens. Kevin wrote travel articles.

Kevin and Mim rode together in silence as Delaware sped by. Out of the window I-95, raised up on vast, rectangular columns, paralleled the train tracks. Mim watched the traffic speed by, glad she was sitting on the train and not driving.

When the train stopped in Wilmington, several people boarded. Idly, Mim read the signs along the platform: ING Direct. She really ought to move money out of her bank account into something that paid interest. The Delaware Theater Company. She remembered with a start tickets to the Kennedy Center in an envelope that was held onto her fridge by a magnet. She couldn't remember for when or for which production.

The train was crossing the Christiana River when Kevin cleared his throat.

"But you do see why I say hellebores are cursed?" He asked. Mim had been looking out over the river at identical rooflines that made her think of the crenulations of a castle.

"I guess I never thought of what happened to Tate in the same light as what happened to Marion Petersfield and Wilson McCoy," Mim said, trying to stifle sudden annoyance. She wished he would leave it alone. She didn't want to be interviewed, to be part of his research. "And I don't believe in curses and neither do you." It came out snappishly. She calmed herself. This was Kevin. It was the way he was. She began again.

"Okay, three people who bred hellebores did not live out their natural lives. People have terrible accidents every day, Kevin," Mim said softly.

"So you don't think my hook is such a hot one?" Kevin eyes were very wide and luminous. Mim shook her head.

"I guess the idea of a curse connected to these plants is an attention-grabber."

"Do you mean cheapshot?"

"No. I mean it's the sort of thing that grabs your attention but, in this case, it might be a little thin...or forced to me. I do like your idea of writing about the human side of plant breeding– the people who focus on finding rare plants. That could be fascinating. What drives people to spend years of their lives concentrating on the breeding of a single plant?"

She looked at Kevin. There was a queer, unreadable expression on his face. She decided to change the subject. Relieved to be away from this particular mine-strewn field of conversation, she held up the conference brochure and asked brightly, "Are you going to attend the pre-conference workshops tomorrow?"

"Nope."

"Then aren't you going up a little early? You know, the main conference doesn't start until the reception tomorrow night. I'm just going up early for the workshops tomorrow."

"I plan to visit a couple of friends while I'm here. You know, Philly is where I started out. I interned on the *Philadelphia Star*. You remember Randy?"

"Your cousin Randy—the detective?"

"Well, he's a detective, but he's not really my cousin. He's actually my uncle. My mother's little brother. He's only four years older than I am."

Kevin thrust a hand into the pocket of his sport coat. It was a deep and soft midnight black. He pulled out the brochure and unfolded it carefully. He held it out to her.

"Maybe we could go over this together?"

6

Mim opened the conference brochure and held it up so both could read it. Kevin pointed to the first event on Friday: "Registration 4-9. Reception 7-9, Juniper Room."

"What happens at the reception?"

"Schmoozing mainly. Usually, it's hosted by one of the corporate trade members. See!" Mim pointed to "hosted by Warner Seeds."

The lectures of the main part of the conference occupied the entire second page. She skimmed over the information about breakfast, but stopped at: "9:00: Welcome, Margaret Stemple, Conference Director." She hadn't noticed that before

Margaret Stemple? Awkward, overweight, Margaret worked at The Garden Center, Mim's local nursery. What was she doing organizing a conference? Mim had no idea that Margaret possessed the kind of organizational skills necessary to run a conference. Clearly, she had underestimated her.

She read: "'9:15: Hellebores of the World, Joachim Muller.' He's an international expert on hellebores and a great speaker."

"Go on," Kevin urged.

"The ten o'clock lecture is going to be really good." She pointed to: "10:15: Double Hellebores, The Delmarva Belles, presented by Darrel and Jenny Taylor."

"The Taylors were some of Tate's good friends. Their nursery is called Locust Hill. It's a Mecca for hellebore enthusiasts—on the Eastern Shore of Maryland."

"What's so special about their nursery?"

"Their plants are outstanding. They have bred doubles in a range of beautiful colors…"

"What exactly are doubles?"

"Oh Kevin! I'm afraid this is going to be a very long weekend for you!"

"Hey, don't worry," Kevin held up his hands to protest. "I'm into this. I just need to get up to speed on the vocabulary."

"Okay. Doubles." Mim was momentarily at a loss.

"Okay. Remember when you were a little kid and you drew a flower?" She looked at Kevin who nodded.

"Well if your drawings were like mine, there would be a circle in the center and four or maybe five half circles around the middle to represent petals."

"Yup."

"Well, that kind of flower exists in nature. It's called a simple flower. It's the basic, no frills flower with a center and a single row of petals arranged around the center."

"Breeders like the Taylors have taken those simple flowers and gotten more petals—a double amount or more. Double flowers are really full and fancy looking. And the Taylors have bred them in a whole range of colors—not just the whites and pinks that are the usual colors of hellebores."

"People who breed plants are always looking to improve on the original by getting more petals, different colors, a better habit…"

"What do you mean by habit?" Kevin looked ever so slightly cranky. Maybe he'd had enough botanical information.

"The shape of the plant," she said briskly. She held up the brochure. "Let's get back to the schedule."

"After the Taylors, there's a break—probably coffee and donuts. And then Benjy Glover is going to speak. He's got a really big nursery in North Carolina. His topic is 'Dreaming of a White Christmas Rose at Christmas—preferably a Double White.' And pigs will fly! He wants to breed a white flower with lots of petals that will bloom *reliably* at Christmas. Anyone who can do that is a wizard! And he would make a fortune."

"What's a Christmas rose? Is it a hellebore?"

"Yes. It's one kind of hellebore. There are a bunch of different species of hellebores, but the Christmas rose is one of the more common ones."

"Why did you say 'and pigs will fly'? "

"Because...because breeding a plant that will bloom on schedule – like at Christmas—is pretty dicey. A lot depends upon the weather in a given year. And Christmas roses can be finicky—at least in acid clay soil and that's what a huge part of the East has. I think they grow better in sweeter soil."

"Are you talking about pH?"

"Yes. We have acid soil. Most people in our part of the world can grow the Lenten rose really well. For us, it's an altogether easier plant. It's big and lusty and reproduces like crazy, but it doesn't bloom until February or March." Mim looked at Kevin, who knotted his brow. "I'm losing you aren't I?"

"No. No, I think I get it. Why is he talking about one that blooms at Christmas if it doesn't do that and won't grow here?"

"Well, breeders are in it for love, but also for money. Imagine if someone could develop a beautiful hellebore that would bloom reliably every Christmas. It would be sort of like a poinsettia. Only it would grow outside in your garden. And being a perennial plant, it would bloom every single year—at Christmas. Outside! Everyone would want one. You'd make a fortune."

"It would be every breeder's dream. But it's just that–a dream. Tate said that the Christmas rose did not cross with the Lenten roses."

"I've got both Christmas and Lenten roses and had them for at least twenty years in my garden. After the first couple of years, the Lenten roses started to self sow and now I've got dozens of these big, tough, bushel basket-sized plants covering the ground in several areas. They are vigorous and healthy and trouble free. That's what they mean when they talk about hybrid vigor. As a rule, my Christmas roses aren't as robust and tend to stay smaller."

"Tate planted some crosses he bred in my garden. I can't remember if he ever said what the parent plants were. They were just tiny seedlings when he'd planted them. He refused to speculate on what they were going to look like. Maybe he didn't know. So far, they haven't bloomed. Maybe this will be the year."

Kevin was staring at her.

"What's next?" he asked.

"The concurrent sessions are right after Benjy Glover's lecture. Have you decided which ones you're going to attend?"

"You mean I get a choice?" Kevin laughed. "You know, this might be a little more than I'm ready for. All I wanted was to get a little background on these hellebore plants."

The train had stopped at a station. Newark? Kevin and Mim watched as the front door of their car rolled open and two women entered, one in shirt sleeves and the other wearing a lime green linen blazer. They brought a waft of spring-like air with them. It could have been early May.

"What do I want to attend?" Kevin yawned.

"There are three choices," she said returning to the brochure and pointing to the section marked 'concurrent sessions.' You have to choose one."

"Why don't you choose for me?"

"I'm going to session "C"—that's going to be about a beautiful garden on the Jersey Shore. Maybe not your cup of tea."

Frowning, she read, "'B' is 'Species of Balkan Hellebores' Barney Staples of Staples Hellebores."

"You know, he sounds vaguely familiar," Mim mused. I think I met him, but I didn't know he had a nursery or, for that matter, that he was into hellebores," Mim said.

She'd never heard of Staples Hellebores. Tate had certainly never mentioned it. And she thought he would have known all about a nursery that was dedicated to hellebores. It must be new.

Staples was not someone in what she thought of as "Tate's group," a tight knit group of breeders who were passionate about their work. Still, the name was familiar.

"I think I met him," Kevin perked up. "Sort of. In Slovenia!"

"Sort of?" Mim asked.

"There was a Barney there who was pretty drunk. Big guy. I think I'd recognize him if I saw him again, but I'm sure he wouldn't remember me." Kevin said dismissively.

"Well, that session is going to be way too much information for your purposes. I think session "A" would be a perfect fit for you." Mim pointed to the description.

"Wow. 'Death by Hellebore.' That's got to be good!" Kevin took the brochure from Mim and read while Mim explained.

"Rose Redfern, the woman who is presenting that session is known, rather unkindly, as the white witch of hort writers. She's going to be giving a more in depth presentation at the workshops tomorrow. I'm going to attend that one. Apparently, she's an expert on phytotoxins," Mim explained. Kevin's rapt expression turned to a scowl.

"Phyto whats?"

"Plant poisons."

Kevin now read and reread the brochure, turning it over with renewed interest. Mim sank into thought. They rode in silence for a quarter of an hour as the train moved as trains did, slowly but relentlessly forward. Outside the window, a fine mist softened the shapes and muted the colors of the passing scenery.

Mim touched Kevin's sleeve.

"You know," she said and felt a lump rise in her throat, "it's not hellebores, but plant hunting that can be cursed. Maybe that's your story. Throughout history, hunting for plants has been notoriously dangerous. Dozens of guys were drowned, gored, eaten by wild animals and cannibals.... They came down with tropical fevers and died of infected wounds." She felt a tear roll down her cheek, but she kept on.

"Tate was hiking in the mountains. He was alone on a treacherous trail. The day before it happened, my friend Katie Hiscock came very near to falling as well. She would have fallen if her friends hadn't been grabbed to stop her from rolling over the edge." Mim took a breath and continued. She could see from Kevin's expression that what she was saying was something he already knew. But she continued. Her words tumbled out like a wall of water crashing through a canyon. Tears rolled over her cheeks. She could stop neither words nor tears.

"The next day—it had been raining. It was very slippery. It was a terrible, terrible, accident, but one that, unfortunately, is not unheard of," she concluded very softly. Tate went out alone and he slipped and fell."

The terrible facts of Tate's death. For the first time, Mim had spoken them out loud. Kevin reached for her hand. She drew strength from the warmth of his grip. They sat for a long time in a comfortable silence, watching a narrow strip of Delaware fly by. Finally, she pulled her hand out of his. She patted his hand and wiped her face. She felt renewed. Lighter.

"You said you want to write about the so-called curse on hellebores. Well, Marion Petersfield or McCoy—what happened to them was a long, long time ago," she continued. "Because they were lovers and because they died—at least she died violently, there is the idea of a curse connected to breeding hellebores. What really puts those two on the map is that they were early enthusiasts for hellebores. They bred really good plants and got people interested in them. And, now, in the garden world, Christmas and Lenten roses are hot," said Mim.

"Hot!" Kevin hooted. "Hot! And why are they *hot?*"

"Kevin, are you aware that you're about to spend a weekend with a hundred or more hellebore fanatics? Better show some respect!"

"Okay. I promise, but the question really was serious. Why are they hot? What's so great about them?"

"They're the perfect plants. If you're a gardener, they do everything right. You can be a black thumb and grow beautiful hellebores. They're evergreen. They bloom in the winter. They're great looking and they self sow like crazy. And deer don't eat them. That's huge!"

"And if you're a breeder, it's very easy to make crosses of Lenten roses and create new plants. Right now there are more people breeding hellebores than you can shake a stick at. In fact, four of the most prestigious hybridizers in this country are on the program—five if you count both of the Taylors. And they're all in perfect health."

"You haven't heard?" Again, that unreadable expression.

"Heard what?"

"You haven't heard," he said again, a quiet statement of fact. She felt her lips form the word 'no,' but no sound came out.

Kevin explained gently that JP Chiasson had been bludgeoned in a burglary two weeks ago. When he had failed to turn up at a party or answer his phone, his fiancée had driven home and found their office trashed and JP dying.

As if somehow to negate Kevin's words, Mim flipped the brochure to the back page. JP Chiasson's name was listed as the speaker for the Sunday brunch. She stared at the description: "Hunting for Hellebores, presented by JP Chiasson."

JP had been on the plant hunting trip with Tate. He had been scheduled to speak and show photos of the Balkan trip at the brunch on Sunday morning.

7

There are places along the railroad line that runs up the coast between Washington and New York where the railroad tracks closely parallel Interstate 95. Sitting next to the window of the third car on Amtrak's Northeast Regional, Mim might have glanced over to the highway and recognized the white Garden Center van. Margaret Stemple was driving.

Margaret was actually beginning to feel more comfortable driving the van. She had made good time until she was about a mile from the Baltimore Harbor Tunnel. There, the heavy traffic forced her to slow to a crawl. When the toll booths came into view, it was stop and go.

She sat in a line of some twenty cars. The white van with the green Garden Center logo and at least a hundred other cars, trucks, and buses inched forward in long lines as they approached the toll booths.

It was, after all, rush hour. And she had been warned.

"I'm telling you— you leave now you will sit in traffic all the way to Philadelphia. Okay. Okay. I am just trying to help. But don't listen to me. You never do." At this, Mother had flounced out of the kitchen— only to return a minute later. She was starting to wind up. Her remarks would go from helpful comments to those all wrapped up in concern, but designed to hurt. It was Mother's usual progression.

"You know, I worry about you. That hoity-toity group of yours, the Horticultural Writers Society," she spat. "Do you really think they appreciate you and all the work that you're doing? You spend far too much time doing their dirty work."

"When I could be home, listening to you," said Margaret inaudibly. She could have shouted it. Mother never listened once she got on a roll.

"You know what I think?" It was a rhetorical question. Mother paused dramatically. Margaret said nothing; she didn't want to know what Mother thought. She went on packing her briefcase.

"They're using you! That's what! And you can't or won't see it. Listen to me. Are you a writer? No. You could be, of course. God knows we provided you with the education for it. But you, with a *master's degree in English literature*! What do you do? You're a laborer in a nursery by day. And by night, you're a go-for. You pick people up from the airport and take them to their hotels. You know, that's what taxis are for. I'm just grateful your poor, dear father can't see how you've squandered your education." It was one of Mother's regular tirades.

When Margaret's "poor, dear father" was alive, he had been the usual recipient of Mother's vitriol. Her father's great failing had been not aspiring to be or becoming chairman of the English Department at Maryland. Instead, he had taught Beowulf, Chaucer, and freshman composition for twenty years. He also owned many other failings that Mother had routinely pointed out before his early death and subsequent beatification.

Margaret missed her father all the time. Sometimes, she missed him so much the ache in the middle of her chest made it hard to breathe.

This morning Mother had surprise ammunition. She had found one of Margaret's newly printed business cards. She must have gone through the room yesterday. She must have gone through the suitcase, too. It was a good thing she'd left her dress and the new underwear in the van.

"What's this?"

Mother held the card up a few inches from Margaret's face. Margaret kept herself from flinching. She stared straight ahead. She had learned not to react. She would never give Mother the satisfaction of a flinch or even a frown. This morning, it was easier than usual to maintain a pleasant expression.

"It's a business card Mother. For my nursery." Though she could feel a coal of anger smoulder in her chest, Margaret responded sweetly. She wanted to deprive Mother of the satisfaction of making her angry, of hurting her. It gave Margaret a perverse pleasure to deny her mother satisfaction.

Not being able to land her verbal blows always made Mother angry. Make that angrier. Mother was always angry. Her efforts escalated.

"Oh my! It's *Heavenly* Hellebores is it," Mother said with choked cheer that ended up a sneer. Then she walked over to the kitchen window. Mother lifted the curtain, and peered outside where Margaret's hellebores stood in neat double rows around three sides of the back yard lawn. "That must be the heavenly nursery!" she said, feigning enthusiasm. She let the curtain drop. "Tell me! Is there a lot of money in it?"

As a matter of fact, there would be money in it. Possibly a fortune! But there was no point in even trying to explain to Mother. Her taste in plants ran to marigolds and roses. Not that she had a clue about growing them.

Mother's escalating tirade had gone on for another quarter of an hour or so before she transitioned to what Margaret thought of as Mother's swan song. Margaret had to get a teaching job like her sister Carol. Then she'd have summers off. Margaret wouldn't leave her all alone for days on end. Anything could happen. She might fall. What would Margaret do if she broke her hip? She could die. She probably would and it would serve Margaret right.

Mother's voice wavered between a self-pitying whine and snide accusation. It happened every time that Margaret left for longer than a working day. This was happening more and more often now that she was taking on more responsibilities in hort writers. Like today.

Margaret handed the woman in the toll booth a five, asked for a receipt, dumped the change into her purse, and accelerated. Traffic thinned. She drove on with increasing confidence and a sense of liberation. It was going to work. Her life was finally on track.

She was going to Philadelphia for a long weekend, to a Horticultural Writers conference that she had put together herself. She was the conference director. Margaret Stemple, conference director! Intense pleasure and a sense of accomplishment washed over her. This was just the beginning.

If all went well, her conference would be the best Horticultural Writers conference in history. She had lined up a who's who of breeders of hellebores, including Joachim Muller, considered to be the world's expert. The response had been overwhelming. The main conference had filled in less than a week! There was a waiting list of fifteen. The pre-conference workshop had not been as successful. She brushed this thought aside.

Her efforts had not gone unnoticed. She'd had congratulatory calls from Binky Kaplan, a past president, and Lin Baldwin, a district director, who had hinted at a bigger job in the offing. Margaret Stemple was not only the best conference director section two had ever had, she was now in line for the presidency.

She thought of the new dress–lavender lace–with pleasure. She thought of her new lavender lace underwear and blushed.

She didn't mind being in a line of cars at the toll booths for Baltimore's Harbor Tunnel. She didn't care that the line of cars moved slowly forward, stopping at the toll booths as each driver rolled down a window and paid the two dollar toll. She slid out of her sweater and cracked the window. In spite of its being December, it was going to be a beautiful, spring-like day.

Mitch, the manager, had taught her to drive the Garden Center's van. First it was around the parking lot after hours and then they'd gone out onto River Road. Later, he'd gone with her to some of the wholesale nurseries above Baltimore. She still didn't like driving on the interstates.

She had looked forward to those lessons with him after the work day ended. Before each one, she had ducked into the ladies room to refresh her lipstick and comb her hair. She should have known. As soon as she got her license, a new responsibility was added to her job description. She had to transport merchandise between stores, something Mitch used to do before she got her license.

She'd been allowed to take the van for the weekend because she was transporting samples along with literature to distribute at the conference. And she would be picking up Mitch at one of the big wholesale nurseries on the way back.

She had memorized the directions so that she could reach the hotel with minimal difficulty. I-76 would take her from I-95 north into Philadelphia. It should show up anytime now. From I-76 she would take 676 into the city and exit on Market Street.

Margaret drove at well under the speed limit, which was mostly 65 miles per hour. After three hours of driving some of the morning's excitement was wearing thin. Highway driving always made her nervous, but today it was more than that. There was so much at stake.

This conference had to go off without a hitch. It had to. She was the conference director. As much as that title could fill her with pride, it engendered fear. Her future was riding on it. And there were still some big problems to be dealt with. Andy Toll had not yet sent her his program. And there was JP's program. That whole business was a mess.

JP's fiancée, Amy Tomczyk, wanted to give his presentation. That would only happen over her dead body! She'd never heard Amy say ten words! It simply couldn't happen if she had anything to do with it. She could imagine Amy standing on stage, a rank amateur, forgetting what she was going to say. No! This conference was going to be perfect! Her fingers tightened on the steering wheel until her hands felt numb. She shook one hand and then the other. She had to stop fixating on problems!

Margaret saw the entrance for I-76 north for Philadelphia the moment she passed it. She was seized with panic. She wanted to stop the van, but she couldn't in the midst of all of this traffic! Then she remembered that, once before when Mitch had given her a driving lesson on an interstate, she had passed an exit. Mitch had calmly told her to drive on, explaining that she could reverse directions by taking the next exit and turning around.

Soothed by this memory, she slowed down to about forty-five and began looking for the next exit. She checked the clock. It was only 11:30! That left plenty of time. Mother's dire predictions of terrible traffic had been wrong.

Still, she had to concentrate on what she was doing. Fixating on how to keep Amy from presenting JP's program was a time waster. She should simply tell Amy that her presentation was not up to standard. Period! She was the director.

She recited the directions out loud. "Exit on I-76 North. Take 676 into the city. Turn on Market Street."

When she got to the hotel, she would need a porter to transport everything into the hotel. She would find her room, have lunch, and then she would begin setting up. Hopefully, by then, Lin Baldwin and her partner John Beam would be there to help.

Just eleven-thirty. Maybe not. She forced her attention back to the road and the directions she had memorized.

8

Mim and Kevin shared a cab to the Bentam Hotel. They arrived at just past two. Although the majority of conference attendees did not attend the workshops and would not show until late tomorrow, some of the people in the lobby had the look of hort writers.

Mim smiled and waved at the familiar faces, but wheeled her suitcase directly toward the front desk. She would have plenty of opportunity to introduce Kevin around and catch up on gossip later. Mim motioned Kevin ahead of her because she knew he had an appointment with his cousin/uncle Randy. Ever the gentleman, he insisted that she precede him. Obstinate, she refused. He insisted. She went to the ladies room.

When she returned, Kevin was concluding his registration and there were two women ahead of her in the line. One looked vaguely familiar and Mim was sure she belonged to Horticultural Writers, but couldn't recall the woman's name. Hard, when you only see these people at most once a year. The woman was wearing clogs with thick socks, trousers, a turtleneck and a scratched and, in places, torn down vest that suggested she wore it when she pruned roses. She carried only a vintage backpack that had once been black. Her garb and a kind of springy athletic bearing announced that she spent most of her time outdoors instead of in front of a computer. She was probably a member associated with one of the botanic gardens or nurseries.

Kevin tapped Mim on the shoulder.

"See you tomorrow for breakfast? I'll probably stay out for dinner tonight."

"Breakfast starts at seven," Mim announced. Kevin grimaced. He was a night owl.

He had already checked his bag at reception. Now, he glanced at his key, pocketed it, and bussed her cheek. He was out the door in seconds.

One person remained ahead of Mim in the line to register. The woman was unfamiliar. Short with a mop of curly, chestnut brown hair, she seemed too elegantly dressed for a Horticultural Writer—even a Horticultural Writer on the town. Her black suit was beautifully tailored. The pencil skirt reached almost to her ankles. Mim looked down surprised. In spite of three-inch high heels, the woman stood barely over five feet tall. A red coat or cape was slung over her left arm and on that arm was a rhinestone—diamond?—bracelet. The hand at the end of that arm was as small and soft and white as a child's. The hands with perfectly oval and polished pearly pink nails, did not look like they had ever held a trowel. Perhaps she was with some other group.

"Reed, Philippa Reed," the woman was saying with a distinct British accent. "I'm with Glovers Gardens." Mim's ears perked up. Benjy Glover who was to present "Dreaming of a White Christmas Rose" was the owner of Glovers Gardens.

It would not be unusual for the head of a nursery to bring staff along, but Mim couldn't figure out what this woman's position at a nursery could be. Secretary? Publicist? Gardeners and horticulturists cleaned up nicely but usually not glitzily.

This woman didn't fit. Girlfriend? She tried to think whether or not Benjy was married.

Mim looked down at her own hands. They were rough and freckled, or were those age spots? There had been too many hours in the sun wielding a trowel for them ever to be soft and white again.

When the woman, now firmly established in Mim's mind as Philippa Reed, took her room key, Mim turned to her.

"Excuse me," she smiled, "I couldn't help but overhear you're with Glovers Gardens. I'm Mim Fitz and will be writing a story about hellebores for *Washington Home*." Philippa turned and extended her hand.

"Philippa Reed. How do you do?" Philippa was gorgeous. Her eyes were remarkable–enormous and brown. Her reddish brown, Shirley Temple locks framed a perfect, heart-shaped face. Her skin was a fine, flawless, luminous cream. Mim judged her to be in her early-thirties.

"Nice to meet you, Philippa. Glovers Gardens is a fine nursery," Mim said. "May I ask what you do there?"

"I'm going to be working on developing perennials—specifically hellebores," she said, thrusting out her chin as if expecting to be challenged.

"Wonderful!" said Mim. The woman at registration was waiting. "Excuse me! My turn to register. See you later."

"See you later," Philippa smiled. She turned and strode to the elevators, three-inch heels clacking so loudly on the marble floor that Mim as well as several other people in the lobby turned to look.

Registration complete, Mim draped her coat over one arm and grasped the handle of her suitcase.

"Oh!" said the receptionist. "There's a message for you." The woman handed Mim a slip of paper. Under Mim's name was written, "I need your rose story no later than Monday at 9 a.m." No name. Mim crumpled Phyllis's message and tossed it into a trash receptacle.

She turned, pulling her red suitcase, and almost collided with a very tall, white-haired man. He quickly stepped to his right to avoid bumping into her. Simultaneously, she stepped to her left. Then each reversed direction so that they still ended up face to face. They stopped and looked at each other. She saw recognition dawn in his eyes, then, something like a wince moved over his features. In a second, it was gone, replaced by a warm smile. He looked familiar; she was sure she had met him and ought to know his name. Close up, his tanned face and pale green eyes were so youthful that the contrast with his hair was shocking.

She smiled as he bowed to let her pass.

"Thank you," she said as she pulled her suitcase past him.

"Let's catch up later," he said.

Catch up later? Who was he?

Mim walked slowly to the elevators where she joined a half-dozen people waiting. She glanced back at the man she had bumped into only to find him looking at her. She nodded back. He looked familiar, but she couldn't place him.

When the elevator arrived, six of those waiting, including Mim, entered. One stepped back. She was a tall blonde. Apparently she preferred to ride in a less crowded elevator.

The elevator doors closed in front of Amy Tomczyk. In the polished brass that framed the elevator she caught a wavy reflection of herself: a slender blonde in a blue pants suit with a black purse slung over her shoulder. On her feet were the Prada pumps she and JP had bought together at the *marché aux puces*, the flea market, in Paris last spring. They had made the trip so that she could meet his family.

Now she was waiting for the elevator that would take her up to the fifth floor–alone. To the room that had originally been reserved for JP and her.

She could see two other people reflected in the brass as they waited for an elevator. They stood apart from her, but she felt that they were watching her—pretending not to, but watching her.

Now even some of their friends avoided her. They had come to the funeral and offered their words of sympathy. And now they didn't know what else to say. Those who did approach her seemed intent upon discouraging her from delivering JP's presentation.

"I'm not sure you should go ahead with this," Margaret Stemple, the conference director had said in a message on her answering machine. She added, "Have you ever spoken in public? It can be a very intimidating up there in front of a hundred and thirty people."

"You don't have to do this, you know," Benjy Glover had offered sympathetically. Most of the others had offered similar advice. Knowing she was shy. Knowing she was the quiet one.

JP had bragged to them all about her. She was the ballast that steadied his vibrant and animated extraversion. She was the quiet, steady power behind his throne.

She had prepared JP's many lectures and put his stunning photographs into PowerPoint format. She had composed and printed out his handouts; she'd written the publicity blurbs. But she had never spoken in public. In fact, she hadn't spoken in front of an audience since the tenth grade when she'd taken speech class. And that hadn't been a roaring success.

Her great talent was organization. She had kept JP's photos and lectures in perfect order. She had stored them by topic and placed each disk neatly in a long metal box that was kept in the office. When he was scheduled to speak, she always made a backup of his lectures on a disk and a flash drive. Just in case.

Her careful practice of backing up JP's lectures had preserved all she had left of his work. She reached her hand into her pocket and felt the flash drive. It was like a talisman. Only about three inches long, it contained two of JP's slide presentations. Thankfully, one of them was his lecture on the Balkan trip. There was nothing else. The thieves had taken everything—their computers, their cameras, their storage disks, their telephones. And they had taken JP.

She felt her throat constrict and struggled for control. The elevator doors opened. She breathed a sigh and stepped inside. Two people followed her. The woman, white-haired and dressed entirely in white, said, "seven please." Amy punched in the number and waited for the man to speak.

"Five," he said. She punched in his floor and felt for her talisman, the flash drive. She enclosed it in a tight fist.

It didn't matter that she had never spoken in public. Why should she be afraid? There was nothing left to be afraid of. The worst had already happened. How could she be afraid when she no longer cared about anything. Nothing was left. Even the pain had burrowed down so deeply into her being that it was surrounded by a great, soothing numbness, a kind of deep, cottony padding all around her.

She felt nothing, feared nothing, cared about nothing but the one thing she must do. Her entire consciousness was directed to one great task. JP had been asked to speak on the species he had observed and collected in the Balkans. And he had wanted to showcase his own work. To do both of those things, he had anticipated this conference with more eagerness and excitement than she had ever seen in him. He had painstakingly sorted through his photos. He had spent months working on his address.

Now that he couldn't do it. She would do it for him. She would show his photos and read what he would have said.

She exited the elevator and walked to room 515.

Amy was too absorbed in her thoughts to have noticed the man who exited the elevator after her. He walked along the corridor behind her and used his key to enter room 513.

Marcus Tydings walked into room 513, set down his handsome leather case and opened it. He placed six starched shirts, socks, and underwear in the drawer of the armoire, hung up two pairs of neatly pressed jeans and his sport coat. He stashed the suitcase. Then he sprawled on the bed while he consulted the hotel book of services.

He called down to order dinner in his room for six o'clock. He chose sirloin tips and added a bottle of cabernet. It would be paid for by the conference because he was supposed to be presenting a workshop tomorrow afternoon on hellebore propagation and care. Philippa would be having dinner with Benjy Glover and the rest of the staff from Glovers, but she would probably sneak over later.

In the meantime, a quiet afternoon and evening would give him a chance to alter his program. Margaret Stemple, the conference director, told him that John Bevins, the scout from Pefect Perennials, would be at his workshop. This was the chance he had been waiting for! If Perfect Perennials wanted one—or more—of his hellebores, his fortune would be made!

Forget telling the conference attendees how to germinate hellebores! He was going to wow that scout with the breadth and depth of his plants.

He wouldn't bother attending the other workshops. After he reworked his program, he could sleep in tomorrow morning. Maybe he'd go to the gym to work out. He might do a little reading, and make sure his clothing was in order.

After decades of indifference, he now took great interest in clothing. His clothes were his signage, an important part of his image. He chose each piece to hint carefully at something about himself that he wanted known. The shirts, sweaters, jackets, and shoes he wore suggested to the world that he had chosen them as a practical necessity, that he cared little for clothing, but had enough money to buy the best.

Like today. His shirt—obviously custom made and very expensive—was a bright, robin's egg blue. It was a color that enhanced his aqua blue contacts. All of his shirts were the same blue color. Georgenti shirts cost a bundle, but they were a business expense. He had them monogrammed with the initials "EH" for Extraordinary Hellebores and deducted them as a business expense from his taxes.

His expensive shirts were a personal emblem; they announced that their wearer was successful enough to have a stack of meticulously laundered shirts on hand—jacquard in winter, a light linen weave in summer. The fact that they were all identical in style and the same color made the point that while he bought good quality, he wasn't overly interested in clothing. Having them all the same indicated that he casually ordered them by the dozen as with undershirts or shorts. A necessity.

The robins egg blue shirts enhanced the deep tan he maintained year round. The tan forged the reputation he allowed, that he was a phenomenally successful plant breeder who spent winters in Vail or Zermatt. He had never mentioned those places and didn't know how to ski. He had no idea how the rumor of his winter vacations started, but he never disputed it.

He never wore dress shoes. On his feet were the custom made boots that advertised that he was first and foremost, a nurseryman, a person who worked outside. That they also added three inches to his five foot eight was an added bonus.

The navy cashmere pullover he was wearing today was a flea market find. Baggy, with a little hole in the back, it was the sweater he invariably wore when he spoke to garden clubs. The hole was a brilliant little boy touch that hinted at vulnerability and won him instant sympathy from the female members of his audiences. He had only to remove his sports coat before one or another of the audience would sidle up and whisper to him that there was a hole in his sweater. He needed both hands to count the women who had offered to fix it for him and ended up doing more.

Image was everything. Marcus Tydings had learned that a little late in life, but he had learned it well. Now it was his mantra. That's what he thought as he regarded himself in the mirror of his hotel room. He never tired of looking at himself, although he made a point of never, never doing so in public.

He hadn't always been this way. From the time he was in high school until just five years ago, he had avoided looking at himself in a mirror. He hadn't liked what he saw there, a thin, timid looking man with what his mother sighed and called "the Tydings chin."

It was odd. He still couldn't remember the exact chain of events that led to what was, for him, an unexpectedly daring act. Five years ago, he had undergone surgery for a chin implant.

It didn't matter how it had come about. That surgery changed his life. The spectacular result, a finely chiseled, Marlboro man face, surpassed his wildest expectations. Even Dr. Van Horton, his plastic surgeon, had been astonished at the change.

Skinny, mousey Mike Tydings with the weak, receding chin, learned with amazement that he was attractive to women. And men, too, for that matter.

Women threw themselves at him. In the beginning, he hadn't known what to do. That changed. He learned swiftly. Now the list of his conquests, if that's what they were, was longer than he could remember.

His magnetism became even stronger when he changed his name to Marcus. The name change was something he had done for himself in recognition of the new man he had become. Most of all, he had done it because he had learned the importance of packaging. Yes, presenting an image was a lesson he had learned very well. He now knew how very much his name, his appearance, how he dressed had to do with how the world received him.

Before the surgery, he had worked as county extension agent in Muncie where he had spoken occasionally to garden clubs and other horticultural groups. His talks, almost always about hellebores and other shade loving plants, were politely but tepidly received.

He stood before the mirror. Bespectacled Mike Tydings, an extension agent in Muncie, Indiana, was gone. The Marcus Tydings in the mirror was a completely different man. His good looks, the expensive shirts and boots, and the tan that hinted at luxurious vacations forged an elegant and mysterious façade. Nothing succeeds like success was ridiculously, absurdly true. Act successful and, sooner or later, you'll be successful. It had certainly worked with women.

It also worked with his speaking engagements. He knew his information had not changed. *He* had changed and that had made all the difference. Now, he was in such demand with garden clubs and small botanic gardens that he had raised his fee and raised it again. The workshop he would give tomorrow would not only enhance his reputation, it would earn him some real money.

It was money he needed to support the carefully constructed persona he showed the world. That included everybody. It was a persona that shielded a different reality. The income he received from selling hellebores—mostly Lenten roses—was a pittance. Of course, he could have earned far more, but his goal had never been to sell thousands of hellebores; leave that to those who were satisfied with the status quo.

His shining goal was to create the one-in-a-million plant that would bring him respect and renown. And it just might bring in enough royalty to last a lifetime

He had "acquired" some excellent stock plants by various means. He smiled at his own ingenuity. His new persona—rich and independent–placed him above suspicion when plants at the nurseries and gardens he visited went missing.

He had recently cultivated a source of exceptional plants from an outstanding British breeder. These and other recent acquisitions—the finest plants available—comprised the foundation of his breeding program. He planned to cull their progeny ruthlessly. He sold the offspring he deemed unsuitable for future crosses. He'd call smaller nurseries to say 'his people might be able to put together some plants for them.'

Nobody knew "his people" were non-existent because he couldn't afford help. Nobody guessed that there wasn't a score of minions to pot up his hellebores. He potted up hundreds himself—always wearing disposable surgical gloves to keep his hands from becoming grimy.

Nobody knew that his office was an old camper that was parked in a field just outside State College Pennsylvania. Or that he rented that field from a farmer. He conducted all business by email and post office box. None of his colleagues had ever visited his nursery. And until his fortunes coincided with the image he projected, no one ever would.

9

Being here at the conference brings back memories of the expedition in Slovenia. I don't think I will ever forget what happened there. Nor will I ever really forgive Tate Adkins for his deceit, for the way that he humiliated me.

I still recall my incredulity, as I stood facing him on that narrow mountain path, and the look of disgust on his face! I couldn't believe it. I simply could not believe it. Could I have been wrong?

No! For the entire week of that expedition, every time I was anywhere near him, I felt his eyes on me. I heard his thoughts as clearly as if he had shouted them.

But when I got him alone—away from JP and the others— he denied himself and he denied me. I knew why. He was afraid to reveal the truth.

I had walked with him and shared my most private thoughts with him. I had told him absolutely everything!

Then he turned on me, denying everything! I couldn't believe it. Finally, we had a chance to be alone together and he was backing away. I remember that I just stood there on that cold, gray mountain, sick and chilled.

I had been so anxious not to miss him that morning when he started out, in my haste, I just grabbed a light jacket and some gloves and left my waterproof parka behind. As a result, I was soaked and very, very cold. I felt so bad that I didn't give a damn about those Christmas roses anymore. I knew even if we both got them, he'd be the one to get all the credit anyway.

After his betrayal of me and that look of disgust on his face, I just wanted to get out of there, to get as far away as possible.

But I didn't. Instead of turning around and heading back to the inn as fast as I could, I just stood there, wretched and soaked through. I couldn't move. It was like every ounce of energy had left me. I was limp from humiliation.

We both just stood there for five, maybe ten minutes? I don't know how long it was. Maybe he was waiting for me to say or do something. Or he was hoping I would go away.

"You know," Tate said finally, "I live with a woman…you probably know…"

"Yes, of course I know," I cut him off because I wanted him to shut up. And I did know. I had run an internet search on her, too.

I knew he was dying to get going. He wanted to be done with me and get moving. He started shifting from foot to foot. He looked over his shoulder at the trail ahead.

"I'm pretty sure what I'm looking for is not too far ahead," he said heartily like he was leading a Sunday school hike. He started walking. I thought about turning back. I should have. I don't know why I didn't. I guess I followed him because I was too exhausted and miserable to do anything else.

We walked for at least another mile. He never turned around once. I actually think he forgot that I was there or maybe he just wished I wasn't.

Then he stopped. I looked up and saw what he saw—a huge colony of Helleborus niger, hanging off a ledge. Pink Christmas roses! They weren't the ones we'd seen the day before, these were bigger and pinker. In fact, they were like nothing I had ever seen. I almost forgot feeling miserable. I couldn't take my eyes off them.

Neither could he. He was so mesmerized by them, he forgot himself and he lunged forward and it was a really narrow part of the trail. He almost lost his balance. I watched him sway back and forth before he regained firm footing. It froze me in my tracks.

For some minutes, he just stood absolutely still—just where he was. His chest was heaving and his breath started coming out in big clouds. So was mine, only I was hyperventilating from a combination of misery and shock. We just stood there for several minutes.

Then I took a better look at that colony of hellebores. Even though you could see them easily, I knew they wouldn't be easy to reach. They were off the trail on a ledge about three feet down over a drop-off. The ledge was plenty wide enough for a perch. You probably could have danced a jig on it, but it just jutted out into thin air. It made me sick to look at it.

Oh, I wanted them! But when I saw what you would have to do to dig them out, it wasn't something I wanted to try. The only way to get close enough to them would have been to climb down onto the ledge.

Okay, it was wide enough for three people. But there were no guard rails—just a lot of air all around it and a fifty foot drop below it.

I really thought Tate would give it up right there. I hoped he would.

But no. All of a sudden—Tate began looking at me with interest. Of course I knew it wasn't because he was interested in me... or my breeding program.

10

Kevin first got the idea for a "curse of the hellebores" story in Slovenia. Walkingtours had sponsored a press trip for travel writers. He had joined with the intention of doing a story on eco-tourism for the *Washington Edition*.

He remembered clearly how it had come about. He and the four other members of his group had just finished following their indefatigably perky tour guide Oriana on a grueling twenty-two kilometer hike.

After five days of hiking, his endorphins were no longer firing or whatever they were supposed to do. He was flat out exhausted. And he found evidence of the recent conflicts utterly depressing. Scattered along the trails were the remnants of people fleeing: shoes, a cooking pot, once even a dead cat. He had no idea that the ethnic war had raged everywhere in this region—not just in Bosnia.

He was exhausted. Even though their luggage was transported by car from inn to inn, he was weighted down. In addition to his day pack, he was carrying his camera, lenses, and tripod. He had hoped to get a second story out of this trip. *The Saber*, the paper he wrote for under the pseudonym Minna Kay, had expressed interest in a photo essay on hiking in the Balkans.

Now he was tired of stopping to set up the tripod and take the photos and then catch up to the others. And the others were tired of posing and falling behind with him.

For the last five kilometers, his longing to stop walking, to be back at the inn was overwhelming. He wanted to take off his boots, to eat, to bathe, and to put on dry clothing. But when they finally reached their destination, instead of the quiet, rustic inn they had left two days before, they walked into a scene of chaos.

Dragan, the proprietor, was collapsed in a large heap on a bench in front of the great hearth. His monumental shoulders shuddered as he wept. His six-year old daughter Nadya sat quietly by his side, her tiny hand engulfed in his, an appendage the size of a dinner plate.

Kevin's first thought was that something terrible had happened to Dragan's wife, who was also called Nadya. Lacking the language to inquire of the other staff and unwilling to disturb the innkeeper, he had gone into the bar in search of English speakers only to find it full of them in similar states of grief.

He recognized members of the same plant hunting party his group had encountered more than once as they hiked. There were about a dozen of them. A few were in their cups, but two were nearly falling down drunk. One, whom the others addressed as JP, had tears streaming down his face. He was muttering to himself in French. The other drunk stood unsteadily and waved his arms for attention.

"It's the curse. I tell you. I should know. I, of all people, should know! Hellebores are cursed."

"Oh shut up, Barney!" one of the women said. "Join the twenty-first century!"

"You know nothing about it!" the man called Barney countered, knocking over a half-filled glass of beer. "Ever heard of Wilshon McCoy? Eh?" Ignoring him, the woman began mopping up the spilled beer with napkins the rest of the table quickly handed to her.

"C'mon Barney, let's take a walk," a stocky, fiftyish man put a friendly arm around Barney and led him from the bar.

"Who's Wilshon McCoy?" a trim, white-haired man asked.

"That would be Wilson McCoy," someone answered.

"Okay, Wilson. Who is he?"

"He's a dead hellebore breeder."

"What happened to him?"

"He was killed—probably murdered."

"And so was Marion Petersfield!" a male voice cut in. "Someone did a job on her! Maybe Barney's not as off the mark as we think."

Kevin sat down at the edge of the group and listened. He learned that earlier in the day one of the plant hunting party had disappeared.

A search party composed of members of the plant hunting group and locals had found him. He had fallen over a cliff. The man's name was Tate and Kevin remembered him from a brief earlier meeting as someone he had hoped to get to know. Apparently, Tate had lost his balance while looking for a certain kind of hellebore which was a plant the party was collecting.

Kevin had never heard of hellebores, but the idea of a curse associated with them fascinated him. He observed that several members of the group gave credence to the idea. As he listened to their stories, he forgot about his hunger, his exhaustion, and his wet clothing.

Recently, he had published an article on actors' superstitions and the origins of "break a leg." It had been very well received and had given him a welcome break from straight travel writing. He decided right there and then that he would write about the hellebore curse.

He joined two of the women, Olga and Katie, for dinner. They all talked for so long during dinner and afterwards by the fire that his clothes dried completely.

He skipped the bath. Before finally tumbling into bed, he wrote for nearly an hour, putting down all that he had learned that night. Tate Adkin's death had been an accident, but at least one of the other two hellebore breeders had been murdered.

Kevin got off the tram some blocks from Franklin Square. He walked the rest of the way to Police Headquarters. All around him, familiar sights brought back memories of his time in this city. The spring like air and the familiar landmarks evoked vivid recollections. Suddenly, he felt younger. His step quickened and he walked taller as if the energy of his youth was returning to him.

But when he reached Police Headquarters, Kevin was escorted to Detective Randall Murray's office by a young female officer with a blonde ponytail who looked to Kevin much too young to be a police woman. Then, he reflected, his fifty-fourth birthday had come and gone and everywhere he went lately—to the dentist, to the doctor–everyone looked too young to be doing what they were doing. For a few seconds, his spirits were deflated. Then he saw Randy and the warmth of a rich, long friendship washed over him.

Randy's face lit up when he saw Kevin. He came forward to greet him, grabbed his hand in a hearty shake and enveloped Kevin's trim body in an enthusiastic bear hug.

Then the men stepped back, each looking the other over.

"How long has it been?" Randy asked, leading Kevin to a chair. Kevin sat down, facing Randy across his desk. It was, he observed, as untidy as ever, covered with piles of paper, photographs, a book, candy wrappers, and coffee cups.

"Going on eight months, I think. How are Sue and the kids? Sue still at Thomas Jefferson?"

"Yeah, and Sarah, too—they're working together. Sarah's a head nurse," Randy said proudly.

"And Johnny?"

"Takes after your side of the family," Randy joked, running his eyes over Kevin's black cashmere blazer and neatly creased pants, acutely aware that there was absolutely nothing about their appearances to indicate they were related by blood. "Tall and skinny like Grandma McKinny. Neat as a pin!" Randy looked around him and laughed out loud. "Not like his old dad."

Randy looked like the former left guard he had been at Lowell High– only many years later and many pounds heavier. He slouched in his chair so that his great stomach rose above huge thighs that strained at his gray pants, giving them the look of giant sausages.

His gray Harris tweed jacket, flung over the back of his desk chair and draping down to the floor, exposed a torn lining. The pockets were stretched beyond redemption and gaped open as if he used them to carry his lunch, which he sometimes did. Today, one of them held a banana.

"You know he passed the bar. He's a lawyer now," Randy said, a big smile lighting a face that was florid and slightly damp along a receding hairline of black hair as stiff and straight as nails.

"Has he found a job?" Kevin asked, falling easily into the warmth of a friendship that had grown golden over the years. It had begun the summer Kevin landed an internship at the *Philadelphia Star*. He had looked up his uncle Randy who had followed a girl friend to Philadelphia after his discharge from the marines. Since then, he and Randy had communicated at least once a month, in person, by phone, and, for the last few years, by email.

"Working for the DA! Right down the street!"

"The apple does not fall far from the tree," said Kevin. Randy beamed. Then his smile faded.

"Remember Pringles?" Randy asked.

"How could I forget? Are they still around?" Mr. Pringle had owned the Corner Coffee Shop where Randy and Kevin had breakfasted each morning of that long ago summer. Finding that they lived in the same neighborhood, both stopped there for breakfast on the way to work. After a week, they were regulars who looked forward to meeting each morning and discussing their plans and, by August, their dreams.

"They were until last month! Of course, old Pringle, he's been gone—oh, probably eleven years now. Molly, that's Pringles' daughter, she took over for him. Did a good job, but she's had it. Sixteen burglaries in twenty years!"

"That never was a great neighborhood," Kevin said, frowning.

"Worse now. Drugs!" Randy spat. He leaned back in his chair, all business now.

"You want to know about JP Chiasson?" Randy said with a strong Massachusetts accent that had survived twenty-odd years on the Philadelphia police force. He leant his chair so far back that Kevin feared it would topple. "Realistically? I'd say drug related. They go in and take everything that wasn't nailed down—wallet, computers, cameras, one of these watchacallit power projectors, even the friggin' telephones! Chiasson and his girlfriend, fiancée, kept all of that stuff in their office, right by the front door. So it was nice and convenient for the thieves."

"The fiancée says she had valuable jewelry upstairs in the bedroom. Wasn't touched."

"Looks like he walked in on it– surprised them. Thing is, the door wasn't forced." Randy shrugged.

"So maybe, it wasn't locked. Fiancée says she forgot something that morning. She goes back inside the house to get it. She *thinks* she locked the door."

"What time did it happen?" Kevin asked, thinking it unusual for a burglary in the late afternoon and early evening. Randy shrugged.

"Fiancee says it's around nine when she gets back to the house. Their stuff's gone. He's there. Head bashed in but he's alive or, I should say, not dead yet–still conscious. Sort of. And jabbering in French. She calls 911. Ambulance comes, but he dies on the way to the hospital."

"Co workers say they saw him after lunch, maybe around two, and, later, he goes to this meeting at Longwood–some kind of plant conference.

Started at three. Supposed to go on all afternoon and, right after that, there was this dinner party for the people at the conference. He was at the conference and he went to the party and then he left. Nobody notices when he leaves or knows why." Randy rotated his head, a movement that generated a loud crack in his neck.

"His fiancée," Randy read from the computer screen, "name's Amy Tomczyk, she says she was supposed to meet him at that party after work. She gets there around 7:30 and they say he's gone. First, she figures maybe he went home to change clothes or maybe he forgot to bring something for someone who is there. She waits. An hour goes by. They only live fifteen minutes away. When he doesn't show up at the party and he doesn't answer his cell—they took that, too–she goes looking for him."

"Like I said, he was still alive when she found him, but he wasn't making sense. He was talking French. He was French. She says he kept saying 'bitch-ette, bitch-ette' like he was going to tell her something else, but he never did." Randy pronounced it 'bitch-ette.'

"Bitch-ette?"

"It sounds to me like "little bitch," but, apparently, it's a term of endearment—in French!" Randy laughed. "Not one I'd get away with using on Sue." He continued, "I say coincidence. But you're right, there is this "hellebore connection," Randy said, wiggling his fat fingers like quotation marks.

"Before he came to Longwood, Chiasson was working at a nursery in England. It specialized in...these same kind of plants. The owner, woman name's Marion Petersfield, 68 years old, white female, British, lives near...." Randy consulted his computer, "near Salisbury. That's in England. Petersfield is some kind of big shot plant lady. She's out walking her dog in the woods. The dog runs back to the nursery—that's where she grows those flowers you're so interested in. Withcombe Nursery."

"Chiasson worked for her? I didn't know that. At Withcombe Nursery?" Kevin stopped writing. He was looking out the window behind Randy's desk at the parking lot, full of police cars that came and went.

"Yeah, that's the place. Chiasson was working there the day she got killed. You know about it?"

"Marion Petersfield was murdered," Kevin said, looking to Randy for confirmation.

"You got it." Randy shifted his bulky form into a more comfortable position.

"She goes out to walk her dog. Someone takes a pipe or a tire iron or something nasty to her head, beats her to a bloody pulp. Dog comes back without her. Guys working for her get worried and they go looking for her. She's still alive—barely. Fully clothed, no evidence of sexual assault—which checks out."

"Wait a *minute*." Randy clicked through several files on his computer. "I got a shot of them."

"Here it is." Randy angled the monitor to give Kevin a better look. He rolled his chair over as a photo of four people filled the screen. "Check it out." Kevin got up and walked around to Randy's side of the desk for a better look. The four wore Wellington boots. Three were wearing the kind of barn jackets that are trendy among young people who never go near barns.

"Which one is Chiasson?"

"Guy on the left. That's Petersfield in the middle." Randy pointed to a white haired woman wearing a skirt, Wellington boots, and a barn coat. Kevin looked at Chiasson. He was of medium height, only slightly taller than Marion Petersfield. Kevin guestimated JP's height to be about five feet eight or nine inches. His blonde hair caught the sunlight, like a halo. He was smiling as if he hadn't a care in the world. A likable face.

"Guy on the right is Robert Marvel," Randy said.

"Big guy!" Kevin commented. Robert Marvel was easily a head taller and a foot wider than JP Chiasson and Marion Petersfield. He was probably twice the height of the fourth figure.

"Who's the other one? " Kevin's gaze settled on the fourth figure. At first he thought, judging from the stature, it might be a child. The face was in the shadow of a large, floppy hat. Wisps of unruly long hair that escaped her hat blazed orange in the sunlight.

"That's Philippa Paxton-Reed. Looks twelve, but she's twenty-nine." Randy clicked on his mouse. A printer on his desk, hidden under papers, came to life, dislodging papers and bits of a tuna sandwich. A photo emerged from under it all.

"Here." Randy handed Kevin the printout. Keven examined it for a few moments.

"Do they have alibis?" Kevin looked up from his perusal of the photo. He was imagining how easily a man of Marvel's strength and stature might wield a lead pipe.

"The three people working at the nursery, their alibis all check out." Randy scrolled down the computer screen. "At least," Randy looked up and shrugged, "they were all together."

"Anyway," said Randy, resuming his story with relish, "after they find Petersfield, she's unconscious, but she's still alive. They call an ambulance. Ambulance comes and takes her to the hospital and the employees—all three of them—they go to the hospital. They sit there together and they wait and they wait until they get the bad news. And while they're sitting there, you know what happens?"

"What?" asked Kevin, without taking his eyes from the photo.

"The place—this Withcombe Nursery —gets robbed. If you could call it that! Funny thing is, only a bunch of plants disappears. There's money in the cash register and lots of plants and gardening stuff. But what gets lifted? Not the plants in the pots, ready to go, which would make it easy to carry them out and load them up. No. Whoever does it, he digs the plants out of the ground—way in the back of the nursery. Alls that's left is holes. Supposedly, these are very, very valuable, special plants that Petersfield didn't want to sell."

"Prime suspect is a guy named McCoy. And…"

"McCoy!" Kevin leaned forward eagerly. "Wilson McCoy!"

"You know who he is?" Randy's eyes widened.

"I've heard of him." Kevin thought back to his conversation with Mim on the train. "I've heard that McCoy and Petersfield used to be close, lovers. They fell out over something that had to do with hellebores."

"Well, they didn't make up," Randy snorted. "McCoy and Petersfield had a big shouting match a week before she gets whacked. He's also the competition. He's got a really big nursery in another part of England…" Randy consulted the computer screen, "in Upper Sackfield. "

"Does anybody know what they argued about?"

"Nope. All anybody heard was an argument. Couldn't make out the words, or so they said."

"What does McCoy say it was about?" asked Kevin.

"He swore up and down it never happened. Nobody actually *saw* him during the argument, but he was at the nursery earlier that day and her workers say Petersfield couldn't stand him."

"So, cops search McCoy's place. They're looking for these stolen plants—all of which are white with lotsa petals. That's rare with these kinds of plants. They find pink plants and what have you, but they don't find a single plant that's like the flowers they're looking for. And he's got an alibi. Two employees say they were with him at his nursery the time Petersfield was killed."

"How far apart are the two nurseries?" Kevin had stopped writing and was looking through the window behind Randy's chair. In the deepening dusk, the police cruisers entering and leaving the parking lot had turned on their headlights.

"Just over forty miles, but the Brits say that it would take two hours to drive. Small roads, lotsa little towns."

"Anyway, they can't get anything to stick, but they're watching him. He's a 'person of interest' in the Petersfield case. And they've got nothing else. And then...This beats all."

Randy looked at Kevin with a cat's-got-the-canary smile.

"One year later. One year *to the day* later. McCoy gets killed. Drives off a cliff! There's a big dent in the back right bumper—like maybe he had a little help."

"So yeah! Maybe growing this watchamacallit flower is not good for your health. Maybe people should grow petunias instead."

"There is another hellebore misfortune story," said Kevin. "Have you ever heard the name, Tate Adkins?"

"Nope."

"He was a horticulturist at Backenbrook Arboretum—and a hellebore breeder. Two years ago, Tate Adkins was on a plant hunting trip in the Balkans to collect new kinds of hellebores. That's where they grow."

"I happened to be there, too. Not with the plant collecting group. I was researching eco-travel in the Balkans with a group called 'WalkingTours' and our two groups crossed paths a couple of times." Randy rolled his eyes at such cushy activities that passed for work, but Kevin, long used to Randy's teasing, ignored him.

"Adkins' group stayed at the same place we did. We got there on the day he died. He went out early in the morning. Alone. He never came back. Apparently, he had been climbing a very steep path when he slipped and fell—a long way down. He was killed."

"There were seventeen other people on that plant hunting trip," Kevin said. "And one of them was JP Chiasson."

Kevin looked up and saw what he hoped would be there: a spark of interest in Randy's brown eyes.

Randy thought he'd be able to stop by the hotel on Saturday night. If that didn't work and getting together proved too difficult, they would talk by phone.

Kevin said goodbye, hailed a cab back to the hotel. The friend he had hoped to surprise visit was out of town until tomorrow. It was just as well. Tonight, he wanted to work.

As he looked out the taxi's windows at the festive shop windows and streetlights garlanded with Christmas lights, he felt the familiar excitement of a developing story. Randy might act indifferent, but Kevin was sure he had seen the bulldog gleam in Randy's eye. Randy would do a little investigating of his own.

In his hotel room, Kevin, with the discipline gained from years of reporting, immediately sat down to transfer his notes about JP and the burglary-murder from his notebook into the growing file in his laptop. He had labeled it "hellebore curse."

Then he went back to the beginning of the notes he had made in Slovenia after Adkin's body had been found. He remembered members of the plant hunting party, in various states of shock and grief, installed in the restaurant where two of the men were already quite drunk, while others huddled quietly together, talking in low voices.

Who had first mentioned a curse? Maybe it was in his notes. He scrolled over a long description of the inn, the commotion, the local police, down to the words he was looking for. He glossed over a list of names until, further down, there it was! He had written: "JP Chiasson, drunk, weeping, French, good friend of Adkins."

He scrolled down to the heading, "curse of the hellebores," the germ of the story he was now following. Under the heading were bulleted notations. He read the first entry, "Barney, drunk, shouting about curse. Mentioned Wilson Mc Coy."

He read on. The second entry was "Marion Petersfield–hellebore nursery—murdered."

He remembered sitting by the fire in the inn and talking to the women—Olga and he couldn't remember the other one's name–while his clothes dried on his body and his hair hardened into stiff peaks on his head. He scanned his writings for the woman's name and found it.

"Katie Hiscock, nursery in Virginia. KH disputes curse notion, acknowledges murder of Petersfield, woman with nursery, England, and McCoy Wilson. Accidental death?"

After he typed in the information Randy had shared, he placed the printout Randy had given him on the desk, flattening it with the palm of his hand. He moved the lamp over for a closer look at the grainy image. Again Marvel's size leaped out at him. His size was menacing, but his face? It could go either way.

JP Chiasson was another case altogether. From the face in the photo, Kevin judged JP Chiasson to be an upbeat, cheerful person. In fact, the man in the photo looked so positive, so together, so on top of the world, it was hard to connect him to the image in Kevin's memory of the blubbering drunk in Slovenia.

He shifted his gaze to Marion Petersfield. What was it about this unsmiling, but not unfriendly face that had inspired such rage? Randy had said she was in her late sixties. Her hair was snowy white, cut sensibly short.

The fourth person was a woman. Kevin checked his notes. Philippa Paxton-Reed. She was young, 29, and small as a child. The hat she wore shadowed her face. All he could see were a pair of extraordinary, large, round eyes.

11

By 7:15 a.m. on Friday morning, Sally Flinn had already set up her tripod in Chanticleer Garden's Asian Woods. A good thing she got here early because today promised to be as warm and sunny as it was yesterday.

She had to move quickly before the sun got high. Even with a polarizing filter, bright sunlight could make her colors dull and her images flat and uninteresting. She checked her notes for the hundredth time. There were still four trees to go for her photo essay on tree bark for *American Gardener* magazine.

She was standing in front of one of them, an Asian species of maple with wonderful jade green bark that was striped with white. First, she photographed the label: *Acer olivarianum*. Then she set up the shot, bracketing for good measure. She moved in closer, took another series. Then she moved back and took several more. Finally, she repeated the sequences using a flash.

After this, what she needed was a sugar maple—a really big one—with deeply grooved, almost black bark. If there was still time, she'd try to get a better shot of persimmon bark.

Yesterday, en route to Philadelphia, she'd crossed into New York and driven south on the Taconic Parkway. Then, at Sleepy Hollow, she'd headed west to pick up route 9. It wasn't a direct route to the Philadelphia area, but there was method in her madness.

She wanted to stop at Wave Hill in the Bronx. Even in winter, the gardens would be lovely. They were so lovely, in fact, that she wandered from garden to garden, reveling in the unseasonable weather and the warm sun on her face…and forgot the time. Three hours later and way behind in her schedule, she got back into the car and promptly spent another two hours in heavy traffic. But, she told herself, she did get some great shots of the dawn redwoods.

She made it as far as King of Prussia before, exhausted from the drive, she stopped at the first motel she came to. It was not a chain, but a mom and pop concern. Inside, she smelled incense being burned in the owner's quarters. She heard, but did not see children, but the man who came to reception was elderly with white hair that contrasted with skin the color of dried oak leaves.

The room was forty-nine dollars, a bargain. But it came with no frills. There was a television, an overhead light, one small dim lamp, and no alarm clock or radio. Fearing she would oversleep, she kept waking and checking her cell phone for the time. At four in the morning, she finally fell into a deep sleep and didn't awaken until six-thirty.

Panicked at the possibility of losing shooting time in the early morning light and not knowing how long it would take to get from the motel to Wayne, where Chanticleer was located, she skipped breakfast.

It was now ten-fifteen. She had taken photos of all of the tree barks except for the persimmon and her stomach was complaining loudly. She decided to stop en route to Philadelphia to have a big breakfast. Then she'd go straight to the hotel. She was looking forward to seeing her friend Mim Fitz with whom she would be sharing a room. Mim would be there already because she was attending the pre-conference workshops.

She was also collaborating with Mim on a book about herbs used as landscaping. Yesterday afternoon, Tom Frank, one of the editors at Foresters had called saying they were interested—very interested. Every time she thought about it, she felt a thrill pass through her. She hadn't told Mim yet. It would be a great surprise. In fact, she would stop and buy a bottle of champagne for them to celebrate!

She was excited for herself, but also for her dear friend Mim. Two years ago, the love of Mim's life had been killed on a plant hunting trip. Mim had been utterly devastated at the time. Before his accident, she had been perpetually smiling and lighthearted. Afterwards, she hadn't been herself.

On Friday morning, just as Sally woke up in the motel in King of Prussia, Mim opened her eyes in her room in the Bentam Hotel. Instead of the usual sense of displacement she experienced upon waking in a strange room, Mim was aware of the placement of the beds, the desk, the bathroom. Not surprising. The layout and furniture in the room were utterly interchangeable with those of most hotels.

In the main part of the room, two queen sized beds—one still made up–were separated by a small bed table that held the telephone. Across from the beds, an oversized blonde oak armoire in department store style dominated the room. It held the television and provided drawers for those hotel guests who unpacked their suitcases, something Mim never bothered to do unless she stayed for longer than two nights. On the walls were pictures of landscapes in soothing shades of blue and salmon that coordinated with the colors of the bedspreads and the wallpaper. Somewhat cramped for space in front of a wall of windows at the far end of the room were an easy chair and a desk. The windows were covered with both sheer and opaque drapes.

She glanced at the clock. 6:30. That left plenty of time to get dressed, grab a quick bite for breakfast and make it just in time to the first workshop "Hellebores of the World" by Joachim Muller. It was Joachim Muller that JP and Tate had met in Bosnia before they joined the plant hunting expedition in Slovenia.

She swung her legs out of bed, intending to take a shower and get dressed. Once up and on her feet, she felt sluggish. It was the kind of wound up, muscle tense exhaustion that comes from inactivity–too much sitting at the computer. What she needed was a workout followed by a hot shower. Maybe a quick twenty minutes would do the trick.

She sorted through her red suitcase and dug out yoga pants and a top. She put them on, put on her black sweater, grabbed her key, and was out the door. She took the stairway down to the ground level, found the exercise room, and entered by inserting her room key. The television was broadcasting a local news channel and the room was awash in fluorescent light, but she was alone. All the better. She turned on the treadmill, ratcheted up the incline, and walked swiftly and slightly uphill for twenty minutes, stopping only once to drink water dispensed from a cooler into the kind of cone-shaped paper cup she had not seen since childhood.

The exercise invigorated her. She felt ready for whatever the day would bring.

Mim dressed and went down to the lobby. A breakfast buffet was set up in a large alcove just beyond the registration desk. There were stations for juice, fruit, coffee, cereal, sweet rolls and bagels lined up along two sides of the room. Freestanding and accessible from two sides were the hot foods in metal serving containers: eggs, bacon, sausage, pancakes.

It was eight-thirty. Kevin was nowhere to be seen. Not that she had truly expected him to be there, but she had hoped he might be and now experienced a totally unwarranted sense of loss. She shrugged off this sentiment. Kevin was a night owl. She wouldn't have bet a nickel on his showing up for breakfast.

She picked up a tray, and inspected the choices before deciding upon orange juice, chunks of melon, sausage, scrambled eggs, and toast. Recognizing nobody in the dining area, she found an empty table, set down her tray, and went back for coffee.

Not more than two minutes later, she looked up and was surprised to see that a short line had formed in front of the coffee station. When it hadn't moved forward after a couple of minutes, several of those waiting stepped out of line to see what Mim observed clearly from her table. At the head of the line was Eric Ferris, otherwise unkindly, although perhaps not altogether undeservedly known as "Eric the ferret."

His nickname had been earned more for his consistently wild and erratic behavior than for his appearance. He was small, about five feet six, and wiry. With no chin to speak of, his head was dominated by an aquiline nose and thick lips that opened to show prominent yellow teeth. Perhaps it was his unappealing appearance that drove him to his bad behavior.

He was, hands down, the bad boy of Horticultural Writers. Rude and contentious, he was an anomaly in this group of generally easy-going people who loved flowers and gardens.

Oblivious to the people behind him, he was slowly filling three cups of coffee. She watched as, methodically, into each cup he dumped four heaping teaspoons of sugar, carefully stirring the coffee after each spoonful. Then, he topped each with a big splash of cream and, again, he thoroughly stirred the coffee. Finally, with great care, he gently pushed lids onto the Styrofoam cups. Finally, he placed the cups of coffee on a tray and, to the relief of those in the line for coffee–now ten strong and growing–he picked it up and headed to the tables.

Curious to see who his companions might be, Mim followed him with her eyes. He set the tray down at an empty table, sat down, and greedily reached for a cup of coffee. Nobody sat down at his table. In fact, nobody sat down anywhere near his table. It was as if a twenty-foot ring around it had been cordoned off.

Apparently, all three coffees were for him. She should have been annoyed with this rude behavior, but instead, all she felt was a tugging at her heart.

"Are you saving these seats for somebody?" Mim looked up to see Wendy Hunsicker, a plump and pretty blonde of around thirty with rosy milkmaid cheeks. She was Rose Redfern's research assistant. Apparently, she also ran interference for Rose, who now stood behind her, dressed in her signature white. Actually, today, it was more accurately cream—an ankle-length knit skirt over which she wore a matching tunic. Draped around her neck was a cream silk scarf patterned with tiny green ferns. She was cradling a cup in extraordinarily long, thin fingers, heavy with rings. Rose was looking off into the distance.

"Please sit down," Mim said. Reflexively, she looked around for J. J Stein ("just J") and Wendy followed Rose everywhere. Wendy helped Rose write her articles and books about herbs, but nobody could figure out exactly what J did.

The pair was nicknamed "the acolytes" because Rose was noted for her knowledge of herbs and plant poisons, something that made her the Horticultural Writer's version of a Druid priestess. Or witch.

Wendy smiled brightly. Rose nodded and sat down. A moment later J arrived. A pale young woman of perhaps twenty-five who used kohl around her eyes and wore her hair, dyed crow black, in a Roaring Twenties' bob with severe bangs, J dressed in unrelieved black. She was carrying a cup of coffee. She must have been at the tail end of the line behind Eric Ferris. She plopped down in her chair.

"That guy...!" In inchoate disgust, J rolled her eyes toward Ferris' table. Then, finding her voice, she said, "How can he even taste coffee when he puts so much sugar and cream in it?"

Rose looked coolly over to where Ferris sat. Her bright black eyes examined him leisurely like a sated snake examining some future but certain meal.

"J, you should drink Rose's tea instead," said Wendy brightly. She addressed Mim.

"Rose mixes her own blend of tea. It's from her garden."

"Really? What do you use in your blend?" asked Mim.

"It's proprietary!" inserted Wendy protectively. Then she smiled and added apologetically, "Rose will have some for sale after her workshop today." Rose gave Wendy a regal smile.

"I don't mind sharing the recipe with Mim," said Rose with *noblesse oblige*. She turned her bright, black, snake eyes on Mim.

"I began experimenting many years ago," Rose fixed Mim with an unblinking stare. "After many, many—*countless* tries really–using only the herbs that I grow and harvest in my own garden, I began to add tea, real tea, which of course I did not grow—except I do have a single specimen of *Camellia sinensis*— that I grow more for curiosity really. Of course, it must be brought into the conservatory over winter."

Mim pictured a gardener in Wellington's toting a large container into an elaborate Victorian greenhouse. Rose smiled and began to make a plucking motion with one hand.

"I have harvested the two leaves and a bud from that plant, but for my tea mixtures, of course, I need much more. Some years ago, I began importing a high quality oolong tea from friends on a tea estate in Sri Lanka. That is the base of the tea, if you will." Rose stared at Mim, but now seemed to be waiting for a response. Mim nodded. Rose continued.

"I have said that tea, *Camelia sinensis* is the base of my mixture. That is true. Tea is the largest single component of my mixture. However, tea comprises less than forty percent of the total. The rest—sixty percent—is an herbal mixture." She aspirated the "h" in herbal. Rose held up a very white, long hand and counted on fingers each of which bore an ornate ring. Mim stared at one ring that was in the shape of a snake.

"Several species of *Monarda*." She pushed three fingers down to tally the monardas. *"Melissa*, of course...." Her pointer finger folded down, forming a fist. She stared at the upright thumb.

"I add a bit of rosemary for its medicinal properties—did you know rosemary is helpful in memory retention? But it is so very easy to add too much!" Rose furrowed her brow, obviously reflecting on efforts gone awry. She settled her hands in her lap.

"Finally, I mix in hibiscus flowers and several salvias. I especially like *Salvia melissodora*. A delightful fragrance!" She offered her cup to Mim who sniffed the complex aroma with pleasure.

"That's lovely! Salvia meliss…?"

"*Salvia melissodora*. Grape sage."

"I don't know it."

"Not hardy here I'm afraid," said Rose. "It's a zone eight plant. Popular in California. I have it brought into the conservatory over the winter." Again Mim pictured the gardener. It was said that Rose lived in a great pile of a house on the Hudson River that had been in her family for generations. It was also said that she was the house's sole occupant. Wendy and J shared a gatehouse on the property. Again, Mim wondered what J did there. Pale, thin, but softly fleshy, she was an unlikely gardener.

Wendy launched into a description of grape sage and the conversation moved to sages in general. Suddenly J started and tapped her watch meaningfully. It was nine-thirty. Rose's workshop began in an hour.

"I'm keeping you from your preparations," said Mim, rising and thinking, and I'm keeping myself from Muller's workshop– already underway. "I am very much looking forward to your workshop. And I plan to buy some of that lovely tea," she added.

Rose nodded with a thin smile, remote and cool as if she had retreated into somewhere far away.

Mim was late for Muller's lecture. She sped toward the Juniper Room where she was to register.

12

A sign in the lobby: "Horticultural Writers Pre-conference Workshops, Registration in the Juniper Room" directed Mim down one flight to a long corridor lined with conference rooms. She passed the Oak Room, the Sycamore Room, and the Maple Room, before she turned a corner.

At first she didn't recognize the woman sitting at the registration table. Margaret Stemple, at least twenty pounds lighter than the last time Mim had seen her, sat at a cloth covered card table in front of the Juniper Room.

Mim took a second look. Margaret had also lost the glasses. She looked positively chic.

Mim looked around. On a breakfast table spread with a white tablecloth, there were four coffee urns and trays heaped with mounds of bagels, Danish, and croissants that looked untouched.

"Gosh, I thought there would be more of a crowd today. The breakfast table looks untouched," Mim thought out loud as she halted before Margaret at the registration table.

Margaret recoiled as if she had been struck. She sat dumbstruck for a moment, then snapped, "You're late. Dr. Muller has been speaking for," she glanced at her cell phone, "fifteen minutes!" Margaret snapped into a perfectly upright position and remained so for some moments. Mim became alarmed. A brain tremor? Then Margaret continued as if the interruption had not occurred.

"There has never been a huge turnout for the pre-conference workshops. We hold them merely for enrichment because some members want to learn more about the various subjects covered at the conference."

"The *conference* filled within a week of the mailing," Margaret went on crisply. "We have twenty people on the waiting list." She looked down and began to study the short list of names on the single sheet in front of her as if she were to be tested on it.

Mim took a second look. Yes, it really was Margaret Stemple, the same big-boned, long-suffering, overweight young woman with the thick, black-rimmed glasses who had worked at the Garden Center, Mim's local nursery, for…for years.

Not only did Margaret sound different from that quiet, self-effacing woman, she looked different. The ugly glasses were replaced with colored contact lenses that turned her eyes a purple-blue and made Mim think of Liz Taylor. Margaret was neatly turned out in gray slacks and a lavender turtle neck.

Maybe Margaret no longer lived with her mother who everyone said and Mim had observed, was a harridan. It was said that Margaret held a master's degree in English although she had worked as a salesperson at The Garden Center—probably at minimum wage.

Now she was doing something else at the Garden Center, Mim couldn't remember. Sally? Or someone else said it had been a promotion. Margaret was conference director! Maybe all of that success came at a price. She must feel stressed. Not surprising. Running this conference would be a headache for anyone. Maybe Margaret would relax when the conference was over.

"I'm sure that smaller, more intimate groups attending the workshops will provide better learning experiences," Mim carefully said, wishing she could withdraw her comment on the small turnout. Margaret's fragile ego was on the line. Even if the conference was oversubscribed, Margaret might equate low attendance at the workshops as a personal failure.

"Not everyone can take off work, you know," Margaret added, somewhat mollified. She still didn't look up, but checked her cellphone. "You are very late for the first lecture. Joachim Muller is the world expert on hellebores. We were lucky to get him," Margaret stated as she checked off Mim's name and handed her a nametag.

"Dr. Muller is speaking in the Oak Room." Then she added dismissively, "Death by Hellebore will be in the Pine Room. The propagation workshop, after lunch, will be held in the Pine Room also."

The door to the Oak Room was closed. Mim pulled it open very gently and slipped into the darkened room. On a screen at the opposite end of the room was the image of a hellebore Mim had never before seen. The long pointed leaves arranged themselves in perfect circles. The bright yellow flowers nodded slightly.

"This photograph was taken in Bosnia, where *Helleborus odorus* is endemic," Muller said in English only slightly accented by a mushy "R".

"What is unusual about this particular site is that not only are these plants a more vibrant shade of yellow than is typical, they are a form of *Helleborus odorus* that is completely evergreen. That's right! Completely evergreen!"

Muller advanced to the next photo and Mim gasped. There stood Tate and a blonde man in the midst of a vast field of yellow flowers. Tate and JP had joined Dr. Muller in Bosnia the week before they went on the expedition in Slovenia. Was that JP? And Tate! A shiver ran down her spine.

"Here are my colleagues standing in the middle of the largest population of evergreen *Helleborus odorus* I have ever experienced in my forty years of plant exploration!" Muller explained. "Moreover, as you can see, these flowers are quite a clear yellow. This photo was taken in Bosnia in the only place I have ever observed this very particular yellow flower color." Beyond identifying them as 'colleagues,' Muller said nothing about either Tate or JP, but he advanced rather too quickly to the next photo.

Muller continued, showing a dozen other species, but Mim could not concentrate. Over and over again in her mind's eye, she saw the image of Tate surrounded by a field of bright yellow hellebores. This was, she calculated, probably the last photo of him that she or anyone else had. She would ask Doctor Muller for a copy.

When the lights turned back on, Muller made his closing statement: "The genus *Helleborus* has been barely utilized. The many species within the genus offer countless exceptional ornamental qualities. The best cultivars are yet to come!"

In moments, Muller was surrounded by people from the audience posing questions. Asking him for a copy of Tate's photo would have to wait. Slowly, she got up and headed for the door.

The next workshop would be Rose Redfern's "Death by Hellebore. " Margaret had said it would take place in the Pine Room.

13

Mim found the Pine Room at the end of the corridor. Beyond it, another turn led to the parking garage. The door stood open. Inside, Rose and the acolytes were visible at the front of the room arranging a row of potted hellebores. There were small bottles of liquid next to the plants. From outside the room, Mim could see the word "poison" written in large, bold letters on each bottle. The poisons!

Mim entered and looked around. No wonder Margaret was touchy about attendance at the workshops! Not counting Rose and the acolytes, she counted only eight other people in the room.

Mim recalled the way Rose's face had faded from pleasant animation when she discussed her tea blend to an emotionless mask at the mention of her workshop. She must have put an enormous amount of preparation into this presentation. Next to the containers of plants on the table was a thick stack of handouts—enough perhaps for fifty people. What a disappointment this small turnout must be! Of course, she would be giving one of the concurrents tomorrow. Would that be under-enrolled as well?

Rose looked at the clock and scanned the nearly empty room. Then she turned to the table at the front of the room and began rearranging the objects upon it. Mim looked toward the still-open door, willing others to enter and fill the empty chairs. The corridor remained quiet and empty.

At five minutes before ten, Margaret Stemple rushed in accompanied by the man Mim had narrowly avoided bumping into yesterday in the lobby. She searched her mind to remember his name. Again she came up empty. When he saw her, he changed directions, came over, and slipped into the seat beside her. Unaware of his defection, Margaret had continued toward the front of the room. When she sensed he wasn't following, she turned around.

"Barney?" she called.

"Over here," he motioned her over. Barney! Thank you, Mim said mentally. She remembered now. Barney Staples. It had to be.

The acolytes began passing out handouts. Rose Redfern moved to the front of the table to address the little group.

"We have a cozy group today," she announced. "Let's make it a bit cozier. Would everyone please move up to the first two rows?" People rose and made their way to the front.

One person remained in the fourth row. Eric Ferris, the bad boy of Horticultural Writers. His chin was lifted and his arms were crossed over his chest. His body language shouted, "Try and make me." Rose looked at him coolly.

"Thank you," she said. Bravo, thought Mim. Rose addressed those sitting in the first two rows.

"This morning we will investigate the phytotoxins within the genus *Helloborus*. Although in modern times, hellebores are known chiefly as garden ornamentals, in antiquity, these plants were regarded first and foremost, not as ornamentals, but as important components of the pharmacopoeia…."

As Rose warmed to her topic, her manner morphed from the cool, remote façade she usually presented to the world to one of very ladylike, but warm, enthusiasm. She was in the midst of a story about the siege of Kirrha and how the Greeks had used hellebore to poison the besieged city's water supply, when Ferris raised his hand and began waving it wildly. Rose looked at him, nodded slightly, and was finishing her sentence, when he blurted out, "Kirrha, how's that spelled?"

Rose repeated what she had been saying. Then she looked at Ferris and said, "Mr. Ferris, you will find that spelling on the first page of your handout." Ferris rifled the handout as though the information had been deliberately hidden from him. Upon finding it, he grunted loudly. Then he fell silent.

Rose went over several species of hellebore, rating them in order of their toxicity. As Mim put an asterisk beside *Helleborus viridis* as being the most toxic, Ferris stood up and exclaimed, "It's hot in here! Can't you open a window?"

Considering the smallness of the group, the response of shushes and shut ups was remarkably loud.

"Take off your coat!" a woman called from the first row. Those near her and that was pretty much everyone else in the room heard her mumble 'moron' under her breath. Ferris grumbled something inaudible and took off his jacket.

It wasn't until Rose began explaining the chemistry of the poisons that Ferris again became restless, squirming in his seat, tapping first a foot, then his pen against the chair leg.

"Two glucosids are contained in the roots and root-leaves of various species of *Helleborus*," Rose stated. "One is a cardiac poison called helleborein. It is soluble in water, but not in ether. The other is a narcotic poison, helleborin. Helleborin is not soluble in water but it is soluble in ether..."

"What's the difference?" called out Ferris. Rose stopped speaking and looked at Ferris. Her face might have registered amazement, irritation, anger, but it was utterly without expression. Only her black eyes glittered.

"Why don't I give you an example?" she asked calmly. "If a person accidentally ingests helleborin, he would become very ill with extreme gastric disturbances. He could even die." Rose paused as if weighing a thought and mused, "He might die or he might not."

"What about the other one, the other poison?" Ferris interrupted.

"The other one is helleborein. It is far more toxic," said Rose. "If one wished to murder someone," her eyes burned into Ferris, "one would use helleborein, enough to cause cardiac arrest."

"You mean a heart attack," corrected Ferris.

"Indeed," agreed Rose. For the first time that morning, she smiled.

Margaret Stemple squirmed in her seat. Finally, finally, Rose Redfern was winding down. She was summing up the information on hellebore toxins. Although Rose had followed the schedule and there were still another ten minutes to go, Margaret was twitching with impatience. She looked around. Nobody else seemed as bored as she was. Barney sat next to her and he seemed to be really interested in what Rose was saying. She glanced sideways and saw that Mim Fitz—she would have liked to vaporize Mim— was listening intently.

It really hadn't been a bad workshop– better than she expected. She just couldn't concentrate on anything but the poor turnout. It upset her because she was the one who had chosen these speakers. Last March when she began planning, it seemed like Rose Redfern and Joachim Muller would be the perfect speakers to round out the conference. She had thought they would offset Marcus–a complete unknown. Now a sickening feeling washed over her. Rose Redfern and Joachim Muller had not been powerful and popular enough to make up for Marcus. If she had asked Andy Toll or the Taylors to take the afternoon slot, the workshops would have been packed....

Instead, she had booked the conference rooms and ordered breakfast and lunch for the lousy twenty-three Horticultural Writers who had signed up for an extra day of workshops. And half of them weren't here! The fact that the main conference was a sellout meant that no money would be lost. Today's losses would be more than made up. But she wanted it to be perfect and it wasn't.

This morning she blamed it on Rose. On the slow, careful way that Rose said things. Boring. And Rose was going to present one of the concurrents tomorrow. Thank heavens it was only a concurrent.

And then there was Eric Ferris. She wished that she had managed to "lose" his application. But she hadn't and, now that he of all people was here, he was sure to make more trouble. Ever since she had beaten him in the race for District Representative—he had nominated himself–he made it clear he disliked her.

She had had it with both of them. With Rose and her deadpan way of presenting information and with Eric Ferris for just being himself. She wanted the workshops to end so they could move on to the more successful part of the conference.

It was all she could do not to rush to the front of the room to regain control. She stood up, but she forced herself to stand still next to her chair. Standing up was a signal that the speaker had gone overtime.

Rose glanced at her, glanced at the clock. There were five minutes to spare. Ignoring Margaret, Rose asked, "Are there any questions?" With all her might, Margaret willed everybody to shut up, but Eric Ferris, of course, waved his hand and then didn't wait for Rose to call on him.

"Could you go over those two poisons again? Helleborin and what's the other one?"

Rose looked at him in that poker face way of hers. You could never really tell what Rose was thinking. Margaret guessed it wasn't good. Rose stood up very straight and tall, straighter and taller than she was already and that had to be close to six feet. Dressed in a slim white skirt and tunic sweater with a scarf that hung down to her knees, she seemed to be looking down at Ferris from a very high place.

"Not again today." She said it like she was brushing away a fly that was bothering her. Then she looked at everyone else in a way that excluded Ferris.

"In conclusion, I suggest that you remember that hellebores are as deadly as they are beautiful." She bowed her head a little. Everybody except Margaret and Ferris clapped wildly.

Finally, it was over. Margaret hurried to the front of the room. She asked that the attendees remain in their seats while she read the announcements. Eric Ferris got up and left. Good riddance! She almost said it out loud.

She quickly read her announcements to the little group that was still sitting there. She skipped the jokes she had planned because people were fiddling with their handouts and squirming in their chairs. She was also supposed to ask if anyone wanted to buy Rose's herbal tea. She skipped that, too. She hurried on.

"Lunch will be served in the Juniper Room and, immediately following lunch, the last workshop of the day, Hellebore Propagation, will take place in this room."

Nobody seemed to be listening to her words as much as they were waiting for her to stop talking so they could jump up and leave. Like in musical chairs. Bitsy Kaplan, with a smile of apology, got up quietly, making an exaggerated show of tiptoeing out of the room. Margaret glared at her.

"Finally, tonight's reception will also be held in the Juniper Room and you can register for the main conference in the hall directly in front of the Juniper Room." Everyone sprang up.

Margaret picked up her briefcase and looked for Barney. He was walking out the door behind Mim Fitz without so much as a backward glance in her direction. Well, she wasn't going to run after him. As conference director, she had responsibilities. She would help Rose Redfern clean up.

14

Mim headed out the door and decided she would stop at the ladies room. Barney Staples walked beside her. Neither spoke. She smiled at him, pointed to the ladies room door thinking immediately that doing so was an unnecessary bit of information. He was probably impatient to get to lunch. But he nodded. And when she came out, he was still there, waiting. As she walked toward him, she took a good look at him.

Now she remembered where she had met him. She had been at a party. He had been in the host's kitchen, pouring wine. She remembered his profile—a great blade of a nose that might have made his face homely, but didn't. In youth, maybe it had. Combined with what she guessed was perhaps three inches over six feet and a thin build, when he was young, it might have made him gawky, an Ichabod Crane figure.

His was the sort of face that gained distinction with age. In his case it made him uniquely handsome.

Now—at perhaps fifty– he moved with a grace unusual in anyone, but particularly in someone so tall. Although his hair was cut very short and combed forward, like Caesar's only without Caesar's receding hairline, it was thick and white. As she approached he met her gaze with eyes that were a pale green and startling against his tanned face. Either he had been somewhere warm recently or he spent most of his days out of doors.

"Hungry?" he asked.

"Very," she answered. Inside the Juniper Room, a table laden with sandwich makings, trays of cold cuts and cheese, lettuce and tomatoes, and assorted breads had been set up along one wall. A sprinkling of horticultural writers had already served themselves and sat at several of the round tables that were covered with white tablecloths.

"How about here?" Barney asked, patting an empty table. She nodded and set her papers at one place while Barney set his beside hers. At a table that would seat ten easily, the two side by side places, marked by their handouts, looked oddly intimate. She looked away, feeling suddenly annoyed.

They heaped their plates with roast beef sandwiches, cole slaw, and potato salad, and returned to the table, balancing plates and cups of coffee. She moved over one place.

"So I can see you," she said. He raised his cup of coffee in a toast.

"Here's looking at you." She did not raise her cup, but smiled, looked down at her plate, and decided to ask a question before taking a bite of her sandwich.

"I'm trying to remember when we met. It was at a party, wasn't it?"

After lunch, Mim and Barney retraced their steps to the Pine Room where the propagation workshop was to take place. A screen had been set up in the front of the room. There was no sign of plants or propagation paraphernalia or the speaker, Marcus Tydings. Mim counted ten people seated in the room.

Mim would have liked to sit in the front where there were a couple of single seats left, but Barney found two seats together in the back of the room. She dutifully joined him there, but her bonhomie was wearing thin.

It was not that Barney had said or done anything wrong exactly. His behavior had been thoroughly gentlemanly. His courtesy was ingrained and effortless. He opened doors and let her proceed through them automatically. He was a good listener whose conversation was a true give and take. It was simply that for someone she hadn't recognized when they bumped into each other, he seemed to know a lot about her and about Tate. Too much. In his conversation, he revealed a command of information about her life and interests that even some of her friends didn't have.

Barney talked about the town in which Mim lived and commented on the labor necessary to maintain her one acre garden. On average, how many hours did she spend gardening each week? He knew that before he died Tate had been moving his plants over to Mim's garden. Had she been obliged to make new beds to accommodate them? He referred to the article "Small and unusual ornamental trees for residential properties" she had written for *Washington Home*. He said it was "unusually sophisticated for a lifestyle magazine."

How did he know all of this? It was beyond unsettling. It was creepy.

She was relieved when, five minutes late, a man, presumably the speaker, entered the Pine Room to begin the workshop. Actually, he didn't so much enter as sweep in, displaying a blazing white smile in a deeply tanned face. Tall, thin, and brimming with energy, he was wearing jeans and an azure blue dress shirt with the sleeves rolled up. He was drop-dead handsome. Throughout the room, women sat up straighter and appeared suddenly more alert.

Margaret Stemple, the conference director who introduced the speakers was not present. The speaker introduced himself.

"My name is Marcus Tydings," he began without preamble. "Is the representative from Perfect Perennials in the room?" Tydings waited, tapping one toe. Heads turned. Nobody answered. A shadow passed over his handsome features.

Then, like sunshine after a cloud, he smiled broadly.

"My nursery is called Extraordinary Hellebores. Today, I'm going to talk about the hellebores I propagate there." He paused.

"We have a lot of ground to cover, so let's not waste any time!" With that, he dimmed the lights. The first photo, a potted Christmas rose in full bloom, burst onto the screen.

"We are all familiar with the Christmas rose, *Helleborus niger*. It's a fine plant that's been around for centuries. It's a classic. Good evergreen foliage. Early white flowers. But..."

Tydings paused for a very long moment before adding slyly, "there are so many possibilities!"

He advanced to another photo of a hellebore Mim did not recognize. It lacked the rich foliage of the Christmas rose, but had dark purple flowers.

"What if I cross the classic Christmas rose with *Helleborus atrorubens*, the plant in this picture? I might get something like this." The next photo showed a Christmas rose with bright pink flowers.

"I developed this," Tydings explained and named a long series of crosses. A woman in the seat in front of Mim was writing frantically to record Tydings's information.

"Or this." A photo appeared of a close-up of a red and white striated flower. Tydings ran through another complicated genealogy.

"Or this…" Tydings proceeded to show a series of flowers—each with a long list of generations of species he had crossed to achieve the pictured result. Mim sat back dismayed. There were no vials of seeds, potting mix, or anything but Tydings and his photos. There was nothing to indicate that the attendees would be doing hands-on propagation. Wasn't this supposed to be a propagation workshop?

Instead of a session that would teach the attendees how to propagate hellebores themselves, apparently, Marcus Tydings understood the term "propagation workshop" to mean showing them the plants *he* was propagating at Extraordinary Hellebores, his nursery.

Suddenly, she was bored and exhausted. Lunch with the unfailingly polite, but all-knowing Barney Staples hadn't helped her mood. She was hyper aware of Barney's presence in the seat next to hers and it irritated her.

To make matters worse, Tydings was describing his crosses with rabid enthusiasm in excruciating detail and kept repeating there was "a lot more ground to cover." She wanted out. She turned and gazed longingly at the door.

She started to cough. At first, it was in little, muted bursts. Then she was coughing uncontrollably. She got up and hastened, still coughing, to the door. When she got there, she took one last look at the screen. Tydings was showing a plant with bright yellow flowers.

"This is my *Helleborus odorus*. I named it 'Sunspot.' Keep an eye out for it. I expect it to hit the market in the next two years. Not only does it have the brightest yellow flowers in the species, it is fully evergreen."

His 'Sunspot' looked a lot like the hellebores that Joachim Muller had shown in his workshop—the ones in the photo with Tate and the blonde man. But that was a species and Tydings said he had "named" his plant. Did that mean it was a named cultivar, registered with the powers that be or just a plant he had unofficially named?

15

Mim inserted a credit card sized key into the slot above the door handle. There was a click, a green light appeared, and she opened the door to room 415. Sally Flinn, with whom she was sharing the room during the conference, had arrived. That fact was evident by the presence of a camera bag the size of a small refrigerator and dresses and outfits, lying across the beds in lifelike but flattened attitudes as if their occupants had suddenly evaporated. The shower was running.

"Hey, Sal. It's me, Mim," she yelled as she banged on the bathroom door.

"Mim! Great! I'll be right out." Sally called out. And she was. In less than a minute, Sally and a great puff of steam emerged from the bathroom. She was enclosed in a huge, white, terry bathrobe with her hair wrapped in a turban of towel that, along with the cloud of steam, made her look like an angelic genie. The two exchanged hugs.

"Ugh, I had such a long drive down today. I had to take a shower and wash my hair. I wanted to get clean and dressed by the time the workshops were over and you got back," she said, bending over and shaking out her hair. She began to rub it vigorously with the towel.

"Are they over already?"

"No. I left the propagation workshop after the first ten minutes. Coughing."

"Have you got a cold?"

"No. I just got bored. I also missed the first fifteen minutes of Joachim Muller's this morning." Sally looked at Mim in surprise.

"That's not like you. You okay?" Sally stopped drying her hair and sat down next to Mim.

"I'm fine. Just lost track of time this morning so I was late. I did get to Rose Redfern's workshop on time."

"What did she talk about?"

"Death by hellebore," said Mim, distractedly. She was thinking about her lunch with Barney Staples. She sat on the bed. Sally was watching her.

"Actually, the Death by Hellebore workshop was very interesting. Fascinating really. Rose Redfern knows her stuff. "

"I left the so-called propagation workshop early."

"You said that," Sally looked at Mim. "Why 'so-called' ?"

"It was all about what Marcus Tydings was doing—my this, my that. Zip information on how-to for the rest of us."

"Sounds like it was pretty disappointing for a propagation workshop," said Sally. "Who's Marcus whatsziz?" When Mim didn't respond, she asked, "What's wrong?" She peered at Mim who had sprawled onto the bed. If the bedspread had been snow, Mim could have imprinted a snow angel.

"Nothing's wrong. I'm just tired. Long day." The look on Sally's face suggested she wasn't buying the tired excuse.

"O-kay," Sally said skeptically.

Mim raised her head from the bed to regard Sally. Then she lowered it and examined the ceiling.

"What do you know about Barney Staples?" Mim asked.

"Not a thing. Except that he left a message for you." Mim's head shot up.

"When?"

"I don't know. The message light on the phone was blinking when I got here. I didn't know who it was for, so I took it. Actually two of them." Sally walked over to the table between the two beds and picked up rose-colored memo paper.

"Here." Sally handed the memos to Mim. "The other one is from your editor." Mim read the first message, "Must have your story by Sunday night at the latest."

"Bitch!" Mim said.

"Who?" Sally asked.

"The new editor! She makes unreasonable demands in the hopes I won't be able to deliver."

"Can't you go over her head?" Sally asked.

"No. Over her head is the publisher who is banging her."

"Bummer!"

Mim read the second message out loud: "Let's have lunch after the workshop."

"Is Barney good-looking?" Sally asked. Mim didn't answer. When Sally repeated the question, Mim snapped back to the moment.

"As a matter of fact, he is. Tall with white hair and very unusual eyes. They're pale green. Like a cat's. Very distinguished looking. He speaks with a British accent." Mim said absently as she took the message.

"Sounds yummy," Sally said looking at Mim whose brow was now furrowed in concentration.

"He must have left this early this morning," Mim said more to herself than to Sally She turned the paper over, looking for more information.

"Is there a problem with that?"

"Yes!" Mim sat up. "This says, 'let's have lunch after the workshop.' How did he know that I would be in that workshop?"

"And today. We did have lunch together," said Mim drawing out the words thoughtfully. "It's just that…it's like he knows me much, much better than I know him." Sally digested this thought, grunting as she combed out tangles from her hair.

"When did you meet him?"

"That's just it. I didn't really remember until today. There was a party at Lin Baldwin's. He was there."

"Today, after Rose's workshop, Barney and I ate our lunch together. And he was talking about that party where we met. It must have been three years ago. I forget who had it and I asked him and he said it was at Lin's. I sort of remember now. It was a big group of people."

"He even remembered details of our conversation that sounded like something I would say. He knows where I live! And he knows where I work!"

"Mim, that's no big secret. I got my conference packet early. It's all in there!" Sally said.

"And he talked about Tate."

"About Tate?" Sally had a look of concern on a face still rosy from her shower.

"He talked about Tate's work like he knew all about it."

"Maybe he was a friend of Tate's," Sally suggested.

"No," Mim said with finality. "I don't think so. Tate never mentioned him. Never. And before today, I had only the vaguest recollection of meeting him or seeing him." Mim kicked off her shoes and lay back on the bed, propping herself up on her elbows.

"Yesterday, when I checked in, I ran in to him. Literally. And he said, 'let's catch up later.' Like we were old buddies. He did look sort of familiar to me, but at the time I really had no idea who he was."

Mim sat up on the bed and swung her legs onto the floor. Sally took a seat across from her on the other bed.

"Another thing. The way he talked about Tate's work. Almost like they were collaborating. The thing is *I* didn't even know all of what Tate was working on."

"Well, there could be several explanations," Sally said.

"Like?" Mim asked irritably.

"Like perhaps Tate talked to him about his work. And he probably remembered you because he found you attractive! Perhaps you have repressed your memory of him because...," here Sally paused and reached for Mim's hands. "You've been living under a rock for two years.Or perhaps...." Mim looked up, waiting for the next words. Sally smiled wickedly.

"Perhaps, Ms. Fitz, you are in the throes of early Alzheimers."

"Not funny," said Mim who really did fear losing her memory. She got up and walked to the window wall and moved aside the gauzy curtain with the attached metal rod. Opposite the window was a brick wall.

"Sorry," said Sally. "But I think it's time for you to join the world again. You should be flattered that an attractive man is taking an interest in you." Mim heard the 'sorry,' but the rest of Sally's words were swept into a deluge of memories from this afternoon. How did Barney Staples know so much about Tate's work? She had never, ever heard Tate speak of Barney. He was certainly not a confidant.

How did he know that Tate was moving his plants to her yard? Where did he get his information? It was as if he had done research on her, something she found not flattering, but creepy.

Sally cleared her throat. She gestured toward a table on which there were two champagne flutes and a bottle of Veuve Cliquot. "On another note. I'm clean and I hope you don't mind if I don't get dressed before we celebrate." Mim sat up.

"Veuve Cliquot! What a wonderful, warm welcome! What have I done to deserve such an honor?" asked Mim.

"Not just you, sweetie. Me, too!" Mim stared at Sally a moment before comprehension dawned.

"No!"

"Yes! They're really interested. I mean, we don't have anything like a contract yet, but they want to publish it!" Sally had a wonderful crooked smile, full of mischief and delight. Now, it reminded Mim of a mischievous Jack o' lantern.

"Hallelujah! I was beginning to think we had done all of that work for nothing," said Mim. "What about Rose Redfern?" Rose Redfern was pretty much the accepted expert on herbs in any form.

"Tom says there's no problem. Anyway, Rose is otherwise occupied," Sally laughed. "Rose is working on a book of plant poisons. Didn't she mention it at her lecture? Plant poisons are her new thing."

"I was so excited when he called! He's going to be here, but not 'til tomorrow or Sunday brunch at the latest. Maybe we can snag him for lunch if he gets here tomorrow?"

"Fabulous. A celebration is in order," said Mim. The celebration was forestalled for a few moments while Sally and Mim took turns working the cork off the bottle of champagne.

"I don't do this nearly often enough," said Mim a micro second before the cork flew. Sally whipped the towel from her head, wrapped the cascading bottle, and poured.

"To *Designing with Herbs*" said Sally. "*Designing with Herbs*," said Mim.

16

Margaret Stemple had stuck her neck out for Marcus Tydings, a complete unknown. In Slovenia where she met him, he had talked about his nursery and his plans to introduce some extraordinary cultivars. He had made a great impression on her.

It later turned out that none of the big hellebore people really knew who he was. Nevertheless, nobody on the committee had raised an objection. That made them all equally responsible.

Anyway, what was the point of being conference director if you didn't have any say in who the speakers were going to be? He wasn't a household name, but she knew he was funny and a good speaker. And she had only put him on the program for an afternoon workshop.

At least, Marcus Tydings had charisma. That was a lot more than you could say for Rose Redfern. And he was a lot nicer to look at.

Margaret had used her influence to have Tydings come to speak at the Garden Center where she worked. After that, he sent her frequent emails.

She had also suggested that John Bevins, the representative from Perfect Perennials attend Marcus's workshop. Bevins didn't attend and she had to skip it, too. She should have been there, if not to give moral support, then in her capacity as conference director. She was supposed to evaluate his performance.

Instead, she had to spend Friday afternoon putting together the conference packets. As conference director, by rights, she should have been able to delegate this task. Foolishly, she hadn't enlisted more help than ultra dependable, extremely efficient Lin Baldwin, the regional director of section two. Lin always brought along another pair of hands, her companion, John Beam. And those two were the equivalent of six ordinary mortals. But Lin's mother had suffered a heart attack and, this morning, Lin cancelled. That meant that John wouldn't be here to help either.

Well, perhaps it was better this way. It would give her an excuse to stop by Marcus' room to ask him how it went. He knew she had stuck out her neck for him. And he had been paid the same as the big name speakers even though he was an unknown. He would be grateful. And she sensed that there was something more…

She looked over the assembled conference packets with pride. They were complete and arranged in alphabetical order. Except for his. She would take it to him. Not now. When she was wearing the new dress over the new underwear.

Now, she looked over to see the caterers busy setting up the bar and laying out the tables for the hors d'oeuvres. She consulted her watch. In exactly one hour and forty minutes, the reception would begin.

Her cell phone vibrated. She checked the screen. Mother. Again. It would be another two hours before Mother would be engrossed in her television programs. Until then, Margaret could count on the periodic calls her mother made when she was bored or angry–which was pretty much all the time.

"You're always gone." "I'm here all alone." "Your *sister* called." That was mother's favorite, the implication being if her sister Carol were mother's caretaker, life would be hunky dory. Ha, Margaret thought. Carol is safely in California, having gotten as far away as possible the minute she graduated from Maryland. Carol has a husband and children. Carol has a life. Carol sends money every month to "help out." Blood money.

Margaret, the younger, plain sister, was destined to take care of Mother in the cramped house in which she had grown up. The longest she had ever been away was during college, when she had lived in the dorm for one glorious semester. Then her father died.

Through the remainder of her years at the University of Maryland and the rest of her adult life, she lived at home with Mother, commuting to school and then to work, and sleeping in the same bedroom she had shared with Carol growing up.

She had joined Horticultural Writers when she was promoted from sales to public relations assistant at the Garden Center. Mitch, the manager, had suggested that she join various garden and landscape organizations and, dutifully, Margaret had done so.

When she went to meetings of the Maryland and Virginia Nurserymen's Associations whose membership was predominantly male, she was ignored politely at the regular meetings and not so politely at the conference socials.

At the Horticultural Writers meetings, predominantly female, she had made friends with shy aspiring writers and soon came to know members of the local media who called her for information on the plants sold at the Garden Center.

Over the years, she had volunteered for committees that did the necessary, but not necessarily glamorous, jobs that needed doing. And she had done those jobs well and without complaining. She had scheduled buses for trips, dealt with caterers, contacted botanic gardens and nurseries for meetings. She had picked up visiting speakers from airports. She had driven them– the shakers and movers of the horticultural world—to the hotels she had booked for their stays. And she had picked up from them new notions of dress and bearing.

She had worked hard and it had won her recognition and respect— even a degree of fame. People looked up to her. Horticultural Writers was her chosen family, her social life, her anchor in what might otherwise be a bleak existence. If it weren't for the hort writers trips and meetings…! She pictured for a split second spending another endless weekend, taking Mother to the grocery store and the hairdresser. But that was no longer the case. She was here. She was respected and, with a little luck, in line for the presidency.

Margaret gathered her thoughts back to the matters at hand. She had to tell Amy Tomczyk, who wanted to take JP Chiasson's place and present his program on Sunday morning at the brunch, that she had not yet turned in her slide shows. She didn't have Andy Toll's either. Friday last week was the absolute deadline. Margaret made a point of previewing any and all slide presentations for quality control. Reviewing Tony's program was a mere formality. He was a seasoned and very effective speaker.

That was not the case with Amy who was not going to speak to the conference if she had anything to do with it. Somehow, she would dissuade her when they previewed JP's program. She had already decided to ask one of the pros to take JP's slot at the Sunday's brunch. Or maybe she could ask several of them to present a panel discussion....

She made a note to ask Andy and Amy for their programs tonight. With Amy, it would be for form's sake. Then she would have to make time—somehow—to preview them.

She turned off her cell phone, got up, grabbed her purse, and headed up to her room. She would have just enough time to change into the beautiful new lavender—lavender!—dress she had bought for this meeting. It was her favorite color and had been an extravagance, but, she reasoned, now that she was Regional Director, she needed to look the part. Anyway, the dress was her only expenditure. The Garden Center paid her transportation, conference fee, and hotel bill. And Horticultural Writers allowed her a generous expense account.

Even so, it was a good deal for hort writers. She had earned her position with hard, unstinting work and deft organization–always behind the scenes. Now, she was ready to enjoy a little attention. She would make sure this conference went off without a hitch. Hopefully, her reputation would make her a favorite for president in the next election.

Forty-five minutes later, showered, perfumed, and dressed from the skin out in lavender lace, Margaret, conference packet in hand, tapped on Marcus Tyding's door. When he opened the door, she was startled to see he was bare chested. He made no excuses for his lack of clothing, nor did he seem surprised to see her.

"Hey, you look great!" Marcus gave Margaret his most fetching smile and watched her melt.

"Turn around," he twirled a finger and she did as he suggested, turning in a circle with embarrassed, mincing steps. She blushed crimson.

"Wow!" he said, thinking that she did have a really fine ass. He had never noticed. "Come on in." She was holding out a large green envelope. He raised his eyebrows.

"For me?"

"It's the conference packet. I...Well, I thought I'd drop it by," she held it out to him.

"Thank you! Thank you." He took the packet in one hand and, laying on the charm, took her hand with the other. "Come, sit down." He patted the bed. She looked around the room for a chair, saw that both the armchair and desk chair were heaped with clothing and papers, and sat down a little awkwardly on the bed. She cleared her throat.

"Well, I uh wanted to know, how did it go? You know, your workshop."

"Great!" he said. He gave her a dazzling smile, then slid his gaze to her remarkable décolleté.

"How many attendees did you have?" She asked. She was aware of his gaze, he thought, though she continued to stare fixedly at his desk. She was also pleased. Why not?

"Uh, let's see. About nineteen, I guess," he lied. "Not a big turnout for sure, but they were a lively bunch. We ran over the time. Lots of questions. I wished you were there." He looked into her eyes and held them. "Uh…Bevins didn't show."

"I heard. And sorry I wasn't. I had to…to put the packets together," she said, out of breath. He watched as her quickening breath heaved those big breasts. He touched her nose with a finger. Her eyes widened at his touch, but she didn't back away.

Slowly, he moved his finger down, over her lips, tracing her throat, and, finally, moving it down into her cleavage. He pretended it was stuck there. She giggled.

He pretended to scold the errant finger, telling it that it was naughty. She laughed heartily. Then he simply pushed her back on the bed and kissed her.

He read in her face a mixture of pleasure and amazed disbelief. It was what she wanted, but she couldn't believe it was happening.

He was pretty sure his initial assessment of her was correct: She was an awkward thirty-five year old virgin with dreams of romance. He intended to give her the romantic treatment of her life.

17

"Where's the Juniper room?" asked Sally. They were walking toward the elevator. "That's where you're supposed to pick up your packet."

"It's one level below reception. I had lunch there after the workshop." Mim swayed just a little and put her hand on the wall for support. "I'm not used to champagne, Sally, I think I'm a little loopy."

"Did we finish the bottle?" Sally asked.

"Almost."

"That explains it. I'm a little tipsy, too," Sally giggled. They had arrived at the elevators. Sally pressed the down button and favored Mim with her lopsided grin. "I just can't believe it. Tom said they might even offer us an advance!" Mim smiled at Sally and at the prospect of their working together on a beautiful book about landscaping with herbs.

The elevator doors opened and Sally, glowing from three glasses of champagne and delighted to see the person standing in the elevator, let out a happy whoop. "Amy! I'm so glad you're here!" And, then, suddenly, remembering what Mim had told her about JP Chiasson, Amy's fiancé, she looked stricken, and moved forward to put her arms around Amy.

"Oh, God, Amy. I'm so, sho sorry!" Sally slurred ever so slightly. Mim watched Amy's face tighten for only a second before it assumed its previous bland, neutral expression. Sally, who tends to be a hugger, had her arm around Amy. Mim thought, from the expression on Amy's face, that it might be unwelcome, but then she saw Amy squeeze Sally's hand in response.

"Amy, this is Mim Fitz. We're rooming together. Mim is the garden editor at *Washington Home*, who also designs gardens," Sally said. "And

Amy is the plant propagator at Stamnitz, biggest nursery in the Delaware Valley. Oops. Here we are."

The elevator doors opened onto a scene of thronging humanity that was nothing like this morning's scene at the workshops. The movement and energy in the crowded room put Mim in mind of a Bosch painting. Horticultural writers who weren't hugging and bussing each other in boisterous recognition or moving toward the Juniper room where the party was to take place, were lining up at a long table to get their conference packets.

Some, who had already obtained the dark green packets, had put on the name tags and were rifling through and examining the contents of green folders emblazoned with the horticultural writers' emblem, the rose and pen, this time in gold. Inside, in addition to name tags, there would be coupons for breakfast and lunch, handouts from the speakers, and brochures from the companies that hosted the cocktail party and lunches.

The trio, Mim in front, flanked by Sally and Amy at her sides, moved through the milling crowd like an ice breaker at the South Pole. In moments, they took places at the end of the line to pick up conference packets. At its head was the table where Margaret Stemple, the conference organizer, was handing them out. Her pale face was grim.

Mim turned her attention to a thin, slightly built man with a blonde ponytail directly in front of her. There was something familiar about him. On a whim, she tapped his shoulder.

"Well, hello there!" Chase Filmore turned myopic gray eyes toward her behind vintage glasses that were set with rhinestones. His long face lit up. "Why do we keep meeting this way?" He gave Mim an affectionate hug.

Mim introduced Sally and started to introduce Amy, someone, it turned out, Chase already knew. Chatting amiably, Chase advanced in the line facing backwards toward Mim, Sally, and Amy.

He was a floral designer whose spectacular arrangements were celebrated and much in demand for toney Washington, DC events. He never advertised. He didn't have to. Knowledge about Chase's extraordinary talent was something savvy Washington insiders shared among themselves. All of his clients came by word of mouth and he was usually swamped.

Lean and wiry at no more than 130 pounds, he had quick, observant eyes behind retro glasses, sparkling with rhinestones. He wasn't a member of Horticultural Writers, but his presence at this conference was no surprise. Chase was an energetic fixture in almost any garden program, plant sale, or conference held in the Mid-Atlantic region or, for that matter, at an event he found to be sufficiently interesting. He frequently traveled to England for the Chelsea and Hampton Court Flower Shows.

"Relatively speaking," Chase explained to Sally and Amy, "Mim and I are neighbors. But the only time we get to spend time together is at meetings. When was the last time we got together?"

"San Francisco! That meeting was three years ago. Three years ago! " said Mim.

"That's where I met Amy and JP!" laughed Chase. Amy smiled tightly. It was clear that Chase had no idea what had happened to JP. Chase's next question would probably be, 'Where is he, anyway?' Quickly, Mim asked a question.

"Are you going to Chelsea again this year?" It wasn't just changing the subject. Mim had joined as an international member of the Royal Horticultural Society. She was toying with the idea of attending the Chelsea Flower Show in the spring. It would be fun to go with Chase.

"I'd love to, but I just got back from England three days ago. I was visiting a dear old friend in Kent.

"Anyway," said Chase cheerfully, "I'm afraid that this year I'll be working non-stop through the spring. I have weddings scheduled for almost every weekend, starting in March!" It was a work load that might have daunted a lesser being, but Chase beamed at the prospect. His glasses glittered.

"And…," he added, allowing a pause to lengthen dramatically, "I am doing arrangements for a dinner…." Here he paused again. He looked at each woman in turn to make sure she was giving him her full attention, before concluding, "At the White House!"

The women let out whoops of excited praise. Mim offered her congratulations. As Sally and Amy offered theirs and asked what Chase planned to design, Mim relaxed. The conversation had drifted into safe waters.

She mused. Why hadn't the conference goers been notified of JP's death? He was on the program. Certainly, no notice of any program change had come in the mail. And there had been enough time. Now, Amy would be bombarded with painful questions about JP from horticultural writers who knew nothing of what had happened.

Perhaps there would be a general announcement—probably not tonight at the reception. Tomorrow morning at the start of the conference would be more appropriate.

Binky Kaplan, a former president, commented on the high cost of mailings to the membership. Emails were free, but perhaps not the most sensitive way to announce JP's passing. That was probably it.

"Oh look!" said Chase. Having obtained his conference packet, he turned back to the women just as the elevator door opened to disgorge another densely packed group of horticultural writers. "That woman in black. She looks so familiar."

As Chase spoke, Amy had reached the head of the line and was busy registering, but Sally and Mim turned to look. The elevator was open. Standing front and center, stood a tiny, striking woman in a sweeping black cocktail dress with a plunging neckline.

"Never mind," Chase waved his hand dismissively. "It couldn't be who I thought it was." He laughed. "I mean that would be impossible." He frowned and stared at the woman.

It took a moment before Mim recognized the pretty woman exiting the elevator as the woman in black with the British accent she had seen at reception the day before. Philippa somebody. Mim couldn't remember her surname.

"She's a hellebore breeder," said Mim. "She works for Benjy Glover at Glover Gardens. British."

"British?" Chase's eyebrows shot up over the rhinestones of his glasses.

"Yes, if I'm any judge of accents."

"Right!" Chase said, but the look on his face announced disbelief. Under his breath, he mumbled something.

"Sorry?" Mim asked.

"Nothing," said Chase.

Amy had finished registering and Sally moved to the head of the line. Amy looked up and frowned.

Philippa was first to exit the elevator. A crowd of merry horticultural writers poured out behind her. It was a ridiculously long stream of people that called to mind those old photos of sophomores crammed into a phone booth. At the tail end of the elevator throng was Eric Ferris, who was eagerly pushing through to get to the front. He kept looking over at Philippa, as if trying to catch her eye. He seemed desperate to catch up with her and was none too careful in the process. He must have stepped on Rose Redfern's foot because she yelped and turned on him sharply. Ferris paid her absolutely no heed, but kept following Philippa, who walked swiftly into the Juniper room, oblivious of his efforts. She disappeared from sight in the packed room.

At the threshold, Ferris paused and searched the room, now thronging with horticultural writers. As if they had purposely thwarted his efforts and were responsible for his failure to catch up with Philippa, Ferris turned around and glowered at a now limping Rose Redfern.

"You are very rude!" cried Rose Redfern in a stentorian voice. Her companions clucked in agreement.

"You're a clumsy cow!" shouted Ferris. People paused in their conversations to turn and stare. Ferris disappeared into the Juniper room. Rose Redfern and her entourage glared after him.

If looks could kill, thought Mim. She turned to Amy, wide-eyed at the scene. "You've just witnessed one of our finest in action!"

"Who *was* that?" Amy asked as she and Mim approached the double doors of the big room. Mim had to move closer to Amy and speak directly into her ear to be heard above the din.

"That was Eric Ferris, sometimes called "Eric the ferret," said Mim.

"Oh! JP told me about him. It's got to be the same guy. He went on the Balkan trip," Amy watched Eric disappear into the crowd.

"Did he? How did he manage to get a spot on that trip? I thought it was for professionals."

"JP wasn't real happy about it," Amy shrugged. "He said something about that guy pulling strings and taking up someone else's place."

Kevin had watched the elevator doors opened and people began to file out, standing at the opposite end of the corridor. He met the large, dark eyes of a beautiful woman with a sense of *déjà vu*. He had seen those remarkable eyes before. He ran through a series of possibilities and came up with the photo that Randy had shown him. If it was the same woman, her name was Philippa. She was heading into the Juniper room.

She was exquisite. He crossed in front of the entrance to the Juniper room to intercept her just as the elevator disgorged its full load of garden writers who streamed tward the Juniper room. Moving quickly, he skirted ahead of the advancing crowd. He almost collided with an older couple arguing about which one of them should have brought along the room key. He followed Philippa into the Juniper room.

"Philippa," he called in a low voice as he approached her from behind. If she wasn't Philippa, she wouldn't respond. But she did. She turned and looked at him with surprise in a pair of amazing brown eyes.

"My name is Kevin Minahan. I'm a reporter for the *Washington Edition*." He couldn't think of what else to say.

"Hullo," she said smiling, waiting. Gorgeous, he thought.

"May I bring you a drink?" Kevin asked, stifling a strange urge to bow.

He returned with her whiskey sour and a Scotch for himself. As he handed her the drink, he felt as if he'd suddenly been struck dumb. Kevin Minahan, veteran reporter, man about town, able to talk to anyone about anything, was tongue tied. Biding for time, he turned as if to observe the surge of humanity that now crowded the Juniper room. At last some small gear shifted in his frozen brain. He turned to her and began, " How long" as she asked simultaneously, "Are you...." They both laughed.

"You first," said Kevin.

"I was going to ask you about your newspaper. That's what it is, isn't it?" He told her that he had worked for the *Washington Edition* for twenty-five years, first as a crime reporter and, later, as the travel editor. Too long, he thought. That probably made him old enough to be her father.

"My turn!" he said. "How long have you been in this country?" he asked. The black dress had a deep décolleté that exposed ample cleavage. Her skin was very fair, flawless, and creamy white, but instead of looking pale, she was luminous. Her hair was curly with a red sheen. Her coloring was extraordinary. He made an attempt to concentrate on what she was saying.

"...three days. It's my first trip to America," she was saying. "I'm going to be working at Glovers Gardens. I'm the new hellebore breeder."

18

Marcus stepped out of the elevator and strode toward the Juniper room. He didn't have to bother picking up his packet thanks to Margaret. Several times he caught her staring at him, a look of confused shock on her face. She had left his room, he realized, without saying a single word.

At the threshold of the Juniper room where the cocktail party was in full swing, he stopped abruptly. Sometimes this happened to him. The old paralysis at the thought of plunging into a social situation would come over him. At those times, he had to catch his breath and calmly tell himself who he was—*now*. Timid Mike with the weak Tydings chin no longer existed. Muncie, Indiana was a lifetime away.

He struck a nonchalant pose and surveyed the room until the pounding in his chest slowed to a normal rhythm. He breathed in and chanted silently, "one-one hundred, two-one hundred, three-one hundred." Then he languidly strolled over to the bar.

Mike Tydings would have asked for white wine, but Marcus Tydings had cultivated a taste for single malt Scotch. Not likely they'll be pouring Laphroig here, he thought to himself. It was a phrase he had appropriated from Tate Adkins. The late Tate Adkins.

Marcus had first heard Tate use this expression at the bar in Slovenia. Tate, as always, had been the center of attention of the male members of the plant hunting party. They had laughed at his comment, not because it was especially witty, but in deference to Tate.

Marcus had been sitting at a table with several of the women. Up to that moment, he had luxuriated in and taken full advantage of their attentions. But seeing Tate as the object of male adulation had awakened a deeper yearning in Marcus. Women were easy. He had more than enough of their company now. More pressing was his hunger for what Tate had: the respect of his male peers.

The bartender was looking at him curiously. Marcus ordered Scotch and soda.

Mim and Amy stopped a few feet from the doors to the Juniper room. The reception was going strong and the room pulsated with life and heat and noise. Amy's eyes scanned the gaggles of hort writers, chatting and laughing. "I'm not sure I'm up to this," she said softly.

"Well, I certainly don't need anything more to drink," said Mim. "I've already had more than my share of champagne and...." Mim looked around for Sally, but saw she had moved off and been engulfed by the crowd, "I'm starving. Do you want to go somewhere else? We could get something to eat." Mim asked. "I think there's a little restaurant on the top floor that's decent and peaceful." Amy looked grateful and relieved.

"I don't think I've eaten all day," Amy said, "but," she hesitated, "are you sure you want to leave...this?" She made a sweeping gesture to indicate the throbbing room.

"Let's go!" Mim answered, rolling her eyes and pointing toward the elevators. Both women walked against the stream of horticultural writers headed toward the Juniper room. They had the elevator all to themselves up to the ninth floor where they exited and walked into a nearly empty restaurant. The hostess seated them at a large, round table that was near the fireplace.

A fire glowed beneath a mantel that was decorated with holly and pine, accented by white baby's breath. The fire wasn't necessary, but it was cheery and appropriate for the season.

Mim smiled contentedly. Amy collapsed into her chair and exhaled audibly.

"Long day?" asked Mim. Even in the glow of the fire, she could see dark shadows under Amy's eyes. The expression of pain in them was so naked, Mim had to look away. It had only been two weeks since JP Chiasson had been brutally murdered. Mim suppressed a shudder.

Tate's death had been far away, but that had made it unreal. In the weeks that followed, she had caught herself hoping to hear his step a hundred times. And then the realization would descend and the immenseness of lost hope would fill the long hours with lead.

Amy and JP were to be married. Sally said they'd lived together for a couple of years.

She and Tate had been all about possibility, Mim thought with a sharp pain.

At his memorial she had met his mother and sister. Mrs. Adkins and Celia, his sister, had been gracious, introducing her as "Tate's little friend from Maryland." A little friend, not someone who was entitled to grieve with the family. It made Mim think of the Spanish proverb, "nobody gave you a candle at this funeral." It meant, more or less, that you don't have the right to complain because you weren't invited and you don't belong.

After the memorial, she'd driven home, booked a flight to France, and sat in a rented room in Aix en Provence where she tried to write without success. She'd begun an affair with a man fifteen years her junior. She had walked the streets for hours on end and, finally, faced reality, and come home.

The reality was this: She and Tate had shared something amazing for almost four months. And now he was gone. He had often spoken of things that they would do together and these things would never, never come to pass. And maybe, maybe had he lived, things might have changed. She'd been mesmerized by Tate, but she also knew that there were things about him that might ultimately threaten a relationship.

It was no secret that Tate had a monumental ego. That he was passionate about his work, married to his work...

"It's very hard seeing everyone. It's the first time since..." Amy's words broke into Mim's thoughts. Mim nodded to allow her to leave the sentence unfinished.

Amy looked spent. She had said she was here to present JP's lecture. She would carry on because he could not. Keeping up the courage to do what she felt JP would have wanted was clearly exhausting her. Mim admired her determination. Her motherly instincts kicked in.

"Let's get something to eat," she said, snapping open her menu.

Over dinner, the two women exchanged basic information. Amy was originally from Colorado. She had studied at Cornell, interned at Longwood, and was currently employed by Stamnitz Nurseries, one of the country's finest. JP had worked there very briefly after leaving England and before taking a position at Longwood.

"You didn't know JP?" Amy's voice sounded weary, but calm.

"No, I never met him. Tate spoke of him and wanted me to meet him, of course, but no," said Mim, thinking that she had heard JP was something of a *very* charming ladies' man. Then she remembered who it was who had said it and deemed it possibly unreliable information. Sally, whose judgment she trusted, said he was a solid friend and an excellent plantsman.

"From what Sally told me about him, I'm very sorry I never got to meet him. Sally liked him immensely." Amy smiled and her eyes seemed fixed on a vivid memory.

"There was nobody like him. He was so alive and so loving." A tear rolled down her cheek, but her face projected an inward glow. "And he was brilliant. He would have changed the entire world of hellebore breeding."

"I wish I knew more about the hybridizing efforts of hellebore breeders," said Mim. "I guess that's why I'm here. I want to learn." Absently, Mim rearranged her cutlery, lining up the bottom of the knife with the spoon. "I grow the plants and I love them, but I've only the vaguest notion of how breeders achieve their goals or how much work goes into breeding them. I wish I knew more." Mim thought of the plants Tate had given her. They had made a little bed along her back walk. Those young plants had yet to bloom. He wouldn't say what they were. It would be a surprise.

Amy had an odd look on her face. She seemed about to say something.

Just then, the waitress arrived and asked them if they wanted anything more. Amy ordered a cup of coffee. When it arrived, she added sugar and began absently to stir.

"You know, if you grow hellebores, you probably know how easy it is to get seedlings," Amy warmed to the topic. "But, very often, they are mediocre. I used to think they were all pretty, but JP taught me to see the differences."

"He was meticulous when he made crosses, because his standards were so high. He had collected outstanding stock plants and kept crossing them to get better and better offspring. He developed hybrids with wonderful traits. It wasn't enough for him to have just a beautiful flower and good looking foliage, he wanted early bloom and unusual color. Yellow. Peach. Red. He wasn't in a hurry like some breeders. He was working toward a perfect plant." Amy smiled sadly. "He had already named it."

"Really! What did he call it?" Mim saw that Amy's beautiful face was suffused with a warm glow.

"Aimee," she said and looked away. When she turned back to Mim her face was streaked with tears, but her eyes were shining. "That's what he called me."

19

"There you are!" called Chase. At his words, Mim and Amy looked up to see Chase approaching their table with Sally and Barney Staples in tow. Chase was his usual, outrageously upbeat self, but Sally looked haggard.

"Mind if we join you?" asked Chase, plopping down next to Mim. Mim looked at Amy for approval, who said, "Please do." Chase introduced Barney to Amy, who smiled and said, "We've met," and to Mim, who didn't stop him, but smiled conspiratorially at Barney.

In moments, the conversation was rolling with Chase keeping it lively. Mim observed that Barney Staples spoke little, but followed closely what was being said. When he commented in his a very slight British accent, it was with intelligence. Mostly, he quietly followed the conversation.

"Where did you go? I couldn't find you." Sally addressed Mim. She was not only looking haggard, she sounded tipsy. Either the champagne hadn't worn off or she had drunk something more.

"I was starving," said Mim. "And I was very, very bad and ordered the fettuccini alfredo, which is very, very good. We came up here for peace and quiet."

"Well, it's a war zone down there," Sally put her head in her hands. All of a sudden, her shoulders shook with silent sobs. Seeing this sudden show of emotion, the waitress who was approaching their table suddenly stopped and turned around.

"What's the matter?" Mim asked in alarm. Sally didn't move her hands.

"Eric the ferret!" said Chase, baring his teeth in a pretty good imitation of a ferret about to attack. He made clawing motions with his hands. Mim tried to peek at Sally's face.

"He says he's going to sue Foresters!" Sally said miserably. She dropped one hand to expose one eye that made contact with Mim.

"What *for?*" Mim dismissively said. Clearly, Sally had drunk more than she could handle.

"He says he had submitted the idea for a book of herbs in the landscape a year ago!" Sally was near tears.

"You didn't tell him about..." Mim began.

"Of course not!" Sally snapped.

"He crept up behind us," said Chase, raising his voice in anger. The shiny stones set in his glasses sparkled as he shook his head with righteous indignation. "Sally was telling *us* about the book and he eavesdropped," concluded Chase.

After a moment in which they all sat in somewhat gloomy silence, Mim reassuringly spoke.

"You know, I wouldn't put it past him to have made the whole thing up. That would be classic Eric Ferris. Out of sheer meanness! Just to spoil your pleasure, perhaps, or to take our idea and try to scare Foresters into thinking he had it first. He likes stirring up trouble. I bet Tom won't give him the time of day!" Mim warmed to the subject.

"Last year Eric threatened to sue Lin Baldwin for a photo she had published that was taken at his garden after he *invited* her to come and shoot," Mim continued, gaining conviction. "Of course, nothing came of it because he had no grounds for suit. They both knew that she had been invited into the garden to take photos. But it still upset her terribly. It turned out that he had submitted similar photos to one of the magazines and was outraged that the magazine had bought *her* photos of *his* garden instead of his."

"Order something nice to eat and we'll talk to Tom tomorrow," Mim concluded dismissing the problem.

The restaurant was slowly filling up. Horticultural writers by ones, twos, and groups of four or more were coming off the elevator into the dining room. While Chase, Sally, and Barney perused their menus, Mim enjoyed a good view of the restaurant entrance. She recognized some of the speakers for tomorrow's symposium. Daniel Cullen, a tall, attractive man in his forties, walked in together with the Taylors, a handsome couple in their vigorous mid-fifties.

She saw Philippa, the British woman, pause in the foyer. She was swiftly escorted to a table where she sat by herself. Where was Kevin?

"My word," said Chase, looking up. "That man is gorgeous. Now I know what they mean when they say 'drop-dead good-looking'!"

Everyone, except Sally, who was still brooding, turned to look. Marcus Tydings stood at the threshold of the restaurant, scanning the room.

"That's Marcus Tydings," said Barney. "He's a breeder. Well, a talented amateur. I believe he operates a small nursery. It's in Pennsylvania somewhere. Mim and I attended his workshop."

"I felt unwell and had to leave before it was over," explained Mim, meeting Barney's eye.

"Mim escaped," Barney laughed.

"Grrrrrrrrrrrrrrrr!" Chase's appreciative growl was loud enough to draw attention from the tables around them. It would be hard to miss, but Marcus did miss it or, at least, appeared not to hear it.

Chase gestured to the empty chair beside him, but Marcus, who saw it, but pretended not to, turned his head from left to right, obviously looking around the room for another place to sit. He swung completely around and saw Philippa sitting alone at a table for two. He walked directly to it. Gesturing with a sweep of the hand to the empty seats, he bent, apparently to ask her if he might join her.

She looked up surprised, appeared to listen to what he had to say, smiled, shook his hand, and motioned with the other hand to the chair across from her. Tydings bowed his head as if in gratitude and sat down.

"Did anyone see Kevin at the cocktail party?" asked Mim, returning her attention to the table and scanning the room.

"I did," said Sally. "I saw him with that British woman. The one with the neckline that plunges to her waist." Chase caught Sally's eye and inclined his head toward the table at which Philippa and Marcus were now engaged in conversation.

"Oh! Guess Kevin didn't get lucky." Sally sat to attention and stared at the table. "That is one beautiful man!"

"I saw him first," said Chase.

Mim glanced at Philippa's table. Beyond it, she saw that Margaret Stemple, entering the restaurant. Margaret systematically scanned the room as if looking for someone. Her eyes stopped at the table where Marcus and Philippa were now in animated conversation.

"Those two make a very attractive couple," Mim said, following Margaret's gaze to Marcus and Philippa. "They look like something out of a Ralph Lauren ad."

Amy stared at the couple and frowned in concentration. Sally studied her menu. Chase sighed dramatically.

"What a waste!" he announced in a jovial tone at odds with an expression of mistrust on his face.

Mim watched Margaret make a wide arc around Marcus and Philippa's table. She's heading for us. Margaret approached slowly as if she were carrying an enormous weight. Her low-cut lavender lace dress flattered her figure, but did nothing for her rather sallow skin and mouse-brown hair.

"Margaret, please sit down" broke in Mim. "You look bushed—but I must say, you are sacrificing yourself for a good cause. This symposium is the best yet! The only thing that could possibly top it would be if David Hawkins were on the program," she gushed.

"The reason that David Hawkins is not here speaking," bridled Margaret, "is that he had a scheduling conflict. And at the times he had available, *all* of our other speakers could not make it! You have no idea how difficult it is to organize a symposium of this size!"

"Oh Margaret! I'm so sorry. I was trying to be ironic. I did not mean to criticize." Mim cursed herself for yet another tactless remark to Margaret who was both hypersensitive and not gifted with a sense of humor. "This is a fabulous conference!"

The others, with the exception of Amy, agreed, all at once chirping like chipmunks with words of agreement and praise. Mim noted that Margaret's eyes were red as if she'd been crying.

Gallantly, Chase rose and pulled out a chair and Margaret literally dropped into it. She looked at Amy.

"Amy," said Margaret in a weary voice. It was as if her defense of the conference speakers had taken up her last ounce of energy. "I must have your program ASAP. I was supposed to have it a week ago." Margaret looked like she was about to crumble. "Do you have it with you?"

"You mean JP's program? The shots of the Balkan trip?" Amy looked baffled.

"Yes. I asked for the presenters' programs over a week ago. I know that...." Margaret paused, struggling with how to express herself tactfully in light of JP's death. Before she could call up the right words, Amy spoke.

"But I sent you a disk!" Amy protested. "Before.... I sent it myself! At least three weeks ago!"

"If you sent it, I never received it," Margaret said tiredly. Seeing Amy's stricken expression, she added, "I'm so, so sorry Amy, but I never received a disk from you or...JP." Amy sat stunned. There was a moment of silence.

"Do you have a copy?" Margaret added expectantly. Everyone looked at Amy, who had gone pale.

"I have *one* copy," she gasped, as if suddenly aware of a disaster narrowly averted. "But I can't...don't have it with me. I mean, not here. It's upstairs—in my room," Amy said, wringing her napkin with both hands. "I'll give it to you first thing tomorrow." Margaret furrowed her brow, then looked around the table. It was clear that tomorrow wasn't good enough, but she didn't want to press the point in front of an audience.

"I need it by eight a.m. sharp," said Margaret briskly. "Please bring it to the projection room at the back of the auditorium. I'll be there." Margaret pulled herself up wearily and said good night.

"I put JP's program on a flash drive," Amy said in a stage whisper that was full of relief. "Actually, it's not in my room. I have it in my purse. I just...can't bear to let it out of my sight," she added, hugging her purse to her chest. "It's the only thing they didn't get," said Amy, suddenly choking up.

"Don't you have a backup?" asked Chase, incredulously. The others looked up from their menus in surprise.

"You should always make more than one copy," said Barney.

"And never, never give your only copy of a program to anyone else," said Chase.

"They took everything. I didn't even think about the program until... when I found it in my jacket pocket. I thought Margaret already had a copy. I sent it weeks ago. I don't know how it got lost." Amy shook her head.

"I never expected it to get lost. I'm afraid I've been..." she searched for the right words. "Not thinking clearly."

Give yourself a thousand points for thinking at all, thought Mim. For getting up in the morning and getting dressed, let alone coming to this meeting to present JP's talk.

"Come on. I've got my laptop and flash drives upstairs," said Mim. "We'll make a backup."

"But it's in Power Point," said Amy.

"No problem," said Mim, "I've got an older version on my laptop, but it should work. I use it all the time. *Bon appetit!*" she wished the others.

As Mim and Amy got up from the table, Barney Staples politely rose, followed by Chase. Barney's green eyes caught Mim's and lingered.

20

Mim fired up her laptop, stood up, and gestured for Amy to sit down. Amy needed no instructions. She seated herself at the desk and deftly inserted the flash drive into a USB port.

"You must have a Sony laptop," Mim commented. Amy stopped still. She said nothing for a moment but seemed to be struggling for a rejoinder. Finally, she uttered a single word.

"Had." It was meant to be a jaunty response, but came out in a strangled voice.

"Sorry," Mim said. "I'm so sorry! I should have remembered."

"It's okay. It's fine. It's just that every once in a while...." Amy exhaled deeply. She addressed the computer and began typing.

"I guess you don't need any instructions on how to use the Power Point program," Mim said as Amy made herself comfortable.

"I could do this in my sleep," Amy said as she now absent-mindedly kicked off her shoes and leaned toward the screen. A swift few clicks later, a file entitled "Balkans" appeared on the desktop.

"Want to see it?" Amy asked.

"Sure!" said Mim, seating herself on the edge of the bed for a better view of the computer screen. Mim slipped out of her shoes while Amy clicked on the file that blossomed into orderly rows of photos. Another click and the show began.

From the center of the screen, a "wallpaper" of overlapping hellebore foliage appeared, followed by a burst of multicolored bloom. Then, a tiny pink dot in the center of the screen moved forward becoming clearer and larger and redder. It split like so many colorful amoebas into letters that spelled out "Hunting for Hellebores."

"Wow!" said Mim. "Did you do that?"

"Yeah!" Amy smiled proudly. "I took a course in animation. I do—did—all of JP's talks for him," she added briskly. She clicked and the next photo appeared.

"Oh!" Mim said breathlessly as a photo of Tate standing next to Dr. Muller in a field of bright yellow hellebores appeared on the screen. Mim stared, mesmerized, filled with conflicting emotions—joy, pain, and an overwhelming sense of loss.

"Dr. Muller showed a photo like that this morning. Only it was just Tate and…I guess it was JP."

"Yeah. JP and Tate were invited to Bosnia by Dr. Muller," said Amy. Her voice was thick with emotion. "It was right before they were going to meet up with the others in Slovenia. Muller's a big authority on hellebores, you know. JP and Tate were the only ones he invited to go."

"Tate told me about Dr. Muller," said Mim. He was excited to join him in Bosnia with JP. That's a great shot."

"Yeah," said Amy. "Should I move on?"

"Sure," said Mim.

The next photo showed smiling members of the plant hunting trip to Slovenia posed in front of a rustic inn. In the background was a jagged panorama of snow-capped mountain peaks.

Tate half knelt in the center of the first row, wearing the red anorak. He was grinning at the camera.

Again, Mim couldn't take her eyes away from the screen. To her utter amazement and consternation, a sob rose in her chest. She tried to stifle it but it escaped her.

"Dammit!" she said.

"Mim," Amy rose from her chair and sat down beside Mim on the bed. "Hey! I know all about you and Tate. I mean, I didn't know you in person before tonight, but JP told me that Tate told him about you." Amy slipped her arm around Mim's shoulders.

"He did?" Mim felt a little flame of joy fire up and then extinguish just as quickly. "I'm sorry," Mim said, wiping her wet cheeks with the sleeve of her sweater. "This is crazy." Mim saw that Amy's eyes were bright with tears.

"I should be the one comforting you," Mim said, embarrassed. Hugging Amy, she let out a long, soft sigh. After a minute of silence, Amy rose and took her seat at the desk.

"*Allons-y*," she said over her shoulder. She pressed her lips together in a smile that looked more determined than heartfelt.

"Wait! Before you advance, that's JP?"

"Yeah! That's JP on the left in the green parka," Amy said. "Right next to him—those are the Taylors—Jenny and Darrel. Lots of these people are here at the conference. They're speaking." Amy tapped at the people on the screen. "There's Benjy Glover, Andy Toll, Katie Hiscock, and Daniel Cullen… They're all good friends, you know."

"You're right! Just about everyone in that photo is here at the conference. I mean…" Mim stopped.

Amy smiled sadly. "Yeah." She stopped and stared at the group photo.

"You know, Mim, Tate was JP's best friend. He really thought the world of him," said Amy. "He said Tate was one of the few people he could really trust," she said, tucking a strand of blonde hair behind her ear. "JP used to say that the world of horticulture could be…a little intense and some of the people who breed specialty plants are…are a little strange. And he's seen what happens on both sides of the Atlantic." Amy stood up.

"Have you ever heard of Marion Petersfield?" Amy asked.

"Yes. Odd that you mention her," Mim said with a dull sense of foreboding. "This is the second time in two days that I've heard her name. She was the hellebore breeder who was murdered–in England? And wasn't she the one who started this whole business about hellebore's being cursed?"

"Yeah. JP worked at her nursery. He was there the day she was killed."

"Oh, how awful!" The sense of foreboding darkened to dread. A saying came to mind, something about coincidence. And levers and pulleys. She couldn't quite remember it.

"JP said he had a bad feeling that morning. As if something was *going* to happen." The hair on the back of Mim's neck rose.

"What did he think would happen?" Mim asked.

"Well, Marion was almost seventy and she had high blood pressure. JP always worried she might have a heart attack or a stroke or something while she was out in the woods alone. She took these really long walks with Phoebe—that was her dog. Marion always walked – at the same time every day—after lunch. Sometimes when business was slow, she was gone for hours. Sometimes she stopped and had tea with her friend. JP pretty much ran the nursery." Amy looked at JP's image as if for corroboration.

"Do you know what happened to her?"

"Well, JP told me. He said that day—the day she was murdered—Marion was gone for a really long time—maybe three hours. They were getting ready to close up when Phoebe came back without Marion and she was acting strange. You know. Whining and crying."

"JP knew, he just knew, that something bad had happened. He and Robert, a guy he worked with, they went to find her. And they did.... not all that far from the nursery. There were these walking paths in the woods and that's where they found her. It was terrible. She was lying on her back, but you couldn't recognize her face–plus she was unconscious. Someone had beat her, really beat her. JP said he knew who she was from her clothes and stuff. Otherwise you couldn't tell who it was. Her face was caked with blood."

"They called an ambulance. They closed up the nursery and went to the hospital. Three of them. There were three people working for Marion at Withcombe—JP and Robert and..." Amy's tone changed, "the other horticulturist, a woman," she said crisply. Then she shot Mim a wry look. "Tate lived with her for a while. Anyway, all of them went to the hospital."

Mim wanted to ask Amy about the woman, but something in Amy's bearing dissuaded her. This wasn't the time.

"Marion lived for a couple of hours. At first, they thought she might, you know make it, but she died. JP thought that was probably for the best. She was pretty messed up. He thought the world of her, but she probably would be brain damaged if she lived."

As Amy spoke, the image of the plant hunting group photo disappeared from the computer screen. It was replaced by a photo Mim had taken on Cape Breton Island of spruce trees in deep snow. Absently, Amy moved the mouse and the plant hunting group reappeared.

"Nobody could believe it. I mean, like everybody knew Marion. Withcombe is a really small town, more like a village, and Marion was sort of a celebrity. You know, with a famous nursery and all. Everyone knew her and everyone knew that she walked her dog every day." Amy shook her head.

"After Marion was killed, well…JP was pretty broken up about it. He said he couldn't sleep. JP was…," Amy struggled for control. She breathed in and floated out her words on the exhale, "he was a softie." She brushed her hands across her face as if whisking flyaway hair. She took another deep breath. Her face became serene.

"Anyway, the next morning, real early, he went back to the nursery. He said he had this really bad feeling. And as soon as he opened the gate, he just knew something was wrong." Again, Amy looked at JP's image for corroboration.

"He went into the shop and looked around and everything seemed okay. He looked in the till. The money's all there. But he kept having this feeling that something was wrong. So he walks out into the nursery. And, way, way back—there was a fence along the back. That's where Marion's best stock plants were growing—the ones she used for breeding—a bunch of them were gone."

"Someone stole her plants?

"Yeah."

"Hellebores?"

"Yeah."

"Did they ever catch the person who did it?" Mim asked.

"No. Never!" Amy put her hands on her hips. Her mouth twisted into a shape that twisted her words. "They never found out who killed Marion, never mind who stole the plants."

Amy shook her head in disgust. "I mean, compared to murder, what's a few plants?"

Then Amy shook her head and made brushing gestures with her hands as if trying to sweep away these unhappy thoughts as if they were annoying insects.

"Well, I remember how proud Tate was of some of his plants. Before I met him, I thought one hellebore was pretty much like another. Now I know that a stock plant could be pretty precious and the result of years of breeding," Mim said.

"Yeah," said Amy. "JP had this idea. Like, at first, he thought that the person who killed Marion stole the plants, too. He thought it was someone who bred hellebores. And that's what the cops thought, too. At least at first."

Amy and Mim turned toward the door at the click of a key in the lock, but the noise must have come from the room next door.

"But JP thought they stole them more out of spite than to actually use them," Amy said.

"Why out of spite?"

"Because you could really mess up someone's breeding program if you stole their best plants."

"Did JP or the police have any suspects?"

"Yeah. At first, JP thought it was Marion's big rival– a guy named Wilson McCoy…She hated him. Funny thing was, they used to be, you know, like close, lovers. That's what JP said."

Wilson McCoy again! Mim felt a frisson of dread.

"Did the police think he did it?" Amy shrugged.

"Yeah, well maybe. At first. Because of the way she was killed—like someone knew her really well and really hated her. The cops called it 'a crime of passion.' But it turned out that McCoy couldn't have. He had this big nursery in another part of England. I can't remember the name. Hours away. Halfway across England. And that's where he was when Marion was killed. Two people vouched for him. After that, JP didn't think he had anything to do with it."

"Did he suspect anybody else?"

"He thought maybe it was some crazy amateur. See, they weren't dead sure when the stock plants went missing. It could have been maybe a couple of days before. Maybe it had nothing to do with Marion's murder. Nobody could remember the last time they went back there and saw them."

"Why did JP think the thief was an amateur breeder—why an amateur?" asked Mim.

"Well, the best breeders have been at it for a long time. They have their own breeding lines and they think their own plants are way better than anything else that's out there. That's how JP was." Amy smiled indulgently. Then her smile faded. She looked angry.

"Another reason he thought it was probably an amateur is because of his own bad experience with amateur breeders. He invited a group of hellebore enthusiasts to our garden. They were all members of the Royal Horticultural Society. In town for a conference at Longwood. Some were Brits. There were a couple of New Zealanders. Most were Americans.

Anyway, one of them stole one of JP's plants *while* he was giving a tour of our garden. It was there when he started. And it was gone when they left!"

"That's incredibly tacky! But how could someone do that without getting caught?"

"JP thought it was maybe someone who was wearing a backpack. And a bunch of people were wearing backpacks. Or, else, it was someone who dropped behind the group and left early. The garden is almost an acre and there are lots of big trees. They were wandering all over the place. No way could we keep track of who was there and who wasn't," Amy held her palms up in a gesture of helplessness at the memory. "Or it could also have been someone who hid the plant and came back for it later—but I don't think so."

"Did JP ever suspect anyone in particular?" asked Mim. Amy crossed her arms and hunched her shoulders as if she were cold.

"Yeah. As a matter of fact, he did. But he could never prove it," said Amy. "He thought it was someone who went on the Balkan trip." Amy pressed her lips shut as if to stop herself from saying any more. She turned to the photo on the screen.

"Did he have any reason for thinking that? I mean, most of those people on the trip are pretty reputable breeders...."

Amy glanced at Mim, looked away, and bit her lip. Mim thought she might be debating whether or not to answer so she said nothing, hoping Amy would fill the silence. Amy looked down at her hands as if the answer were written on them. She took a breath about to begin, then seemed unsure how to start.

Mim thought if she said anything, Amy might change her mind and clam up. She held her breath and waited.

"On that plant hunting trip to the Balkans..."

Mim nodded encouragingly, willing her face to look neutral and not too interested.

"They collected seeds and plants everyday. They kept everything they found in their rooms. Everybody had a little stash of plants and seeds and stuff. After... what happened to Tate ...after that happened," Amy looked imploringly at Mim. "Tate's plants disappeared. "

21

After Amy and Mim left the restaurant, Barney ordered a dessert wine and Chase ordered the "Bentam Bomb," a giant ice cream sundae. It was so formidable that even Chase could not contemplate finishing it. He asked for two more spoons and urged Barney and Sally to help him. After the first reluctant bite, Sally ate with relish, something that improved her mood immensely.

Halfway through the sundae, Chase, who had eyes only for Marcus Tydings during dinner, now took a casual look at the man's table mate. Then he looked again, hard. Good grief! he thought. That's Pippa. That's Pippa! I'm sure of it. What could she possibly be doing here?

He thought back to the first time he had seen her. It was two weeks ago in the airport lounge as they waited to board for the flight to London. It was hard to ignore someone with the face of an angel, that carrot red curly hair, and those enormous brown eyes. What really made her stand out was her pacing, nervously back and forth, back and forth on three-inch stiletto heels that clicked on the terrazzo floor.

Their overnight flight originated at Dulles. He had brought a book and planned to read himself to sleep. That way, he'd be as fresh as possible the next day.

But she was seated next to him. Extremely nervous, she had chatted all night—almost hysterically at times.

Now, Chase thought about getting up and re-introducing himself, but decided against it. It's wasn't the best time for that. And, in the very unlikely event that he was wrong, it would be best to confront the woman when they were alone.

As he watched, the woman rose, shook hands with Tydings. His eyes followed her as she left the carpeted restaurant. When she reached the marble foyer, he could hear the tapping of her high heels. She had an energetic walk that made the mass of her curly hair bounce.

The tapping was right, but the hair was different. The color was wrong. This woman's hair wasn't carrot red. It was chestnut brown.

Mim stared at the computer screen. One of the people in this photo stole Tate's plants! How could someone–supposedly a friend–stoop so low?

Then she remembered. JP thought it was an *amateur* breeder who went on the Balkan trip. That narrowed the field.

It meant that JP suspected one of the non-professionals in this group, thought Mim, scanning the photo. Andy Toll, the Taylors, and Benjy Glover could not be considered amateurs. That left a big field. There was Rose Redfern and Margaret Stemple and Katie Hiscock and Marcus Tydings or...her eyes moved to a short man wearing a baseball cap.

"Who's that?" amy looked to where Mim was pointing.

"That's you know—we saw him tonight. The guy nobody likes."

"Eric Ferris?"

"Yeah, that's his name."

Eric Ferris. Mim stifled irritation. She wouldn't put anything past him.

"Who's the guy in the hat. The one who's looking away from the camera?" asked Mim.

"Him?" Amy pointed.

"That's Barney!"

"Barney Staples?"

"Yeah. He was at our table tonight. He used to teach at Delaware. He retired. He's getting into hellebores." Amy did not continue. Did that mean that JP suspected Barney Staples? For reasons inexplicable to herself, she hoped not. Mim waited, but Amy said nothing.

Did Amy consider Barney a professional? Mim glanced sideways at Amy to read her expression. Amy's brow was deeply furrowed. Mim ventured the question foremost in her mind.

"Did JP ever tell you who he suspected?" Amy turned her face to Mim with no change of expression.

"No. He wasn't sure," Amy's answer was clearly without conviction. She was a lousy liar.

"Not even a little suspicion?" Amy just shook her head. She didn't meet Mim's eyes. Mim thought she was certainly holding something back.

Mim looked from one face in the photo to another. She recognized many of those in the group. Her gaze settled on a tall woman with blonde hair. She was one of the strangers in the photo.

"Who's that woman in the back row?" Mim asked.

"That's Olga. I can't remember her last name. She's Russian and works at the Botanic Garden in Moscow."

Mim looked at a small, childlike figure at the end of the front row. He or she, probably a woman judging from the size, was wearing a broad-brimmed hat that cast a shadow over the face.

"Who's ...?" Mim began, just as the phone jangled. Both women turned toward the interruption. Mim got up to answer.

"Susan is right here," said Phyllis Butner without preamble. "She has written an outstanding piece on African violets."

"Well, I have written my piece on hell...Christmas roses and will have it to you well before the original deadline," said Mim.

"*Christmas* roses will be *tres passé* by January, " Phyllis said.

"Oh! No no!" countered Mim with authority. "Not at all! There could not possibly be a better time for this article. First of all, Christmas roses don't bloom until after Christmas in our area. And secondly, I am also covering the Lenten roses that bloom in early spring. Christmas and Lenten roses will be a perfect subject for the January issue."

If Phyllis was bothering to telephone her at her hotel, Mim guessed, the change in subjects had not been cleared with John Winkler, the publisher of *Washington Home*.

"And I have dynamite photos!" Winkler was a stickler for good photography. Mim was sure she could obtain outstanding photos from the presenters at the conference. There was a silence on the other end of the line.

"You realize," Phyllis finally spoke, "that *you* have put Susan through a lot of work for nothing!"

"It was not *my* idea to have her write about African violets! Or anything else," said Mim heatedly. She stifled her anger and said softly, "I write the garden articles because I am the garden editor."

"Fine!" snapped Phyllis. She slammed down the phone. Mim took a deep breath. She returned to the desk where Amy was sitting, gazing at the group photo. Amy turned to Mim with a questioning expression.

"That was my editor. Where were we?" Mim asked.

"You were asking about the people on the expedition," Amy said. "They weren't just Americans. There were horticulturists from all over on that trip—from Germany, Moscow, and I think maybe Belgium."

Mim moved her eyes to the center of the photo. The knot in her stomach loosened.

JP, tan and blonde, had his arm around Tate's shoulder. On their faces, Mim read the excitement and satisfaction, the passion for what they were doing.

The Taylors were standing behind Tate. Jenny wore her strawberry blonde hair in a Gibson girl hairdo. A few strands had escaped charmingly. Next to her, distinguished with his white hair and beard was Darrel. Wearing identical yellow rain gear, they looked comfortable and contented; they had probably taken many such plant hunting trips before.

Likewise, Andy Toll, tall and relaxed, seemed in his element. Next to Andy, Katie Hiscock, clad in her signature purple, looked as if she were bursting with joy. To Katie's left stood Margaret Stemple in a mouse gray parka. Or maybe it was lavender. She seemed to favor lavender. Someone really ought to tell her. ... It was hard to read the expression on Margaret's face. She had to be pleased to have escaped her dreadful mother long enough to take a trip to the Balkans!

Rose Redfern's wore beige pants and parka, a change from her signature white, doubtless a color concession to the rugged surroundings. Next to Rose was Eric Ferris, grinning rat-like into the camera.

A little apart from Margaret, Rose, and Eric, Marcus Tydings looked like he was posing for a clothing ad. He, too, was wearing a red anorak, similar, or, perhaps even identical, to Tate's. But Marcus sported what looked like a fashionable version of tan safari pants and a broad-brimmed, Australian-style hat. He was smiling with his teeth. It gave him a wolfish look.

Everyone in the photo was looking at the camera except for the man Mim now knew was Barney. He was standing in the back row, looking off to the side.

The phone jangled again. Thinking it was Phyllis again, spewing more vitriol, Mim answered it gruffly.

"Amy?" Mim held out the phone to Amy and said, "It's for you."

Amy accepted the phone with a baffled expression.

"Margaret," whispered Mim. Amy took the phone and spoke briefly. She hung up.

"She was calling to remind me to bring her the program tomorrow morning. First thing!"

"How did she know you were here?" Mim asked. Amy shrugged.

"You know, I *know* I sent her that program. Three weeks ago! She must have lost it." Amy plopped onto the desk chair.

Mim wanted to get back to the subject of Tate's stolen plants. As they clicked through the photos, she waited before bringing it up. Finally, she said casually, "So, JP didn't know who might have taken the plants? He must have had some suspicions...."

Amy paused, apparently searching her memory. Then, her expression changed. She seemed to have come to some kind of decision and she wasn't going to part with any more information. She simply shook her head.

Amy advanced to a photo of a beautiful hellebore. The plant formed a perfect mound of satiny, dark green foliage. It was covered with deep pink flowers that, unlike the hellebores in Mim's garden, were held up above the clump.

"That's gorgeous!" said Mim. "It's the best looking hellebore I have ever seen!"

"That's one of JP's best stock plants," said Amy.

The next photo was a landscape shot of a snow-capped mountain range, obviously taken on the trip to Slovenia. In the distance were colorful dots—the plant hunting party hiking into the gray landscape.

"See how tiny the people are. JP did it to show the scale of the landscape," said Amy proudly.

"Wait!" Mim cried. She made out a tiny red dot. Either Tate...or Marcus. She moved closer to the screen, but that made it worse. With advancing years, she was losing her close-up vision. It was impossible to make out more. Amy watched her patiently. She looked at Amy and nodded.

Amy advanced to the next photo. It and most of the photos that followed were macro shots of various species of hellebores. The images were crisp and clear. Interspersed with groups of plant portraits were shots that JP had taken to show the scale and character of the landscape. Sometimes, Mim saw tiny colored dots in the distance. They had to be members of the plant hunting party. Each time she bent close to the screen to try to identify who they were, her farsightedness made them disappear into the background. Frustrated, she sat back.

Seen in the distance, the people, tiny in their colorful rain gear, were a foil to the gray landscape and the vastness of the terrain. JP was a superb photographer.

After the shots of the expedition, there were three photos of a large group of hellebores. In each, there was a little placard bearing the date. The first one read "March, 2002." Several hellebores were in bud and one was showing lavender flowers. Amy advanced to another group. The date was March, 2004. In this photo, three of the hellebores were in bloom. Two were a deep mauve color, but one was closer to a real purple. In the last photo, dated March, 2006, one hellebore shone a satiny blue-purple. It held its flowers proudly above the clump. Amy advanced the program and a circle appeared around this plant.

"That's 'Aimee'," said Amy, her voice choked with emotion.

"That's incredible! It's really blue!" said Mim.

Amy advanced to the last photo. Hellebore flowers popped out of the computer screen and came together in a stunning collage.

"Did you do that?" Amy nodded as a tear rolled down her cheek. It's amazing!" breathed Mim. "And that's a terrific lecture!"

Mim was disconcerted to feel her own eyes tear up. JP had been a great photographer and although Mim knew nothing of breeding, she could guess what a triumph it was to achieve a blue-colored hellebore. Nevertheless, it was Amy's skillful manipulation of the photos that put the program over the top. She fished in her floppy black bag until her fingers found her flash drives.

"You go girl!" she said, handing Amy two flash drives. "Make yourself a second copy." Amy looked doubtful for a moment, then she smiled and thanked Mim.

After Amy copied JP's program, she asked if she could save a copy on Mim's laptop. It was a safety measure, she said tactfully. The real reason, they both knew, was that she knew Mim wanted to see it again.

Amy worked fast, but when she was done, she literally sagged with fatigue. She rubbed her eyes and yawned.

"Have you been sleeping well?" Mim asked. Amy just looked at Mim not so much ironically, but as if she was trying to remember the last time she slept.

"At all?"

"I know I must be sleeping, but I always wake up with the feeling that I've been lying awake all night," Amy said. "I know this is weird, but I have a feeling I have to protect something. It's like I have to stay alert and keep watch. But I'm not sure for what." Mim met Amy's eyes and saw in them the unspoken 'there's nothing left.'

"Maybe you'll get a good night's sleep tonight," Mim suggested. "Your work is done. JP's program is beautiful. If you didn't do anything else but stand up there and advance these photos, you'd impress everyone. You've done a terrific job. You deserve a good rest." Amy seemed almost dopey with fatigue, but her tired face flushed with pleasure.

"JP was so excited about showing the Balkan slides at this symposium. And he wanted everybody to see Aimee," Amy said. "I have to do this for him. Thank you for all your help!" She groped under the desk to retrieve the black heels she had kicked off earlier. Then she headed, shoeless, for the door, yawning. At the door she stopped, bent over wearily, and put her shoes back on.

"Wait! Your key!" Mim handed her the key.

"You know, I'm right above you," Amy said. She pointed toward the ceiling. "This is 415, right? Thanks again!"

After Amy left, Mim went to the bathroom and ran a comb through her hair. She applied a subtle, flesh colored lipstick.

It was just nine o'clock. She decided to look for Kevin and see what he had learned at his meeting with Randy.

After Amy pressed the "up" button and while she waited for the elevator, she wondered if she had told Mim too much. Learning that Tate's plants were stolen had upset Mim. She could see that. She liked Mim and had felt instantly comfortable with her—so much so, she had almost said more. They only met each other a few hours ago! It was better that she had not mentioned the glove.

She could never tell Mim that. It had haunted JP. Sometimes he had trouble sleeping when he thought about it. Mim was still raw. It would only hurt her.

Amy waited for the elevator for what seemed like five long minutes. She watched as numerals lit up for each floor the elevators passed, but it seemed that every time they ascended to the fourth floor, the elevators returned to the lobby again.

The day had seemed endless. Her legs and back ached from standing. She just wanted a hot shower and bed.

Just as she decided to try the stairs, she saw that one elevator was ascending quickly; it wasn't making any stops. Amy hoped this meant it would be empty. She didn't want to have to talk to anyone. She stepped in front of the ascending elevator's door and waited.

When the doors rolled open, she saw it was not empty. Amy looked down at the floor, but not before she caught a glimpse of the woman in a black dress who was standing in one corner of the elevator, as far away from the other person as she could be in such a small space.

Without looking directly at him, she knew that the other occupant was Marcus Tydings. He'd been on the Balkan trip. She could feel his eyes on her.

Something deep in Amy's memory stirred. She didn't try to find the memory. She didn't want to know what it was. Though she couldn't say why, she felt suddenly and deeply uneasy. She wished she had taken the stairs. Now, the feeling was so strong, one part of her wanted to stay where she was and wait for another elevator.

Instead, her tired feet won out and she stepped into the elevator. After giving the two people the faintest of nods, she turned to the controls to punch in her floor.

Amy saw that the five was already illuminated. They were all heading to the same floor. Damn. She punched in nine.

All at once, her thoughts were flying, digging up memories and swiftly dropping them as not relevant. What was setting off these sirens in her head? An animal instinct made her not want to expose her back to the people in the elevator. But just as strongly, she didn't want to face them. A no-win situation. She turned sideways, leaned back against the wall, and looked down at the gray and maroon swirl patterns on the carpeted floor.

The elevator door rolled open at the fifth floor. She pretended to be fishing around in her purse when the other occupants exited. She felt the two people glance her way as they passed. They paused outside.

It seemed like minutes before the elevator doors rolled closed again and she was alone. She was trembling. She longed to be inside her room with the door locked.

On the ninth floor, she held the elevator door open while she counted, very slowly, to fifty, then hit the button for five and rode the elevator back down. When she stepped out, she saw that Marcus and the woman were now walking together. No longer the strangers they had seemed in the elevator, they were holding hands. Somehow, she was not surprised. The way they had stood in the elevator had seemed too posed. That deception, too, fit with the warning signals flashing in her mind.

To put a little more distance between herself and Marcus Tydings and his girl friend, she paused in front of the elevators and, again, fished in her purse, this time locating her room key. When the couple had progressed a good way down the hall, she followed slowly.

A small part of her felt foolish. Why should she avoid these people? Marcus Tydings had been on the trip to the Balkans with JP. Although she didn't think he and JP had been good friends, she really should talk to him, at least say hello. She just didn't want to.

What was it about him—about both of them—that made her feel this way? She couldn't put a finger on what it was, but something was making her uncomfortable. If this was paranoia, she didn't care. She was far too tired to fight it. She didn't want to know about it. All she wanted was not to have to interact with them.

When Tydings stopped and reached into his pocket—probably for his room key—she felt relief. In moments, they would be gone and the corridor would be empty. As she slowed her pace to almost a stand still, her relief changed to horror. As Amy watched, the pair walked on and entered the room next to hers.

There was nothing to do but follow slowly. Amy was trembling by the time she reached 515. Shakily, she inserted her key and opened the door to her room. She groped for the light switch, turned on the light, and immediately felt rather than saw that something was different. Someone had been in her room.

Standing with her back to the door, she scanned the room. Everything was the way she left it, but somehow different. On the luggage rack, her suitcase was open. She was pretty sure she left it that way, but it looked different. She remembered rummaging through it looking for a shirt. Now the clothes in the suitcase seemed too neat.

On top of the dresser in front of the mirror were her hairbrush and comb, not the way she left them. She was sure of that.

Then she saw the bed. It was turned down and there were two little pieces of candy on the pillow. She let out a choked sigh. Relief flooded over her. Housekeeping had been here. That was all.

Still, she double locked the door. And felt horribly alone. Wanting some sense of connection to the world, to other people, to what was normal, she walked to the television, picked up the remote, and clicked "on." A point of light appeared and began to spread across the dark screen.

She crossed to the bed and picked up one of the foil-wrapped pieces of candy. It looked like chocolate. Too tired even to unwrap it, she stepped out of her skirt and collapsed on the bed. Lulled by canned laughter, she fell into dreams.

22

After Amy left, Mim decided to go downstairs and socialize. She took the elevator down. Mim spotted Kevin in the lounge area. A section of the lobby adjacent to the bar had been fitted with couches and comfortable club chairs. It was partitioned off the rest of the vast room by banks of potted plants. Mim touched the leaf of a large palm. Fake.

She was not surprised to see Kevin in the lounge and also not surprised, and a good bit relieved, to see he had acquired an entourage—all female, of course. This was the Kevin she knew and loved. Sally's remark that Kevin was goggle eyed over Philippa dismayed her. She liked to think of Kevin as immune to feminine charms—even those as enticing as Philippa's. She didn't like to think there was a chink in his armor, that he was vulnerable to someone like Philippa, and she felt a motherly urge to keep him safe.

As she approached, she saw that he and his following had commandeered an entire alcove within the lounge area. Kevin was sitting in the middle of a sofa like a pasha, albeit a buff one, flanked by his harem, a couple of whom sat in easy chairs. The coffee table in front of the little group was laden with a wine bottle and several half-empty glasses.

On his right was Mim's friend Katie Hiscock, garden editor of the *Fredericksburg Star* and the owner of Bird's Nest Garden in Fredericksburg, Virginia. Katie's salt and pepper hair had been cut short and curled in ringlets around her permanently tanned face. Her eyes were magnified behind huge glasses and she was dressed in her signature purple, a long, full skirt topped by a baggy, purple sweater. But then, thought Mim, Katie was tiny, a dynamo in constant motion. Anything she wore would appear baggy on her tight, wiry body.

On Kevin's left, Rose Redfern, sat queenly and elegant in a long, flowing creamy white crepe skirt and the long white tunic sweater she had worn for the class. Her hair was a white cloud. On her ears, huge diamond studs glittered in complicity with Rose's black eyes.

Mim had a new respect for Rose and she was delighted to see Katie, one of her favorite people. Mim turned first to Katie Hiscock who rewarded her with a grin that lit up her eyes. Katie rose to hug Mim.

"Hey girl! How are you? I was hoping we'd get together. It's been way too long!" Katie gestured to Kevin, "And lookee who I found. We were in Slovenia together!"

"I think you know everybody?" Kevin said as if it were he, not Mim who was a longstanding member of Horticultural Writers. He stood and pulled up a chair for Mim.

Mim nodded to Rose, fascinated by the way her eyes glittered in the light of a candle lamp on the table. She was reminded of the way snake's eyes were supposed to mesmerize their prey.

Two deep lines ran from Rose's narrow nose and disappeared into the down-turned corners of her thin lips. Rose's was a mouth unused to smiling. Then Mim considered that Rose must be at least seventy. Who knew what she had lived through? Life can be unkind in the events it dishes up.

Rose's appearance had doubtless contributed to her moniker, "the white witch." So did her interests. Most of the herbalists Mim knew made perfumed sprays, potpourri, and tussy mussies from herbs. Rose's fascination was with their darker sides. Her workshop this morning demonstrated that her knowledge of plant poisons as well as the history of their use was deep and wide.

The acolytes sat facing Kevin and Rose. Just 'J' with her kohl-rimmed eyes was wearing unrelieved black. At the other end of the fashion scale, sweet-faced, honey blonde Wendy Huntziger looked like the quintessential farmer's daughter in a denim skirt. A blouse patterned with rose-colored flowers matched her rosy cheeks and strained over her ample bosom. Wendy was Rose's secretary and it was rumored that it was she who researched and wrote Rose's books.

"Yes," said Mim smiling at the acolytes. "Nice to see you all! Mind if I join you?"

"Please do," Katie said enthusiastically. The acolytes murmured polite assent. Rose sat silent with the thinnest of smiles on her lips. Mim guessed that, for Rose, her expression passed as a warm welcome.

At that moment, a middle-aged, very tired-looking cocktail waitress with wispy blonde hair that had suffered too many encounters with a bleach bottle approached the group. She asked if there would be anything more.

Mim ordered Irish coffee, Kevin, another Scotch. Katie was still nursing her beer and the acolytes were still sipping wine. Rose declined. Kevin turned to her.

"I'm very much looking forward to your talk on …phytotoxins," he said, catching Mim's eye for approval. She smiled as Kevin engaged Rose by asking her about the toxins found in the black hellebore or Christmas rose. Rose warmed to the subject and the acolytes attended to her every word although they must have heard it all many times before. Mim, who was still thinking about the group photo of the plant hunting team and the stolen plants, leaned back and glanced at Katie.

"How well do you know Barney Staples?" she asked quietly. Katie gave her a big smile.

"You interested?" she asked, teasingly.

"Is he single?"

"Divorced…wait! Maybe not yet. Still in progress, I think," said Katie. She sat up and adjusted her glasses. "Seriously, Mim, are you interested? He's a good-looking man."

"Just routine curiosity. I don't really know him, except to say 'hi'." He was in the workshop this morning and he sat at our table at dinner. It's the first time I've spent more than ten minutes in his presence." Mim thought of the way his eyes met and held hers when she left the restaurant. A very good looking man. But one who seemed to know too much about Tate and too much about her.

"I guess I'm asking because you were on the plant hunting trip together. I thought you might know a little about him."

"Well, lemme see," said Katie, rolling her eyes up to the ceiling. "I was sort of interested myself at the beginning of the trip…You know. He's got that sexy British accent."

"And?" Mim prompted.

"He wasn't interested in me," said Katie bluntly. "But that's okay. Barney's really not my type. He's nice and all that, but—like when we would all gather in the bar at the end of the day–he was always the first to go back to his room. I think he reads a lot. And, you know me. I like to be where the action is." Katie grinned.

"Oh," she added, "And, to me, he seemed kinda proper. Like he doesn't want to get his hands dirty. First thing he did, before he even touched a plant, was to pull out his gloves and put them on. And they were always brand clean—like he brought along a bunch of them and never wore them twice."

"You know, the other guys, like JP and Tate, they don't—didn't– sweat the small stuff." Katie got a funny look on her face. She stopped talking.

"Katie!" Mim said sharply. Katie came to life.

"Like I was saying, Barney is kinda too proper for me. But he's a good guy."

Gloves. The faceless phantom of her nightmares arose in Mim's mind. As always, he dangled a single glove from his upraised hand. His eyes bored into her ferociously.

Was it malevolence? Or was it a warning? Or, it suddenly occurred to her, an entreaty? Her scalp prickled. She made herself think about something, anything else. What came to mind was the afternoon that Tate had prepared to leave for several days in Bosnia after which he would join the expedition in Slovenia. She had watched him while he packed. He was pleased she had bought him an anorak but a little surprised by its bright red color. Mim remembered him folding it into a small duffle and how surprised she had been at how very little else he was taking.

He had said he would be bringing back much more. Plants.

She looked at Katie, envying her that she had gone on the trip to the Balkans. Now, Mim wanted to know everything. It was now or never get-it-over-with time. She plunged ahead.

"How did you all know that Tate had fallen?" Mim asked. Katie stiffened. For a long moment, she didn't move. Then, she turned very slowly toward Mim and took her hand.

"I'll tell you," she said, meeting Mim's eyes. "That morning, JP wanted to get a group photo and he got everyone to meet outside the inn. The guy who owned the inn was going to take it. That was really early.

After that, half of us went back inside and went back to bed. We were pretty exhausted by then and the weather was crummy. But Tate left." Katie sighed. "I didn't see him go, but I knew he was gone. I wanted to ask him something and he wasn't there." Katie met Mim's eyes. "You know, I don't remember anymore what it was I wanted to ask him."

"So he left early..." said Mim, putting Katie back on track.

"Yeah and, well, it was after lunch when...I guess Tate and JP were supposed to do something together and when Tate didn't come back, JP got really worried." Katie looked at Mim imploringly. Her eyes were magnified by her glasses. "It was really rugged terrain. I almost fell the day before..."

Mim read Katie's thought. If it had been Katie who had fallen to her death, perhaps Tate would still be alive. Mim reached out to hold Katie's hand.

"So JP went to look for him?" Mim patted Katie's hand and took hers away.

"Yeah! Most of the guys went along and JP had the owner of the inn—Dragon, weird name—he called the local police. But, they all went in different directions. Do you know Marcus Tydings?"

"I don't really know him, but I know who he is," Mim answered. "I went to the first fifteen minutes of his workshop on propagation."

"Just the first fifteen minutes?" Katie asked.

"It looked like all he was going to do was show photos of his own work," said Mim.

"Why doesn't that surprise me?" Katie laughed. "Marcus Tydings has a healthy ego. He's very easy on the eyes though. He's a real ladies' man."

Mim recalled how this evening in the restaurant Marcus had come up to Philippa's table and introduced himself. She remembered Chase's growl of approval at Marcus' good looks.

"Yeah, I guess Margaret put him on the program, I wouldn't be surprised if she had a little crush on him herself," Katie said.

"Marcus went looking for Tate?" Mim asked.

"Marcus was the first one to find Tate."

"Not JP and Andy, then?" Mim asked.

"Well it was really all of them, but Marcus kind of went on ahead. That's what I heard. He saw Tate first. He and Barney were together. And they got the others." Katie checked Mim's face. "I'm sorry, Mim. I'm just blabbing away like an idiot. I'm sorry." Katie glanced at Kevin and Rose, who, thankfully, seemed to be engrossed in conversation. J and Wendy were listening to Kevin and Rose.

"Please! Don't be sorry. I need to know everything," Mim took Katie's hand again and squeezed it. "Really."

Mim sat back, taking in this new information about Tate's death. She was quiet for so long that Katie began to look alarmed. "I'm fine Katie, really!"

"So, Barney. You want to know about Barney," Katie said with enthusiasm, looking relieved to be moving on to a safer topic.

"Sure," said Mim, still imagining the men finding Tate. She took a deep breath. She would find out everything she could about Barney. She wanted to know what he did, if he would be classed as an amateur and, thus, be one of the suspects in the theft of Tate's plants. Most of all, she wanted to know how and why Barney knew so much about herself.

"What does he do?" Mim asked.

"Well, he's English. The word is he used to be a professor in England. He's got a little nursery. Staples Hellebores. In his backyard, I think. Anyway, that's what somebody said. He's just starting up. Barney wanted to get some good stock plants." Katie paused, seeming to have come to the end of her information. Then, she sat up straight, remembering more.

"You know who else you should ask about Barney."

"Who?"

"John Beam. Barney is—or was— on the staff at Delaware Hort. I think he taught botany. John could tell you all about him."

"John and Lin aren't here."

"She's one of the organizers," Katie protested.

"Apparently, her mother went into the hospital yesterday."

"I believe that Katie could tell you all about that," Rose Redfern's commanding voice overrode their conversation. Katie looked at Rose questioningly.

"Kevin is interested in plant patenting," said Rose, giving Kevin a big smile that for her must happen only once in a decade. Kevin, having charmed the white witch of the West, was grinning like a pig in swill. Mim coughed.

The conversation turned to plant patenting. Katie was telling Kevin about 'Katie's L'il Lass' and 'Katie's Kurls,' two cultivars of coneflowers she had discovered. The former, unlike coneflowers that reach four or five feet tall, grew only to a neat two feet. The latter had flowers with tousled petals, not unlike Katie's curly hair.

"So, a cultivar is like a clone?" asked Kevin. Mim looked at him in surprise. For a scant afternoon and evening at this conference, Kevin, a dyed-in-the-wool urbanite travel writer, was already starting to talk like a gardener.

"Exactly," said Katie. "A cultivar is a clone. And, to be registered in the Cultivated Plant Code under its special name, it has to be different from all other cultivars. Also, when you grow it, you have to be able to reproduce its special characteristics reliably. Most often, that is by asexual reproduction."

"Asexual reproduction?" Kevin smiled. "Sounds kinky."

"It means not by seeds," Katie shot him a grin, then continued earnestly. "For a plant to make seeds, it takes two sexes, usually on separate plants–but unlike with animals and humans–you can also get exact duplicates of a parent plant by dividing it into smaller pieces." Katie's large glasses slid down her ski-jump nose. She pushed them back absently and continued her explanation.

"But dividing is a pretty slow process. Depending on what it is, let's say from a single outstanding plant you get up to two or, maybe even four, divisions per year. At that rate, you'll starve to death if you're trying to make money sellin' plants. It'll take a lifetime to get enough of them to make marketing worthwhile," Katie explained, keeping an eye on Kevin to see if he followed her explanation. Kevin nodded. He appeared absolutely, totally engrossed.

"With some plants, you can also take root cuttings—little pieces of root—from the plant you want to duplicate. You just cut the roots into little pieces and put them in a flat of growing medium." Katie indicated the size of the little pieces with her fingers as she spoke.

"Will that get you a clone?" Kevin asked.

"Absolutely," replied Katie. "But you will have to grow that plant up and that takes time, too. And if the plant has been on the market for a year, you can't patent it. So the thing is to find or develop a really fab plant, make a trillion copies, and hit the market all at once."

Mim sipped her Irish coffee and looked out over the lobby. She saw Eric Ferris heading toward the lounge with a man she had never seen before.

Eric was talking non-stop as he steered his companion toward the lounge. When they got closer, Mim examined the man with Eric. She'd never seen him before. A new horticultural writer? Some innocent who hadn't yet felt the full force of Eric's personality? The man looked about forty-five. He was dressed in jeans and a sport jacket. He had a kind, patient expression on his intelligent face.

Totally absorbed in what he was saying, oblivious to everyone but his companion, Eric ushered the man to a sofa and two club chairs that formed another conversation grouping a few feet behind Mim. Two potted palms and a tall banana plant occupied the space between Mim and Eric's back. If she turned sideways to face Kevin and the women on the couch, she could see Eric and the stranger out of the corner of her eye.

She saw Eric raise his arm and snap his fingers for the waitress' attention. She was taking an order from another group of people. She looked up, nodded, and proceeded to the bar. Eric sat up and kept snapping his fingers loudly until the waitress came over, clearly annoyed.

"Sir," she said, "I'll be with you as soon as possible. Those people have been waiting…patiently." She emphasized the last word, turned and started back to the bar.

"I'll have a martini and my friend would like…?" Eric shouted loudly at her back, turning to his companion. The other man gestured no. He didn't want anything.

"Now!" Eric roared so loudly that everyone in the lounge stared at him.

Kevin's eyebrows rose as he met Mim's eyes. Katie stopped talking. Rose stared at Eric for a long moment. Suddenly, she was standing. Startled, the acolytes stood, too.

"Excuse me," Rose said. She walked toward Eric. J and Wendy quickly gathered up their packets and purses and followed. Wendy turned back awkwardly to nod an excuse to Mim, Kevin, and Katie.

Eric was speaking so animatedly, he didn't notice Rose's approach. The trio formed a half circle facing him. He stopped in mid-sentence and looked up, irritated.

"You are a disgrace to this organization," said Rose in a loud, clear voice. "Why don't you leave before—"

"You're the disgrace!" Eric's loud outburst cut off her words. On his feet like a cat, he stood with his chin thrust inches below Rose's. "You don't even write your miserable books! And you know what? Everybody knows who does. Little toady here does it all, don't you, you with your dyke friend!" he sputtered, glowering from J to Wendy, whose chin began to quiver.

Rose's mouth was a blood red slash across a face that had grown whiter than her sweater. Her eyes bored into Eric like obsidian darts. If she truly had been a witch she would have turned Eric to stone. But, instead it was Rose who turned. She walked stiffly away. The acolytes scrambled after her. And Eric remained standing, an angry little man.

His companion looked at Eric with what was probably amazed disgust, turned, excused himself, and hurried after the departing trio.

"Fuck!" roared Eric. Then he noticed that Kevin, Mim, and Katie were observing him. "What are you looking at?" he sneered. He strode off.

"Who *is* that man?" Kevin demanded. "He can't be a horticultural writer!" Kevin had risen to his feet and now looked around as if surprised to find himself standing. He plopped down on the sofa.

"Ooooh yeah," said Katie. "That's our boy, Eric Ferris."

"Does he always act that way? What's the matter with him?" Kevin's eyes were wide with disbelief.

"Well," considered Mim, "that was a tad rude—even for Eric. Nobody knows why he acts that way."

"One of these days, he's gonna mess with the wrong person," said Katie.

"He may have already done so," said Mim. Katie met Mim's eyes.

"You're right. Did you see the way she looked at him?" Katie asked with a little shudder. "Woo-hee! I mean, I like her well enough, but I sure wouldn't want to cross Rose Redfern!"

"I wouldn't cross a woman who knows her way around all those phytotoxins," laughed Kevin.

The Eric episode had shaken Kevin, Mim, and Katie out of their various stages of alcohol-induced stupor. All three were now wide awake and full of nervous energy. After several conversational topics, Mim led the talk back to the trip to the Balkans.

"Let me see now," said Katie. Kevin wanted the names of all the people who had gone on the plant hunting expedition. "There were eighteen of us. Or was it nineteen?"

Kevin took out his notebook.

"There was Tate." Katie spoke to Kevin, but Katie cast a quick glance at Mim, listening in the depths of a big, overstuffed chair. She used one finger to push her glasses back into place. "Barney Staples. Most of them are here at the conference," Katie turned to Mim. "And there was JP Chiasson. I guess it does look like hellebore breeding is cursed!" Katie gave Mim a sad little smile. Then she looked at Kevin. "But, where was I? A passel of us single women—Margaret Stemple, she's the director of this conference, Olga, a Russian horticulturist..."

The man who had sat with Eric Ferris walked by. For a moment, he looked as if he might stop. He gave Mim, who alone noticed him, a thin smile. He walked on.

"We shared a bunk room," Katie was saying as she ticked off the names of the women on the fingers of one hand. "There were the Taylors and, the men,

Andy Toll, Benjy Glass and...Marcus Tydings."

"There's a group photo of everybody who was on that trip," said Mim from the depths of the club chair. Both Kevin and Katie looked at her.

"Amy Tomczyk showed me JP's photos—the ones she's going to show Sunday at brunch," said Mim. "Everybody who went on the expedition is in it. You're in it. So are JP and Tate." She felt her voice give a little at Tate's name. "JP must have got someone else to take it because he's right in the middle of the picture—with Tate."

Remembering that both Marcus and Tate had worn red anoraks, Mim asked, "Did it rain a lot?"

"Actually," said Katie. "They told us to expect plenty of rain and we all brought rain gear, but we had pretty good weather until...the last... well, what turned out to be the last day."

"The expedition ended with Tate's accident?" Mim asked. She was staring across the lobby but seeing the mountains in JP's photos.

"Yeah. Yeah it did." Katie looked down at her hands folded in her lap. "After that nobody had the heart to do any more collecting. JP–JP took it very hard. That…day, JP came back bawling like a little baby. Then he and Barney got stinking drunk." Her glasses slid down her nose. She readjusted them and reached for Mim's hand.

"I'm making you sad. Again. I'm so sorry," said Katie, a big tear running down her own cheek.

"No! I'm glad you told me. I wanted to know everything. Really." Mim patted Katie's hand again. "Thank you." Mim looked at Kevin meaningfully. She repeated, "I have to know everything." She was ready to hear anything else he had to say and he knew it. Sometimes she thought Kevin could read her mind. He nodded.

"I was on a press trip with WalkingTours. We were there for two days while we used the inn as a base. And we all ate together so I knew who Tate was," Kevin said, gazing across the lobby.

"That day—the day of the accident–we had been hiking all day. I was really looking forward to reconnecting with him when we got back."

"When we got there—the inn was in an uproar. And… we found out what happened. That's when we met," he looked at Katie who nodded in agreement. "We talked for half the night."

"Nobody wanted to go to bed," said Katie. "I guess it was nobody wanted to be alone."

Kevin, Katie, and Mim sat silent for a few minutes. Then Katie yawned and stretched.

Kevin asked Mim and Katie if they wanted another drink.

"Lord no! Thank you for asking." Mim's languid voice came from the depths of her chair.

"I'm good. Thanks," said Katie.

"Do you think Amy might let me see her program before Sunday?" Kevin asked. Mim sat up.

"I'd love to see it, too," said Katie. "JP was an artist with his camera."

"I'm sure Amy won't mind. Come on," said Mim, already on her feet. Kevin looked confused. He looked at his watch. Katie wrinkled her brow.

"It's ten-thirty. Don't you think that's kind of late to intrude on someone," Kevin said, checking his watch again. "And do you know what room she's in?"

"No, no. We don't have to wake her. Amy left a copy of JP's program on my laptop. I'm sure she won't mind if we look at it."

23

For the second time that evening, Mim fired up her computer. The screen lit up and she found the icon entitled "Balkans." When she clicked on it, neat rows of photos appeared on the screen just as it had when Amy first opened the file. Katie and Kevin seated themselves on the bed across from the desk.

"Want to see it as a slide show?" Of course they did. Mim turned to the computer screen, clicked the mouse, and the title shot appeared. Again, the center of the screen bloomed with handsome hellebore foliage followed by blooms. They seemed to be growing out of the computer. Then a ghostly title emerged, becoming clear and large. "Hunting for Hellebores."

"Nice, huh?" Mim asked.

"Did Amy do that?" asked Kevin.

"Yup."

"She's good!" said Katie. "That's animation. Can you do it again?" Mim obligingly closed the file, then opened it again so that the title shot reemerged in all of its glory.

"She's very talented," Kevin agreed, leaning forward to watch the hellebores fill the screen.

The first photo showed Tate and Joachim Muller standing in a field of yellow flowered hellebores. Katie leaned closer.

"What are those?"

"They are *Helleborus odorus*. This photo was taken right before Tate and JP joined up with your group in Slovenia. They spent three days with Dr. Muller in Bosnia."

"Those are unusual for the species. Most *odorus* flowers are sort of chartreuse," Katie said.

"I went to Dr. Muller's workshop this morning. He said he'd never seen *odorus* flowers that were this particular shade of yellow...and evergreen," said Mim.

"They couldn't be evergreen," said Katie.

"Yes, he said they were and that they were unusual in that regard," Mim recalled.

"You bet your life they're unusual. I wish I had some," said Katie. "With the right marketing, I could be set up for life."

Mim advanced to the next photo. It was on this photo—the shot of the assembled plant hunting group—that they lingered.

"Oh, look!" breathed Katie. She stood up the better to see the photo. "There we are. I remember that!"

"That's JP next to Tate," Mim said, turning to Kevin. She scanned the faces around the two men in the center. Somewhere in this picture was the person who had stolen Tate's plants.

"I remember him," Kevin said. "He was three sheets to the wind that night."

"He was a good man," said Katie with a catch in her voice. "He had a big heart. Those two, JP and Tate—they were the future of hellebore breeding."

"You know, the others—like the Taylors—have already found their niche. Locust Hill's got some incredible doubles. Andy's got a really unusual striped form and a million other plants. But you got the feeling with JP and Tate that they were going to do something really amazing. They were going to set the hellebore world on its ear."

"How could they do that?" asked Kevin.

"Well, imagine if someone could produce a red-flowered hellebore that flowered *reliably* around Christmas," said Katie.

"Isn't that what—who's the guy who's speaking tomorrow on 'dreaming of a white Christmas?'" asked Kevin.

"Benjy Glover," said Mim.

"He's talking about a *white* Christmas rose," interjected Katie, "and even that's a big, big stretch if you want it to bloom reliably at Christmas time. What if someone actually produced a red Christmas rose that bloomed at Christmas—sort of like a hardy poinsettia—only much, much better."

"That's got to be the holy grail of hellebores," said Mim. "Whoever did that really would be set for life."

"More realistically, JP had some early-blooming purples," said Katie. "And Tate. I'm pretty sure he was working toward a plant with fragrance."

"I wish…I only wish I had known more about Tate's…" Mim said, unable to finish the sentence. Katie got up and gave her a bear hug. Mim squared her shoulders and grinned.

"How about a blue flowered hellebore?" she asked. Katie's eyes lit up and moved to the screen.

"Does JP have a blue?" Mim only smiled at Katie's question. Before she advanced the photo, she took one last look at the group. The two men at its center radiated vigor.

"You do get the feeling that Tate and JP were the center of things. They were both so full of life," she said, her voice caught. She saw that Kevin and Katie were watching her.

Kevin half rose, looking quizzically at Mim.

"Hey, we could do this tomorrow." He gestured toward the laptop which still displayed a group of plant hunters.

"No. Please! Let's see the rest of the program," said Mim.

"Sure?" asked Katie.

"Of course!" Mim said in a businesslike tone. She turned to them, two wonderful old friends. She sighed, and decided to open up as she had not done to anyone. She found that she could speak calmly.

"For the record, Tate and I had been together for not quite four months. They were absolutely the best months of my life. You know how people say, 'life couldn't get any better than this?' Well, that's how it was." Mim held up a hand to stop what she knew she couldn't bear: Sympathy.

"I feel grateful—really, really grateful– that we had even that short time together. But…one of the things that…I regret. I am so sorry I didn't know more." Mim looked at Katie. "About Tate's interests." Mim laid out these facts dryly.

"You know more about his breeding program than I do. I never even met his best friend JP. He told me about…about the people who are at this conference—the breeders. But a lot of what we talked about was all going to happen…in the future." She waved her hand toward an imaginary horizon. "It was just a beginning. In the grand scheme of things, you could argue that we didn't even know each other that well." Mim looked at Katie.

"I *was* going to meet his plane at Dulles," Mim said, suddenly struck by the memory. "Thank you, Katie, for sparing me that!" Mim patted Katie's shoulder. "I would have…I would have been there waiting, if you hadn't called me from London."

"It was JP. He told me to call you. He knew about you and Tate. He didn't want to be the one to break the news because he didn't know you." For the second time, Mim was warmed with the thought that Tate had told JP about her.

"And he knew we were friends," Katie softly continued. "JP noticed things."

All three looked at JP's image in the group photo. Then Mim asked, "Okay?"

"Yeah," said Katie. Kevin nodded and Mim advanced to the next photo. Kevin and Katie settled themselves comfortably on the edge of the bed.

"Wow!" said Katie. "That's one good looking plant! Look at those flowers—how they stand up above the clump."

"Is it unusual for the flowers to stand up like that?" asked Kevin.

"Yeah—not unheard of, but most Lenten roses tend to carry their flowers lower among the leaves. That makes the flowers harder to see," explained Katie.

"Amy called this plant Aimee's grandmother," said Mim.

"Who's Aimee?" asked Kevin.

"JP called Amy 'Aimee.' It's kind of a *double entendre*. A play on her name and the French word for "beloved"—or something like that. He was using this hellebore as a parent, or rather, a grandparent of generations of even better plants. And when he was satisfied with an outstanding descendant from his crosses, he was going to introduce it as 'Aimee' in honor of Amy, his fiancée."

"That's so romantic!" said Katie. "I wish someone would do that for me!"

"Katie, what are you talking about? You have two coneflowers named after you already! 'Kate's Little Lass' and 'Katie's Kurls.'"

"But *I* found those. It's not like some gorgeous hunk named his most fabulous plant for me as a token of his undying love!" Katie sighed. "And JP was a beautiful man! Olga, the Russian woman, stuck to him like glue."

Katie had been divorced now for five years, thought Mim. Recently, she had been, sequentially, in a couple of relationships, but neither man had been "the one." She was lonely. Mim recognized loneliness when she saw it.

She advanced to the next slide, a panorama of stark gray mountains with tiny colored dots in the distance.

"Lookee! There we are!" said Katie. She took off her glasses and leaned forward. "Oh my God! There I am!" She pointed to a purple dot. "Those yellow ones must be the Taylors." Mim could barely make any of them out.

"It's really rainy looking in this picture. That means it must have been taken ... well, it was on the last day." Katie pointed to the screen that showed a spray of multicolored dots. "See! There are only," she counted, "nine of us in this shot. Some folks stayed in the inn and went back to bed. It was cold and rainy."

"Usually, Tate and JP left together at the crack of dawn while the rest of us were still in bed. Except that day. The last day. Tate went off alone." Katie looked off in the distance, envisioning the events of the last day in Slovenia.

"It started drizzling—off and on." Katie hugged her arms close to her body.

"I mean, the day before, I slipped and fell. Even without the rain, I nearly rolled right off that mountain!" Katie shuddered. "Jenny grabbed my leg. Olga got a hold of my backpack. If they hadn't...." Katie caught Kevin's eye. He had heard her tell the same tale at the inn. Katie looked into Mim's face. Her eyes were big as if pleading for Mim to understand.

"On that last morning, like I said, Tate went off alone. JP didn't go with him. He wanted to get more pictures. I think that's why he took it so hard. He blamed himself for not going with Tate."

"Anyway, this must be some of us heading out on the last day. By the time this picture was taken, Tate...Tate was already gone. He left right after JP got the innkeeper to take the group shot. I remember, Tate was on his way out and JP made him stay and wait to be in the picture."

"As soon as the innkeeper snapped the picture, he took off like a shot…by himself," Katie met Mim's eyes. "He couldn't be in this picture," Katie explained.

"Oh," was all Mim said.

She advanced through the rest of the photos without the pleasure that she had felt previously. Seeing the photos had made Mim feel closer to Tate. Now, when she saw a tiny red dot in the vast gray landscape, she told herself, it would be Marcus Tydings, not Tate.

They had come to the end of the program and were looking at the last slide, the beautiful 'Aimee', when Sally returned. She looked wretched. She flopped on her bed and covered her eyes.

"Sally?" Mim asked. "What's the matter?"

"You don't want to know!"

"Just tell me," Mim got up and sat on the bed beside Sally.

"Good night, ladies," said Kevin, discretely. "Let's talk tomorrow."

"Bedtime," Katie said, gathering her purse and a purple shawl. "I'm bushed. I drove up from Fredericksburg this afternoon. She leant over and bussed Mim's forehead and blew Sally a kiss. "G'nite!"

Mim hugged Kevin and Katie. When they closed the door behind themselves, Sally spoke.

"I ran into Tom. He said they're going to have to clear things up with Eric Ferris," she spat out his name, "before they can give us a contract. Ferris claims that a book on herbal landscaping was his idea. That he offered it to Mari Yokomoto when she was still working at Foresters. She's at New Garden now. They're not going to offer us anything until they are satisfied …"

"Sally, excuse me, but I happen to know that Mari couldn't and can't stand Eric," Mim broke in. "It won't be hard to prove he doesn't have any grounds to sue Foresters! Eric is a born trouble maker. My God! You should have seen him tonight with Rose Redfern!"

"I honestly think that's all this is. Maybe we can talk to him…"

"Oh right!" Sally's voice dripped with sarcasm. "I tried! That's what's so bad," Sally said bitterly. "After I talked with Tom, Chase wanted to cheer me up. He suggested going to a bar where there was supposed to be karaoke. He thought it would be fun. So I went. After a while, Eric came in."

"I stupidly—stupidly—thought maybe I could talk to him. I just went up to him. I didn't even get a word out. I didn't say boo. As soon as he saw me, he started yelling at me! He *wanted* everybody to hear. He said we were trying to cheat him. The whole conference was there! Everybody stopped what they were doing and just watched us. It was horrible!" Sally sighed wretchedly.

"What did you do?" Mim asked.

"I came back here." Sally said miserably. "I hate him. I hate him!"

"Sally, Eric Ferris is all hot air and venom. Everybody knows it. He's really good at being bad and making trouble." Mim caught Sally's eye. "The only thing to do is to ignore him."

"Then why is Tom...?"

"He's just doing what he's supposed to do. Being careful. Don't worry!" Mim stood up. "Mind if I take a shower?"

By the time Mim stepped out of a quick shower, Sally was in bed and asleep. In spite of—or possibly because of—her run in with Eric, Sally must have fallen asleep almost instantaneously.

Mim switched off the light and lay back. For a few moments as her eyes adjusted, there was complete darkness and then, as always in hotel rooms when she wanted to sleep, lights from the corridor shone in under the door and light from the city found its way between the cracks in the curtains. Slowly the room started to illuminate. It was one more hurdle between Mim's whirling thoughts and sleep.

After a few moments, in addition to the light–the whole hotel seemed to vibrate with a constant rumble. It sounded like water boiling and someone lifting the lid off a pot every now and then to check the contents. Mim rolled over, facing away from the door and closed her eyes. Immediately, the photo of the plant hunting group with Tate and JP flashed in her mind's eye. She saw again the jagged mountain range that had taken Tate's life. The vision of the mountains both sickened and fascinated her. More troubling, it provoked a gnawing feeling that there was something she had to find in that rugged, forbidding landscape. She had no idea what that could be.

By contrast, Amy's task was clear if not exactly simple. She was carrying out JP's role in this conference.

There was something else Mim envied that she didn't like to acknowledge. Amy had the right to carry on for JP. Whether legally or practically, Amy was JP's acknowledged executor.

Mim didn't even have a thorough idea of what Tate's accomplishments in hybridizing had been. She knew he had been a perfectionist. She also knew that he had already developed an early-flowering salmon colored double. She knew it was special because the blooms it carried high above the clump appeared earlier than usual. Was it fragrant? She had no idea. It had seemed that a lifetime stretched out before them. She would have years to learn about his work. There had been no hurry.

He had lined her woodland path with tiny plants of a hellebore he said would take another year or so to bloom. It was to be a surprise for her. When they did bloom, he said, they would host a party to celebrate. But that promise, like everything else in their all too brief relationship was part of a future that ended in the Balkans.

He had talked about a trip to visit his family in Maine in the summer. That pleasant prospect had been cruelly altered into a trip to his funeral. In Portland, she finally met his mother and sister in the sprawling white house in which Tate had grown up. They greeted her kindly, surrounded in their grief by a mob of lifelong friends and family. She was alone. Returning home alone had been the most wretched journey of her life.

Pointless and masochistic to dwell on it! She concentrated on the bittersweet knowledge that Tate had told his best friend about her.

A vision of the vast mountains where the two men had gone to collect plants flashed across her inward eye. Above dark slopes, she could see jagged peaks that dwarfed the people on them to tiny specks of color. The red dots weren't Tate, Katie had said. They were Marcus Tydings. But all of them? Something stirred in her memory, out of reach.

She pictured again the group, gathered in front of the inn, smiling for their picture. And she felt a jolt of revulsion. One of those smiling people had benefited from Tate's death. One of them had stolen the plants that Tate had collected.

The eyes of the phantom flashed in her mind's eye. Were they menacing or beseeching? And if they were the latter, what did it want of her? Was she supposed to find out who the thief was?

She slipped out of bed and moved through darkness to the desk as if drawn by some invisible cord. She turned on the computer. As it ground and grumbled to life, she looked over at Sally's bed. Sally stirred, but did not wake.

The answer was in the picture of the plant hunting group. It was staring her in the face if only she could see what it was. There they were. And one of them, someone in this photo had stolen Tate's plants. Mim thought if she looked hard enough this photo would yield a clue.

She brought her attention back to the task of observing the group and what could be deduced from the way that these people had arranged themselves. Vague memories of the sociology course rose. Wasn't there something about distances between people–how far apart they stand when they are talking?

This group wasn't engaged in conversation, they were posing. But you could look at the people in the group, not as individuals but as a mass with an outline. She squinted her eyes and, instantly saw that there was a big difference between the right and left sides of the photo. The clique of breeders who all knew each other clumped together on the right side of the photo. They were standing close together, touching. Directly behind Tate and JP, with his arm around Tate's shoulder, the Taylors leant over them slightly. Behind them and slightly overlapping was Benjy Glover. Andy Toll stood beside Barney, who was looking off to the right, but very much a part of the group. Katie Hiscock stood in front of them, next to Tate. Visually, when you squinted your eyes, the "in" group formed a solid clump.

The closeness of the in group may have alienated the others, but it didn't cause them to gather closer together. The other members of the plant hunting party left open space between themselves and their neighbors. She decided to go over the photo, person by person, observing facial expressions. Maybe she could glean some information if she examined each person's body language.

They had strung themselves out loosely on the left side of the photo. In some cases, there was plentiful space between people. Less well known to each other, each stood separate, not touching or only barely overlapping with his or her neighbor. There were Olga, and the two men Katie had identified as the Germans Peter and Hanno. Eric Ferris, wearing a baseball cap with two cameras hanging from his neck, was standing on the left side of the photo, near Margaret Stemple. Although, they stood next to each other, they might have been on different planets. His stance gave new meaning to the phrase, "lonely in a crowd." He was turned ever so slightly to his right. It was not hard to imagine Ferris stealing Tate's plants out of sheer spite. But to the best of her knowledge, he was a photographer and writer—not a nurseryman. He would gain nothing by stealing plants, except perhaps, malevolent satisfaction.

Margaret stood just slightly apart from the group. She was wearing a tan jacket. Her facial expression was difficult to see.

Peeking over Margaret's left shoulder was a person, who, judging from size, had to be a woman. The brim of the hat curled over the top of the face revealing only one, large brown eye.

Marcus Tydings knelt farthest left. He had positioned himself a foot or two clear of the group. He was with the people in the picture, but apart. The gray-green landscape encircled him like a frame. The bright red color of his parka enhanced the frame effect and made him pop out of the background. He was wearing an Australian hat, with one side of the brim turned up. He smiled a canine smile—all teeth.

What struck her now was something she hadn't noticed before. His posture. Marcus Tydings knelt in a posture identical to the two men at the heart of the group. Mimicking the leaders, he was kneeling on his right knee. Unlike them, he had separated himself entirely from the group. Or, was it the other way around? Had the group isolated him?

Rose Redfern, resplendent in beige just behind Tate, bridged the gap between the breeders on the right and the 'out-group' on the left. Mim could well imagine that Rose identified with the breeders, but that her personality distanced her from them.

At the extreme right was Barney Staples. She examined him. He was the only one not looking directly into the camera. Clearly, Barney was talking to someone outside of the photo. From the look on his face, the exchange appeared to be a pleasant one. His white hair was longer in the picture than the military cut he now wore and it was tousled. There were laugh lines around the one eye she could see. It was the same handsome, pleasant face she had enjoyed seeing across the table earlier this evening.

Was she talking herself into Barney's innocence?

JP had told Amy that he thought the person who stole Tate's plants was an amateur breeder who had gone on the trip to the Balkans. It was unclear whether JP considered Barney Staples an amateur or a professional. If he had taught at Delaware, he was a professional horticulturist. He had a small backyard nursery. She knew several people with big, thriving nurseries who had started out that way. For the time being, she classed Barney with the professionals.

Mim's eyes burned. She checked the time. Midnight. She got up, tiptoed to the bathroom. While she drank a glass of water, she summed up what little she had gleaned from studying the group photo. Perhaps the most important thing was that a good number of the plant hunters were at this conference!

Barney, the Taylors, Andy Toll, Benjy Glover, Katie Hiscock were here. So were Eric Ferris, Marcus Tydings, Rose Redfern, and, of all people, Margaret Stemple, who was the conference director! Another thing: with the exception of Margaret, Eric, and Katie, all of the others were presenters at the conference. And JP had been slated to give a talk at Sunday's brunch.

24

Amy arrived at the auditorium, as she had promised Margaret Stemple, at five minutes before eight. She was there to give Margaret one of the flash drives containing JP's photos that she had copied on Mim's computer. Margaret was nowhere in sight. She tried the door. Locked.

She paced back and forth in front of the auditorium door for what seemed like a half hour. But it was only a few minutes past eight, when Margaret rushed up, burdened with a bulging briefcase in one hand, apparently so heavy that its weight unbalanced her gait. She walked as if one leg were shorter than the other. She held a stack of papers under her other arm. Her face was gray with fatigue and her eyes were red-rimmed. She did not acknowledge Amy except to hand her the stack of papers while she rummaged in the briefcase for the keys to the auditorium.

Amy followed Margaret into the projection room, waiting for her attention, for some sign that the other woman was aware of what she was doing. Margaret seemed so distracted, Amy felt uneasy about giving her the memory device.

"Is there a special place that you want this?" Amy asked, looking around to see where the other programs might be kept. "I wrote JP's initials on it…"

"I'll take it," said Margaret, reaching for the small stick on its looped cord. Amy pressed it into Margaret's hand uneasily.

"Margaret, would this be a good time to preview my presentation?" Margaret stared at the flash drive as if seeing it for the first time. Without taking her eyes from it, she spoke in a weary voice.

"I just can't do another thing right now," she said, waving Amy away. "Later. Later."

Then she sat down and began shuffling through her papers. Finally, wordlessly, Amy turned and walked away.

Mim was trudging up what seemed like an endless gray slope. Rocks rolled out from under her feet and she stumbled more than once, each time catching a heart-stopping glimpse of the abyss just inches away. Every now in the distance, she caught sight of Tate's red parka. It wasn't Marcus. It was Tate. She knew it was. She was following him and getting closer.

Then someone stepped in front of her, blocking her way and obscuring her view. She tried reaching for that person to turn him around so that she could see who it was. Several times she grasped the slick, wet surface of the person's parka. It slipped from her fingers. Finally, she lunged forward to grab it, latched on to fabric, but the person disappeared. She found herself holding a glove. She stared at it in horror. She tried to scream, but no sound came out. Behind her someone in the group of people posing for a picture laughed an eerie bogyman laugh.

With that laughter ringing in her ears, Mim sat up in bed. It was all a dream. A new spin on the glove nightmare. It was Saturday morning. She was at the Symposium.

She looked over at Sally's bed and saw it was empty. She hadn't even heard her get up and get dressed.

She looked at the clock. It was ten minutes past eight. In spite of the lateness of the hour, she felt as if she hadn't slept at all. She felt as fatigued as if she had really followed Tate up a mountain. Her head felt thick, filled with something dense and cottony.

Across the room on the desk, an asteroid shower flicked across the computer screen. It was her screen saver. Last night, after searching again through JP's photos, she had stumbled into bed without shutting down the computer. She had found nothing obvious. That the expedition had divided itself into two groups was not surprising. The "in group," if that's what it could be called, had come about honestly. She was sure they would not intentionally exclude people. It was simply that these breeders and growers had all known each other long before going on that trip. Their professional paths overlapped. Most important, they all shared a passion for their work. It was no surprise that they became friends. Mim thought of them as the "eastern hellebore mafia." Beyond the fact that they may have appeared an exclusive clique to others on the trip, nothing had leapt out at her.

But she had come away with something she couldn't put her finger on—some niggling intimation that sparked in her mind, but stayed out of reach. Like a picture that flashed on a screen somewhere at the back of her brain, it was a visual memory snatched away before she could comprehend it. She thought it was like seeing the train of a dress slip out the door before she could see the wearer. No matter how she tried to sneak up on it, the picture quickly eluded her efforts to capture it.

It had to be there. She would look until she found it. If she studied JP's photos hard enough, she might recapture the elusive image. She sat down at the desk. When the icon for JP's presentation appeared, she opened it and chose the "slide show" option that would automatically advance the photos. As she rummaged in her suitcase for clean underwear, as she laid out the clothes she would wear today, Mim glanced at the changing photos.

Damn. It was late. She had barely enough time to shower, get dressed, and get breakfast before the program started at nine. She took one last look at the computer screen before heading into the bathroom to shower. There, again, was a panorama of gray mountains, studded with tiny dots of color.

When Mim scanned the breakfast area for a place to sit, she saw Kevin alone at a table. It was early for him to look so cheerful, and alert. Freshly showered, dressed in his signature black, a black t shirt, black slacks, and a black blazer, he was tucking into a stack of pancakes and sausages with gusto. He wished her good morning with his most charming smile—a straightforward, I'm-happy-to-see-you grin. Kevin always made her feel better. He made the world a better place. She felt profoundly grateful for his friendship.

She wished him good morning feeling somewhat less cheerful and alert than he. She set down her tray laden with scrambled eggs, toast, orange juice, and coffee. Right now, only the coffee looked appealing.

"Have you seen Sally this morning?" she asked.

"Yes. We had breakfast together—Sally, Amy, and I. They finished about ten minutes ago. I'm on seconds." Mim looked at the sausages and a stack of five pancakes and the trim man devouring them and thought 'unfair.'

"Do you know where they are?"

"Yup. They went to see if Amy could run through her program on the big screen in the auditorium." Kevin speared a chunk of sausage with his fork and waved it vaguely in the direction the women had gone. "Amy's got the jitters and the director—Margaret, is it?—seems kind of out-of-it."

"Margaret is wound up tight and touchy as hell," said Mim. She took a sip of her coffee. "You know, I've known her for years, though not really well. Frankly, I was surprised at first that she was capable of running the conference. I think it's a stretch for her and the strain is showing. But she's doing a fantastic job even if her bedside manner is off-putting."

"She hasn't done well by Amy. She lost JP's program that Amy says she sent weeks ago and now she's supposed to preview Amy's talk, but hasn't made herself available." Kevin speared a chunk of pancake. He chewed and swallowed.

"Sally thinks," continued Kevin, touching his napkin to the corner of his mouth, "that Margaret doesn't want to preview it because she doesn't want Amy to give the talk. Amy says that she keeps making comments about how Amy has never spoken in public before."

"I think Margaret's got her ego all wrapped up in this symposium. She's pretty touchy about criticism—even when it isn't meant to be," said Mim. "You weren't with us at dinner last night. I said something like 'the only thing we don't have is David Hawkins' and she got her back up." Mim took a bite of her scrambled eggs.

"David who?" asked Kevin. Mim took another bite and swallowed.

"David Hawkins is one of the shakers and movers in the world of plants in general and hellebores in particular. Among the *cognoscenti*, he is a household word." Mim peeled open a little jelly package, scooped some onto the tip of her knife, and spread the jelly on her toast. Kevin continued to slice and devour his sausages.

"With the exception of David Hawkins, Margaret got all of the big names in the world of hellebores to give lectures. This is an amazing symposium and she wants it to be perfect. I'm sure it will be. I'll say something to her." Mim took a sip of her coffee.

"You've seen JP's photos," she added. "They're spectacular. All Amy has to do is advance them and give a little bit of background. She'll get a standing ovation."

Halfway through her coffee, Mim felt herself become come alive. As the caffeine worked its magic, her surroundings came into clearer focus. She watched as her fellow horticultural writers headed to the buffet and returned carrying trays of breakfast. Holding their trays, they scanned the room for empty tables or tables with friends. Others finished breakfast and chatted with friends as they sauntered toward the auditorium.

Mim saw Philippa heading toward the buffet. A second later, she reappeared, carrying only a cup of coffee or, perhaps, tea. She was scanning the tables. Mim saw a flash of recognition as Philippa spied Kevin. Kevin had not, as yet, seen her.

Philippa approached their table. At the last moment, she changed course. She might have changed her mind because she saw Mim or simply changed her mind. In any case, she disappeared from view. Mim looked at Kevin, who had not noticed.

Then she spotted Sally and Amy waiting in what was becoming a very long line at the coffee station. She looked to see what was causing the pile up and was not surprised to see Eric Ferris, slowly emptying a package of sugar into his cup.

"He's a piece of work!" said Kevin, who had watched the entire incident. "Why does he act that way?"

Mim shrugged. "Everybody asks that question. And nobody knows the answer. It's like he actually works hard at being obnoxious."

Sally and Amy, both carrying styrofoam cups of coffee sat down at the table with Kevin and Mim.

"Any luck?" asked Kevin.

"We couldn't find Margaret earlier. And now she wants to have her breakfast," said Amy. "Maybe I can practice over lunch."

"We did find Eric," laughed Sally.

"We noticed. He really likes sugar," said Kevin.

"Oh that! Classic ferret behavior! No, I mean we found him earlier. He was over his head into his element!" Sally and Amy exchanged amused looks. Mim looked at Sally, waiting for an explanation.

"He was trashcan diving! Sunk up to his butt in a trash can. He had taken off the lid of a trashcan down the hall from the auditorium and he was inside digging around!"

"Did you ask him what he was looking for?" asked Kevin.

"No. We just stood and watched. And when he came up for air, he gave me a dirty look," laughed Sally. "And he leered at Amy!"

Kevin followed Mim, Sally, and Amy as they entered an auditorium that was almost full. The cheerful din of one hundred and thirty people chattering and finding seats was punctuated by little cries of recognition as horticultural writers recognized friends and colleagues they hadn't seen since the last meeting.

Kevin couldn't help but smile. He felt a little like a spy. He was someone who didn't even own a trowel in the midst of more than a hundred "garden geeks"– a term Katie had used last night. He looked out over the sea of horticultural writers. These people were wildly enthusiastic; they lived for plants. They died for plants.

Virtually all of the seats in the back three-quarters were already taken. They walked further along the sloping aisle.

"Looks like we're going to have to sit up front," said Sally, leading the little group down a side aisle. "Look, there's Chase and the row in front of him is empty."

They had almost reached the more sparsely populated front few rows when Kevin's cell phone rang out "Hail to the Chief."

"Save me a seat," Kevin said to Mim. He pointed to the phone, turned around, and headed for the lobby. As he walked up the slight incline out of the auditorium, he pressed the "talk" button. Behind him, probably on the stage, he could hear someone was setting up a microphone, banging it in the process and sending booms out over the sound system.

"So how goes your flower show?" It was Randy. "Anyone else get cursed?"

"So far, so good," replied Kevin. "Any news on your end?"

"That's why I'm calling."

Sally, Amy, and Mim found four seats together in the second row. Mim placed her purse on the seat next to her to save it for Kevin.

As usual, the front row was nearly empty. With the exception of the speakers, who sat together in a little group near the stairs to the stage, only two other people occupied seats in the first row. Eric Ferris lounged front row center with his arms extended over both neighboring seats. It was probably intended to look like a relaxed pose, but Ferris seemed to be twitching with energy. His head darted back and forth, though there was little to see on the stage.

Near the speakers, but a few seats apart from them, Philippa's chestnut curls were bent over a huge purse in which she was fumbling, apparently looking for something, but not able to find it. After what seemed a futile search, she plopped her purse on the seat next to her with exasperation.

When they had settled themselves, Mim found herself directly in front of Chase, who tapped her on the shoulder in greeting. Mim turned around and chatted with Chase and Katie Hiscock, seated next to him.

Kevin dropped into his seat. He leaned over to whisper to her just as Margaret Stemple, looking surprisingly slim and elegant in a black pant suit, walked to the microphone on stage. He stopped, sat back, and waited.

"This morning, I have a very difficult announcement to make," Margaret's voice caught. She looked down for a moment, before regaining composure.

"JP Chiasson, one of our dear friends and colleagues," she stopped and struggled for control. When she continued, it was in a strangled voice. "JP...was murdered...during a robbery in his home two weeks ago."

After that difficult start, her words began to tumble out as if she were eager to be done with the terrible announcement. A low rumble rose to a roar as those who had not already heard the news took it in. A sea of hands waved. Several horticultural writers stood up to be acknowledged. It was a full five minutes before the room quieted.

Margaret took a deep breath. "I know that you have many questions, but please! Please! I cannot answer them now!" She hung her head. Those who were standing sat down. People lowered their hands. Finally, Phyllis spoke.

"We will miss him terribly in our social and professional lives and we will miss his presence and his contribution to this conference. Please let us take a moment of silence to remember JP." She said nothing about Amy.

The silence that followed was absolute. Amy sat as if cast in stone.

"Now," Margaret concluded the silence. "I would like to welcome you to the Horticultural Writers District II Conference, Focus on Hellebores. And I would like to dedicate this conference to JP Chiasson!" There was sustained applause. Kevin leant over to Mim.

"That was Randy. They've found JP's computer and the other stuff that was stolen."

Margaret had started speaking. Mim just looked at Kevin and rolled her eyes toward Amy. He should share the good news.

"No no! It's been trashed. Dumped in a creek. All of it! Computers, cameras, printer, telephones!" Kevin whispered. "I made a list of everything they found. Show you later." Kevin sat back and turned his attention to the stage.

"Why?" Mim asked stunned. "Why would somebody steal a person's electronic equipment and then dump it in a creek?"

"Maybe," whispered Kevin, "something happened that made them have to get rid of it quickly."

"Dumping it into a creek defeats the whole purpose of theft!" she said. There were shushing sounds around them.

"Later," Mim whispered and turned her attention to the stage

"It has been my great pleasure," Margaret beamed, "to consider this amazing group of horticulturists to be both colleagues and," with a face-splitting smile, she gestured to the group of speakers sitting in the front row, "friends!"

"When I first met her," Chase leaned forward to whisper to Mim, "Margaret worked as a salesgirl at the Garden Center. She didn't know that zinnias were annuals!"

"Right!" breathed Mim. Six or maybe seven years ago, Margaret had been an awkward, nearsighted woman who slouched perpetually in an effort to shave off some of her height which Mim estimated to be about five foot nine.

"The Garden Center promoted her from sales to programs," said Chase. "And voila!"

"How do you know all this?" asked Mim. Chase only smiled knowingly.

"Ah, the healing power of gardening," whispered Mim to Chase, only half joking. Now she took a long, hard look at Margaret. She looked an entirely different person from the shy, overweight young woman she had known.

"Does she still live at home with her mother?" Mim asked. Chase shrugged.

The change had to be more than superficial. Margaret must have overcome enormous difficulties at home. Mim remembered that three, maybe four years ago, Margaret had no car and couldn't drive. Mim had driven her home after a lecture when she found out that Margaret would otherwise have to take several buses to get there.

Margaret wanted to be dropped at the corner. Mim insisted on taking her all the way home. Too late, she understood Margaret's reluctance. Mrs. Stemple was sitting on the front stoop, waiting to pounce. Although reputed to be an invalid, she had jumped to her feet like a cat when the car pulled up and scowled as she approached the car. She looked inside to see who was driving.

Mim thought that Mrs. Stemple suspected Margaret of having a male friend because when she saw the driver was Mim, her demeanor changed. Margaret introduced her, making the point that they'd been at the lecture together in a way that made Mim feel they were in collusion. Poor Margaret with that harpy of a mother!

Maybe Margaret's acceptance and success in the Horticultural Writers Association was giving her a way out of that dreadful home situation. From all accounts, Margaret was an outstanding regional director—if over-sensitive. And all the accolades she received must do wonders to bolster her confidence. If she worked half this hard at her job at the Garden Center, Mim thought, she would be considered a very valuable employee indeed.

Whatever it was that had engendered the change, Margaret had metamorphosed into someone who could organize an outstanding conference. That *had* to affect her home life. Perhaps she could stand up to her mother now. Then Mim remembered Mrs. Stemple's strongly down-turned mouth, her darting, suspicious eyes, and her wheedling, insinuating manner of speech. Maybe. Maybe not

"In praising hellebores, it is impossible to lay it on too thick. They are superb plants. They have natural grace of form, elegant bell-shaped flowers, and beautiful deep-cut foliage, which is evergreen in most varieties; yet they are hardy and reliable, flowering in the worst months of the year when even the early bulbs prefer to stay underground."
Anne Scott-James, *Down to Earth*

25

Joachim Muller was the keynote speaker. This morning, his presentation, Hellebores of the World, was a shorter version of the workshop Mim had attended the day before. In the workshop, Muller had shown a photo of Tate and JP standing in a vast field of *Helleborus odorus*. Mim felt herself grow tense when he approached that part of his lecture. She braced herself for that photo to flash on the huge screen. But today, perhaps out of sympathy for the deceased, perhaps to condense his lecture, Muller only showed one photo of *Helleborus odorus*. It was a close-up of a single specimen. And he had gone over it briefly without much comment.

Mim was both disappointed and relieved.

Muller finished his presentation. There was applause and Margaret Stemple was back on stage, introducing Jenny and Darrel Taylor. Their Locust Hill nursery on Maryland's Eastern Shore was a Mecca for hellebore enthusiasts. Mim relaxed.

The Taylor's lecture was brain candy. They showed photo after photo of flowers in their Delmarva Belles series. The flowers were all doubles and each one had been more beautiful than the last.

"Wow! Did you see 'Speckles,' the white one with the red spots? " asked Sally. "That was terrific! Boy, the Taylors are going to be a hard act to follow!"

Amy looked stricken. Sally patted her hand and said, "Oh, Amy, I'm sorry. I didn't mean you. Don't worry!"

"Easy for you to say," said Amy, looking at an audience that was still clapping enthusiastically. "Maybe Margaret is right and I should leave lecturing to the professionals."

"Don't let Margaret get to you," said Mim. "They're going to love you."

Margaret took the stage to announce a fifteen minute break. There would be refreshments in the hall outside the auditorium. They stood up and joined the crowd in the aisle, heading toward the hall.

Mim had thoroughly enjoyed the lectures but wondered whether Kevin had been bored by all of the "hard core" horticulture, complete with botanical Latin.

"What did you think, Kevin?"

"It was really interesting," he smiled at the women as he said this, "*surprisingly* so. I enjoyed it!"

The crowd of garden writers moved slowly down the aisle until they reached a bottleneck near the door. The exit was clogged, probably by those queuing for refreshments set up on the other side of the door. Suddenly, Margaret Stemple was at Mim's side.

"Can you help me pour drinks?" she asked, addressing Mim, Sally, and Amy. "I've got to get this moving." Sally looked at Amy and they said simultaneously, "Sure!" They followed Margaret who pushed her way through the crowd. Mim stayed with Kevin. She wanted to hear Randy's full report

"I'll help," called a deep voice right behind Mim. She turned to see Rose Redfern, moving swiftly through the crowd that parted miraculously like the Red Sea before Moses. But people flowed into the gap after her, trapping the acolytes as surely as the sea had drowned Pharaoh's army.

Mim caught glimpses of Rose as she passed through those waiting to exit. As usual, her white hair was pulled into a chignon at her neck. She was dressed in a white turtleneck and white slacks. Mim looked sideways at Kevin, who was also watching Rose. Their eyes met and Mim knew they were thinking the same thing. It was one of the many things she loved about Kevin. They were on a wavelength. Either he read her thoughts or they had come to the same conclusion simultaneously. Why on earth would Rose want to pour coffee and hand out sweet rolls in that outfit?

As soon as they cleared the doorway, Mim steered Kevin to a quiet bench. He sat down and she sat beside him.

"Okay. Tell all!"

Kevin pulled out his notebook and read out the highlights of the stolen goods. Among other items, two computers, two cameras, a printer, and telephones had been found in a creek not two miles from JP and Amy's house, apparently dumped over a week ago. Probably immediately after the theft.

"Maybe the thieves had to get rid of the stuff in a hurry," Mim mused. "But why?"

"Randy thinks that the bludgeoning made the stuff too hot," said Kevin, handing Mim his notebook.

"Here is a complete list of everything that was recovered." Mim took the notebook and scanned the items. The list was long and included thousands of dollars worth of computers, printers, a slide scanner, two hard drives, cameras, and telephones.

"Randy thinks that JP walked in on the theft. He was struck from behind with tremendous force. Randy says there are tire tracks on the lawn area indicating that the thieves arrived at the house first. When they left—that would be after JP got there and they had already loaded up their van—tire tracks point to a van–they had to drive onto the lawn to get around JP's car. Randy thinks he must have run into the house to see what was going on. When he got inside, he was hit over the head. Maybe they realized how badly he was injured and dumped the goods so there would be no chance they could be traced."

"I guess if JP died, it was no longer just robbery. It was murder," Mim stated grimly.

"And that means the police will put a lot more effort into the hunt for the perpetrators," said Kevin.

That explanation made sense, Mimi thought, but something bothered her. She wasn't satisfied. Why would the thieves stop barely two miles away from the scene of the crime to dump stolen goods? They might be seen. If she were in their position, she would drive as far away as possible. She would make sure nobody saw her.

Mim looked over to the refreshment table, where the crowd had now thinned enough to reveal a woman in a maid's uniform and Margaret, handing out sweet rolls, while Sally, Amy, and Rose Redfern poured drinks.

Eric Ferris walked up to the table and regarded the three women pouring coffee. Of the three lines for coffee, he chose the one where Rose

Redfern would have to serve him. He waited while she poured him coffee, tasted it, and handed it back to her. She glowered at him and gave him another bag of sugar. He tasted it again and again handed it back. She took it from him, turned, presumably to dump in sugar from a larger container. She gave it back to him. He tasted it and, apparently satisfied, turned from the table grinning.

"What about the disks?" Mim asked. Amy had mentioned that all of their storage disks were stolen along with the other things. "There aren't any disks on the list."

"What disks?" asked Kevin, pulling his gaze away from Ferris.

"Amy said she backed up all of JP's photos and lectures on disks," Mim explained. "They kept them in a big metal box on his desk. The box was taken." Kevin knitted his brow.

"Randy didn't mention any disks. Or any box. He read me the official list of all of the articles found and I wrote it down," said Kevin, wrinkling his brow in an effort to remember. "I wrote down everything he said. You saw the list. He never mentioned a metal box or any disks."

"Mim, this bench was fashioned to mortify flesh. Let's have a coffee and sit in the auditorium where the seats are padded."

"Wait! Please Kevin! Just a minute. We can't bring coffee into the auditorium anyway. Maybe the thieves kept the disks," she mused. "But why would they bother?" Mim held onto Kevin's arm to keep him from rising. He settled back onto the bench with a sigh.

"Why? Maybe they just dumped everything else and forgot the disks. This was a burglary. They're in a big hurry with lots of adrenaline pumping. They just want to toss the stuff and get away as fast as possible," Kevin theorized. "What's so important about disks anyway?"

"Amy said that all of their photos were on disks. JP was a great photographer and Amy carefully copied his photos onto disks by category, both the personal and the professional ones."

Kevin shrugged. He said, "That's not likely to be useful to anyone but themselves....unless there was something on those disks that could somehow profit somebody else. But what would that be? What exactly was JP's research?" Kevin had stopped squirming on the bench and now looked intrigued. "What would he have stored that could be worth stealing?"

"Certainly not the personal photos and they couldn't use the professional ones," Mim mused out loud. "But he might have kept a photographic history of his crosses."

"Crosses?" Kevin raised his eyebrows.

"Using two parent plants with outstanding characteristics to create an offspring that shares those traits," explained Mim. "I could ask Andy Toll or the Taylors how they keep their records."

"I thought that plants got cloned," said Kevin.

"You're forgetting. Nobody bothers to clone a plant unless it's a real winner," said Mim. "Cloning takes big bucks."

"But I don't see how someone could profit from just a photographic record," said Kevin, rising. "If someone kept JP's records, they still wouldn't have the plants needed to get his results. And why would anyone want to start all over from the beginning. From a marketing standpoint, all you need are the really good end results." Kevin was moving toward the refreshments. Mim got up to follow.

"I guess you're right," said Mim. "I still don't get why they would bother with disks." They stood in front of a tray of sweet rolls. Mim used a napkin to pick up an almond-filled croissant. She handed it to Kevin.

"Eat! You need more padding!" Kevin took the croissant and bit into it. He chewed, swallowed quickly. "Look. When they got there they probably just grabbed whatever was in sight—box of disks included," he decisively concluded. Kevin looked at Mim and waited for her to agree.

"But then why didn't they dump the box of disks with the rest of the stuff?" Mim persisted. Kevin shrugged.

"Maybe they forgot. Or maybe the cops didn't find them." Kevin was done with this subject. He finished the croissant and reached for another.

"Or, maybe the thieves kept them?" Mim persisted. Kevin gave her a look and chewed slowly.

"It just doesn't fly," he finally said. "Judging from what is on them—other than personal shots—it's photos of plants, lectures about plants, and maybe a record of plant crosses. Right?" Kevin looked at Mim. "Okay, if someone actually stole them and actually meant to keep the disks, wouldn't that mean it's got to be someone associated with plants, maybe with hellebores?" He popped the last morsel of croissant into his mouth.

"Yes," Mim uttered assent, and a new possibility dawned. What if someone could benefit not from copying but *destroying* JP's work? That would mean that his murder had not been a chance confrontation with thieves, she thought.

It would mean whoever did it was someone he knew or someone who knew him. But Kevin was right. Even if he lost every single photo and note, JP would still have his plants. Amy said there were no plants missing.

"What if whoever stole the equipment was also planning to steal the plants and panicked when he saw JP," said Mim. Kevin looked at her patiently.

"If you were going to steal plants, you would steal plants first, not electronic equipment," he said. Kevin was right. Probably just thieves. She just wanted to make a connection because someone had stolen Tate's plants and might benefit from Tate's efforts. Mim dismissed the whole argument and moved with Kevin along the refreshment table.

Now that the greater mob had been fed and watered, one woman from the catering staff was clearing the refreshment table while Margaret attended to stragglers. Rose, Sally, and Amy had been relieved of duty. Rose had disappeared. Sally and Amy stood nearby, eating Danish and drinking coffee.

"Coffee, tea, lemonade?" asked Margaret, checking her watch. "You've got three more minutes."

"Yes. Coffee please!" said Mim. "Me, too," said Kevin.

Margaret poured their coffees briskly.

"The conference is outstanding," Mim said meaning it sincerely, but also hoping to mollify Margaret after her previous gaffs. Margaret smiled tiredly. "How are you holding up?" Mim added.

"I'll be fine as soon as today is over," Margaret said. Her cell phone rang. She rolled her eyes. "Mother—again." She moved away to speak privately. Mim heard her raise her voice to say, "not until tomorrow. Tomorrow!"

26

By the time the break was over, most horticultural writers had already returned to their seats. The clamor of voices faded obediently to a rumble as Margaret took the stage to introduce the next speaker. Sally and Amy scurried back to their seats in the front of the auditorium. Kevin and Mim followed close behind.

"How'd she get up there so quickly?" asked Sally, plopping into her seat as Margaret adjusted the microphone. "Wasn't she just serving coffee in the lobby?"

"I've never seen her move so fast," said Mim, who had always thought of the conference director as somewhat phlegmatic. Now, Margaret, this new Margaret, this ultra efficient woman who seemed to exude confidence, looked out over the filled auditorium with an unmistakable expression of pride.

"She's done a fantastic job so far," said Mim. Remembering the insistent ringing of Margaret's cell phone, she added, "and if running this conference isn't enough, her mother keeps calling." To herself, she said, "her awful mother."

"Before we hear what Benjy has to say about white Christmas roses," Margaret spoke into the microphone, "I have a couple of announcements." The noise level in the auditorium dropped to near silence. "First of all, the concurrents will be held right after lunch. So, please take out your pens and write this down! I'm going to read the rooms where they will be held." Margaret looked down at her notes.

"Okay. Those attending session A, Death by Hellebore with Rose Redfern, go to the Pine room—that's two or three doors down from where we had the reception last night. Got that? The Pine room for Death by Hellebore."

"If you're going to session B, 'Species of Balkan Hellebores' with Barney Staples, meet in the Oak room, that's right next to the Pine room. And finally," Margaret beamed at the audience, "Session C, that's 'Hellebores at Cullen's Cottage' with Daniel Cullen, will meet right here in the auditorium. Everyone got that?"

Margaret repeated the locations for each concurrent session.

"Immediately after the concurrents, we will have our lunch break in the Juniper room."

"Right after lunch, please come directly back here to the auditorium for our last presentation of the day. I know you are all looking forward to Andy Toll's lecture, Little Shop of Hellebores. And we all know that's going to be good," Margaret winked—winked–at Toll who was sitting in the front row. "Andy's lecture will begin promptly at 2:30. So please be on time."

"And now for tonight," Margaret beamed. "This is going to be a real treat! We get to see Longwood Gardens all dressed up for the holidays! You'll have a nice break after Andy's lecture—time to get ready for tonight's banquet at Longwood Gardens!"

"The buses that will take you to Longwood will be waiting for you right in front of the main entrance of the hotel. They're going to leave at exactly 6:05. *Exactly*. The reason we're going early is so you'll have some time at Longwood to look around." Margaret paused. "That's *exactly* five minutes after six! That means you will have to be *on* the bus by 6:00 o'clock." Margaret looked over the sea of horticultural writers. She smiled

"So I am asking for your cooperation. *Please*! Please be outside in front of reception by 5:45. We will begin boarding then. Please!" she added coyly.

Mim noticed Marcus Tydings walking—no! He was sauntering down the aisle back to a place in the front row. He reminded Mim of a model at a fashion show. When he sat down in his seat, a few seats down from Eric Ferris, he lounged sideways, half turned from the stage, as if he were sitting for a portrait in profile. He met Mim's eye as he perused the audience behind him.

On stage, like any good speaker, Margaret turned her head to address parts of the room. As her eyes scanned the audience, a smile lit up her face. She looked like she was about to take a bow. But when Marcus took his seat in the front row, the smile froze on her face. Her eyes darted wildly around the room and returned each time to a point directly in front of her and then roved frantically around the room again.

The change in Margaret's expression was dramatic. Mim looked at the faces around her to see if anyone else noticed. Sally was fumbling in her purse. Chase was scribbling in a little notebook. Nobody else seemed to notice the change in Margaret's demeanor. She looked at Kevin, who was looking at the space where Philippa had seated herself. Philippa was now invisible behind the other members of the audience.

She looked back at Margaret who was scanning her notes as if she couldn't find what she was looking for.

Mim looked around again. Hadn't anyone else noticed? Marcus Tydings was still displaying his handsome profile. Front row center, it looked like Eric Ferris noticed the change in Margaret. He seemed to be staring at Margaret, challenging her to speak. He seemed to be enjoying her discomfort. Typical.

Beyond Ferris, in the little group of speakers, Benjy Glover was gathering up his notes in preparation for his talk. Andy Toll was chatting with Joachim Muller. In the lengthening silence, Daniel Cullen raised his head and regarded Margaret.

On stage, Margaret shuffled her notes and looked up. She reshuffled them and looked up again. But each time she seemed about to speak, she stopped and looked down at her notes again. Her expression suggested she was about to announce the end of the world. People who had been chatting, riffling through purses, and reading, started, one by one, to stare at the stage. Little by little, the tension in the room ratcheted up until it seemed there was an electric buzz in the air.

There is nothing more disturbing for an audience than a speaker who freezes. Around her, Mim observed that people, disturbed by the sudden change in mood, began sitting up, squirming, and looking around.

In less than a minute, something had changed profoundly. There, before Mim's eyes, the jaunty, confident conference leader morphed back into her old self, awkward, insecure Margaret Stemple who lived with her harpy of a mother. Even her carriage had changed. A few minutes ago, she had stood tall. Now she slumped into the lectern as if she needed support to stand.

"Okay," said Margaret finally. The audience breathed a cumulative and audible sigh of relief.

"Anyone who is driving to Longwood and will not be riding the bus, or if you are..." Margaret stopped, out of breath. She took a breath and continued. "If you are not planning to attend the banquet, please let me know. I will be outside the auditorium door after our final lecture." She cleared her throat, but still her voice wavered.

Benjy Glover was poised on the edge of his seat, doubtless waiting for his introduction. Margaret glanced at him and nodded her head.

"And now," she began in a voice that began with a waver, but gained strength, "it is my great pleasure to introduce Benjy Glover," Margaret smiled. "Not only is he the owner of an outstanding nursery, Glovers Gardens, he is an outstanding breeder, a wonderful fellow traveler, and a good friend. Benjy's talk is entitled Dreaming of a White Christmas Rose...at Christmas—preferably a double." Margaret's smile was now so broad it looked like her face might split open, but it didn't reach her eyes.

"Benjy, come up and tell us about your white Christmas roses!" Glover rose, ascended the steps and took over the lectern.

As Margaret exited the stage she glanced nervously toward the front row. Mim looked over to those sitting there. At the far end, the little group of speakers sat politely waiting for Glover to begin. A few seats down from the speakers, Philippa massaged her fingernails. Dead center in the row, Eric Ferris twirled an amulet that hung from a string around his neck. He turned to follow Margaret's progress. Sitting at the opposite end from the speakers, Marcus Tydings eyes also followed Margaret.

Mim couldn't look at Marcus without thinking that like Tate, he had worn a red anorak on the plant hunting trip to the Balkans. In her mind's eye, she could see the cold gray mountains and the people in that vast landscape, diminished to tiny specks of color. Marcus was the red fleck. JP had considered Marcus an amateur. And Katie had said he "dabbled" in hellebores. Was he the one who had helped himself to Tate's plants?

She would make a point to talk to him before the conference was over. She wasn't sure exactly what she would say or how to say it, but she had to try to speak with the people who had been on that trip. Now she brought her attention back to the present.

27

The lights dimmed for Benjy Glover's talk. A close-up of a double white hellebore flower filled the screen.

"We breeders like to have a goal," Glover began. "I have been dreaming of creating a big, beautiful white Christmas rose that blooms *reliably* at Christmastime."

"As you all know, the Christmas rose, *Helleborus niger*, can bloom in December," Benjy Glover said, "but it is generally a smaller, somewhat less vigorous plant than the hybrid Lenten roses —at least in our soils and in this climate. Moreover, the flowers of the Christmas rose are, as you know, generally single whites."

"My goal has become the creation of a hybrid that has the vigor of a big, robust Lenten hellebore, *Helleborus x hybridus*, with the early bloom and more upright flowers of the Christmas rose, *Helleborus niger.* In short, I want very early, pure white flowers that stand up *above* a big, healthy clump of dark green foliage. I'd also settle for white flowers with a clear red streak as long as the flowers are doubles." This last remark drew guffaws.

What Glover wanted was the impossible.

"I know what you are thinking. You're thinking, that's impossible, he's crazy." Glover paused. "Maybe. Maybe I am. But did you know that some fine interspecific hybrids have been created using *Helleborus niger?*"

Kevin leaned over, "inter-whats?"

"Crosses between two species," whispered Mim.

"Didn't he just say it we are supposed to think that's impossible?" Kevin spoke so loudly, there was a chorus of shushing behind them.

Mim waited for the shushing to subside and the shushers to shift their attention back to Glover. Then she bent close to Kevin and spoke in a soft whisper.

"There are more than just the two kinds of hellebore. The Christmas rose and the Lenten rose are just the most well-known species," explained Mim. "There are lots of different species."

"Look!" said Mim as a photo of a cream colored hellebore appeared on the screen. It was a young one with silver veins in its leaves. The flowers stood above the clump, reminding Mim of an African violet. "See the one he's showing now? That's a cross of a less-known species with the Christmas rose."

"This is *Helleborus x ericsmithii*," said Glover. It was named to honor pre-eminent hellebore breeder Eric Smith, who with Helen Ballard developed some incredible plants." Another hellebore appeared on the screen. "And Helen Ballard is commemorated in this plant–the hybrid *Helleborus × ballardiae*."

"Here's another shot of *Helleborus x ballardiae*," said Glover of a large close-up. " It is a cross between *Helleborus lividus* with *Helleborus niger*. So you see that *Helleborus niger*–the Christmas rose–keeps popping up. It has the capacity to cross with other species."

"With that in mind, I selected this plant," he said, "because it was extremely floriferous and bloomed in mid-December." The screen lit up with a photo of the fullest, most impressive Christmas rose Mim had ever seen. Mim counted eight, nine, ten, eleven white flowers arching above an enormous clump. A murmur of surprised commentary arose from the audience.

"I crossed that Christmas rose with these Lenten rose crosses." A photo of gorgeous Lenten roses in shades of white to white striped red appeared on the screen.

"The next slide illustrates the results of my first efforts at crossing *Helleborus niger* with *Helleborus x hybridus*," Glover said, then advanced to a photo showing containers of soil with nothing growing in them. The audience howled with laughter.

For the next half hour, Benjy Glover continued to regale the audience with the saga of his frustratingly disastrous attempts to breed an outstanding December-blooming hybrid hellebore. He advanced quickly through photos of hellebores that were archetypical Christmas roses to those of archetypical Lenten roses to photos of foliage with no flowers at all. Finally, he paused at a photo of several people standing in what looked like a nursery.

"In conclusion, I want to say that although there have been plenty of bumps in the road, I haven't given up on my breeding goal," Glover was saying. "Some years ago, I had the pleasure of visiting Withcombe Nursery in England. As you may know, that was the late, great Marion Petersfield's nursery. It closed after her tragic death." He paused.

"I took this photo while I was there—that's Marion on the right." Glover used a laser pointer to designate Marion Petersfield, a very upright looking woman, probably in her late sixties, with a cloud of white hair. She was wearing a skirt, hose, sensible shoes, and a barn coat. Kevin recognized the photo. It was the same one that Randy had copied for him.

Glover moved the pointer to the center of the group and pointed to a man with a shock of blonde hair. Good grief! thought Mim, that's JP. She looked over at Amy. She was leaning forward, eyes were glued to the screen. The color had drained from her face.

"This is JP Chiasson. We are horrified and deeply saddened to learn of his passing. As you know, he would have spoken to you at this seminar tomorrow morning...." Again, Mim remarked that there was no mention of Amy's taking JP's place. Glover continued, "He was a fine breeder. I first made his acquaintance at the time I took this photo. He was working with Marion Petersfield at the time of my visit." Glover shook his head as if to brush away negative thoughts.

"You know, when things like this happen it almost makes you believe those old wives tales about hellebores and curses." Glover cleared his throat. Mim looked around. Was she imagining it, or was there a ripple of consensus passing through the audience?

She looked at Amy, who sat with her head bowed low. She was perfectly still.

"But I prefer to look on the bright side even though I know I need a lot of help," Glover was saying. He moved the laser's red arrow to a small figure in coveralls, Wellington boots, and a cap. "This very lovely lady was Marion Petersfield's right hand girl and now she is going to be mine."

"She will be sharing with us some of the hellebores developed at Withcombe, and she will be joining us at Glovers Gardens!" Glover gestured toward the front row.

"Come on up here, Philippa! Please, everyone, welcome Glover Garden's newest employee, Philippa Reed!" From her seat in the front row, the British woman stood and walked up the stairs to the stage. Benjy Glover put his arm around her shoulder.

"As you can see," Glover said, "she's even prettier in person." Isolated catcalls greeted this remark. "She's got the most beautiful head of red curls," here Glover took a closer look at Philippa Reed's auburn hair. "Sorry. I remembered incorrectly. She's got the most beautiful head of curls I've ever seen *and*," here he looked into her face, "... the eyes of a doe." There were a few more catcalls.

"Hey, guys! Take it easy! We don't want her to get the wrong idea. This is her first time in this country. I don't want to scare her away before she helps me breed a spectacular white Christmas rose!" There was an enthusiastic round of applause.

"Thank you, Mr. Gover!" said Philippa into the microphone. "I hope I can live up to those expectations. If I am not mistaken that would be a Christmas-blooming, large clump *niger-hybridus* cross in pure white or white striped double flowers. Anything else?" She looked at Glover.

The audience roared.

"Well, I'll do my best," Philippa said. She nodded to the audience and amidst thunderous applause exited the stage.

Glover checked his watch. "We've got three minutes. Are there any questions?"

Amy got up and bolted from the auditorium.

Chase Filmore watched as Philippa Reed returned to her seat. I'm sure that's Pippa! The name's different, but those big brown eyes are unmistakable. He's right. She has the eyes of a doe. The hair's different, but Glover thought it was red, too. She probably dyed it. I'll have to check.

But he said this is her first time in this country. How can that be when I sat next to her on the flight to London! That was only two weeks ago. We chatted for hours! She told me she was a nanny, working outside Philadelphia. And she said her name was.... Chase tried to recall. The name eluded him, but he remembered that it was hyphenated and it wasn't just "Reed." Parker-something. Proctor?

He had made small, subtle overtures to the woman, smiling at her and, once, catching her eye and waving. These efforts had met with no response beyond cool, dismissive glances and, the one time when Chase had waved, the woman turned her back!

Chase considered asking Benjy Glover about Pippa. Then he reconsidered. He decided against it. It would be like telling him that his new employee was a liar.

Maybe she is a liar, thought Chase. And maybe she's embarrassed that she lied to me. Or maybe she's got a twin. Or a sister who looks just like her.

Then a thought struck Chase. Maybe she simply doesn't remember me. Her hair and those big brown eyes are memorable. But I look pretty much like lots of guys my age, Chase thought with a wry smile. Better not to say anything to anybody until I have a chance to talk with her.

28

In the applause for Glover's lecture, Mim got up and followed Amy. She met Kevin's eye in passing. As usual, she read in his expression that he concurred with her inclination to follow Amy.

When Mim reached the lobby, the refreshment table had been cleared of food trays and coffee pots. A woman in a black maid's uniform whipped off the white table cloth and began stuffing it into a plastic bag. Two men advanced. One had an Errol Flynn mustache. They were about to carry the table away. Amy was nowhere to be seen.

"Has anyone seen a blonde woman? She just came out of the auditorium," said Mim.

The hotel employees stopped what they were doing and stared at Mim. I spoke too fast, thought Mim. She decided to try out her very poor Spanish.

The man with the Errol Flynn mustache tried to hide a smile. Maybe they didn't speak Spanish either, she thought ruefully and I sound like an idiot. Then the woman came to life.

"Sí, sí. Esta en el baño." Baño, baño, thought Mim.

"The ladees room," nodded the woman, making sure that Mim understood. She gestured down the hall toward an alcove marked by signs that bore the international symbols for restrooms, silhouette figures of a man in pants and a woman wearing a skirt.

"Thank you! Muchas gracias," said Mim, already in motion. She walked briskly down the carpeted lobby and turned into the alcove. When she opened the door, she heard a quiet whimper. Amy. She was in one of the toilet enclosures.

"Amy, it's me. Mim," Mim said, addressing the feet in the corner stall. There was no reply. Mim waited for what seemed like a full minute. Then the door opened and Amy appeared. Her face was blotched red from crying. She looked at Mim, but said nothing.

"Come on. Let's go get a drink," Mim said.

"No, Mim. You'll miss…" Amy began.

"Don't worry! Come on!" Amy followed without further protest. She walked limply after Mim. They took the elevator up to the street level where Mim was sure they could find a restaurant or a bar.

"What do you feel like—coffee?" asked Mim.

"Can we just take a little walk?" Amy asked. "I've had too much coffee already. And it's a little too early for anything stronger. Can we take a walk?"

"That sounds great," said Mim, steering Amy toward the door. Outside the air was fresh and still unseasonably warm. Mim was wearing her long black sweater jacket over matching pants. Amy wore a jacket of a very fine Harris tweed pattern with gray slacks. The jacket fabric was lightweight enough to allow for graceful gathering at the cuffs and waist. The result was a contrast of traditionally masculine fabric with a very feminine blouse style. The jacket was stunning in itself and terrific on Amy's tall, slender figure.

"I like your jacket. That's a beautiful cut," said Mim. Amy walked a few steps without comment.

"It's from Paris. It was JP…JP…." Amy's voice caught. "He…always brought me the…He had great taste." Amy pressed her lips together as if to stop a flood of words or tears. They walked on in silence.

From time to time, Mim glanced at Amy. She walked with her head held high, but her eyes seemed to be fixed in the kind of stare that sees only inward.

Amy rubbed the sleeve of her jacket to feel its substance. She remembered picking JP up at the airport. He had been red-eyed, exhausted, but so excited and pleased with his present for her that he made her open the package containing the jacket in the airport.

He did love her. She was his Aimee. But why, why in his last breath had he not called out for her?

The horrifying scene played again in her mind's eye. She came into the darkened house and saw something on the floor. She must have turned on the light because then she saw JP lying on the floor in a pool of his blood. His eyes were wide and fixed on the door. He said it over and over, "Bichette, bichette, bichette."

In shock, she had followed his eyes and looked through the door to the empty porch beyond. The light was on. Outside, it looked as it always had, normal, undisturbed, safe. The porch and the garden made sense. Inside was the terrible unreality. The horror of it washed over her again: the office in utter disorder, the blood, JP. Her thoughts cycled back to his words: "Bichette, bichette, bichette."

She surfaced and looked around. They had wandered into Chinatown. She ganced at Mim, walking quietly beside her. Amy felt a surge of warmth. She hadn't known Mim for more than twenty-four hours, but she felt she had found a friend.

"Mim, thank you for… I really needed some fresh air. Thank you!" Amy stopped walking and examined her surroundings. "Do you know where we are?"

"I think we just walked in a big circle. The hotel should be a couple of blocks in this direction," said Mim pointing down the street. They walked on and Amy's thoughts wandered back.

Once, soon after she and JP moved to the house in Gladwynn together, JP had called her "Bichette." Thinking it was a French term of endearment, she hadn't paid much attention. But he had so quickly and insistently corrected his mistake, reiterating that she was his "Aimee" that the incident lodged in her memory. At the time, she thought that "bichette" might be a French way of saying "bitch," which made JP's quick correction all the more endearing and understandable. Afterwards, she looked up the word in the French-English dictionary. It meant "hind," an old term for a female deer.

"You know, that lunch was surprisingly good!" said Sally. She was sitting with Mim and Amy at a big round table in the Juniper Room. "I've never had kielbasa before. When I heard what lunch was going to be, I didn't think I would like it. But I did. And I ate way too much of it," she said, patting her stomach. "It's a good thing that Andy Toll's up next. If anyone can, Andy will keep me awake."

"It was really good," said Mim, who looked over at Amy. Amy hadn't touched her plate. She was sipping water and staring into space.

"Where's Kevin?" asked Sally. In contrast to Amy's preoccupied presence, Sally was animated and behaving more like her old, bouncy self. She must have fully recovered from her run in with Eric Ferris. Even though, Mim thought sadly, a book contract would not be forthcoming until Tom could sort things out.

"Over there," Mim rolled her eyes toward a table across the room. Kevin, all smiles, was sitting next to Philippa Reed. Smitten, Mim thought as she watched Kevin looking ingratiatingly at the British woman.

It bothered her. The simple reason would be that she was jealous. Philippa Reed was a beauty. And Kevin was her good friend and even if there was no romance, she had a proprietary interest in him. So, yes, she felt the tiniest bit of jealousy. But it was far more complicated than that.

Call it intuition. There were times when simple gut feeling worked better than reason. And this was one of them. Her instinct was flashing "wrong, wrong, wrong." Something did not compute.

"He's really turning on the charm," said Sally, rising and looking at her watch. "Hey, I gotta go back to the room before the next session. See you in the auditorium."

"I should have known," Amy said softly as Sally galloped toward the elevator. It was the first thing she had said all during lunch. It took a moment to register that she had spoken.

"Known what?"

"Who she is." Amy gestured with her eyes toward the table where Philippa sat with Kevin.

"You know her?" Mim asked with surprise.

The tables around Mim and Amy emptied as the others made their way to the rooms where the concurrents were being held. Amy remained rooted in place. She seemed reluctant to make any effort to move, to continue on with a day that must be taking a huge emotional toll. Mim stayed with her.

Across the room, Kevin and Philippa Reed rose from their table. Kevin threw his head back in laughter at something Philippa said. Together, the pair walked toward the auditorium. Kevin made sidelong glances at Philippa as they moved forward. Both seemed oblivious to those around them.

"They were lovers," Amy spoke in a monotone. Mim glanced back at the retreating couple. Did she mean Kevin and Philippa?

"That was when he worked at Withcombe…in England with Marion Petersfield."

"You mean Philippa and…" Mim began. Amy finished her question.

"JP. Yes, JP," Amy said, staring at a spot in the center of the table. "You know, when I first saw her here at the conference, I had this bad feeling. I thought she looked familiar, but I couldn't place her," said Amy. "I must have seen her in one of JP's photos, but it didn't click then." Amy shook her head. "I had this really bad feeling. It was almost as if I already knew….Then when Benjy Glover showed that photo and she came up on stage, I knew for sure."

Chase Filmore hurried by en route to the auditorium. Seeing them, he stopped, waved, and waited. Feigning impatience, he put one hand on his hip and began tapping his foot. Mim made the faintest movement of shaking her head. Chase nodded, pointed in the direction of the auditorium. Mim nodded to him and he continued on his way, one hand raised in a vaudeville exit flutter. Amy seemed to have noticed nothing of this exchange. She seemed oblivious to everything but her narrative. She continued in a flat, unemotional voice.

"I think they lived together for about a year. You know what?" Amy looked at Mim. "After they broke up, he didn't even like her. She did something…" Amy shrugged her shoulders to indicate she didn't know what it was. "She did something that changed his feelings for her." Amy ran her hand down the fine wool of her jacket sleeve as if she were stroking a cat.

"Do you have any idea what that might have been?" asked Mim. Amy's face was pensive. Her eyes seemed to be following some inner vision. They widened as if they had spotted what they were looking for, but she shook her head slowly.

"No. He never really said anything about her that was negative. Maybe it was from what he didn't say," Amy sighed deeply. "It was a feeling I got from the way he looked and held himself when he talked about her. I mean, he didn't really talk about her much at all, but when he first mentioned her…it was the way he said it. And the look on his face." Amy glanced toward the auditorium and slowly rose from her chair.

"How did he look?" said Mim, standing and gathering up her folder.

"Horrified," said Amy. She gathered her purse and stood up. "I'm going to take a nap."

"Good idea," said Mim.

As Amy waited for the elevator to take her to her room on the fifth floor, she drooped against the wall. The fact that JP's former lover was here was bad enough. That she was so beautiful rocked Amy's world.

He only called her "Bichette" once and, she remembered how he corrected himself immediately. Immediately! As if he had said something horrible. I was always "Aimee." Amy stroked the fabric of her jacket. Absently, she held up one arm to examine the gathered cuff on her beautifully tailored jacket. Aimee. That's what he called me.

"Bichette was his name for her," Amy said out loud. Staring into the distance, she mentally placed the final pieces into a puzzle. There was sadness in her face, but also relief. She had solved the puzzle of JP's last words.

Maybe Dr. Garvey, her grief counselor was right: When someone dies it must be like the lights going out in a big building. And the person dying is left stumbling in the dark. And maybe, he finds a dim light bulb hanging in one of the old storerooms and recognizes someone there. And he calls out her name. *Her* name.

29

It was clear that Daniel Cullen's presentation was the most popular of the concurrents. Mim entered an auditorium so packed she wondered if anyone was attending the other sessions. In contrast to the morning lectures, the first few rows were filled. Anticipating a good show, horticultural writers were clustered as close to the screen as possible. The closest seat to the stage that Mim could find was in one of the back rows.

It was a good show and it got better. Cullen opened with a photo of his home, Cullen's Cottage. It was idyllic, painted a crisp white and set off by a rose-covered arbor. Around the house was a succession of gardens brimming with hellebores and many other perennials. Flower borders flanked a central vegetable plot which was contained within a white picket fence. There was also a greenhouse, winter quarters for his collection of tropicals that spent summers on the patio.

If the setting was idyllic, his hellebores were over the top. Cullen was showing a plant with yellow double blooms growing in a field of deep, almost black purple-flowered plants.

"When I first gardened with hellebores, I was fascinated by them. Now, what keeps my interest is how variable they are," he said. "There is no end to their potential." He flipped through a series of close-ups of flowers that began with white singles, moved through white doubles into white flowers with rose markings. From rose colored flowers, he moved through purple to those so dark, they were almost black. He concluded this series with yellows and, finally, a salmon colored flower with a ruff of crinkled petals around the center. This last drew gasps of appreciation from the audience.

As Cullen clicked through the series of flower close-ups, he threw out the names of the species that had contributed to each hybrid. It was more information than Mim could absorb, so she sat back and simply enjoyed the photos.

The audience was rapt. You could have heard a pin drop. Mim sat back to watch the show, but she couldn't keep her mind from wandering. She had seen Kevin walking with Philippa in the direction of the auditorium. She wondered if he decided to attend Cullen's presentation instead of Rose Redfern's talk on plant poisons.

The dimmed lights made it too dark to see if Kevin was in attendance. All Mim could make out were row upon row of heads.

Her thoughts turned to Amy, hopefully, able to nap upstairs in her room. Amy staggered under the combined weights of her grief, still so new and raw, and her apprehension about giving JP's presentation. The last thing she needed at this conference was the presence of JP's former lover. Another coincidence.

It seemed to Mim that this conference was fraught with coincidences. Taken singly, each was unremarkable. It was not unreasonable that Amy should be here or that Philippa should be here. Or even that her dear old friend Kevin, a travel writer, should have crossed paths with Tate in the Balkans and, because of Tate's death, elect to write about the curse of the hellebores and come to this conference.

Taken altogether, there were too many coincidences. The worst was the fact that both Tate and JP, in their prime and at the forefront of their field, should die. True, Tate had been engaged in dangerous work. But JP's death, in his home in the peaceful Pennsylvania countryside...!

And why had the thieves taken everything connected to his work and then discarded it?

The people and events that circulated around hellebores and this conference formed a web of coincidences that challenged reason. Mim didn't believe in curses. Coincidences made her think again of the science fiction writer Emma Bull's words, 'coincidence is when we can't see the levers and pulleys."

It was all too connected. A chilling new thought gripped her. Could Tate's death be connected, too? No.

After the concurrent sessions, horticultural writers gathered outside the auditorium in anticipation of the final lecture, Andy Toll's "Little Shop of Hellebores." Kevin walked up to Mim.

"How was Rose Redferns talk?" Mim asked.

"Really interesting," Kevin said, pulling out his notebook. "Listen to this! In ancient times," Kevin read, "hellebores were used in a concoction to summon the devil. "

"Sounds like useful stuff," Mim said. Kevin ignored her remark and continued.

"Hellebore poisoning was also used in warfare. The Greeks used it to poison the water supply of Kirra—that was a city they besieged. And it worked! Everyone got the runs and the city fell."

"Alexander the Great and…," Kevin looked down at his notes, "Don Alonzo de Aquilar, who fought the Moors at Granada– the last Moorish stronghold in Spain–died from hellebore poisoning."

"Apparently not one, but two poisons are extracted from hellebores. One is a narcotic. And that species would be…," he looked up waggling his eyebrows, "*Helleborus niger*. The other poison, helleborein, can cause cardiac arrest and there's more of it in another species, *Helleborus viridis*."

"Kevin! Listen to you speaking botanical Latin! You're becoming a plant nerd!"

"Is that a compliment?"

"Actually, yes," Mim said. "So you enjoyed her lecture?"

"Yes. Very much. She's a very dramatic speaker. Want to hear more?" Kevin smiled, turning over a page in his notebook with a flourish.

"Helleborin has an unpleasant taste which makes it difficult to use in poisoning."

"She said that?" Mim asked. Kevin nodded.

"Makes it sound like she tried," Mim mused.

"She also said that, for poisoning, the other one, helleborein, is much more useful because it tastes sweet. "

"Good grief! What else did she say?" Kevin closed his notebook.

"That's about it," he concluded. Then, apparently remembering something important, he held up one finger.

"Oh! I almost forgot! One of the most interesting things she mentioned was about the derivation of the name 'hellebore.' It comes from the Greek."

"And?" Mim prompted. Kevin grinned wickedly

"It means 'food to kill'."

Mim and Kevin stood in front of the auditorium, waiting for the last lecture to begin. Barney Staples joined them. Mim and Barney had not spoken since the propagation workshop.

"How are you feeling?" Barney asked. Mim was at first confused by his question. She had almost forgotten her escape from Tyding's workshop.

"Oh! Much better, thank you! How was the rest of the workshop?"

"You dodged about two hundred bullets. Everyone envied you!" Kevin raised his eyebrows and Mim explained to Kevin how she had left Marcus' lecture on propagation.

"Apparently, Tydings has crossed a lot of plants," Barney laughed. "I think he showed his audience every one of his favorites!"

Mim asked Barney, "Do you know Tydings well?"

"Actually, no. I first met him…" Barney hesitated, swallowed, and glanced at something over her head. "On the Balkan trip," he concluded. She turned to see what he was looking at. She saw nothing.

"He has a nursery. Have you been there?" Mim asked. This question he answered directly.

"Nobody—at least nobody that I know—has been to his nursery." He must have read Mim's expression as curiosity because he continued. "Perhaps it was sheer devilment, but everybody on the Balkan trip made a point of asking him if they could visit."

"And?"

"Everybody got the same story. Apparently, he is very worried about security. He says he travels a lot and doesn't have what he feels to be adequate security, so he wants to keep the nursery 'off the map'—that's how he puts it. All anybody's got is his post office box number in State College, Pennsylvania." Mim examined Barney. She was thinking of the plants that were stolen from Tate.

"Sounds like he's hiding the holy grail of hellebores," she said. Barney laughed.

"Maybe he thinks so. Not likely. But I will say this, he has tremendous enthusiasm and, no doubt, will eventually develop some good plants." Barney paused. "He knows his stuff."

30

Kevin slipped away while Mim and Barney were talking. Mim looked around. Not only was he nowhere to be seen, but everybody else had moved into the auditorium. The lecture had started.

Mim entered the auditorium with Barney following. Andy Toll was showing a close-up of a beautiful white, double-flowered hellebore to a murmur of appreciation from the audience as Mim slipped into the seat beside Sally. Barney took the next seat.

"This is hybrid 'Mrs. Betty Ranicar'," Toll was saying. "It's been a star at Preeminent Plants ever since we obtained our plants from the breeder, John Dudley of Tasmania." He advanced to the next slide which showed the entire plant.

"Where's Amy?" whispered Sally.

"Taking a nap," said Mim. "Where's Kevin?" Sally pointed to the front row, where Kevin was sitting next to Philippa Reed. His head was inclined toward Philippa as she spoke into his ear.

"We've been deserted," smiled Sally. Mim didn't smile and felt truly deserted as she watched Kevin and Philippa. Ridiculous, she chided herself and turned her attention to Andy Toll.

"...A very vigorous plant," Toll was saying. It does come almost completely true from seed, but so far, anyway, it hasn't produced much seed." He advanced to another white flowered hellebore.

Why would Marcus be secretive about his nursery? What did he have to hide? Mim thought again of Tate's missing plants.

"*Helleborus x nigercors* 'White Beauty'—whew! That's a mouthful!" Toll was saying. "It's one of the rarest of the Lenten roses, the reason being that it is a sterile hybrid between *Helleborus niger* and *Helleborus argutifolius*." He advanced to a close-up photo of the foliage.

"Look at the gorgeous silver veining on the leaves! In a well-drained, somewhat dry site, this is a big, vigorous, and very easy-to-grow perennial..."

From the audience came the sound of snoring. Toll stopped speaking, surprised. With his hand shielding his eyes in a pantomime of scanning the horizon, he searched the audience and found the offender, sitting immediately before him in the front row. He pointed dramatically to the culprit.

"Eric! Eric!" Toll called and the audience, realizing who it was, burst into laughter. The snoring continued. Mim half rose to get a better look. Eric Ferris was sound asleep with his head thrown back and his mouth agape.

Benjy Glover rose from his seat and tapped Ferris on the shoulder. Ferris sputtered and snorted. Glover tapped again, harder. Ferris rolled over to one side. Glover held up both hands in a gesture of helplessness. Then, suddenly, the volume of the snoring diminished to a low, vibrating rumble.

"I guess we can live with that," Toll said. "I didn't realize how helleboring I was." The audience laughed and settled again into the program and Ferris was forgotten.

After Toll finished, Margaret Stemple returned to the stage. With anxious glances at the still-sleeping Eric Ferris, she dismissed the conference, repeating the instructions for meeting the buses that would take attendees to the dinner at Longwood Gardens. Mim had been so engrossed in Andy Toll's presentation that she forgot all about Ferris. And so, apparently, had everyone else.

Horticultural writers streamed up the aisles toward the exits and out of the auditorium. One of the last to leave, Mim looked back and saw Margaret walking toward Eric Ferris, still asleep in the front row.

Chase Filmore and Katie Hiscock were waiting by the exit. "We're going to the Market," said Chase. "Want to come?" He looked from Mim to Sally to Barney. Barney excused himself. Sally checked her watch while Mim debated internally.

"I need a nap," said Sally.

"Mim?" asked Chase.

Mim returned from the market with aching feet. Sally's bed was unmade and empty. The television was tuned to Home and Garden TV. A woman in black was faux finishing a wall to make it look like marble. The bathroom door was closed. Sally was probably taking a bath, Mim thought enviously. Clearly, resting in the room rather than exploring the market had been the wiser choice, she thought as she took off her shoes and stretched her toes.

And these are my sensible shoes, Mim thought, regarding her black, slip-on flats. She sat down on the bed and massaged one foot and then the other. In a few moments, the insistent pain diminished as circulation returned. She tried standing up and found her feet had revived. She walked over to the bathroom door and tapped on it. "Sally, I'm back!"

"Wait! Wait just a minute. I want you to get the full effect!" The bathroom door opened a crack. "Close your eyes!" Sally commanded.

"Okay. They're closed."

"Ta da!" Sally emerged from the bathroom, fully dressed, arms raised like a Broadway dancer.

Mim opened her eyes and got the full effect. Sally was resplendent in deep purple velvet harem pants. She wore a knee length shirt of ivory silk so fine, it was transparent. A black bolero, embroidered in gold, covered places that by dint of its fine fabric the shirt could not.

"Wow! Where did you get that outfit?"

"At Rita's Resale, the consignment shop in Milbury. Isn't it great? Fifty bucks!"

"Gosh, I would have thought any consignment shop in Milbury would be knee deep in Ann Taylor or Lily Pulitzer," said Mim, thinking of her visit to the quaint, decidedly affluent, and seemingly conservative little Connecticut town where Sally lived.

"Oh, there's plenty of that, but there are also a few eccentrics in the hills," Sally smiled. Mim looked at herself in the mirror. She was already wearing the black slacks she would wear tonight along with her favorite knit jacket. She planned to change out of the paisley blouse she had worn all day into a white silk shirt for the festivities tonight.

"By comparison, I will be a very plain bird indeed," Mim muttered, slipping into the white silk shirt. She studied herself in the mirror. "In fact, I could be taken for part of the wait staff."

"Wear your Indian necklace," suggested Sally. "That'll jazz it up."

"Good idea." Mim fished in her jewelry case and held up the heavy antique necklace. The memory of the day Tate had given it to her flashed with a bittersweet aftertaste. It had been their one-month anniversary. She took a deep breath.

Then she put it to her throat. Made of old silver, articulated with delicate chain, the necklace draped gracefully, encircling her neck and dropping to a "v" shape below her throat. She turned to Sally.

"That's perfect! You are the soul of understatement with a dash of pizzazz!" Sally said approvingly. Then she frowned, "You sure I'm not overdressed?"

"You look fabulous. Let's go! I'm looking forward to just *sitting*. Sitting on the bus to Longwood and sitting at the dinner. And eating! I'm hungry. While you were lolling on your bed all afternoon resting, I was force marched through the market with Chase and Katie. We must have covered five miles."

"Did you find anything for your godchild?" Mim grimaced.

"Yes, but upon reflection, I'm not sure his mother will appreciate it." She held up a boomerang. "It is handmade."

Sally and Mim were half way to the elevator when Sally stopped.

"Oh! Damn! I forgot *Rain Gardening*!" Sally smacked her forehead with the flat of her hand. *Rain Gardening* was a book Sally had written and photographed. Despite good information and great photography, it had fallen between the cracks because of an upheaval within Wallace Editions, the publishing house. "Lin Baldwin wants to do a review," she called over her shoulder, running back to the room. "Don't wait! I'll take the stairs down."

In less than a minute Sally was back in the room. Her half of it was decidedly less neat than Mim's, but, she excused herself, she had come farther and had made stops along the way, taking photos and promoting her book. A one-woman dog and pony show.

Next to her bed stood the black bag she carried to lectures. It contained all of the handouts, notes, business cards, and whatever promotional material the nurseries and seed companies handed out. The book wasn't there. She tried her suitcase. Nothing. Then she remembered. She had shown Mim the photo of Daniel Cullen's garden.

She strode to the desk on Mim's side of the room. There it was! In picking it up, she jogged the mouse on Mim's computer and the screen came to life. Filling the screen was a rose colored hellebore. Mim must have left her computer on and let it run all day long.

Should she turn it off? Maybe Mim wanted to leave it on. Or maybe she just forgot. She'd been out all day. Sally stood for a moment, staring at the screen, undecided. Then she shrugged. Perhaps, to be on the safe side, she would leave it on....

The photo changed to a panorama of mountains, speckled with colorful dots. Taking her glasses off, she bent forward for a closer look. It was spectacular! The colors reminded her of a Turner painting. The mountains were revealed in soft shades of gray. Streaming from the lower left and getting smaller as they moved into the distance were members of the plant hunting party. She could make out heads and legs, but it was the stream of colors against a field of green that captured her eye. Sally was charmed by JP's use of colors and contrasts. He had used his camera as an artist used his paints to create a picture that was both informative and beautiful.

The photo disappeared and was replaced by another one of the same scene taken at a different angle. In the distance, high on the mountain, Sally thought she saw a very tiny red dot.

She looked closer. Hadn't Mim said that Tate left the group and went off by himself? If the red dot on the mountains was a person, it could be Tate. Unless someone else wore a red parka. Did Mim know?

The photo faded into another shot of hellebores, obviously growing in the wild. Sally reversed the photo and, again, she was looking at mountainous terrain, speckled with people who registered as colorful dots. If she leaned forward, she could see a small red speck—this one looking very like a person, high on the mountain. When she put on her glasses, the spot disappeared.

She looked at the clock. 6:03. There was no time to shut down the computer even if she wanted to. If she didn't hurry she'd miss the bus. They would be loading now. Sally grabbed *Rain Gardening* and dashed out the door.

Mim reached the lobby in time to find the swarm of garden writers heading to the waiting buses. She joined the crowd and was carried with it to the driveway where Margaret was pacing back and forth. She held a clipboard, presumably holding a list of those who would be riding the buses to Longwood.

"We're running late," Margaret announced. "Please keep moving!" Margaret checked off each person who boarded the bus on a sheet attached to her clipboard. Mim noticed that she seemed to know almost everyone by sight. Once in a while, she scanned the person's nametag. This was made easier by the fact that few garden writers had bothered to take coats on this unusually balmy night.

Mim kept turning around to see if Sally was following. When she reached the bus, she stopped and said to Margaret, "Sally is still upstairs. She'll be here any minute." She hoped that Sally, who so easily got caught up in what she was doing and could so easily forget the time, would make haste.

"That's okay. The last bus will wait for another five minutes," Margaret assured her, taking her arm and gently urging her forward. "But please, since you're here, get on this one. We're going to need to fill every seat."

"Sally will be here any second," Mim told Margaret, looking back at the door of the hotel and willing this to be so. She saw Daniel Cullen and the Taylors hurrying toward the buses. Behind them came three more horticultural writers. Sally was nowhere in sight.

"Don't worry. That's why the third bus will wait for stragglers. I promise: We won't leave her or anyone else behind! But we need to fill every seat. Please board. I'll tell Sally you've gone on ahead," Margaret said, checking Mim's name off the list on her clipboard.

"Come on Mim," said Chase Filmore who was standing in line with Amy. "Sally will be fine." Mim followed Chase on board the first bus.

Margaret followed them up the stairs and looked around at the full bus.

"Is Eric Ferris on this bus?" Margaret called out. A few people turned to inspect the back rows of the bus.

"Not here!" someone called.

"Praise the Lord!" said another voice. There was a burst of laughter and a chorus of "Ahmens!"

Margaret exited the bus. Mim watched through the bus's window as Margaret handed her clipboard to Katie Hiscock and returned to the hotel. A few seconds later, the bus pulled away en route to Longwood Gardens.

31

Sally decided against taking the elevator. Too slow. It would be stopping at every floor to take on stragglers who were running late. She walked swiftly to the exit sign at the end of the hall.

As she opened the door, she heard the sound of footsteps coming from above. Someone else hurrying to the bus. She took one step forward and halted. Those descending the stair—and there were at least two of them—were engaged *sotto voce* in a furious exchange. She couldn't make out the words, but felt rather than heard frantic emotion.

Deciding to avoid causing embarrassment to the speakers, she stepped back into the hallway. She decided to wait for them to pass and then follow at a discrete distance. She stepped quickly back into the hall, but the big door, fixed with a hydraulic safety device, would not be hurried. Standing in the empty hallway, Sally watched, mesmerized as the door closed in slow, deliberate millimeters.

Suddenly the voices stopped. For several seconds, there was only silence and footsteps. Sally cringed. The footsteps were loud and near now. Whoever it was had probably seen that the door was open and had stopped speaking.

Uncomfortable moments passed as she braced for a confrontation, for a head that would peer around the door to find her standing there. She heard one sentence, spoken in a harsh whisper that rang with Biblical finality: "He will sleep for a good, long time." Then the door clicked shut.

The sound of steps in the stairwell faded. Sally waited for thirty seconds and poked her head around the heavy door. She considered the curious statement and wondered, who was going to sleep for a very long time. Curiosity aroused, she began to skip down quickly so she could see who had uttered those words.

Nevertheless, by the time she arrived at the first floor, those descending the staircase had already left the stairwell and were, very likely, in the lobby. Sally looked all around the lobby. The only horticultural writers in evidence were two decidedly un-athletic looking women, who certainly hadn't taken the stairs. Through the large, glass entrance doors she could see a few horticultural writers walking toward a bus.

As she hurried to catch up, she saw who they were. Rose Redfern, tall and elegant in a flowing white coat was striding toward the bus with her acolytes scurrying to keep up. When Rose reached the gaggle of hort writers that was forming a line to board, she turned around and looked directly at Sally.

A long white Isadora Duncan scarf was knotted around her neck. Her hair was white, her coat was white, but her eyes were black and gleaming. For a long moment, they bore into Sally. Then Rose turned around and began moving in the slow line that would board the bus.

Was it Rose Redfern who had uttered those strange words? Did she know who overheard them? Sally shuddered. She followed Rose with her eyes until the woman disappeared into the bus.

Sally walked swiftly and took her place at the end of the line. She looked to see who else was ahead of her. Some, she knew. And there were some she knew only by reputation. Andy Toll was deep in conversation with a man who, she surmised from their conversation, made his living photographing gardens and plants. Behind them was Marcus Tydings, whom she didn't know, but recognized. He was impossible to miss! He seemed to be attending to Toll's and the other man's conversation, but they were too engrossed in what they were saying to take notice of him.

Katie Hiscock was standing next to the bus door, checking off the name of each person who boarded.

"I love your...your costume," Katie gushed when she saw Sally. "Harem wear isn't it?"

Costume! Harem wear! Sally nodded ever so slightly and produced a tight little smile. A slow flush rose on Katie's cheeks.

"Have you seen Mim?" Sally asked in as neutral a voice as she could muster in light of Katie's remark. With a helpful flourish that hinted at an apology for her tactless remark, Katie scanned the list on the clipboard she was holding. Before she could speak, a breathless voice answered for her. It was Margaret Stemple, directly behind Sally.

"She left on the first bus," Margaret gasped. Catching her breath, she added, "I asked her to board instead of waiting for you."

"Thank you very much, Katie!" Margaret said, briskly taking back the clipboard. She scanned the names on the list. "It looks like everyone's accounted for...except... surprise, surprise! Eric Ferris!" She rolled her eyes. "I checked the lobby, the bar, and the restaurant for stragglers. I wish he had let me know he wasn't coming," she muttered more to herself than to the women.

Sally broke into a spontaneous smile. It would be just fine with Sally if Eric Ferris never attended another Horticultural Writers meeting. Apparently of the same mind, Katie caught her eye and smiled conspiratorially. Sally decided to forgive Katie for her "harem costume" remark and grinned back. They boarded the bus together in a glow of mutual bonhomie.

They found an empty seat directly in front of Marcus Tydings, who was sitting alone. Gorgeous Marcus Tydings! He was breathtakingly handsome...and unmarried or so the gossip had it. Sally turned around to face him. Katie introduced her. Marcus responded, producing a couple of cards so swiftly, it appeared to be slight of hand.

"Wow. Do you make things disappear, too?" Sally asked.

Marcus stared at her, a look of horror on his handsome face.

"I mean," Sally said quickly. "You know...like magic," she said, handing him her card. "You were really, really quick with your card. I mean, well...Never mind. Just a joke!" Embarrassed, Sally studied the card he had given her. Next to her, Katie writhed and jostled Sally as she hauled up her purse from the floor and rifled through it for one of her own cards to give Marcus.

"I got new cards. I know they're here somewhere." She rifled through the bulky bag. "Damn! Can't find them. This purse is like a dryer. It eats things!" Katie abandoned her search. "Sorry."

Marcus' card was the most beautiful and simple one Sally had ever seen. She rubbed it between her thumb and pointer. It was soft enough to suggest hand-made paper, but stiff enough not to feel flimsy. Next to a photo, or drawing—in the dim light on the bus, she couldn't tell– of a deep red hellebore flower it read: "Marcus Tydings, Esq.,

Extraordinary Hellebores." There was a website and a phone number. No address.

"This is a beautiful card. And this hellebore is so unusual with those pointy petals. It looks like a poinsettia," Sally gushed. Marcus grinned disarmingly.

"I specialize in hellebores," said Marcus, "that are extraordinary. I've named the one on my card 'Joel Poinsett'."

"Isn't that..." mused Sally.

"The guy who found the poinsettia," blurted Katie.

"Right," said Marcus. "He was an ambassador from the US to Mexico. And a botanist. He found the poinsettia—*Euphorbia pulcherrima*—and sent it back to his home—which was in South Carolina. The colors were perfect for a Christmas plant and it bloomed at the right time." Marcus smiled a perfect smile. His teeth were straight and white in his tanned face.

"I admire him because he was a Renaissance man," said Marcus quietly. He turned very slightly as if something across the aisle had caught his attention. Both women were rewarded with his stunning profile.

"Wow!" said Sally. "I mean, well, the color of this hellebore is perfect." She held up the card. "Wouldn't it be great if it bloomed at Christmastime?"

"Actually," said Marcus, drawing out his words, "I am very close." Scenting a story as well as a coup for her nursery, Katie sat up to attention.

"How close?" she asked.

"I am hoping to introduce within the next five years—or sooner. Of course, it depends on a number of factors—what I find this spring. I am working on fragrance."

"Fragrance! Oh, be still my heart," enthused Katie. "That's...that's fab! Great!" Katie bounced in her seat. "We could do a great big ol' photo spread next December. Hey, Marcus—how about a little free publicity! It would be fantastic for your nursery."

"Where is your nursery, Marcus?" Sally asked.

"I'm in Pennsylvania." Sally waited to see if any further description was forthcoming. Marcus smiled again displaying fine white teeth that would have qualified him for a teeth whitening commercial.

She waited, smiling. He smiled back at her. Finally, she said, "Pennsylvania's a big state. Are you in the Philadelphia area?"

"No." Marcus shifted in his seat. He smiled indulgently.

"Look," he said conspiratorially, meeting her eyes with a twinkle in his, "for the present, I feel that for the operation of my nursery, but mostly for my personal life I have to…" he paused, searching for the right words. "I guess you could say, I prefer to keep a low profile. Right now, I really don't need or want any publicity. I can live peacefully. I can work without interruptions. I can travel as much as I like–that's something I enjoy doing–without worrying about stock plants that are…invaluable, irreplaceable." Big smile. Perfect white teeth.

"You go on plant hunting expeditions, don't you?" asked Sally. "You were on the trip to the Balkans with Andy and the Taylors."

Marcus'eyes narrowed and his expression cooled a degree. "Yes," he said. "Yes, I was. Katie was also on that trip." He nodded toward Katie. A muscle in his cheek twitched. His face took on a thoughtful expression.

"That was…a very, very sad expedition. As you may know, Tate Adkins suffered a fatal accident on that trip. An excellent breeder." Marcus shook his head. "A great loss." He turned and looked out the window.

"It really makes you wonder if there might not really be a curse on hellebores," he mused.

"Is that what you think, Marcus?" Sally asked. He shrugged.

"As Katie here very well knows," he leveled aqua blue eyes at Katie and then at Sally, who could have swooned, "plant hunting is inherently dangerous. Katie barely escaped a dangerous fall in Slovenia."

"Where we look for new hellebore blood, if you will, the terrain is usually unforgiving," he went on. "The places are remote and not serviced by the kind of supports we take for granted here—rescue squads and emergency rooms."

"You mean, if there had been a rescue squad and an emergency room, Tate might have survived?" Sally was stunned.

"I can't say that. What I mean is that plant hunting takes place in dangerous terrain that is usually far from helicopters and hospitals. Tate Adkins slipped off a steep path that must have been fifty feet above where he landed. I—I got to him first."

32

Look at them all. Snobs and fools! Those breeders who had no time for me in Slovenia are going to have to sit up and pay attention! All of these people who think they are so smart will finally understand that they underestimated me.

Like Tate underestimated me. Back in Slovenia, Tate ignored me until the moment he saw those pink Christmas roses hanging off the mountain. Then, all of a sudden, he was interested in me because he thought I could be useful. All of a sudden, he noticed me because I could help him get what he wanted. He needed me.

So what did he do? He slipped off his backpack and handed it to me without one single word—as if, suddenly, we were big buddy collaborators on this plant acquisition trip. And without one word, he got down on hands and knees and crawled over to a ledge that jutted out over thin air. He lowered one leg down. Real slow. He got the other leg down and sat with one arm on the trail—more for a sense of security than anything else because there was nothing to hold on to. But he kept it there like a security blanket. When he bent over to dig, he looked like a contortionist.

Just watching him so near to that drop off took my breath away. I felt like I was frozen in place. I actually started shaking in sympathy.

Without taking his eyes of the hellebores, he motioned to me with the hand that was not on the trail. I moved a little closer. It was not close enough for him. He pointed to a spot next to the drop off the way you might order a dog. I moved nearer to where he pointed. He saw I was still holding his backpack.

"Put that down!" he actually snapped at me. So I put it down and he snapped again, "Not there!" Then he took a breath. He didn't look at me. He just kept staring at the hellebores like they were keeping him calm. He lowered his voice and said very distinctly like he was talking to a very small, not very bright child,

"Put the pack down on the other side of you and move closer. I'm going to hand you a plant."

So there I was, his minion. I thought about that look on his face. He pitied me. I disgusted him. And now he was treating me like a half-wit servant.

I should have said, "fuck you" and gotten the hell out of there. But I didn't. Instead, I did exactly what he ordered me to do. And I hated myself for following his orders, and for being afraid, but I hated him more.

He was arrogant and, worse, dishonest. He denied his feelings for me. I am sure it was to maintain his precious image.

But did I tell him to fuck himself? No. Like a lackey, I crept a little closer with my hand stretched out as far as it would go. It didn't quite reach. And it was trembling. He looked at my hand with disgust and he gave me a look.

I took a step closer. My legs were shaking, too. I saw him look at them and close his eyes for a second as if praying for someone else to miraculously appear. But there was only me.

33

A stream of horticultural writers exited the buses, passed through the entrance building, and began to traverse the garden that stretched between the entrance building and the vast conservatory.

"Oh look! That's fabulous. Fab-u-lous!" Tiny, feisty Bitsy Kaplan, a horticultural educator from the Philadelphia area known for her exuberance was in the vanguard. Chase, Amy, and Mim followed close behind. Bitsy had put into words what everyone else was thinking.

Most stood as if mesmerized, looking around them at grounds that sparkled with lights. They were a sophisticated—even slightly jaded—group when it came to horticultural splendor. And they were transfixed by what they saw.

Before them, on either side of a broad walkway, a double row of Christmas tree shapes formed from lights illuminated the way. Above the lower row of trees, great oaks and maples had been wrapped with white lights that silhouetted their shapes against the dark sky. In the distance, fountains shot dazzling streams of water into the night air. Above them dangled snowflakes of glittering, white lights.

When they had crossed the grounds and stepped into the conservatory, Chase, Mim, Amy, along with half of the first bus, stopped in their tracks to admire a display of what must have been a thousand poinsettias, half red, half white. In their midst rose winterberries, their leafless stems studded with jewel-like, bright red fruit.

Cameras flashed. A few organized souls pulled out notebooks and recorded the scene for their publications. Mim snapped a series of poinsettia shots. Amy stood still and looked around her, a dreamy smile on her face.

"Gorgeous!" Chase breathed. He reached into a small, neat pouch on his waist and pulled out his digital Minolta. He carefully framed a photo, took aim, held his breath, but just as he was about to snap the scene, someone stepped in front of him. It was Philippa, the British woman.

"Excuse me!" Chase called. There was no response. "Excuse me!" he said as loud as he could without shouting. Bitsy Kaplan and three or four others turned around, but the woman didn't budge. She just stood there, her back to Chase.

"Pippa!" Chase shouted. Immediately, the woman spun around. Her brown eyes were wide and startled. When she saw Chase, her pupils narrowed in recognition. Then, she looked determinedly at the floor and walked swiftly away. Amy, standing next to Chase, tensed. She followed the departing woman with her eyes.

"Did you see that?" Chase asked.

What Mim had seen was Kevin. He had suddenly emerged out of the crowd and hurried after Philippa. If he had noticed Mim, he'd been too intent on catching up to the British woman to acknowledge her. She followed him with her eyes until he disappeared behind a giant palm.

"Did I see what?" Mim asked distractedly.

"I'll go find us a table, okay?" interjected Amy. Before Chase or Mim could reply, Amy turned and headed toward the main part of the conservatory where glass and cutlery sparkled on pristine tables covered with white tablecloths. In the center of each table stood a small, but exceptionally full and brilliant red poinsettia plant in a foil clad pot and tied with a red bow.

For Amy, it had all come together in the instant Benjy Glover had shown his photo of the staff at Withcombe. All the disparate strands of information came together in a single fabric. The woman looked oddly familiar. The photograph at Withcombe Nursery was like one she must have seen among JP's things. It all clicked into place.

When Benjy Glover introduced her, Amy knew, she just knew, that Philippa Reed was the person JP had called "Bichette."

JP had never hidden the fact that he'd had a relationship with a fellow employee at Withcombe. It never bothered her. Why should it? JP was forty when they met. It would have been weird really, if he had not had a relationship before he met her. And in the one or two times he had come anywhere near to mentioning it, Amy knew that the woman had done something that alienated him during the time they worked at Withcombe.

What she had never imagined was that his previous lover had been so beautiful. Now that she saw her, Amy wondered if the part about the woman's being repulsive might have been wishful thinking? She had turned this idea around in her mind many times before. As always she came to the same conclusion. No, it wasn't wishful thinking. It was something else. JP had communicated as much with his mobile face and hands as with his words. Amy's impression had been formed over their two years together, not by words but by expressions and gestures.

But that was all before Amy had seen Philippa—before she had seen what a beauty Philippa was. Is that why *she* had been the last word on his lips? And now it flashed before her: JP lying on the floor. His eyes were wide open but not seeing Amy. He was staring at the door and calling out over and over, "Bichette, Bichette" as if inviting the woman to come in.

At this terrible memory, a wave of nausea washed over Amy. She lurched to the nearest table and bent over it, gripping it so hard her knuckles turned white and the poinsettia in its glittering wrapping trembled in the center of the table.

Then the worst of it passed and she lowered herself into a chair and tried to remember what Dr. Garvey said. Her grief counselor was the only one she could talk to about it. She told Amy that it is part of the physical process of dying when people remember birthdays that took place a half century before or call out for the companions of their school days. Even so, it tore her apart that his last words as she knelt over him had not been "Aimee, Aimee."

And now that Amy saw Philippa, she thought that maybe it was too hard to forget such a beautiful woman. She remembered the whistles and catcalls Philippa got when she walked onto the stage. Philippa was beautiful. She was tiny and delicate.

Amy was five foot eight. That was only an inch shorter than JP.

"She answered to her name," Chase broadcasted so that people turned around. "I called her 'Pippa' and she turned around!" He was oblivious to the stares of the horticultural writers. "That proves it!"

Proves what? Mim searched her mind for what exactly it proved. Chase turned back to the display of poinsettias and winterberry and raised his camera.

Cursing what was becoming a less-than-phenomenal short-term memory, she asked Chase, "Tell me again. What does it prove? And how do you know that woman?" Chase gave Mim a chiding you-weren't-listening look and fired off three quick photos before answering. Then he lowered his camera and looked at Mim.

"She's the one I told you about—the one on the flight to London," he answered petulantly. He pressed a button on the back of his camera. It sounded its closing ding dong and was silent.

"And, as I said, I don't really *know* her. She's just someone I met on the plane–on the flight to Heathrow when I went to London." Chase looked down at his camera. "No point in putting it in its case," he muttered to himself. Then he turned to Mim, "At first I wasn't sure. She looked just like the woman I sat next to, but her hair is a different color. The woman on the plane had carrot red hair. So I thought maybe she was just someone who looked a lot like the woman on the plane."

"I checked her hair," he said triumphantly. "It isn't hard to see the top of her head. Red roots! She's got red roots! I'm positive it's the same person! Have you seen her eyes?"

"Yes," said Mim. "They are remarkable."

"Who's the guy from Glovers Gardens?"

"Benjy Glover."

"Well, he nailed her when he introduced her. He said, 'She's got the eyes of a doe!'"

"Yes," said Mim, thinking, 'the eyes of a doe'. A doe. The description triggered the same sense of relevance it had earlier when Benjy Glover had introduced Phillipa during his lecture. She searched her mind and, again, came up empty.

She sighed as she paused to examine a bunch of winterberry. The stems were tightly packed with the biggest, reddest berries she had ever seen. Chase glanced at it, but was now too engrossed in his story to pay attention to the variations in varieties of winterberry. They moved back so that those waiting behind might get close to the display to photograph it. They began walking. After a few steps, Chase stopped abruptly.

"On the plane—she sat next to me—she told me that her name was Pippa. And you saw how she answered to that name didn't you? She turned around when I said 'Pippa'," Chase concluded with a note of surprised triumph in his voice. He straightened the pouch at his waist and now replaced the camera.

"Now I'm sure she's the same person!" Chase said.

"Chase," said Mim, "her name is Philippa. Maybe she thought when you said 'Pippa' that you were saying 'Philippa'."

"How do you know her name?"

"I was right behind her at reception. I heard her say her name. And Benjy introduced her..."

"Maybe Pippa is a nickname," interrupted Chase stubbornly. "It's got to be because it doesn't sound like a real name," said Chase, dismissing the possibility that Philippa was not the Pippa he'd met on the plane.

"Chase, when Benjy Glover introduced her as Philippa Reed, he also said this was her first time in...." Again, Chase didn't let Mim finish.

"I *know* that she was sitting next to me on the plane!" he insisted. "You know how some people get real chatty when they're nervous? Well, she couldn't stop fidgeting and she chatted all night. I had a book with me. I don't think I ever opened it. I think she was very nervous about flying. She told me she had been an *au pair* for a family in Philadelphia."

"Philadelphia? But didn't you fly out of Washington?"

"Yep. Dulles. She did too. Said she had come down to Washington for a day of sightseeing before flying home."

Mim was listening with half her brain. The other part was still trying to connect with Glover's description of Philippa. She kept thinking, 'the eyes of a doe.' What was so significant about that?

"She told me her name was Pippa. And then the stewardess called her—Miss something hyphenated. Began with a 'P'," Chase said. "I just remember thinking it sounded very English."

"Hyphenated? Was part of it 'Reed'?"

"I don't remember."

"Benjy introduced her as Philippa Reed."

"I don't remember her last name. But I know it's her. It's Pippa," Chase mulishly concluded. They started to walk toward the main section of the conservatory where tables had been set up for the dinner.

"She said she was an *au pair*?"

"Yes. And not to be snotty," said Chase, lowering his voice, "doesn't she look the part? I mean, she's a young, very pretty woman who's—well, actually, she *is* a bit over-dressed," he said. "She wants to see a bit of the world before she gets married and settles down." Chase and Mim stepped to one side of the aisle to let a speedier group of horticultural writers by.

"Ouch! That's a bit sexist, isn't it? That woman is a plant breeder. She worked at Withcombe Nursery, one of the finest in the world!"

"I know, I know, but…." Chase paused to find the right words. "That doesn't seem right either. She just doesn't seem right here. She doesn't seem…she's too…"

"Young? Pretty?" offered Mim.

"Yes, that and too…flighty, too un-serious to be a breeder," concluded Chase.

At that moment, Philippa and Kevin in animated conversation, crossed in front of them, oblivious to their presence. The pair was making their way through the dining room, apparently looking for a table. Chase and Mim watched as Kevin would gesture toward a table and Philippa would reject it and move on, her head thrown back in laughter.

"I rest my case!" said Chase.

34

Amy sat alone at a table on the outskirts of the great room. It nestled among great silver urns that supported Christmas trees, trimmed in silver and pearly white. It was private, but offered a direct sight line to the podium where the after dinner speaker would hold forth. She had draped her jacket across one chair, a scarf across another and laid her handbag on the table in front of a third place.

"Good job, Amy," said Chase, sliding into the chair next to her. He unsnapped the camera bag around his waist. "*Mon dieu* this is awkward. And, compared to what some people are lugging around…! I could never be a photographer."

"What are you going to do with your photos?" asked Mim. Most of the people here would use photos in their publications. Chase was a floral designer and not associated with a magazine or newspaper.

"Client education. I'm putting together a brochure. I want my clients to see the possibilities. I am so very tired," he sighed, "of being asked to do Christmas arrangements of pine and baby's breath tied up in red ribbons!" He rolled his eyes. "That's what they all ask for. I can't work that way! I need to be free to express myself creatively."

Mim thought of the bunches of baby's breath she bought every year to add to arrangements of pine and other evergreens cut from the garden. To these, she added red ribbon. She did the same thing every year. Maybe Chase had a point.

Chase had a reputation for designing with refreshing and unusual material. People loved his work. Now looking around, she agreed that there were endless and unusual possibilities for holiday decorations. Near their table was a bed with a ground cover of crisply variegated white and green sedge that looked like it was striped with snow. In the center of the bed ran a row of winterberries, heavily laden with candy-red fruits. Utterly simple and stunning.

That gave Mim an idea. She looked at her watch. By the look it–the waiters and waitresses who had begun serving at the far end of the great room–it would be at least ten minutes before their dinners would be served.

"Would you excuse me?" she asked Chase and Amy. "I'm going to get some photos of holiday arrangements with unusual material. Unusual combinations. Wouldn't that be great for my gardening column? Be back in a flash."

Mim picked up her camera and went back to the entrance where she had seen an exhibit of winterberries and red osier dogwood stems. She had used winterberry in arrangements, but never the red dogwood stems.

She examined the dogwood stems. They were striking in their simplicity. Some were a deep maroon and others a reddish-salmon color. Then she thought about Awful Phyllis, the editor. Where Mim saw brilliant color and clean lines, Phyllis would see sticks. To Phyllis, a garden column had to be about flowers—preferably big red ones. Phyllis could not possibly last at the magazine forever, but, in the meantime, maybe Mim could find some flowers for the foreground.

Mim moved around the display. Bonanza! There were dozens of big, red poinsettias. She squatted and aimed her camera to catch a perfect poinsettia flower in the foreground. Filling the background, in focus, was a spray of brilliant red dogwood stems. Behind them were other stems— salmon, maroon, and cherry red—all hazily out of focus. The effect was stunning.

She snapped several shots, then, for an even better angle, she sat on the floor. Her black knit trousers were supposed to be washable wool. She hoped this was true. She took four more photos. Then, still sitting on the floor, grateful for digital photography, she paused to review them.

"Here!" Mim heard a male voice say in a harsh whisper.

"He can see us!" A female voice, protesting, agitated.

"No, he can't." It was the man again. "I need it. Can you get it?"

"Marcus, I promised! He has already seen it."

Marcus? Did she mean Tydings? Mim sat still as stone. She couldn't see who it was and she realized that whoever it was couldn't see her.

She thought about standing up and announcing her presence, but her curiosity won out. She stayed perfectly still with camera aimed, should the pair happen to move around the display.

"Trust me. He'll never know." The words were dismissive. "For Christ's sake, they all look alike. He will *never* know."

"I have got to go. Kevin is waiting." The "got" spoken crisply, without the broad, drawn-out American "o" clinched it. British.

"Get it for me! Please! I need it."

Mim caught sight of Philippa Reed as she clacked back on spike heels to the part of the conservatory where the dinner was being served. Mim sat still and waited for the man she guessed was Marcus Tydings to walk away. She waited for some minutes. No sound. Perhaps he had already gone. She was about to get up when she heard movement on the other side of the display. She saw Marcus Tydings saunter toward the tables and the crowd of horticultural writers. Waiters were moving about the tables, serving the dinner.

When Mim got back to their table, she found Chase sitting with Sally.

"Where's Amy?"

"She's practicing her presentation for tomorrow..." began Sally.

"Margaret kidnapped her," interjected Chase.

"Where are they practicing?" asked Mim, looking around the room for a likely place.

"Not here," said Sally dryly.

"Back at the hotel," said Chase, enunciating each word, "with that bitch."

"At the hotel!" Mim was amazed. She looked at Amy's place. "We haven't even eaten yet."

"I know! Amy and I tried all day to have Margaret watch Amy run through her photos. Every time Amy asked her, Margaret said she was too busy," said Sally with rising indignation. "She couldn't be bothered today, so she takes Amy away tonight. Before dinner! If it had been me, I wouldn't have gone."

"How did they get back to the hotel?" asked Mim, thinking Amy would go anywhere and jump through any hoops to show JP's photos. But this was too much. Margaret took herself far too seriously and her officious behavior was getting ridiculous.

"Apparently," said Chase, "Margaret drove instead of taking the bus."

Mim stewed. Amy, in her grief, had dragged herself to the conference to carry on for JP. And Margaret! From the getgo, Margaret had done nothing but make it difficult for Amy. She had not bothered to make herself available to go through Amy's presentation. In fact, she had been quite unavailable. Until tonight!

She took Amy away from the dinner back to the hotel where she could badger her with no one around for moral support. Amy didn't even get to eat her dinner!

Margaret's behavior went beyond being uptight. It didn't make sense…unless whatever had caused her to freeze on stage yesterday was still bothering her. Margaret had been utterly unable to speak for a minute or two right before Glover's talk. The tension in the audience had been palpable as it waited for her to begin speaking. Perhaps previewing Amy's talk was just a good excuse to absent herself from speaking responsibilities tonight? Maybe Margaret feared another attack of stage fright.

If it was stage fright. Considering how she seemed to have enjoyed being on stage earlier in the day, that seemed unlikely.

Whatever caused her to freeze in front of the audience this afternoon had to be something else. It could have been something Margaret saw in the moments she stood on stage facing the audience.

Marcus Tydings had sauntered down the aisle to his seat in the front row. Rose Redfern, too, had returned to her seat right about the time that Margaret froze. And Eric Ferris. He was sitting right in front of Margaret. Was he sleeping? She didn't think that would bother her. Later, when he did fall asleep, everybody else had found it funny. His loud snoring had been taken as just one more incidence of Ferris's typically outrageous behavior.

Whether it was Ferris or Marcus Tydings or Rose Redfern, Mim bet that someone or something had spooked Margaret in the moments before Glover's talk.

After the talk Margaret seemed to have recovered. She had carried on, with less enthusiasm, but she had carried on. It hadn't been stage fright that kept Margaret from the dinner at Longwood. And Amy.

35

"Mind if we sit here?" asked a tall blonde woman standing next to a dark haired man whose height she topped by several inches. Lin Baldwin and her partner John Beam!

"Hi! Lin! John! Of course! Please sit down! We thought you weren't coming," said Mim, belatedly remembering the reason Lin and John hadn't been at the conference. "How is your mother? We were so sorry to hear of her illness."

"Mom is much better. And stable. Thank heavens!" Lin and John sat down.

"It was Lin's mother who insisted that we come to the dinner tonight," said John, looking fondly at Lin. "I think she got a little tired of Lin hovering over her."

Sally knew Lin and John well, but Mim introduced Chase.

"The lectures have been fantastic! I just wish that I could have attended all of the concurrent sessions. You and Margaret have done a terrific job lining up speakers!" Mim said sincerely.

"Well, we were pleased to be able to include so many experts in the field at this conference. In fact, we were amazed that we got as many as we did," Lin said with evident satisfaction. "Of course, we were sorry not to have Dave Hawkins speak. He has such a busy schedule. We couldn't find a time when he had a free weekend that overlapped with everyone else." Lin looked up and adjusted her glasses. Apparently recognizing someone scanning the tables for a place to sit, she motioned him over. It was Barney Staples.

Chase leaned over to Mim and whispered, "Now, that is eye candy. Alas, of the wrong persuasion. Not as pretty as the cowboy, though. Hmm, wonder where he's sitting." Chase began scanning the room.

"What cowboy?" Mim asked.

"Have you seen him?"

"Chase, I have no idea who you're talking about."

"The drop dead gay man who came into the restaurant last night and sat with Pippa. He wears cowboy boots! And tinted contact lenses."

"You mean Marcus Tydings. Tinted contact lenses! And how do you know he's gay?" Chase just looked at Mim and rolled his eyes.

Mim wanted to ask Chase about the tinted contact lenses, but at that moment Barney Staples arrived at the table. Barney stood talking to John Beam. She remembered that they had worked together at Delaware Hort. Lin leaned over to Mim and gestured to the three still-unreserved seats.

"Gosh, I didn't think," muttered Lin to herself. "Are you saving these for somebody?" she whispered. Mim caught Sally's eye and looked at Chase. Both shook their heads.

"No," said Mim.

"Have a seat Barney," Lin called out jovially.

As soon as Barney sat down, two more horticultural writers appeared and took the remaining places.

Mim heard them ask Barney about his trip to the Balkans. The table was large, the noise level in the room was high, and she had to strain to hear. She heard something like "reason for going." Most of Barney's response was too low to hear. She made out "stock plants." Lin Baldwin, who was sitting closer, stood up.

"Barney has retired from academia." She raised her wine glass. The others followed suit. "Barney is starting a hellebore nursery. He brought back some wonderful hellebores from the Balkans. Here's to Barney and Staples Hellebores!"

Mim froze. Were some of Barney's new stock plants the hellebores that Tate collected?

After the toast, Barney was engaged in a conversation that Mim couldn't hear. By this time, everyone had drunk at least one glass of wine and the noise level in the vast room had escalated to a roar.

It was such that Chase could speak to Mim in a normal tone without being overheard. Sally, on his other side was deep in conversation with John Beam.

"Do you know what I heard?" Chase began slyly. "Our distinguished Brit has an interesting past!" Chase bent closer to Mim's ear. "He's illegitimate." Mim gave Chase a look.

"Not his fault, certainly."

"Mim, my dear. That is not the point!"

"What is?"

"Who his mother was!"

"And that would be...?"

"First, let me put this in perspective," said Chase. "You are doubtless aware of the superstition swirling around hellebores?"

"*Ad nauseum*, actually. You speak of 'the curse of the hellebores'.."

"Well," Chase paused dramatically, "his mother was the one who started it. She was a famous hellebore breeder who was murdered. Maryann Peterson."

"Marion Petersfield?"

"Yes—that's her name! He was her love child. Isn't that delicious?" Chase squirmed with delight. Mim looked over to where Barney sat. His eyes met hers. She nodded to him, and looked away, feeling a combination of guilty blush and scalp prickle.

She sat still as stone. When she didn't react, Chase examined her face. He looked clearly disappointed at her reaction.

All she felt was mental nausea. There were too many coincidences and too many deaths and no good explanations.

"How come his name is Staples?" she finally asked.

"He was adopted by an aunt and uncle. He took their name."

"How did you find out all of this?"

"I am a shameless eavesdropper. My information is the best—I got it directly from the horse's mouth. I sat behind Staples and Glover at lunch. Glover was badgering him. He kept asking 'wasn't he related' because 'he was the spitting image' of Maryann whatsername. Staples finally spilled his guts."

Lin glanced at her watch. "Good heavens! It's 8:00. I'm on in fifteen minutes. I'm supposed to stand in for Margaret tonight. She isn't feeling well. I wish I was here earlier to help her out." She picked up her purse and rose from the table.

"I'd better stop at the ladies' room first," Lin said. Mim stood up, too.

"I'll go with you. Sally?" Mim asked. Sally shook her head.

As Mim followed Lin who was walking swiftly, weaving between tables, she asked, "Did you say Margaret wasn't feeling well?"

"She's got the curse," said Lin. Lin bent toward Mim and said conspiratorially, "she's been having problems. She was doubled over at the hellebore society meeting," Lin paused. "Could be the beginnings of menopause."

"Did you know that she took Amy Tomczyk back to the hotel with her to preview Amy's program?" Lin stopped walking. She furrowed her brow.

"Are you sure?" Lin looked at her watch. "I talked with her not an hour ago. She said she had terrible cramps."

"Well, maybe she felt dreadful and wanted to make someone else suffer," Mim said uncharitably. "Margaret took Amy away from the conference to preview her program because she was too busy to look over Amy's program today. Margaret insisted that Amy go with her back to the hotel so they could go through it together."

"But...." Whatever Lin was going to say died on her lips. She frowned and walked more slowly toward the ladies room.

"What do you think of Barney?" asked Lin as they stood side by side, washing their hands.

Mim thought about what Chase had said. Barney was the love child of Marion Petersfield. Did that mean his father was Wilson McCoy? Or... someone else? Perhaps if the father had been someone else, that could be the reason for their split and the curse idea.

She wouldn't think twice about someone's being illegitimate. Being a 'love child' ought to have a certain cachet. Yet she couldn't help associating him with—not a curse exactly—but something that was dark and ugly.

From the moment she stepped on the train, the notion of a curse on hellebores kept raising its ugly head. She didn't find it titillating and she didn't believe in curses. It was simply that she associated it with death. And the death that mattered to her was Tate's. Lin was staring at Mim's reflection in the mirror.

"I don't know him well enough to make any kind of judgment," Mim said truthfully. "Katie Hiscock said he was in the midst of a divorce."

"Yes, that's true," Lin said. She turned to face Mim and smiled broadly. "He's a really nice guy, you know. And he asked all about you."

Lin went off to fulfill her role as conference director in Margaret's absence. Mim returned to the table to find Chase gone. Perhaps he had gone off to find more enthusiastic ears for his sensational gossip. Across the table, Barney was talking with John Beam. She heard snatches of team and player's names. Mim moved over into Chase's seat, the better to talk with Sally, although, at first, they sat in silence for several minutes. Then Sally came to life.

"I heard the weirdest thing," she said suddenly. Mim just looked at her. She wasn't sure she wanted to hear about anything else that was weird.

"When I went back for my book, I decided to take the stairs down. I thought it would be faster. I opened the door to the stairs and I heard someone coming down ...." Sally leaned closer to Mim and lowered her voice.

"I heard someone say, 'he's going to sleep for a very long time'." Mim's expression must have been unsatisfactorily ho hum, because Sally retorted, "But it was the way it was said. Mean and kind of angry."

"Who was it?" Mim asked sensibly. "And who were they talking about?"

"I'm not sure, but...." Sally paused.

"But who do you think?" Mim asked.

"Well, when I got down to the lobby, whoever it was had already gone outside. Then when I went outside, Rose Redfern turned around and looked right at me. I mean, right *at* me. She gave me this, this *evil* look. Like she knew I was the one on the stairs and heard what she said." Mim could well imagine Rose's look.

"Did she say anything?"

"No. But when I got on the bus, she gave me another look."

36

Dinner was over. Sated diners sat more quietly than before. They were drinking de-caf and waiting for the after dinner speaker to begin

"Are you going to eat that trifle?" Sally asked Mim.

"Hello? Hello Everybody!" boomed a voice over a loudspeaker. Mim looked up and recognized Perry Ricketts, the after dinner speaker. The brochure had described him as "plantsman extraordinaire." He was standing in front of a microphone while behind him two waiters were setting up a screen. Mim checked her phone. It was ten past eight. All around them, people dutifully scooted their chairs around to face the point where Ricketts was standing at a podium.

"I guess I'm going to have to introduce myself," Ricketts announced. "Margaret Stemple had an emergency," suddenly his voice boomed. Those seated at the tables immediately around him gestured furiously for him to turn down the sound.

As Ricketts bent over the podium, adjusting the sound, the light illuminated the tonsure of his white hair, fine as dandelion down, a luminous halo around his solid, shiney bald pate. He looked up and asked only half jokingly, "Where's Margaret when you need her? How's this?" Nods of approval greeted the more modulated level of sound.

Lin hurried to his side. They conferred for a moment. Then Ricketts airily waved Lin away. In spite of what he said about needing Margaret, he didn't need the help of her stand-in.

Belatedly registering Sally's request for the trifle, Mim pushed the little compote toward her.

"Here, have it! I'm not hungry." Mim said. She wasn't hungry; she was annoyed all over again at Margaret for taking Amy away.

Mim noticed that while she was still facing the table, all around her, people had adjusted their chairs to face the speaker. Absently, she turned her chair toward the speaker, but her thoughts were still on Margaret's strange behavior.

The alteration in Margaret's demeanor had begun with something that happened either before or during Andy Toll's presentation. What could have spooked her so? Immediately, Eric Ferris–front row center— sprang to mind.

Mim could imagine him stretching and yawning ostentatiously before falling asleep. But that didn't strike Mim as particularly threatening.

Then there was Marcus Tydings. Mim was willing to bet that Margaret was sweet on him. Had he said something to her? Whatever had happened, Margaret was back at the hotel, ostensibly tutoring Amy, but more likely licking her wounds and gathering strength for tomorrow.

Mim politely turned her attention to what was now a little makeshift stage with screen, podium, projector sending forth a beam of white light, and Perry Ricketts. He was a well-known, much feted horticulturist. His business cards read: "Perry Ricketts, PhD. All things horticultural," which Mim interpreted as she was no doubt intended to as "omniscient grand master of horticulture." Some in the horticultural world thought of him as "pompous Perry" or somewhat less delicately simply as "Pricketts."

He was a member, but kept his distance from society meetings and he did not hobnob with other members. He was a good speaker and photographer, but it was hard to want to give him his due because he was so terribly sanctimonious.

Just enjoy it, she commanded herself. His presentation would be beautiful photos of beautiful gardens. That would be just the soothing balm she needed.

Perry Ricketts never cursed. Curse words were what ignorant people used because their vocabularies were not sufficiently rich to express themselves meaningfully. But if he were to curse, he would surely have done so tonight. He was beyond vexed. As he set up his computer and presentation, he reviewed all of the reasons why he should not have agreed to speak to this group.

In spite of the fact that he was a member in good standing– he sent in the eighty dollars every year to pay for a membership as a business expense that gave him exposure on the website–the Horticultural Writers Society had balked at his fee. Furthermore, they had not expected to pay his travel expenses because he lived in downtown Philadelphia, just a few blocks from the hotel. Margaret, the director, had offered to allow him to ride on the bus. The bus!

Then, *two days ago*, she had telephoned and reminded him to speak on "something relevant" to hellebores. Hellebores! As if sustainable gardening, a subject on which he was the acknowledged international expert, were not of supreme relevance in every area of gardening!

But tonight was the final indignity. In addition to having to bring his personal projector because the one belonging to this pathetic organization had needed repair, Margaret was not here. She had assured him she would be available to assist him. He checked the time. A mere fifty-five minutes ago, she had appeared before him and simply announced that she had an emergency. You *are* an experienced speaker, she had reminded him. Then she left. Simply left him alone to carry on by himself.

Best to get on with it and put it behind him. He checked the microphone, stood up straight, and began.

"Before I start, I've got a question for you," he moved away from the podium with microphone in hand. He was jacketless in a white shirt and bow tie. His trousers were a black so deep, they looked like velvet. His chest and arms were trim and rather slight in contrast to large hips.

"How many of you do not—*do not*—have a television in your home?" A scattering of hands fluttered above the tables. Ricketts scanned the room from one end to the other.

"What's that supposed to mean?" asked Sally who had inhaled the trifle. She rose and picked up her camera bag. "There's something I forgot to get. Be back soon." She walked away quickly.

Chase appeared, but vacillated about where to sit until a pristine trifle lured him across the table. Mim watched Chase gleefully commandeer the extra dessert. After a couple of bites, he began twitching his eyebrows and rolling his eyes. With mild alarm, Mim wondered if Chase were suffering a sugar high. Then she realized he was trying to signal to her. She turned to see Barney standing next to her chair.

"I was hoping to have a chance to speak with you," Barney softly said. And I with you, thought Mim. "Maybe after Perry's talk?"

"Sure," said Mim. Barney smiled and walked across the room toward the doors. Apparently he wasn't going to spend the next forty minutes listening to Perry Ricketts either.

"Not bad. Not bad," Ricketts said, counting the hands of the television-less Pointing to a gray haired woman sitting directly in front of him, he asked, "how long has it been—how long have you been clean?" Did he say "clean"?

The woman, with a mop of curly gray hair and what looked more like the body of a twelve year old than a mature woman, stood up. Standing, she scarcely topped the heads of those seated around her.

"Three years. It's been three years! It broke and I just never got around to getting another one," she said, raising a fist, gray panther style. Over a white satin blouse, she was wearing a navy velvet jumper that looked like it came from the pre-teen department. There were hearty cheers from the audience.

Ricketts held up one hand, "That's a great start. A great start!" Not bad for horticultural writers.

The clapping died out. As the woman sat down, she disappeared from Mim's view, but Mim got a good look at her table mates. Marcus Tydings was at the table, but had pulled his chair so far out that making any kind of conversation would be impossible. Bitsy Kaplan was chatting with Katie Hiscock over the space he had vacated. When the head across from them moved, Benjy Glover came into view. Suddenly, like schoolchildren caught talking in class, they stopped and turned to face Ricketts.

In the posture of an evangelist, he was gripping the podium with both hands. He scanned the audience, now silent and waiting for the important thing he was about to say.

"I have been clean," here he paused for effect. "No television whatsoever! For twenty years!" There was a trickle of polite applause. A number of garden writers gave each other quizzical looks.

"I guess he's telling us that if we have TVs we're ignoramouses, thought Mim, looking ruefully at the empty dessert plate. She wished now she hadn't been so generous. Sighing, she looked around and spotted Sally, camera and tripod in tow, making her way around the tables with difficulty now that everyone had adjusted their chairs to face the podium.

"What I want to know is if I get rid of my TV, will I be saved?" asked Sally, as she returned to the table. Still standing, she began to remove her camera from the tripod.

"Amen," said a voice from a neighboring table that was echoed back in stage whispers.

Sally plopped into a chair. Deftly, she folded the tripod and stashed it, along with her bag, under the table.

Ricketts had been espousing a "dichotomy of untrammeled nature and minimal human intervention" in reverent tones for perhaps five minutes when Mim idly glanced around and saw Philippa gazing fixedly across the room. Mim followed the direction of her gaze and found Marcus Tydings, who was returning the attention. Mim looked away quickly, conscious of having stumbled upon what seemed at once intimate and, she analyzed her impression, clandestine.

Why clandestine? And what was Philippa to *get* for Marcus that *he* couldn't find out about. Who was "he"?

Ricketts had advanced to a photo that showed a mossy path leading between tall white birches. At the base of the trees was a carpet of blood root. Gorgeous, thought Mim. As she shifted in her chair to get a better look, she saw Kevin incline his head toward Philippa to say something. Philippa pulled her gaze away from Tydings as if her eyes were taffy. Slowly and with reluctance showing in every cell of her body, she bent toward Kevin to hear what he was saying.

Mim looked back at Marcus Tydings. His eyes were fixed on Philippa. His face was a blank. When Mim turned back to Kevin and Philippa, she saw that although Philippa leaned toward Kevin to hear what he was saying, she was smiling across the room at Marcus. Kevin appeared unaware of the exchange.

That was quick. Last night in the restaurant, they had appeared to be perfect strangers. The progress of their relationship had been lightening fast. Then she remembered how their apparent meeting in the restaurant had reminded her of mimes.

After Marcus entered the restaurant, he had scanned the room and found Philippa sitting alone. He had paused at her table and appeared to introduce himself and ask her permission to sit there. She had nodded her head and extended a hand to be shaken. Their gestures had been a little too clear.

She was willing to bet that Marcus and Philippa knew each other very well. For whatever reason, they wanted to appear to be strangers.

For all of Chase's assumption that Philippa was an airhead, Mim thought there might be more to the British woman than met the eye.

Chase insisted that Philippa sat next to him on a flight to London two weeks ago. That she said she had been an *au pair*, named Pippa, with a hyphenated surname. If that was true and Philippa/Pippa had been on that flight, why was her name different now? And why did she let it be known that this was her first trip to the States? That's what Glover had said. Her first trip.

If Chase was right, it would mean that Philippa had been here two weeks ago. Why would she go to the trouble of returning to England and then coming back again in the course of three weeks? It was more reasonable that Chase was mistaken.

Then again, there was her connection to JP. Glover had shown a group shot taken at Withcombe that showed both JP and Philippa. They had both worked at Withcombe until Marion Petersfield had been murdered. Philippa was JP's lover. Amy said that Philippa had done something that repulsed JP.

A sudden thought struck Mim. Marion Petersfield had been brutally murdered. If JP had been repulsed by something that Philippa had done, could it have something to do with murder? Her imagination was overheating. If JP were anything like Tate, he would never have allowed a murderer to go free. Better to concentrate on more mundane questions. Like why was Philippa flirting with Kevin while she was making eyes at Marcus?

Ricketts had reached the culmination of his presentation. In spite of the fact that they were horticultural writers, they were responding to his photos. In fact, as he looked out at the audience, he saw that he had them in his hand. He advanced to the next photo. What must have been a thousand clumps of blood root bloomed on a mossy hill. It was a stunning photo—one of his best. He checked to see what the reaction was. Transfixed expressions. He rewarded their interest with information about the moss and the bloodroot—how ants carried away the seeds for the eliasomes on them.

"Would you please explain that? What is it? Eli-something?" A man speaking from somewhere in the middle of the room. He explained. How each seed had a protuberance called an eliasome that ants found a desirable food source. They carried away the seed to their underground tunnels and, in so doing, planted them and spread out the colony of bloodroot.

He looked up and saw that people were beginning to squirm in their chairs. Quickly, he advanced to the next photo. It was a close-up of self-sown *Houstonia* growing in moss. A hand waved, but the woman didn't wait for him to acknowledge her.

"Could you tell us the common names?" Shouted out rudely, suggesting neglect on his part.

"Bluets or Quaker ladies," he snapped. And with that, the magic that had been building was gone. He forwarded to his next-to-last photograph. It showed the sun backlighting a field of grasses that looked as though they were on fire. Often, this photo drew gasps of awe. Not tonight. He surveyed the crowd. Deadheads. There was a general restlessness that stopped just shy of outright rudeness. Well, not entirely. Directly in front of him, two women were giggling at some private joke. Stupid dolts! Around the room, several people had risen from their tables and were making for the rest rooms. He observed the group in front of him with disgust.

Horticultural writers! Half of them couldn't tell you the difference between monocots and dicots. Make that 95%.

His final inspirational photo was the highpoint of his presentation. Usually, he described how he had designed this part of his garden so that the sun highlighted the grasses early in the morning and, again, late in the afternoon. How the color of the grasses changed from the most delicate of spring greens, how they bloomed in summer, and how they dried to an almond color in winter.

But why throw pearls to swine? He passed it over with a simple, "my garden on a late winter afternoon." Why waste energy on this room full of cretins? Might as well get this over with and get out of here. He forwarded to his last photo. Usually, after the remarks about the grasses, he would conclude with something like, 'that bed of grasses was once two perennial borders. I have simplified my garden to a few strong elements and I find that, for me, less is definitely more.' Not tonight.

"Thank you," he concluded, smiling broadly.

"It's getting late," Ricketts announced, looking at his watch. He wanted it to be over, to be on his way home with the speaker's fee in his pocket. It was a larger one than they had at first offered. He had insisted upon his due.

"How about if we save any questions for tomorrow at breakfast?" he said, thinking, they'll have forgotten by then and I'll be home in bed.

He reminded himself to smile, to be humble, patient and courteous. Tom Frank, the editor from Foresters, was sitting at table six. He inclined his head in a kind of bow. Then Ricketts turned and began dismantling the electronic paraphernalia.

The sound of applause gave way to the din of a hundred thirty garden writers rising from their chairs and the clatter of dishes as the wait staff began clearing the tables.

In Mim's mind's eye, she was still seeing the photos of the moss under birches, of the bluets. And the bloodroot!. How wonderful to preserve a garden's perfect moment! It reminded her of JP's photos and with that thought the glow vanished and was replaced with a flush of annoyance at Margaret Stemple.

It was a shame that Amy couldn't have stayed longer. Mim decided to stop by and check in on Amy when she got back to the hotel. She wanted to make sure Margaret hadn't rattled her.

37

One hundred and thirty horticultural writers rose from their tables generating a roar of conversation that was punctuated by the clack of china and cutlery being gathered up. The wait staff had moved in with less than gracious haste to clear the tables.

During Ricketts's talk, Mim had decided that she could ask Barney about the Balkan trip on the bus ride back to the hotel. With that plan in place, she had lost herself in Ricketts's gorgeous photography and almost forgotten Barney. Now that the show was over, she was thinking about how to start a conversation that would glide effortlessly to the Balkan trip. But Barney was nowhere to be seen. Maybe he was outside. Mim let herself be carried along in the crowd as it moved toward the doors.

Horticultural writers stepped out of the conservatory into cool, balmy air. As they crossed the garden, the small groups that returned to the waiting buses, walked mostly in companionable silence. The high spirits of the earlier evening had mellowed to a comfortable camaraderie.

No one hurried. It was a night that invited lingering. Slowly, very slowly, the horticultural writers ambled through the garden, lingering in the magic of the brilliantly lighted trees and fountains. Here and there, they stopped and formed clumped silhouettes that stood out against the shimmering, dancing water.

Chase reappeared and joined Sally. As they walked ahead, Mim slowed her pace and strayed behind the pair, turning the events of the conference and the evening over in her mind. She stopped beside a pool of fountain jets to watch the dazzling water shoot up into the night sky and hurtle down, sending droplets like tiny comets into the air. Beyond this halo of diamantine lights, an invisible cloud of mist floated outward. It touched her cheeks in a cool, watery caress.

Immediately, as he always did when it rained, she thought of Tate. Tate alone on the mountain in the rain. And with that thought there had always come a punch of pain that took her breath away, and when that pain subsided, the dull ache of loneliness and loss.

But this time, it was different. Instead of ache, the mist was a balm—it felt as if Tate were gently touching her face. She had a profound sense of connection with him. She was filled with a conviction that they were moving together toward …she tried to put a word on it and came up, not entirely satisfactorily, with 'peace'.

She turned away from the dazzling fountain and, momentarily blinded by the lights, walked right into Marcus Tydings.

"Sorry! I didn't see you. The light from the fountain blinded me," she said. Now or never she thought. Seize the day!

"You went on the hellebore expedition to Slovenia, didn't you?" she asked rhetorically.

"You are the second person to ask about that this evening," Marcus answered coolly after a pause. Mim's eyes focused enough to see a wariness in his face. He stepped back slightly away from Mim.

"That's odd," he said.

"Really? It is probably because everyone at this conference is interested in hellebores. Wasn't that expedition primarily a search for hellebores?" she asked in a tone as neutral and disarming as she could muster, but the irony was there and he heard it.

"That's correct," he said, turning away. He seemed to think better of leaving. He faced Mim and spoke.

"The primary focus of that expedition was hellebores and yes, I was on it," he said with both irritation and satisfaction in his voice. "But so were a number of others who are at this conference." His implication was not so much 'why don't you ask them?' as it was solidifying his position as one of their group.

"Andy, the Taylors, Benjy, Barney. Even Margaret, the conference director. They were all there." Mim waited for him to continue. He didn't. She prodded, wincing as she spoke the first words that came to mind.

"I heard there was an accident…?"

"Yes," he quickly answered as if he had been anticipating the question. "Unfortunately, you heard right, one of us," he solemnly said, "Tate Adkins, a horticulturist with the Backenbrook Arboretum, suffered a fatal accident on that trip."

One of *us*, why did it bother her that he put himself in company with Tate? Marcus had been a member of the expedition, after all.

"Did you know Tate?" he asked.

"Yes," Mim answered.

"Plant hunting is inherently dangerous," he shrugged.

"Why is that?" Some of her irritation seeped into the question and she knew immediately that he felt it. He glanced at Mim and half turned.

"Well," he said a little tartly, "for starters, we go to remote and dangerous places ..."

Mim was thinking, *we*! *We* go to dangerous places! She was defensive because Marcus Tydings was usurping what belonged to Tate. But annoyance and irritation would not illicit the information she wanted. She mustered control and asked flirtatiously, "Why do you do it?"

The change in his bearing was instantaneous. It startled her. Apparently Marcus Tydings disliked challenge, but Mim bet he was comfortable with the flirting game. He fixed her with aqua blue eyes that made her think about what Chase had said. Tinted contacts.

"Breeders, like myself—we play a dangerous game," Marcus said holding her eyes. "Hunting for hellebores is even more dangerous than for other plants." As he warmed to the topic, he seemed to warm to Mim. He gazed at the beautifully lighted garden. Now he favored her with a captivating white-toothed smile and those amazing aqua eyes. If his face had a caption, it would read: "Swoon now."

"First of all, the lesser known species grow in the most remote places. Secondly, there are people, many sensible people among us, who think accidents happen because hellebores are cursed," he smiled at her, again flashing white teeth. He turned his aqua-blue eyes on her and looked deeply. Caption: "I'm the James Bond of plant hunters."

"Is that what you think?" Mim asked all innocence. Marcus's smile faded, but Mim now had the sense that now he was enjoying their conversation. He exhaled and looked up at the dark sky. After a pause he spoke.

"Yes. That is what I think," he said with conviction.

"About a curse? You actually think there's a curse?"

"You cannot separate the misfortune that befalls many of us from the kinds of places we go to find hellebores," he answered.

"Well," she said. "You must know. I guess you travel frequently. Have you been on many plant hunting trips?" Tydings looked quickly at Mim and looked away.

"I am always botanizing," he said. He smiled.

"Really!" Mim gushed. "Where do you find your plants?"

"In so many places." He stated it patronizingly and with finality. He started to walk toward the entrance.

"You know what I heard about that trip to the Balkans," she put in quickly. "I heard that Tate Adkins' plants were stolen." Marcus walked on as if he had not heard her.

Mim looked at Marcus's departing form. He had heard her question. Even in the dusky light, she could see his shoulders stiffen as if he were hunching them to ward off a blow. If she had solved the mystery of Tate's stolen plants, it was oddly unsatisfying.

Slowly, she walked toward the entrance, frustrated by the encounter with Tydings. Accusing him would accomplish nothing. She had no proof.

She walked on. Memories of the evening flew at her.

Barney Staples had sought out their table. He wanted to talk. Maybe he could tell her more. She would wait for him by the buses.

Chase, new to the group, but, as usual, already plugged in to the information pipeline, had disturbed her with his gossip about Barney. He was the son of Marion Petersfield. What unbelievable bad luck! Through no fault of his, in her mind, it linked him to ...to something that made her profoundly uneasy.

Why did he want to talk to her? Sally had hinted at romance. Now that she thought about it, the overtures he had made since the beginning of the symposium had more to do with fulfilling some sort of duty than with any romantic notions on his part.

He knew too much about her. And he knew a lot about Tate. Was it possible that he and Tate had become friends in Slovenia? Even if that were true, his command of the facts of her life and Tate's made her deeply uneasy.

With effort, she pushed these thoughts away and looked around. Somewhere among these people slowly returning to the entrance was Kevin. This sophisticated man of the world was inexplicably gaga over Philippa. She simply could not understand Philippa's appeal. But then, she was a woman who judged women by a different standard than men did. Philippa was undeniably beautiful.

It looked like imperturbable Kevin had fallen hard. And it wasn't reciprocated. She thought again of the looks Marcus and Philippa had exchanged during dinner.

Why hide their relationship—if that's what it was? And why did Chase, who usually knew everything about everybody, think Marcus was gay? And if he was gay, what was he doing with Philippa? And why would Philippa eat dinner at Kevin's side when, if looks could be believed, she would prefer to be with Marcus? Maybe she could get Philippa alone.

Mim quickened her pace. A few yards ahead, she caught sight of Sally and Chase as they disappeared into the entrance building. By the time she got to the building, they were through it and out the door on the parking lot side where she caught up to them. Together, Sally, Chase, and Mim joined the large group of horticultural writers waiting to board the first bus. As she moved forward in the throng of those waiting, she felt a tap on her shoulder.

Someone spoke very softly into her left ear.

"Will you meet me in the bar at 10:30?" She recognized the voice and turned only part way around to answer him. Kevin.

"Sure," she agreed. "Ten-thirty," she said, thinking, even as she answered, that she had no idea what time it was currently. When she turned to ask him the time, he had been absorbed into the crowd behind her.

Just as suddenly, Barney was by her side.

"I came in my truck," he said. "How about a ride back to the hotel?"

This scenario was not the one she anticipated and she surprised herself at how utterly and completely dead set she felt against it. Why didn't she want to ride back to the hotel with Barney? The practical, logical part of her thought riding back to the hotel in his truck would be an ideal opportunity to question him about the Balkan trip and hear what he wanted to say, but the intuitive part heard a warning bell ringing dimly in the far reaches of her brain. She decided against it. Several excuses popped into her mind. She could say she had to interview someone on the bus ride back to the hotel. Barney could meet her for breakfast in the morning. She was mentally chiding herself for dereliction of duty when she remembered how often her gut feelings trumped logic. But then logic intervened. What could possibly happen between here and Philadelphia?

"Sure," she said.

38

Under the big lights in the parking lot, Barney's Ford pickup looked black. When they got closer, she saw that it was dark green. It wasn't parked very far from where the buses were standing. Even so, as she walked with him toward the truck and away from the buses and the throng of horticultural writers, Mim felt as if a lifeline were slipping through her fingers.

They walked in silence. Once, she glanced sideways at Barney. His eyes were fixed and his face was grim. He looked as though his thoughts were somewhere far away. It seemed he had forgotten her. However, when they reached the truck, he became politely attentive. He opened her door and made sure she was comfortably seated before closing it. Once behind the wheel, he reminded her to put on her seat belt. Then, with a click, he locked the doors. At that, she felt the hair rise on her neck.

Barney drove confidently—fast, but not too fast. She watched streets, lights, houses fly by. This was not the route the bus had taken to Longwood. Apparently, Barney was taking another route.

"Lin said you are leaving academia and starting a nursery," she said to make conversation. "I guess John Beam was one of your colleagues at Delaware Hort? Will your nursery be your...," she paused, thinking that she couldn't say "main source of income"—too nosey. "Your full time work?" He didn't answer. She waited. He seemed a million miles away.

"Barney?" He glanced at her. His eyes widened.

"I was wondering about your new nursery," she said. He sighed.

"Staples Hellebores is a bit of an overstatement, I'm afraid. What I have are some excellent stock plants growing in the back yard of my soon-to-be former wife's house. I shall have to move them."

"Oh," Mim said. "Sorry. Divorce is pretty awful, isn't it?" She could write a book about it.

"Actually, in my case, it has worked out better than anticipated. So far, it has been quite straightforward. But that is because my wife and I are in complete agreement. We first considered divorce about seven years ago. And then we came to the States and, for a while, the new jobs, the new house in the new country were distractions. It was a relief to get away from England and some … associations there." Mim thought immediately of Marion Petersfield.

"However, for Sandra, my wife, and me, the basic disparities are still there," Barney continued. "You know it was Tate who helped me to, to—I suppose the phrase would be—'to take control of my life'. We hit it off on the Slovenia trip. He was a 'seize the day' sort of person. He encouraged me to do just that."

"I took his advice to heart. I retired from Delaware Hort. I purchased a small acreage for a nursery. I'll build on it later. Right now I'm letting a house nearby. In a way, I am starting a new life."

Barney drove on. For several minutes, neither spoke. Mim looked out the window. All she could see were the black shapes of trees and lights from infrequent houses.

"Are we still in Philadelphia?" Mim asked, wondering at the dark countryside outside the pickup's windows,

"As a matter of fact," Barney smiled over at her, "we're not. We are at my nursery." He slowed the truck, made a turn onto a small road, and pulled into a driveway that stopped abruptly twenty feet in. The headlights illuminated a field. As far as she could see, there was no house, nothing around. And no rows of hellebores. She turned to him testily.

"What you offered was a ride back to the hotel!" He held up a hand to silence her.

"I'm sorry. Very sorry! I have something important to tell you. I simply could not speak of it around all of those people." He turned off the ignition. They sat in darkness. He was silent.

"Barney. I want to go back to the hotel. If you have something to tell me, please do it now!"

"I am afraid that what I will tell you may be…upsetting and, perhaps, unlucky. I've only told one other person…"

"Unlucky? Don't worry," she snapped. "I don't believe in bad luck and curses," she said, feeling for the first time—just for a fraction of a second— that there might, indeed, be something to them. It was this strange place and his odd behavior, she told herself. He was being dramatic. She changed tack.

"Okay. Please tell me what is on your mind," she had meant to ask softly, patiently, to humor him, but the question came out as a command.

"It's about Tate." Mim froze. It was the tone of his voice. She knew this would not be a friendly reminiscence. Her command of herself suddenly slipped away. She tried to say something and nothing came out. When she finally spoke it was in a kind of breathless croak.

"Tell me."

Barney let out a sigh. "I'm not certain exactly where to start," he said. He looked over at her. Even in the dim light, she could see anguish in his face.

"On the Balkan trip. Tate went out that morning—that last morning— by himself. When, when he didn't come back, JP rounded us up—the men—and we went out to look for him. When we...that would be Marcus Tydings and myself—we were the first to reach him—when we located Tate in the place where he had fallen...he was holding, actually he was clutching a glove. Tightly. His fingers were...locked on it," Barney said miserably.

"The others caught us up and, well, we all saw the glove and remarked upon it."

"Katie told me about that," Mim said. Barney slowly nodded his head several times before continuing.

"We carried Tate back to the inn. You must imagine, there was a lot of confusion. A local policeman and his assistant showed up. The owner of the inn became quite emotional. Somehow, in all of that, the glove went missing."

"It was all so very shocking. We were exhausted. And when someone— JP I think—noticed that the glove was missing, we couldn't agree upon the last time we had seen it. We argued about it. Some of us thought that perhaps it had dropped on the ground as we carried Tate back to the inn. JP and I went out to look for it. We didn't find it. Then we thought the police might have taken it, but our attempts at communicating with them were in vain."

Mim sat like a stone, listening. Barney paused and something between a sigh and a sob escaped him.

"I know we did not drop it en route to the inn. And I know that the police didn't take it. I saw the glove later."

"Where?" she breathed.

"Someone had tossed it into the fire, into the fireplace. The inn was heated by wood and there was a very large hearth at one end of the lobby. I saw the glove. It was burning."

"Are you sure that…"

"I recognized it absolutely. I know with certainty it was the same glove." Barney took a deep breath before plunging on. "Because it was one of mine."

Mim felt her blood turn to ice. She sat very still, dumbstruck. Was this some kind of confession?

She looked out at the darkness around the truck. She could make out a very large tree—from its shape, probably an oak. In the distance a light went on—a tiny rectangle of brightness. She realized she was holding her breath waiting for something to happen.

She let it out when Barney started the ignition. He backed out of the driveway, then picked up speed. He had fulfilled his mission and now he wanted it to be over.

"I've thought about this a great deal," he said. "I have no idea how that glove came to be…in Tate's hand. I do not think that he had been wearing it," Barney paused. "I took several pairs along on that trip—I always wear gloves—eczema." He turned his hand palm up, apparently to exhibit the effects of his allergy. In the dim light of the truck's cab, Mim saw nothing but the palm of his extended hand. "I never noticed that a glove was missing until, until after I saw the one that…that was burning."

Mim sat stunned. A glove. Again a glove. The nightmare of the phantom holding up a bloody glove came back to her in vivid detail. Barney was saying something. With effort, she concentrated on what he was saying.

"… Back to my room and checked. Four pairs of gloves had been worn and were soiled. Another four were on top of the dresser in my room. Our group occupied the entire second floor. Nobody locked his door. Anyone could have popped in and taken a pair."

"I don't believe it was Tate." Barney inhaled a long, shuddering breath. He stopped the truck at the stop sign at the end of the small road. He looked over at Mim.

"Why not Tate?" Mim asked.

"Don't know," Barney shook his head. "It doesn't calibrate. Thoroughly out of character, I suppose. Mind you, I didn't know Tate before we went to Slovenia. I got to know him there." He looked at Mim again. "I liked him a lot." He paused for a long moment before continuing.

"I am sorry, but …I felt I had to tell you this. I thought you should know." He stopped speaking, swallowed, and looked determinedly out his window. When he turned back to her he said, "I have run through this over and over again. I have wracked my brain for two years. I thought that there must be some simple, logical reason. Perhaps Dragan—he was the owner of the inn—or his wife had found the glove on the floor and tossed it into the fire. Before we left, I asked him. Dragan spoke English."

"What did he say?"

"He was offended at the idea that I thought he would throw away a person's glove. He was very emphatic. He showed me a basket full of things—hats, gloves, key rings– that had been left behind by other guests."

"I have come to the conclusion that, for whatever reason, the gloves had to be taken from my room by someone in our party. Until later that day, we were the only guests in the inn. Perhaps to cover the theft, whoever took the gloves, threw at least one of them into the fire. But…" Barney looked pleadingly at Mim, "that doesn't explain how Tate came to be holding it. And, I have wondered, if, perhaps…." Barney sighed loudly.

"If what?" Mim braced herself.

"If Tate were not alone on that last day," said Barney miserably.

This last statement hit Mim like an electric shock. A panorama of snow-capped mountains flashed on her mind's eye. Barney's statement was electrifying, but strangely unsurprising.

She turned to her window. Outside was the peaceful night with lighted houses between dark fields. Inside the cab of the truck, wild thoughts spun in her brain. Previously unformed, unexamined, inexplicable notions glommed together in a dark, cancerous growth.

Barney had turned the truck onto a busier road. Now, there were more lights, houses, stores, all looking exactly as they should. She sat motionless.

"I thought you should know this. It's important to know…" She sensed that he was looking over at her. She turned to meet eyes that were full of sadness. "I'm sorry. Nobody else knows," he sighed.

"But, you said you told someone else about it. Who is that?" Mim asked. Barney paused for so long, she thought he hadn't heard. Then he spoke.

"I told JP."

39

Barney insisted upon dropping Mim in front of the hotel before finding a parking place in the hotel lot. Now that he had divulged his information, she thought, it seemed he wanted to get away as quickly as possible. Still dazed from hearing his story, she walked slowly toward the hotel entrance and dropped onto a bench.

A new image rose in her mind's eye: a burning glove. And with that vision, disquieting information. Tate may not have been alone. Not alone. What did that mean? That someone had seen him fall and, for whatever reason, not alerted the others? Or? The alternative was too horrible to contemplate.

She remembered the dream, the bloody glove, the intense, glittering eyes in the phantom's otherwise featureless face. When the nightmares started, she had found those eyes menacing. Was their fierce gaze not so much menacing as beseeching? Was there something she had to do?

With blood drumming in her temples, she watched as the last of the buses now disgorged its passengers. Enjoying the balmy night, horticultural writers ambled slowly toward the hotel. A few stood in small groups talking. Nobody seemed to notice her. Good. Right now, she wanted to be invisible.

A group that included Chase and Sally approached. As she watched, Kevin and Philippa brushed by them. Kevin, who was saying something to Philippa, made eye contact with Chase and Sally and gave a slight nod. Philippa looked straight ahead. As she moved past Chase, who was staring at her with open curiosity, a flicker of impatience passed over her pretty face.

Mim, who never wore a watch, called out to Chase, strolling along beside Sally.

"Do either of you have the time?" she asked in a deliberately casual tone. Chase turned in half a circle before he found Mim in the shadow where she was sitting.

"Mim! I didn't see you! Without consulting his time piece which she knew was a vintage superman watch, he said "nine-fifteen. I checked when we got off the bus." He paused. "Everything okay?

"Fine. I'm just enjoying this warm evening."

"Mim?" Sally was suspicious. "Come have a nightcap with us," she coaxed, walking over to where Mim sat.

"I'm supposed to meet Kevin in a bit, but before that, I'm going to see if Amy is done rehearsing." Mim held up a small bag as she rose to her feet. "She missed dinner. I brought her a doggy bag. Did Margaret say where they would be rehearsing?"

"Probably in the auditorium," Sally suggested. Inside the lobby, the three parted. Chase and Sally headed for the lounge area. Mim continued to the stairs and down to the lower level and the auditorium. It didn't look promising. It looked creepy. The few security lights on in the lower level cast a dismal green light over the corridor.

She had just rounded a corner when she heard footsteps. She stepped back into an alcove and waited, not exactly sure why she had this urge to conceal herself. A moment later, Marcus Tydings walked by. Or almost walked by. Just past her, he turned around and looked directly at her. He flinched. Then, without a word, he hurried on.

Mim's heart was thumping in her chest. She waited a full minute. Then she walked swiftly to the auditorium door, opened it, and peered inside. It was dark. Nobody was showing JP's program in there.

She decided to try Amy's room. There was plenty of time before Mim had to meet Kevin. She would knock very softly in case Amy was sleeping ....

Mim joined those at the elevators. They were an older crowd waiting to return to their rooms to get some sleep. Two elevators came and went before there was room enough for Mim to enter. She got in, flattened herself against the wall, reached out to press five, and waited while the elevator stopped at every floor to disgorge tired hort writers. Finally, it reached Amy's floor.

Amy's room, 515, was indeed directly above hers. She tapped softly on the door. When there was no answer, she tapped again louder.

"Who is it?" Amy's voice sounded tired.

"It's Mim!" The door swung open immediately, as if Amy had been standing right behind it. She was wearing a long, oxford cloth nightshirt. Her eyes were red from crying. She looked wretched.

"Amy! What's the matter?" Mim reached out and took Amy's hand.

"Margaret has canceled JP's talk," Amy glumly announced.

"What! That's ridiculous! Did she see your program?"

"I showed her the first ten or twelve shots and she said that was… enough." Amy's face crumpled. She began to cry. Between sobs, she tried to explain. "With…without JP here…no p…point in it."

"No point in your giving JP's program?" Mim asked. Amy nodded miserably.

"That's outrageous! There is no one better than you to do it," Mim said crisply. "I'll talk to her." Amy shook her head.

"It's too late," she sniffed. "Sh…she's got Andy…and Benjy…a panel discussion."

"You mean she's already got a panel discussion organized for JP's slot?" Mim was furious. "That's outrageous," she said again. "What's the matter with her?" Amy just shook her head. She looked tired and defeated, but calmer. Every now and then a little hiccoughing sob escaped her.

"You must be hungry. You missed dinner," said Mim, handing Amy the doggy bag.

"Thanks, but I'm okay. Not hungry now. Maybe later," she took the bag and put it into a small refrigerator. "I ate all the chocolates."

"Chocolates?" Mim asked hopefully. She had given away her dessert.

"The ones housekeeping leaves on your pillow…I was saving them," Amy said, but seeing Mim's interest, added, "Sorry. I ate them all."

"Gosh, Sally and I didn't get any chocolates on our pillows."

"Really?" asked Amy. "Maybe it's kind of a, you know, a VIP thing for the speakers. Because, you know, this room was free. The speakers got their rooms free."

After Mim left in search of Margaret, Amy lay on the bed. What was she thinking? No way could she take over for JP. Margaret was right. Now Amy didn't want anyone to see her in her failure and shame. In particular, she didn't want Philippa to see her. The plan to give JP's talk had been wrong from beginning to end. But now that her mission was gone, the great weight of her loss came crashing down. She felt utterly miserable and alone.

The room started to spin. Suddenly, she was so tired, she couldn't keep her eyes open. Her mind felt clouded. Her thoughts wandered. Mim was going to try to talk to Margaret. It was good of her to try. But it wouldn't work. Amy's last thought was that maybe she really ought to tell Mim what JP had said about the glove. Then she sank gratefully into oblivion.

40

Mim took the stairs down one floor and went to her room. Sally wasn't there. But she had been. Pieces of her harem outfit were scattered around the room. The bolero was draped over the TV. The pants looked like two deflated balloons on the floor beside the bed. The transparent blouse was on the bathroom floor.

She checked the clock. Nine-fifteen. Over an hour to blow before meeting Kevin in the bar. She took the stairs down. The ground floor door opened onto the elevator hall. Mim saw Margaret waiting for the elevator. One arrived. The doors rolled open.

"Margaret, wait!" Mim called as Margaret was about to enter. "Wait! Please, wait!" Margaret turned around reluctantly. She stayed where she was as Mim approached. She watched in obvious irritation as the elevator door slid shut behind her.

"About JP's presentation…" Mim began.

"Yes?" Margaret straightened. She eyed Mim warily.

"Is it true that Amy isn't going to present JP's program?" Mim kept her voice neutral. She was overwrought at Barney's disclosures. She ought not take it out on Margaret.

Margaret's eyes focused on Mim. Her words were staccato.

"Amy is *not* going to show JP's photos because she just didn't feel up to it," Margaret said as she hoisted her briefcase onto her hip and turned away, signifying that the conversation was over. She pushed the up button to summon an elevator.

"She wants to give the program! The question is, why don't you want her to give it?" Mim asked Margaret's back. She had tried to speak calmly, but failed. She wanted to shake Margaret and scream.

"This is a *professional* conference. It is the most professional conference this organization has ever hosted. I asked some of the *professionals*—Benjy, Andy, the Taylors, to do a panel discussion in that slot," Margaret said to the elevator door. "Benjy says he's got more photos." Margaret slapped at the call button. Her movements were sloppy. She turned sideways, not meeting Mim's eyes.

"Look," she said tiredly, "Amy is a sweet young woman and she was JP's fiancée, but she is no speaker." Mim took a deep breath, trying not to let her anger show. She began calmly.

"Don't you think, for JP's sake, we should at least let her show his photos? As a tribute to him? This will be the very last time we all have a chance to experience his participation on that—or any other—expedition."

"Look," Margaret said wearily, glancing at Mim and then looking away. "I had to skip the dinner tonight just so that Amy and I could go over her program and...."

"You dragged Amy away from dinner on the pretense of looking at her slides when you had already arranged a panel discussion!" Mim shouted, losing control.

Margaret leant toward Mim and snapped back, "The panel discussion was a safety measure. I knew that her presentation would be substandard. And I was right! Frankly, we won't be missing anything."

"What do you mean?" Mim asked incredulously. Margaret shrugged.

"I know that JP was supposed to be a great photographer, but from what Amy showed me, I was not impressed," Margaret said dryly.

"Are you kidding? They're fabulous!"

"You've seen them?" Margaret's face took on an expression of surprise that bordered on shock. Her mouth worked as if she were silently talking to herself. Mim met her eyes and Margaret looked away.

"Well, I wasn't impressed," Margaret finally said. "Look Mim, I am dead tired. It's been a very long day. I've got to get some sleep." The elevator arrived. The doors rolled open and Margaret entered.

"What I think is that we are being deprived of an outstanding presentation," Mim loudly stated. Two horticultural writers who were walking by slowed and looked over at Mim and Margaret who punched in her floor. Mim could see that her jaw was working as if she might cry or scream. Instead, Margaret's mouth froze in an ugly twist. When she spoke, her words were as twisted as her face.

"I have worked so hard…." The rest was indistinguishable. Margaret struggled for control and moved to one side of the elevator compartment behind the closing doors. Now all that Mim could see was the back of the elevator.

"Those photos were fabulous!" Mim shouted to the space between the doors. "It's a real loss to this conference that she won't be giving JP's program! A terrible loss. Terrible!" The doors closed firmly. The elevator began its rumble up.

Detective Randall Murray walked into the hotel's crowded bar. Christ, where did all these people come from? He was supposed to meet his nephew Kevin at nine-fifteen. Kevin would be on time and, dollars to donuts, he would be with a woman.

He scanned the tables. In the farthest corner, he saw an angel, a knockout, with big eyes and a shining mass of chestnut curls. He couldn't see who she was sitting with, but he made a calculated guess. He headed for the far corner, maneuvering his bulk slowly through the throng. Bingo! It was Kevin all right!

Kevin introduced Philippa to Randy. After a few pleasantries, she excused herself. As she clacked away, Randy stared after her.

"Philippa Reed! Isn't that…? That's the one in the picture, only she lost the hyphen and the rest of her name!" he said incredulously.

"Yes. She goes by Philippa Reed now. She was in the picture you gave me of the staff at Withcombe Nursery." Randy just stared at Kevin, eyes bulging in his round, ruddy face. When he finally spoke, he said, "Hey, maybe you should be the cop and I should travel around the world! What's she doing here?"

"After Withcombe closed, she took a job with a nursery in the States. It's sheer chance that the guy who hired her is at this conference and wanted her to attend." Randy scowled. Kevin knew why. Randy mistrusted all coincidences. It was a mindset that came with being a detective.

"You got any other surprises for me?" Randy asked, drumming his sausage fingers. Kevin smiled.

"Nope. That's it. How about you? Have you got something for me?" Kevin knew from the gleam in Randy's eye that information would be forthcoming.

41

Mim stared in frustration as the elevator doors closed. Margaret had arranged for a panel discussion to take the place of JP's presentation.

"Demented old cow!" said a voice behind her. Mim spun around. There stood Philippa Reed, wearing or, as it stuck Mim, very nearly losing the top half of her plunging décolleté black dress. The material gaped, revealing the ivory curves of Philippa's breasts. A red coat was draped over her arm. Before Mim could say anything, Philippa spoke.

"You're with that Washington paper," said Philippa. She moved toward Mim, holding out her hand. "I'm Phillipa Reed. We met at reception."

Mim shook a hand so soft, she had to stifle an urge to look down and examine it.

"Yes, I remember. Are you enjoying the conference?"

"Yeh. Very much," Philippa said. She brushed away a curl that dangled prettily above one eye with a hand that was very small and white with long, perfectly polished nails.

"Do you work with Kevin?"

Mim explained that her magazine was another Washington publication but that she and Kevin were old friends.

"Friends?" Philippa queried coyly.

"Yes, really, just friends," Mim countered. "I gather you're not too fond of Margaret Stemple. The 'old cow' part. Unless, of course, you were referring to me?"

"Oh, no, not you!" Philippa laughed and two dimples charmingly appeared. This woman had everything.

"I hate her! Manipulating and…" Philippa stopped as if she couldn't find words with enough venom to express her feelings.

"Yes," said Mim to what was unsaid. She changed the subject. "Speaking of Kevin…where is he?"

"In the lounge. He's with his friend Randy. They're talking old times." She smiled again. The dimples reappeared in her glowing ivory cheeks. "I decided to leave them to it." Philippa stepped closer and conspiratorially asked, "Can we talk?"

Mim looked around for a clock and saw the time. Nine-twenty. Plenty of time until she had to meet Kevin in the bar. She wanted very much to talk with Philippa, but she wondered why on earth Philippa wanted to talk to her. About Kevin? After an evening of making eyes at Marcus? This was going to be interesting.

"Let's find a place to talk," Mim said to Philippa. She looked at the groups of horticultural writers taking up the chairs around the lobby. The lobby was too public. And she didn't want to go to one of their rooms. There was always the bar, but Kevin and Randy were in there. And it would probably be three deep in horticultural writers.

"Where?" Philippa echoed her thoughts.

"The hotel is a madhouse. I took a walk this afternoon. There's a place just a block away," Mim offered.

"That would be super!" Philippa said.

"Do you mind stopping at the ladies room?" asked Mim, cursing her teeny bladder.

"I was on my way when I saw you," dimpled Philippa. They walked across the lobby to a short corridor that housed a water fountain, telephones, and restrooms.

When Mim emerged from the toilet stall, she washed her hands. Philippa was standing at the sink, applying lipstick. Then, she fished a small jar of cream out of her purse. This she applied diligently, taking care to massage the cream around each cuticle. She capped the bottle, dropped it into the purse and looked up.

"Ready?" Philippa asked, examining her soft white, perfectly manicured hands. Her long nails were a soft salmon color.

"How do you keep your hands looking so good?" Mim asked, stuffing hers into pockets. She occasionally sprang for a pedicure because they lasted. The very few manicures she had ever had never made it longer than a day or two. Somehow, she always got her hands into dirt. "I mean, you're a propagator, right? Don't you have to work in the soil?"

"Yeh," said Philippa, holding out her hands to admire them. "Two things. Lotion–plenty of it. And gloves."

Together Philippa and Mim walked through the crowded lobby and out into the night. Outside in the balmy air, the two women slowed their pace to an amble. The mellow night made them feel easy. They might have been two old friends out for a walk. Mim's black uniform-sweater, as she thought of it, was just the right weight for the warm night. Philippa's red cashmere coat would have been too warm. She flung it like a cape over her shoulders.

The effect was dazzling. Five Japanese, businessmen from the look of their well-tailored suits, stared openly, probably hoping that the beautiful woman with the flowing chestnut-colored hair was a lady of the night. Philippa seemed oblivious to them. When she passed by with not the slightest notice of their presence, one of them made a comment in Japanese. The others broke into guffaws.

Mim and Philippa walked another half block in silence.

"Here it is," said Mim. Smitty's Bar took up the ground level of the Residence Hotel. They entered and took seats at a corner table. The bar sported a collection of antique signs, graffiti on the walls, and old photographs that had been artfully arranged by a decorator. Despite its Philly paraphernalia, Smitty's bar was not a hangout for locals. It had filled with businessmen, including more Japanese, probably from the same conference. They were into their cups and making what were probably raunchy comments, but thankfully, in Japanese. There was a trio of brightly self-conscious, thirtyish women wearing nametags, identifying them as participants of some other weekend conference.

They found a table in a quiet corner. Philippa draped her coat on the back of her chair. With that, her expression turned sly. She looked straight at Mim and spoke.

"You were watching me at dinner. Me… and Marcus. I saw you. Marcus did, too. He told me you were watching him."

Benjy Glover was enjoying bourbon in the lounge with Darrel and Jenny Taylor. It was so utterly and unusually peaceful. Then he realized why. His phone had not rung all afternoon and evening. He patted his jacket pocket for the phone. It wasn't there.

Then he remembered. Just before his lecture, he had taken it out and switched it off.

He hoped it was still in the auditorium! He excused himself and sped to the auditorium. When he opened the door, the great room was dark.

The switches for the overhead lights would be near the stage, but, after his eyes adjusted, the low lights along the aisle were enough to allow him to make his way to the front row.

Working from the corner of the front row, he bent and ran his hands along and under the seats. About halfway along the row, he started as his hand touched something soft. Someone sitting there in the dark. He recoiled with such violence that he fell back against the stage.

42

The waiter in Smitty's Bar was well over six feet. He had to bend almost double to take Mim's order for a glass of Cabernet and Philippa's for a whiskey sour. After he left, Mim turned to Philippa.

"I noticed that you and Marcus Tydings seemed to be communicating during the dinner. The reason I paid attention is because, as I said, Kevin is a very old, very dear friend of mine." Philippa gave Mim a look.

"And, yes truly, he is just a friend. But I care about him. He seems to have taken an interest in you. I guess I was curious to see if you returned the sentiment. It seems you don't."

"Oh, no! That's not true!" Philippa's great brown eyes grew wide and earnest. "Kevin is a lovely man. I like him very much!"

"But there's someone else?" Philippa squirmed at the question. She examined the votive candle glass in the center of the table, twisting it around. When she looked up, her eyes were pleading.

"Please! This cannot come out. Not now! Please! If I tell you, you can't tell anyone! If people, if Mr. Glover finds out, it will destroy us!" Philippa's eyes brimmed with tears.

"By something 'coming out,' do you mean the fact that you and Marcus are...?"

"Yeh!"

"Why? I doubt anyone would care," Mim said. Then a thought arose, "unless...is Benjy ..uh...fond of you?"

"No! It's not like that!" Philippa snapped. "It's business. *That's* the problem." Philippa opened her bag and pulled out the little jar of cream she had used in the restroom. Without looking at what she was doing, she began furiously massaging one finger at a time. As she massaged, she spoke.

"Mr. Glover has offered me a very good position for my....what I can bring to Glovers."

"I worked under Marion Petersfield at Withcombe." Philippa looked at Mim to see if the name registered. Mim nodded.

"She was my godmother," Philippa continued. Aha, Mim thought. The waiter reappeared with their drinks. When he left, Philippa continued.

"Withcombe produced the finest hellebores in the world. I helped develop some of them." She looked up as if waiting to be challenged. Mim nodded. Philippa seemed almost disappointed at Mim's easy agreement. She continued.

"The nursery shut down when Marion was killed. You probably heard about that." Philippa looked inquiringly at Mim, who nodded, encouragingly.

"It was terrible! The nursery closed. A nephew inherited it and he wanted to sell it. We couldn't afford to buy it. I had to find work and the only thing I could find at the time was at—Binghams— as a propagator. Binghams is the largest nursery in England. I think, that winter, I plugged geraniums for every window box in the UK." Mim smiled.

"That must have been a big change after working at Withcombe," Mim said. And a real come down after working at such a prestigious nursery.

"It was ghastly—the worst time of my life. I could barely make it through a day. To make matters worse, I was living in a horrid little bedsit in Lower Bodham. Ha! Well named, I'd say. That's where Binghams is located—if you know London at all, that's about 35 kilometers out the M5." Philippa took a sip of her whiskey sour. Her eyes traveled around the room without stopping anywhere. She began to describe her time with Binghams, enumerating the factors that made it the worst time of her life.

"I had very little money. All I could find was a dreadful bedsit. The landlady was demented. The room was not much bigger than the bed. My window looked over a car park. The one person I knew who worked at Binghams was on maternity leave. I had just moved out of a great, posh flat I shared with … with a friend." Philippa's lively description ground to a halt.

"That would be JP Chiasson?" Mim thought so, but wanted to make sure. Philippa dropped her head as if she had received a blow from behind. Looking down, she opened her purse and pulled out a tissue and ran it along the tips of her nails. After a long moment, she looked up, she smiled bright as a bird, and spoke lightly.

"Yeh. He was a great guy. Did you know him well?"

"Actually, no. I know someone who was a friend of his."

"Oh," Philippa said. "You mean that American girl. He got engaged to her. She's here at the conference."

"Amy Tomczyk," Mim offered.

"Yeh! JP was a good man. I'm so sorry. It's terrible what happened to him," she chirped nervously. "I still can't believe it." She replaced the jar of cream into her purse and crumpled the tissue.

"How did you hear about it?" Mim asked. Philippa looked up startled, a deer in the headlights.

"Oh! Mr. Glover! He telephoned. Because he knew that we—JP and I– worked together at Withcombe. We lived together." She looked at Mim.

"You know that. We split when the nursery closed. JP came here—to the States." Philippa glanced quickly at Mim. Then she looked across the room to where two waiters stood. She continued, chattering nervously.

"Amy, the tall blonde woman," Philippa was saying. "I'm sorry for her, too." She lunged for her whiskey sour and took a long draught. And coughed.

"Well, you must know JP was a great photographer," Mim said.

Philippa nodded her head. "Yeh, I heard you talking about his photography to that great cow."

"Margaret?"

"Herself!" said Philippa indignantly, meeting Mim's eyes. "She can't keep her hands off … off the men. She invited them to this conference just so she could get her hands on them."

That would be Marcus, thought Mim.

"Do you think that the men at this conference are taking a great interest in her?" asked Mim. If it was true that Margaret had invited Marcus to speak as a way to pursue a romance, it wasn't working.

Mim recalled how Margaret had entered the restaurant the night before, and glared at the table where Marcus and Philippa were sitting. And she had gone out of her way to walk around it.

Philippa threw back her head and laughed heartily. When she stopped, she was short of breath. Then, as if Margaret had been put in her place and there could be nothing more to the subject of JP as her former boyfriend, his new fiancée, or his unfortunate demise, she hurried back, relieved, to the more interesting details of her own story. She took a deep breath.

"Like I said, working at Binghams was the worst time of my life. Every night, going back to that sorry little bedsit and listening to that demented old landlady and her demented programs on the telly."

"Then, one day—a Friday it was. I remember I had no plans and I was dreading the weekend. A letter came. It was from Mr. Glover offering me a position at his nursery. It was brilliant!" Philippa's eyes shone at the memory of it.

"When he visited Withcombe—that was back when Marion was still alive—he said if I ever wanted a job, he'd hire me. And I did write him, but I never got an answer until then. That letter was brilliant!"

"Not only that. He invited me to go on a plant hunting trip to the Balkans. He said he'd arrange everything–all expenses paid! Fancy that! He said when we got there we could talk about the position at Glovers. If we couldn't come to an agreement, there would be no strings attached. That's what he said: 'no strings attached!' Of course I'd have been demented not to take him up on his offer. So I did." Overwhelmed at her good fortune, Philippa seemed to have lost the thread of her narrative.

"Let me guess," prodded Mim. "You met Marcus on that trip."

"Yeh! I did!" Philippa's surprise at Mim's perspicacity turned to gravity. Her large eyes became solemn. "And we had to keep it quiet. It wouldn't do for all of those breeders and such to know our business." She leaned forward so that the candle illuminated her face from below. Her eyes glittered in a shadowy elfin face.

"The thing is," she began in a low voice, "We couldn't let on that we were—you know. And right now, Marcus is not in a position to expand his nursery. He's putting all of his capital into research and development."

"For the time being, see, the best thing for both of us would be for me to work at Glovers," Philippa looked up at Mim to see if she understood the logic of this plan. Mim nodded.

"It's a great salary and I'll be on this side of the pond," she brightened at the thought. "We'll only be about two hours apart!"

"But you don't want Benjy Glover to know that you and Marcus are close because it's a conflict of interest?" Mim suggested.

"Well, yeh!" Philippa glanced at Mim as if she were mentally challenged. She lowered her voice. "Marcus is the *competition* and...." She stopped suddenly as if she had decided better of what she was going to say.

Marcus as *the competition*? To the best of her knowledge Mim had never heard Marcus mentioned as a bright light in hellebore breeding. She would certainly have remembered if Tate had mentioned him. And what had Katie said? He *dabbled* in hellebores. Barney had been more flattering: "he knows his stuff." Margaret had put him on the program, but Margaret may have had other reasons.

Marcus had certainly presented Philippa with a very positive picture of himself. Was she that naïve? Mim considered Philippa's glowing face, her utter confidence in Marcus. She was in love.

Granted, Philippa may have worked at Withcombe because she was Petersfield's godchild. Could she possibly be as naïve as she appeared to be? Did she really believe that Marcus Tydings would produce the hellebore that would set the horticultural world on its ear? Love is truly blind.

Kevin was nursing a scotch. Randy took a long draught and finished his beer. He signaled to the waitress for another. He sat back and twisted his head, producing a loud crack.

"As a matter of fact," said Randy, enjoying the moment. "I happened to hear something that might interest you." Kevin smiled.

"You're not gonna believe this!" Randy shifted in his chair so that he was closer to Kevin, the better to be heard above the din in the bar. "You remember that guy Wilson–McCoy Wilson?" Kevin nodded, all ears.

"And the old lady who got her face bashed in?"

"Marion Petersfield, yes."

"Turns out, he whacked her, after all!" Randy slapped the table with one meaty hand.

"I thought Wilson had an alibi." Kevin recalled his notes. "Didn't his employees say he was at his nursery when it happened?" Randy grinned.

"Two witnesses. And the cops judged them to be credible! Very credible!" Randy looked at Kevin. His eyes gleamed with more to come.

"Wilson, the old bastard, he goes and turns back the clocks. Don't that beat all! Just enough to give himself time to get back. Then, he calls this meeting with his staff at three o'clock so everyone remembers the time!"

"Didn't anyone have a watch?" Kevin protested.

"Guess not. They were working in the greenhouse on a big rush order. After the meeting, they go back to work. He turns the clocks to the right time. Nobody ever figures it out."

"How do you know what happened?" Kevin asked.

"After we talked, I emailed a guy there. Cop. He calls me back. Says there's a new development. A suicide letter!"

"From Wilson?"

"Yeah! Seven years late! Sent by Wilson's 'solicitor'!"

"To the police?"

"No. Turns out he's got a nephew or something. Solicitor is instructed if Wilson dies, he's gotta wait seven years and then send this letter. To a guy named Staples. Barney Staples."

43

"Philippa, there's something I have to ask you." Philippa looked wary.

"Have you met Chase Filmore?" The change in Philippa's ingénue demeanor was startling. She narrowed her eyes like a cat. Mim plunged onward. "He says, he was your seatmate on a flight to London two weeks ago."

"The chappie with the sparkly specs?" Philippa asked testily. "The one who keeps staring at me like a demented….? Words failed her.

"He's just trying to get your attention. Because he thinks he sat next to you on a flight to London. He also said your name was Pippa, you were an *au pair,* and your last name was hyphenated."

Philippa sat in a petulant silence. It reminded Mim of a young child angry at being told out. Mim waited. Philippa was staring blankly at the Japanese businessmen, oblivious to the effect it had on them. As Mim watched her face, she seemed to see thoughts pass through Philippa's mind. She turned to Mim.

"Okay," she blurted. "Pippa is my nickname. And that name I used…I was married. I'm divorced now—have been for years." A flush colored her pretty face as she explained in rapid fire statements.

"Marrying *him* was a mistake! Stupid sod!" She rolled her great eyes heavenward and circled them down to meet Mim's eyes. "See, I used my old passport. I used my married name for the flight. I couldn't use my new passport because they stamp the date in it when you come into the country."

"What about the *au pair* story?"

"I already told you, Mr.Glover isn't to know that Marcus and I are... you know," she trailed off. "What was I supposed to tell him?" She twirled one chestnut curl around a finger.

Mim waited for more. After a few moments, Philippa let out a long sigh. She explained.

"Thing is, I wanted to see Marcus. He arranged for me to fly to Washington three weeks ago. He met me there. I brought Marcus some of my plants, the ones I developed at Withcombe." Philippa looked to see if Mim understood these were outstanding plants, developed at a legendary nursery. Mim nodded.

"Bringing plants into this country is not exactly a walk in the park. You must declare them to customs and you must go to a special office for an inspection. There must be something called "a phytosanitary certificate" to bring them into the States. It's a great production, I'll tell you. Marcus had to be there to receive them. Thing is, I couldn't bring in plants for Glovers at the same time."

"Or Benjy would know you were giving some of your plants to Marcus," Mim concluded.

"What I gave Marcus wasn't what Mr. Glover needs," explained Philippa. "He has very different breeding goals."

"But maybe part of your arrangement with Benjy was that you bring with you what you had developed at Withcombe?" Philippa twirled her glass. For a long moment she seemed to be engaged in an internal conversation. Then she looked up at Mim.

"This is between us?"

"Fine," agreed Mim.

"Yeh." She looked at Mim ruefully. "The deal was that Glover gets everything."

"But surely Marcus has his own valuable stock plants. And he probably found some good material in the Balkans?" Mim prompted, watching Philippa intently, now almost sure Marcus stole from Tate. Philippa and Marcus were not scrupulous about how they acquired plants. Was it possible that Philippa had taken the plants from Withcombe Nursery when Marion Petersfield was killed? Was that what horrified JP?

"Marcus already has outstanding stock plants. And we found good material in the Balkans. What I brought him were some Withcombe plants that would advance his breeding goals," Philippa explained.

Glover seemed to be bent on pursuing a white Christmas rose. Was that what Marcus wanted to do?

As if reading Mim's thoughts, Philippa spoke.

"It is not a real conflict of interest because Marcus' breeding goals are very, very different from Mr. Glover's. Glover is very keen on developing a double white that really blooms at Christmas," Philippa explained earnestly.

"What about Marcus? What does he want?"

Philippa leant toward Mim.

"Red!" she excitedly said. "A Christmas blooming red! But here's the thing…," she lowered her voice to a whisper. "With fragrance! Marcus wants fragrance," she gushed.

Tate had wanted fragrance, too. Mim quelled the anger that threatened. She had to keep a cool head. She changed the subject. Mim remembered what Barney had said about visiting Marcus's nursery.

"While you were in the country, did you visit Marcus's nursery?"

"We didn't have time. Marcus had to be in Philadelphia for a conference. We drove up there. See, there was a meeting on hellebores," she explained. "Some of the horticulturists at Longwood wanted to form a hellebore society."

"Why didn't you fly into Philadelphia?"

"I couldn't! See, everyone was going to fly to Philadelphia for the meeting. We couldn't take a chance on them seeing me!"

"So you didn't attend that meeting?"

"No! How could I? Mr. Glover was there," Philippa looked at Mim incredulously. "I told you…we couldn't let anybody see me there."

"Did you visit anyone else while you were there?" Mim asked very softly. She watched Philippa intently. Philippa's eyes widened with fear. Huge and frightened, her eyes again conjured the image of a deer in the headlights. A deer in the headlights. A doe. And then it hit. Philippa was Bichette—the little doe.

JP's last words had been 'Bichette,' his nickname for Philippa.

Philippa smiled brightly. "I've got to go," she got up and began gathering up coat and purse.

"You saw JP, didn't you?" It was a flying hunch, but it stopped Philippa in her tracks. She all but fell back into her chair. She stared at Mim for a moment and then began to cry.

44

"You went to JP's house, didn't you?" Mim asked. Philippa hung her head so low Mim couldn't see her expression. Philippa's shoulders shook. She curled her hands into fists.

"Did you go to JP's house?" Mim repeated.

"Yeh," Philippa said almost inaudibly. She opened her hands and cupped them around the whiskey sour glass. Slowly and carefully, she turned it completely around as if something important rested on her performing this task correctly. She turned it once, twice, three times.

"Did you see JP?" This time Philippa brought her head up and looked into Mim's eyes with a pleading expression.

"No! No! I never saw him. I knocked and knocked and no one answered. I didn't know!"

"Didn't know what?"

"That he was dead!" Philippa shouted. People around them stopped speaking and looked toward their table. Philippa glared back at them.

"You knocked and nobody answered?"

"Yeh!"

"What made you go to his house?"

"I wanted to see him. There was something I wanted to say to him. Personal." Philippa crossed her arms over her chest as if to indicate that she would not elaborate.

"How did you know he would be there? Wasn't he supposed to be at a meeting at Longwood?"

"I told you. Marcus and me, we were there, too. Only I couldn't go inside or let anyone see me. Marcus found a private place for me to wait—where nobody could see me. He said he would be back in two hours, but it was much longer. Then I saw JP come down the corridor. I heard him say he was going to go back home to get something." To Mim's quizzical look, Philippa snapped, "I don't remember what."

"I sat there for a little while. In that little room. It was dead quiet. I had nothing to do just sitting there in the dark. And then I saw this cabbie drive up. Somebody got out and, then, the cab just stayed there. That's when I had the idea to go to JP's house."

"How did you get there?" Philippa gave Mim a look.

"I took the cab, of course! I gave the driver his address and the cabbie drove me there."

"How did you get back?" Philippa rolled her eyes.

"I took the cab back! The cabbie waited for me. I knocked and knocked on the door. When JP didn't answer, I finally left. What was I supposed to do?"

"Did you look inside—like through a window?"

"I tried. There was a big glass window in the door. It was so dark inside, I couldn't see anything. I was standing on the porch and the light was on and all I could see was my reflection in the glass."

"What did you do then?"

"I told you. I took the cab back to Longwood. It wasn't all that far, but it cost me! Forty-seven dollars! I didn't have enough money to pay the cabbie. But he was a good sort. He said I could post him what I owed. He gave me his card." She fished in her purse. "I have it." She handed it to Mim, who examined it.

It wasn't just the fact of the cabbie's card. Mim couldn't say exactly what it was, but she believed Philippa's story. If someone had asked her, she would have said 'because it all fits together' or 'intuition.'

Philippa had gone to JP's house on the night of the murder, had knocked and waited, but got no answer because, inside, JP lay dying. Philippa stood under the porch light. JP saw her and called out to her. Bichette.

"Did you hear anything when you were knocking at JP's door?" Mim asked, watching Philippa's expressive face. Her forehead wrinkled for a nana second, then smoothed.

"No," she said simply.

"And then what did you do?" Philippa looked annoyed, but not at Mim's question—at the memory.

"Then I went back to Longwood in the cab and sat in that bloody room for another bloody hour and a half until the bloody meeting ended."

Mim paid the tab. She and Philippa left the restaurant. The Japanese businessmen watched Philippa leave.

The women walked in silence for the first block. Then Philippa stopped abruptly.

"Marcus doesn't know I went to JP's house," she said.

"And Benjy doesn't know that Marcus and you..." said Mim, thinking 'are a number,' 'are friends'? She didn't finish the sentence.

"Right!" Philippa laughed nervously. "I don't want Benjy—Mr. Glover–to find out about us. And it would be better if Marcus..." she hesitated.

"Doesn't know you went to JP's," Mim finished. "I won't say a word to either of them or to anybody in this plant world. But Kevin is a very good friend. He isn't a horticultural writer. I don't want to keep anything from him." They walked on.

From the way her face worked, Philippa was about to protest vehemently, but as they rounded the corner they saw an ambulance parked directly in front of the hotel's main entrance. Medics carrying a stretcher emerged from the hotel. They passed with their burden under the lighted marquis, illuminating the recumbent figure of Eric Ferris, obviously unconscious. Even from across the small street, Mim got a good look at him before he disappeared into the waiting vehicle.

"I know him," Philippa cried out, wrinkling her delicate nose in disgust. "He's dreadful! Demented! He came to my room last night!"

"He did?" Mim asked astonished. That was outrageous even for Ferris. "What did you do?" She remembered Ferris stepping on Rose Redfern as he followed Philippa at the reception. But going to Philippa's room! It seemed like Ferris's obnoxious behavior was escalating. Like some disease. Weren't they always talking about serial killers escalating on the TV crime shows? Maybe aberrant asocial behavior was the same sort of thing?

"Luckily, Marcus was with me. He told that man to get lost," Philippa said with satisfaction.

"Did he?"

"What?"

"Get lost?"

"Yeh! Marcus said he'd take care of him if he bothered me again," Philippa said proudly. "Marcus is a complete gentleman. Not like some who can hardly wait to get into your knickers. Marcus treats me like the queen."

They crossed the street. On the sidewalk opposite, a little knot of people stood in the shadows. By virtue of her white clothing, one of them stood out. It had to be Rose Redfern. She walked up to a thick set man with straight, jet black hair. She must have said something important, because he turned away from what he was doing and began talking with her.

As Philippa and Mim got closer, Mim looked up and saw that Rose, speaking in a low voice to the black-haired man, stared stonily at the departing ambulance. J, a few feet away, might have been chiseled of stone. She stared into space. Only Wendy Hunsicker took notice and greeted Mim with a teary smile. Mim wanted to ask her what happened, but Wendy seemed so upset, Mim decided against it and entered the lobby with Philippa at her side. Kevin would know.

"There you are!" Kevin boomed as he strode across the lobby on cue. He addressed Mim. "I waited in the bar for you." Then he turned to Philippa. He seemed about to say something to her, then decided against it. Instead, he addressed both of them.

"I see you've met." Philippa gave Mim a quick little conspiratorial glance.

"Yeh!" Philippa giggled, but now the look she shot Mim was pleading.

"We decided to have a drink," said Mim, responding to Philippa's silent plea with a reassuring nod. "What's going on?"

"It's your ferret friend," said Kevin. "The Christmas rose guy—Glover–found him in the auditorium. He's been in there out cold since the lectures ended. Could be a heart attack."

Philippa yawned, unmoved by the news. "G'night," she said. "I need my beauty sleep." She bussed Kevin; then she moved forward and embraced Mim. "Thanks!" She clacked away to the elevator.

45

"Good night, Pippa!" Kevin called after Philippa.

"Pippa?"

"That's short for Philippa," he smiled goofily.

This was going to be more difficult than anticipated. Irritation, like bile, rose in her throat. Mim did not suspect Philippa of being anything other than self-absorbed. After talking with her and hearing her narcissistic take on Marion Petersfield's murder and her scant sympathy for JP's death, she could not fathom Kevin's interest in a woman who was as shallow as she was gorgeous.

As they walked toward the bar, Mim could hear an excited, electric buzz coming from both bar and lobby.

"Maybe the sauce béarnaise was laced with caffeine," she said, looking around. It was more than just the number of people in the lobby. They seemed to be all elbows and knees, moving about. A little loud music and some flashing lights and it could have been a disco scene.

"It was dead quiet before they found Ferris."

"Do you know what's wrong with him?"

"Unconscious. Looks like it could be a heart attack," Kevin shrugged his shoulders. "Hotel staff called 911. He hadn't budged since the last lecture."

"Good lord! I peeked into the auditorium when we got back from Longwood. I didn't see him. It was pretty dark, though."

"Why did you do that?" Kevin asked.

"I was looking for Amy." Mim explained that Margaret had taken her from the dinner, ostensibly, to practice her presentation. She finished by telling him that Margaret had bumped Amy from the conference.

"You're kidding! That's going to be a big loss to the conference," said Kevin.

"That's not all. I've got a lot to tell you. Is there anywhere we can sit and talk?"

Kevin and Mim stood in the lounge and looked around for a place to sit. The lobby was so crowded that all of the little alcoves were taken up with animated horticultural writers. Even if they could find places to sit, the noise level would make conversation difficult.

"Want to go outside?" Kevin asked.

"Sure. It's a beautiful night. And I don't need anything more to drink," Mim said. As they walked through the entrance doors, Mim saw Rose Redfern being ushered into a police car by the stocky, black-haired man she had seen before.

"Look," she said to Kevin.

"That's Randy," he looked over at the man, surprised. The man gave Kevin a quick wave, jumped into another car, and was off."

"Your uncle Randy?" Mim asked.

"Yep."

"He's with Rose Redfern!" said Mim in surprise. "Good grief!" She looked around for the acolytes. They were nowhere to be seen. "I wonder why she's going off in a squad car."

"Good question." They looked at each other, and simultaneously arrived at the same thought.

"Do you think that..." Mim started to ask. "No! I can't believe..."

"She must hate Ferris," Kevin countered.

"It's like he's gone out of his way to be rude to her," said Mim. "You saw him in action last night, but you missed him the night of the cocktail party. He stepped on her and then gave her a dirty look because she had been in his way."

"He's a foolish man to mess with a woman who knows her way around all of those phytotoxins."

"Wait a minute!" Mim scolded. "We are jumping to conclusions. Rose would never do anyone harm." As she spoke some of the half-joking rumors about the 'white witch' came to mind. The dead husbands.

Before she finished the thought, *Hail to the Chief* rang out. Mim jumped at the sudden sound of Kevin's cell phone. He answered, listened for a moment, and said, "I'm with someone who might know. Hang on." He turned to Mim. "What's valerian?"

"Valerian?" Mim asked.

"Yup. It's Randy. He wants to know."

Mim dismissed the first valerian that came to mind. That was a common name for *Centranthus*, the rosy red garden flower that shared a name with an herb. If this had anything to do with Rose, it would be the herb valerian.

"Well, it's an herb. It's used for its calming and relaxing effect. And as a sedative and sleep aid," she said, rummaging through her memory. Years before, when she had worked on an herbal cook book, she had made a valerian tonic with an alcohol base. She still had it in her pantry and used it every now and then for insomnia.

"Oh! And it was used for shell shock during the Blitz in London," she remembered. Kevin relayed this information to Randy. There was a pause. Then Kevin said, "Randy wants to talk to you." He handed Mim the phone. Mim more or less repeated what Kevin had just relayed to Randy. Then Randy asked, "I need to know how much of this stuff you need to take to overdose."

"Gosh. It's pretty harmless. I'm not an expert, but I do remember reading something about a woman who tried to commit suicide using valerian."

"How much did she use?" Randy asked.

"She swallowed a bottle of pills and slept for twenty-four hours."

"That's it?"

"As far as I know. I've never taken much of it myself, except once in a while when I can't sleep. I make my own."

"How do you do that?"

Mim explained that she grew the white-flowered plants and harvested some of the roots for a sleep tonic. Randy asked a few more questions, thanked her, said good bye, and hung up.

"He'll call you later," she relayed to Kevin.

"Maybe Rose gave Ferris valerian to knock him out," Kevin speculated. "It looked like they were taking her to the station."

"When Philippa and I walked back from the bar, I saw Rose go up to Randy—I didn't know then that he was your cousin—*your uncle*–Randy at the time. I saw her go up to him. She said something to get his attention.

And they talked for a bit. Then Philippa and I went inside. That's when we met you."

"Do you think she did it—put Ferris to sleep–maybe as a service to the conference?" Kevin asked, only half joking. "And then she turned herself in?"

"I don't know," Mim said thoughtfully. "If anyone had a reason to give him a knock out drug, it was Rose. But Rose's specialty—besides poisons—is herbal teas. It wouldn't be easy to give someone valerian without their knowing it. It has a musty taste—like old cheese or dirty socks." Kevin wrinkled his nose.

"Making a tea out of the dried plant is the easiest way to use valerian, but the taste is a real drawback."

"Is there another way of using valerian?"

"Well, I always make an alcohol-based tincture. It lasts longer because the alcohol acts as a preservative. You can use food grade alcohol—that's the standard way of extracting plant compounds for tinctures. It's much purer and cheaper than buying them. But I make my tinctures out of white rum. That way, most of what you taste is the rum." Mim reflected a moment, then continued.

"But Rose mostly makes teas. She sells them, too. For teas she'd have to use the dried plant," said Mim, thinking of the discussion of teas with Rose and the acolytes at breakfast. The only bottles of tinctures Mim had seen were the poisons made from hellebores.

"Wait a minute!" Mim said excitedly. "Sally told me she overheard someone say something like 'He's gong to sleep for a very long time!'"

"Was it Rose?" Kevin asked.

"She didn't see who it was, but she said that right afterwards. Rose gave her an accusing look."

"An accusing look?" Kevin sounded skeptical.

"My guess is that it was Rose. Whoever it was said, 'he's going to sleep for a very long time.' I think she gave him valerian. Then she told Randy about it. Why else would she be getting into a squad car? And why would he be asking about valerian?"

"Right," Kevin agreed. "I guess we'll find out more when Randy calls." They had reached the end of the first block. The block ahead of them was darker. Kevin took Mim's elbow as they stepped off the curb.

"Could you put the dried plant into coffee?" Kevin asked. She turned to him.

"Sugar—lots of it– might disguise the taste of the valerian! This morning at breakfast, Ferris held up the line for coffee while he poured spoonful after spoonful of sugar into his coffee."

"And then, during the break! He made a special point of having Rose Redfern serve him. Remember? He kept tasting the coffee and making her give him more sugar!"

"So she had opportunity," Kevin said.

"Yes!" Mim said excitedly. "Ferris, most likely to bedevil Rose, came to her to be served. She could have masked the taste of the valerian with plenty of sugar!" Kevin frowned.

"Do you think he overdosed on the valerian?" Kevin asked.

"As I told your uncle Randy, I've never heard of anyone having any kind of lasting effect from valerian. It makes you sleep and diminishes anxiety. That's it," said Mim. She looked around. They had wandered only a couple of blocks from the hotel and found themselves in a warehouse district. Big trucks were parked along the street.

"By the way, did Randy say anything about the things stolen from JP and Amy's office?" asked Mim. "I asked Amy again about the box of disks. She says it was a long metal box. It was filled with disks and it is definitely missing. All of JP's photos were on those disks in addition to some of his presentations."

"No disks. No metal box. After I told Randy what you said about the disks, he sent people back out there to look for them. They did a thorough search and found zip." They crossed another street and turned right. "What about plants? Did you ask Amy if there were any plants missing?"

"Yes," replied Mim. "She said, as far as she could see, they were all there."

"What did you and Pippa talk about?" Kevin asked. Mim took a deep breath. She had no idea how Kevin would take the information she had gleaned from Philippa, but she felt compelled to tell him.

"Well," Mim decided to plunge in, "she told me that she and JP lived together when they worked at Withcombe. He called her 'Bichette.' By the way, that is French for 'doe'."

Kevin stopped walking. "Bichette!" he sputtered. She could almost see the thoughts move across his face. He scowled.

"Wait!" Kevin shook his head as if to adjust his brains. "That's what...."

"JP said before he died."

"According to whom?" Kevin asked.

"Kevin, *you* were the one who told me that 'Bichette' was the last word JP ever uttered!"

"We have only Amy's word for that. Nobody else was there!" Kevin retorted testily. "Amy could have whacked him. And she is completely impartial!" he added ironically, enunciating each word as if Mim were hard of hearing. "Amy was there!"

"Well, so was Philippa," Mim retorted. "She *told* me that she went to JP's house on the night of his murder."

"Wait, wait, *wait*!" Kevin erupted. "Are you trying to suggest that Philippa had something to do with JP Chiasson's murder!" His face registered incredulity, but Mim noted he had switched from using 'Pippa" to the more neutral "Philippa.'

"She wasn't even in the country!" Kevin protested.

"Actually, she was."

"And how do you know that?" Kevin demanded.

"Philippa...told me," said Mim, having narrowly avoided using the words "admitted it."

"She said she was here a couple of weeks ago. And she flew back to England the day after JP's death. Chase Filmore sat next to her on the plane. They talked all night. She said her name was Pippa and that she worked as a nanny for a couple in Philadelphia..." Kevin gripped Mim by the shoulders.

"Why would she fly here two weeks ago, fly back to England, and then return? That doesn't make sense," Kevin said testily. Mim squirmed out of his grip.

"To make a long story short, she was bringing in plants for Marcus Tydings, but she has a job at Glover Gardens and didn't want Benjy, her boss, to know she had imported plants for someone else."

"Marcus Tydings?" His tone and the silence that followed revealed this was not a complete surprise.

"Yes." It was all she said, but it had been enough.

As Philippa, the goddess, tumbled from her pedestal, she felt Kevin's disappointment transferred to herself. The messenger must be slaughtered.

Kevin stopped walking and stood staring at a street light that rendered his face greenish white. He turned to Mim.

"Philippa did not kill JP Chaisson!" Kevin said with finality.

"Kevin, I know that," she said and realized that she meant it. Philippa Reed might be shallow and naïve, but Mim was convinced she was not a murderer.

"No. Absolutely not. For starters, she isn't big enough to bludgeon someone. I'm just saying that she was here. Two weeks ago." She continued.

"Philippa was in this country at the time of JP's death and she did go to his house," Mim said gently. Kevin said nothing. With the streetlight now behind him, she couldn't make out his expression. She decided to soldier on. She wanted to get it over with.

"Philippa told me that there was a conference at Longwood. She wanted to talk to JP and when she saw him leave the conference, she took a cab to his house. When she got there, she knocked on the door and he didn't answer. After a while, she left. The cab waited for her the whole time." Mim reached into her bag and pulled out a card. "She gave me the cabbie's card."

Kevin was about to take the card when he grabbed Mim's arm and turned her around.

"What's the matter?" Mim asked.

"Better part of valor," Kevin replied in a whisper, adding, "mugger." He locked his hand on her wrist, propelling her swiftly back the way they had come. She turned her head to look back and her knees turned to water.

Behind them, moving steadily toward them was a dark figure. He was holding something. A glove? A gun? She couldn't tell. All she knew was that the figure had no face. It was as if her nightmare had come alive.

With Mim's arm locked in Kevin's iron grip, they alternately ran and speed walked back to the hotel. When, stepping off a curb, Mim stumbled, Kevin dragged her forward until she regained her footing. Not until they reached the welcoming aura of light and humanity at the door of the hotel, did they stop. They turned around. The man without a face had vanished.

Now a chill, solid as a freezer door, closed between them. The immediate danger had been a distraction. Without speaking, they walked into the lobby where Kevin, having dispatched his duty to protect them, abruptly said good-night. Before she could respond, Mim was standing alone in the lobby.

Rose Redfern was also alone. She sat in the same alcove Mim had shared with her on a happier occasion along with the Acolytes, Katie, and Kevin. Now that seemed like an event from the distant past instead of, Mim realized with astonishment, just last night.

Something about the way Rose's shoulders sagged made Mim approach her. She saw that Rose's long fingers kneaded her scarf. Her face projected anguish.

"Is everything okay?" Mim asked. Rose's black eyes glistened with what Mim thought were tears.

"I don't know," Rose exhaled shakily. Some of the pain faded from her features. An expression of grim resolve replaced it. She grasped Mim's hand with icy fingers.

"Something terrible is happening here. Something terrible!" Rose fixed Mim with her black eyes. She sat up straight and lifted her chin. Her body language said she had something difficult to say, but she was going to say it– truthfully and thoroughly.

"I have just come from the police station," she articulated the words "police station" distinctly so that there would be no confusion as to where she had been.

"I went there because I gave Eric Ferris a sleeping draught—valerian it was. It was very wrong of me to do so!"

"You gave Eric Ferris valerian," Mim repeated. It was just as she and Kevin deduced. "And then you spoke with the police." Rose blinked at the interruption. She continued as if Mim had not spoken.

"During the break in the lectures this morning…" Rose looked at her watch. "It was very nearly yesterday morning, I was serving coffee and he—Eric Ferris–came up to where I was serving—deliberately. I know it was deliberate," Rose's black eyes bored into Mim.

"Perhaps you observed the other night–we are not friends," Rose continued in a calm, factual voice that was like a recital—probably what she had told Randy more than once. All the while, her voice continued calmly, her hands clutched and twisted her scarf.

"I gave him just enough powdered valerian to make him sleep for perhaps three or four hours. Five at the outside. Not a bit more." She nodded her head. Her shoulders sank. "I don't know what happened," she shook her head miserably. "I don't know why I did such a thing. I suppose I was angry."

"Well," said Mim sympathetically, "if it's valerian, it will wear off, won't it? It's safe enough." Rose fixed Mim with her snake stare. She let go of Mim's hand and held up her bony arm to consult her small, gold watch. "It is now almost midnight. Eric Ferris drank that coffee at ten o'clock –very nearly *yesterday* morning!" Her arm fell limply into her lap. Her fingers found the scarf.

"There is something else," Rose said. Fitfully, she looked off across the lobby as if trying to find something there that would make everything alright.

"You were at the workshop on Friday morning. You remember the vials of poisons I showed the class?" Mim saw that Rose was now searching her face anxiously for affirmation. Mim nodded with a chill that reached her heart.

"There was one vial of each of the poisons—helleborein and helleborin. Do you remember?"

"Yes," said Mim, holding her breath and hoping that what Rose was going to tell her was not what she feared it would be. But it was.

"They're gone," said Rose. "Gone."

46

Mim slept lightly, her mind hyper-alert. At a dull thumping sound, she surfaced quickly. Fully awake, she opened her eyes to darkness. She listened for a minute to rumblings and knocking sounds, surely nothing more than the normal workings of the old hotel.

Events of the previous evening came flooding back in bewildering confusion. Dinner at Longwood. Barney's confession in the truck. Rose Redfern's strange story. Walking with Kevin. The faceless mugger!

The mugger had made the nightmare real. Kevin had chalked it up to a thug in a ski mask—someone hanging around the hotel district for easy prey from out of town. What Mim could not get over was the pursuer's uncanny resemblance to the ghoul of her nightmares.

Now, jumpy and uneasy, she had a deep sense of dread. Being followed by a faceless man had been bad enough, but to make matters worse, she and Kevin had parted on a sour note because had thrown tact to the winds and told Kevin what she had learned from and about Philippa.

"She was JP's lover," she remembered saying. "Bichette. She was bringing in plants for Marcus Tydings."

And then there was the troubling encounter with Rose. After that, she rode up to the fourth floor awash in a mixture of misery and dread. She was sorry for her lack of tact. Sorry for blurting out what she knew of Philippa and sorry for upsetting Kevin.

All of it, circling around the unspeakable notion that Tate might not have been alone, instilled a premonition of something she couldn't name. She tried to find a word for the sense of foreboding and came up with 'evil.' Somehow it was too feeble a word for the magnitude of her dread.

A loud thump. She woke fully with every nerve tingling.

She glanced around swiftly, fearful of what she might see. Light from the corridor seeping under the door silhouetted Sally's sleeping form in the bed next to hers. Finding nothing out of order, she scanned the room from one end to the other. Everything was as it was when she went to bed. That left only the bathroom....

She turned her head toward the window looking for the square of light around the curtain that wasn't there. It was still dark outside. It was still night.

She made her way noiselessly around Sally's bed. The bathroom door stood ajar. With a pounding heart, she reached her arm into the bathroom and felt with her fingers for the light switch. She flipped a switch and jumped at the noise of the fan. Quickly, she fumbled for a second switch and was rewarded with a bright fluorescent light that illuminated every inch of an empty bathroom.

She took a deep breath. There, beside the sink, were their cosmetics, their toothbrushes. There were Sally's clothes in a heap on the floor—something she found at this moment oddly comforting. She turned off the fan, but stood letting the light wash over her until the thumping in her chest quieted.

Then she turned off the bathroom light and stood for a moment to adjust her eyes to the sudden darkness. A moment later she could make out the frame of light around the door to the hall. A piece of paper had been pushed under the door—the bill.

Her nerves were firing crazily. She leaned against the wall and closed her eyes, willing the jumble of thoughts to settle into order, willing calm to return.

When she opened her eyes, she jumped. Sally was standing next to her. She took a long, shaky breath and looked at Sally. In the dim light, her eyes were huge.

"Mim, what's the matter!" Sally said in a voice that tried to sound authorative, but came out as a weak plea. "Something is bothering you. Please tell me!"

"Let's sit down," Mim said. It took a moment for her to slow her still spinning thoughts and speak. Where to begin? How to begin? It seemed like it had all started when Kevin showed up on the train. There were Amy and Marcus. JP was murdered. Tate had been clutching a glove that belonged to Barney Staples. Eric Ferris! Rose Redfern! Tate might not have been alone. It was all too much and too confusing.

Instead, she simply told Sally about the faceless man who had followed them on their walk last night. She omitted the part about her recurring nightmare. Mim had not shared that with anyone.

Like Kevin, Sally was concerned about the incident, but she, too, thought the man was a mugger, out to accost out-of-towners.

"I'm sorry that you had to experience that!" Sally said sympathetically. "Unfortunately, it happens. Now," she said, patting Mim's arm, "what you need is some sleep."

"There is something I have to do first," Mim said, walking to the desk. The laptop was on, sending showers of meteorites across the screen. She hit a key and the computer began buzzing and beeping through its opening sequence. The photo of a snowy Cape Breton scene popped clean and bright and white on the screen.

"Why are you doing that now?" Sally asked. "You need sleep."

"It's got to be here," Mim replied. She opened JP's presentation.

"What could you possibly hope to find in JP's photos? Mim, look at you! You're a wreck. What you need is sleep! Go to bed!" Sally sighed. "You've gone over those photos a dozen times already!"

"You know, I don't really know what I'm looking for. I just know that it's here!" Mim began advancing the photos. The hellebore wallpaper that Amy had created in Photoshop appeared on the screen. A pink speck appeared, advanced, and blossomed into the title "Hunting for Hellebores."

"What's here?" Sally asked.

"The person who took Tate's plants is in these photos! Whoever took the glove is in the photos, too!"

"What? What glove? What are you talking about?" Mim looked into Sally's questioning face and realized that too much had happened. She had not told Sally about her strange ride with Barney to his field. As she tapped the keys, she ticked off the salient points of that incident, omitting the part about Tate's not being alone. With each new bit of information, Sally seemed more confused than ever. And Mim was too involved in her mission to stop and explain in greater detail.

Amy woke up to find herself kneeling in front of the toilet. Nausea washed over her. A monumental headache pounded at her temples. Each time she leaned over the toilet bowl to retch, the pain in her head ratcheted up, unbearable.

After what seemed like an hour, her stomach quieted. She stood up dizzily and made her way back to bed. She climbed back into bed and lay awake in utter misery, wishing she had never come to this conference, wishing she had not tried to carry on for JP, and mostly, longing for him.

47

Mim opened JP's program again while Sally sat on the end of the bed and looked on in dazed confusion.

"After the dinner...you went to Barney's nursery? Where is it?" Sally ventured. The next question died on her tongue. "Barney's glove was....?" She shook her head, too sleepy and confused to formulate more questions. She sank into thought while Mim opened JP's file.

Mim advanced to the first photo. Although she knew what to expect, her breath still caught at the sight of Tate and Joachim Muller in Bosnia. All around them, the ground was blanketed with yellow-flowered hellebores. This photo was similar to the one Joachim Muller had shown at the end of his workshop. In that one, it had been JP and Tate standing in the field of flowers.

While Mim stared at the photo, something triggered in the back of her brain. She tried to capture the thought. And failed. After a few moments of fruitless efforts at recollection, she advanced to the next photo. It showed the whole group standing in front of the inn.

Dead center, JP on the left and Tate on the right struck identical postures, each kneeling on the right knee. It reminded Mim of the football team shots you saw in high school yearbooks. JP had thrown an arm around Tate's shoulder.

Their faces glowed with pride, with pleasure. Everything about them—their smiles, their postures—radiated confidence. The way they had arranged themselves spoke volumes.

What had Katie said? They were the 'future of hellebore breeding'. Something like that. And now, both of them were gone.

With a deep sadness, she brought her attention back to the task. She had gone over these photos a half dozen times and found nothing. Yet she knew it was here. She couldn't say why or even what it was, but she knew these photos held the key to everything.

Again, she noted how the entire group split into two sub groups. It was a social graphic. The members of the insiders group stood actually touching each other. Those who hadn't been close friends before the trip stood at polite distances apart.

Mim had gone over this photo so many times, she almost felt that she had been in Slovenia and observed the social dynamics first hand. She could well imagine the warm camaraderie of the group of breeders who were friends. For them, the expedition would have been like a being at a party that went on for days. And she could also imagine what it would be like to be part of the group, but not part of the inner circle, to be politely included in the activities, but not in the after-hours gatherings in someone's room, in the jokes, the gossip.

Her eyes settled on Rose. Rose Redfern stood off center and seemed to belong to the periphery of both groups. The expression on her face was, for Rose, a very pleasant one. Rose would have been indifferent to the social subtleties. She would have been satisfied intellectually. For the time being, Mim chalked up Rose as a very unlikely thief.

Again, Mim was about to start on to the far left and begin again with Marcus Tydings and the members of the "out group." A new thought stopped her. What if JP was wrong? What if the person who stole Tate's plants was not an amateur as JP had said? Maybe Tate had found a hellebore that was so unusual one of the breeders coveted it. Maybe the person who stole his plants was one of the insiders.

This time, she started on the right side of the photo with Barney Staples. Barney was starting a new life. He had bought a field to begin his nursery. He would need good plants. Barney was wearing gloves. He had gone out of his way to tell her why and that it was his glove that Tate had been holding. His glove had been thrown into the fire.

What did that mean? Had Tate borrowed Barney's glove, taken it without asking? Barney hadn't thought so, but it was possible. Tate was always in a hurry. He moved fast toward his goals, not bothering to stop for obstacles in his way. But why would someone throw the glove into the fire?

Could Barney be lying? Was telling her about the glove a ploy? Was it his way of avoiding suspicion in the event someone remembered what his gloves looked like?

Had Tate been alone? She couldn't bend her mind around the alternative.

She perused the photo. There was Benjy Glover, leaning over JP and Tate. He was hell bent on producing a white Christmas rose, a double that bloomed reliably at Christmas time. He was so desirous of new material that he was hiring Philippa who had brought him plants developed at Withcombe, perhaps the most celebrated hellebore nursery in the world. JP had been repulsed by something that Philippa did. Had she stolen the plants that went missing when Marion Petersfield was killed? Benjy Glover was no fool. Did he really think Philippa would be the ticket to his goals, or was it the plants she could bring?

There were the Taylors, Katie Hiscock, and Andy Toll. She could not bring herself to imagine that one of these people had taken Tate's plants. She sat back in her chair, staring at the photo. It was here, but she couldn't find it. She felt defeated. Too much had happened. The circular nature of her unanswered questions exhausted her.

Mim looked up from the group photo and, again, a memory flashed, but disappeared before she could catch and examine it. She sat silent for a minute, trying to capture that elusive, niggling thought. It was gone.

She moved on to Danny Cullen. He had a small nursery that was well-established and respected. He was known to have the most unusual species and perhaps the most ornamental display of hellebores in the country. He was a passionate collector. Collectors can be ruthless in their desire for new and ever more exotic acquisitions. Had he seen what Tate collected and not been able to find it for himself?

In Cullen's presentation, he had shown some examples of *Helleborus odorus.* The species had been called "odorus" because it had a fragrance. Tate had been breeding for fragrance. Mim remembered her chagrin that she hadn't known Tate's breeding goal until Katie mentioned it.

Cullen's presentation had not been the only one that mentioned *Helleborus odorus!*

Suddenly, Mim grabbed the mouse. She reversed to the first photo in the program. It was the image of Tate and Joachim Muller standing in the field of yellow flowered hellebores.

"He used this photo of the yellow flowers of *Helleborus odorus* to make a point," she mused. She turned to Sally.

"He said he had studied hellebores for forty years and they could still surprise him! He said he had never seen this species in an evergreen form and with flowers so intensely yellow!"

"Who?" Sally bellowed in frustration. "You have lost me completely!"

"Joachim Muller. Muller is the world expert on hellebores. The world expert! Except for these plants that they saw in Bosnia, Muller said that he had never seen evergreen *Helleborus odorus* with flowers this yellow and this bright."

"So," said Sally.

"He also said that the species *Helleborus odorus* was rare outside Bosnia. And that the ones with bright yellow flowers were only from this one place they had stumbled upon in Bosnia!" Sally looked annoyed.

"They were in Bosnia the week *before* the expedition in Slovenia! The week before!"

"You weren't at the workshops. Muller showed this photo—actually one like it– and said that *Helleborus odorus* with yellow flowers grow only in this one place in Bosnia. Then, on that same day, I went to Marcus Tyding's lecture. And guess what he was growing?" Sally raised her eyebrows wearily.

"He was bragging about his brightly colored *Helleborus odorus*. He showed a picture of a row of them he is going to introduce as 'Sunspot'! He said they were evergreen! A couple of his plants were blooming and the flowers were bright yellow!" Sally stared at Mim blankly.

"Don't you see? Marcus Tydings stole Tate's plants! Tate brought plants he had collected in Bosnia with him to Slovenia when he joined the expedition there. After his accident, Marcus helped himself to them! How else would he have an evergreen *Helleborus odorus* with those bright yellow flowers! The odds are infinitesimal that he bred a plant like that by himself."

"The world *expert* on hellebores *never* saw a bright yellow blooming plant that was evergreen until he went on the expedition to Bosnia! JP and Tate were with Joachim Muller *before* they joined the plant hunting expedition in Slovenia!"

"Wait!" Sally held up a hand. "Let me *try* to get this straight. Are you saying that Tate got a plant that was evergreen with the yellow flowers in Bosnia and then he took it with him to Slovenia?"

"Yes, that is exactly what I said. And Tydings stole it!" Sally stood silently digesting the information for a minute. Then she asked, "What if he didn't?"

"He did. I'm almost sure of it! I talked with him last night after dinner. When I brought up Tate's missing plants, he pretended not to hear me. I thought he was guilty, but I couldn't prove it. This is proof!"

"What are you going to do?"

"I don't know," said Mim.

Mim was staring at the photo of Tate and Muller, standing in a field of yellow flowered hellebores. She was almost certain that it was Tydings who had stolen Tate's plants. Now Tydings planned to market an evergreen form of *Helleborus odorus* that had bright yellow flowers. He called it 'Sunspot.'

Mim recalled the strange conversation between Tydings and Philippa during tonight's dinner at Longwood. Tydings had wanted something from Philippa and she was afraid "he" would find out. Would that be Benjy Glover?

Tydings appeared to be ruthless in the way he acquired plants. If he had taken Tate's, it would not be his only dodgy acquisition. Philippa Reed, clearly madly in love with Tydings, had provided him with plants promised to Benjy Glover as part of her employment agreement.

What to do now? She began, idly, to click through the rest of JP's program.

Sally watched quietly as Mim mulled, only half observing the images. She advanced the photos automatically. Half way through JP's program Sally came to life. She jumped up and leaned over Mim's shoulder.

"Wait," Sally shouted. "Go back!" Mim reversed to the prior photo. It showed a few of the plant hunting party in the foreground. In the background were the mountains.

"That's the one! That's the one!" I forgot to tell you. There is a red dot up on the mountain! Look! It's probably Tate! Look up there on the right." Mim leaned forward and then leaned back, trying to focus on what Sally saw. All that was visible to her was a kind of multicolored texture that could have been anything at all.

"Where?"

"Right there!" Sally pointed to a spot on the mountain. Mim squinted. Nothing. Now that her forty-eighth birthday was behind her, she was becoming increasingly more farsighted. For the first time, recently, she had actually checked a large print book out of the library. She shrugged. It was pay back time. For years, she watched as her nearsighted friends coped with glasses and contacts. Now she had joined the be-spectacled. She couldn't even see the dash board of her car without help. And she had gone so far as to envy Sally when, in order to examine something close up, Sally simply took off their glasses.

"I don't see anything," Mim said. "I'm farsighted. If I get close it gets blurry and if I back off, it's too far away." She looked at the photo for a full minute. She sat back, momentarily defeated.

"Wait a minute! Photoshop!" Using the little magnifying glass symbol in her Photoshop program would make it easy to blow up a photo. She accessed the program and opened up the photo of the mountain.

Using the tool, she clicked on the red dot in the photo several times, enlarging it until the entire screen was filled with one part of what had looked to Sally's naked eye like a reddish spot in the rocky texture of the mountain. Then Mim clicked on the section of the photo Sally had indicated. A pixilated, but identifiable image appeared. Mim and Sally stared in horrified amazement.

"Oh my God!" whispered Sally.

48

Margaret Stemple got out of bed. There was no point in trying. Sleep was never going to come. She might as well get ready for the day. There was still a lot at stake. She just had to get through this day. Only one more day and she could relax! One more day.

In the shower, she let hot water pound on her stiff back and neck. Rather than soften her stiff muscles, the force of the water struck like a shower of pebbles.

She stepped out of the shower and turned off the water. She wrapped herself in a towel. She used a dry washcloth to wipe steam off the mirror.

Her face showed every second of the tension, the worries, the sleeplessness. The conference was a success, but it hadn't delivered what she had expected.

She looked into the waste basket where the discarded lavender underwear lay amidst tissues and crumpled papers.

She hated him. From start to finish, he had used her! He had charmed his way into the conference, and insinuated that the speaker's fee she had offered was paltry. And, like a fool, she had upped it!

Well, there was no way Perfect Perennials was going to take one of his cultivars and put it into production. She would see to that! A few words in John Bevin's ear would make sure of it. Marcus Tydings could just crawl back to his obscure little nursery wherever that was!

And then there was Eric Ferris. Why had she ever let him attend? She could have so easily prevented it! She smashed her fist down onto the vanity. Pain shot up her arm and unleashed a storm of tears.

Mim and Sally stared transfixed at the image on the computer screen. When Sally spoke, Mim was too far away to hear. She couldn't take her eyes from the blow up of Tate on the mountain.

The pixels that made up his image were so enlarged they feathered at the edges, but it was Tate. Definitely Tate. She would know him anywhere. One lock of his black hair fell over his forehead. He was wearing the red anorak she had bought for him. He had joked about the color, saying it would keep him from getting lost.

She gazed fixedly at the photo. One of his arms was raised as though he were greeting someone. Below him was a broad, dark gray slash. She accessed the Photoshop tool that allowed her to move from one area of the image to another. She moved the tool along the dark slash.

It was a ledge! Tate was standing, no, crouching, on a ledge. The hair rose on Mim's scalp.

Thoughts, memories flew at her. Katie had said that every morning, Tate and JP had gone off together early. Except…except for the last day. On that day, JP stayed behind to photograph the expedition. He wanted photos of the group and the scenery where hellebores grow. While he took his "atmospheric" photos, Tate went off without him. That was why JP blamed himself.

This photo must have been taken on the last day of Tate's life. The picture on the screen–not Muller's photo or the group photo–was the last photo taken of Tate alive.

The last day! She was looking at Tate on the last day of his life. And then it came to her with a terrible certainty. JP had inadvertently documented not just the last day, but the last minutes of Tate's life.

The realization hit like a punch in the gut. Tate, crouched on a ledge. High on the mountain. This picture might have been taken only minutes—perhaps seconds– before he fell!

Suddenly, Mim started to shake uncontrollably. Sally looked at her with terrified concern, then grabbed a sweater and wrapped it around Mim's shoulders. She put her arms around her friend and tried to turn Mim's face away from the image on the computer screen.

Mim shoved Sally away. She glued her eyes to the photo. She had to hold him there, keep him safe on the ledge.

Sally said something, but, to Mim, her words were an indistinct hum. After some minutes, the photo was replaced by a scene of Cape Breton in the snow. Mim hit the space bar to restore the photo of Tate on the mountain.

"Mim!" Sally's voice broke through now, coming nearer from far away. It was annoying, a mosquito buzzing, an alarm beeping. Mim kept her eyes riveted on the screen, on Tate.

"Come on. Please Mim! This is making you crazy! You haven't slept. You need sleep!" Mim registered dispassionately that it was Sally who sounded crazy. Her words edged on hysteria. She felt Sally take her arm and try to pull her up. Mim didn't resist so much as sink into her own leadenness. When Sally couldn't budge her, she reached for the mouse in Mim's hand.

"No!" Mim screamed, springing to life. She wrenched the hand holding the mouse away from Sally's grasp. With her movement, the image of Tate on the ledge shot away and disappeared. Both women turned to the screen. Tate was gone. In his place on the stony, textured wall of a mountain was the clear outline of a glove.

49

I don't think I've ever been as cold as I was on the mountain in Slovenia. I stood there shaking from the cold and from watching Tate, balancing on a ledge that jutted out over thin air. He took forever to dig out a pink Christmas rose. He was meticulous. Finally, when he was done, he handed it to me. I put it down beside me.

Now wouldn't you think he'd have been satisfied with his precious hellebore? There he was, twisted like a pretzel, balancing on a ledge over a drop off so steep I couldn't bear to look. But no. One wasn't enough. He had to have another one.

While I suffered from hypothermia, he spent five minutes fussing over the next one and making sure that not one tiny rootlet would be left behind. I remember my relief when he finally finished digging it out. I reached out my hand and took the plant and set it beside the first on he had dug out. It fell over and some of the soil came off.

"Be careful with it!" he snapped at me. Okay, I know he was touchy because he was afraid of falling, but his tone incensed me.

I hated being there as his lackey. I hated helping him after he wounded me, denied me, insulted me, and made me stand a foot away from a sheer drop off. I hated myself for being afraid and for helping him. But most of all, I hated him.

I felt this rush of anger rise up inside me. Even so, everything would have been alright if he hadn't had to have a third plant. Two weren't enough! He was so greedy! He had to have three. And you can be sure, the third one wasn't for me.

As he was digging it out, I said (and I couldn't control the anger in my voice), "Be careful, Tate." And he gave me that look. What was it? Annoyance. Yes. But so much more than that. When I got back, I actually consulted a dictionary to be certain there was no stronger and more accurate term for it. There isn't. The word is "disdain." Simple and succinct, it means "scorn, contempt, to consider beneath *oneself, to deem unacceptable." In short, it perfectly summed up the way I had been treated by JP and his little clique ever since I joined the expedition. And now Tate was treating me just like the rest of them did.*

Of course, at the time, I couldn't concentrate well enough to put a word to his look, but I deeply felt what he meant. Without thinking, I calmly repeated, "You really ought to be more careful!" And then I simply gave him a little shove. Not hard. Just the sort of friendly little jostle you do when you're joking with someone.

Now here's the thing. It was all his fault. That little push was not enough to send him over the ledge. But, of course, because he knew he was perching on that narrow ledge, he overreacted. He tried to grab my hand and reached out too fast and too far. It was his own movement that made him lose his balance. He wanted to grab my hand. All he got were the fingers of my glove. I watched his face with fascination as my glove slipped off in his hand. It was like slow motion. Perhaps it took only a second or two, but it seemed to go on for so long. And in that time, I saw the expression on his face change from surprise to understanding.

50

Barney Staples lay awake, remembering a spiteful letter delivered to him seven years after it was written. He knew it word for word. Now, though he had moved far away from his origins, he was beginning to understand that he could never escape them. Perhaps evil is carried in the blood.

Rose Redfern sat motionless. On her cheeks were tears of regret and shame. Why had she done it? Why had she stooped to react to Ferris? Too deflated to move, she was still sitting in the lobby where she had remained since she came back to the hotel in a squad car. She hadn't gone to sleep at all.

Margaret Stemple took two aspirins, lay back on the bed, and stared at the fire prevention sprinkler on the ceiling. This morning was supposed to be her moment of triumph. In spite of some setbacks— Marcus Tydings, first among them– the conference was an unprecedented success. Bitsy Kaplan had given her a big hug yesterday. Benjy Glover had left a congratulatory message. In spite of it all, she had a sense that nothing was ever really going to change.

Marcus Tydings had gone to bed soon after returning from the dinner. He stirred in his sleep. There were noises coming from the room next to his.

When the next wave of nausea struck, Amy stood up. With her first step, she tripped on the bedspread and landed squarely on both knees.

Pain shot through her. She lay in misery for a moment. She was going to be sick. She eased herself up and crawled to the toilet, dragging the bedspread along with her. When she reached the toilet, she pulled herself up over the rim and vomited. Then she rolled onto the bathroom floor and closed her eyes.

In room 415, Mim and Sally huddled before the computer as though before a fire. The first dull light of a December morning showed around the edges of the curtains.

Mim stared at what looked like a tan glove. Always a glove! She glanced sideways at Sally. Did she see it, too? Or had Mim's imagination come completely unglued?

"Doesn't that look like…?" Sally began.

"A glove?" Mim finished Sally's question with one of her own.

"Yeah! Can you move…" Before Sally finished speaking, Mim began to move the Photoshop tool along what appeared to be an arm.

Mim accessed the tool that decreased the image and clicked on it once, twice. The arm attached itself to a jacket. Above the jacket was a head. She traced the figure down to legs that stood slightly to the left and above the ledge. She sat back

"I thought…," said Sally. "Wasn't Tate…?" She didn't finish, but Mim knew that the word Sally had not uttered was "alone."

51

"Mim, are you okay?" Sally asked.

Mim nodded, vaguely registering Sally's question. She was staring at the photo. Okay? She wasn't okay, if 'okay' meant everything was hunky dory.

Enormous images crowded her mind. So many coincidences. Too many coincidences. Kevin on the train, telling her he had been in Slovenia with Tate. Kevin, telling her about JP's murder. Amy, serene and shy, trying unsuccessfully to deliver JP's program. A newly metamorphosed Margaret Stemple putting roadblocks in Amy's way and breaking down right before Glover's talk. Barney Staples knowing too much about her and Tate. Eric Ferris needling Rose Redfern and ending up in the hospital. Phillipa Reed's disclosures. Marcus Tydings!

And, finally, the most shocking knowledge of all. Tate hadn't gone off by himself. He had not been alone. The eyes of the phantom in her nightmare appeared before her. She realized those eyes had not been menacing as she had feared, but entreating her, pleading for...justice. Now, the glowing eyes faded away. She knew she would never see them again.

"Are you okay—really?" Sally's voice was shrill. "Mim!" she shouted. Sally's voice was the verbal slap in the face that jolted Mim out of her reverie.

"Yes. Yes. I think I'm okay. For the first time since I got here, I feel like...like I have found what it was I was looking for."

"Do you think...I mean...Should we do something?" Sally asked.

"I've got to think," Mim sat back. "What time is it?" She looked at the window. Still no daylight showed around the curtains.

"It's six o'clock."

At that moment, a resounding thump on the ceiling startled them. Sally looked at Mim.

"That's Amy's room! She's in 515—right above us!" Mim said. "It sounds like she fell."

"I'll call her," said Sally. She dialed reception and asked for Amy's room. She listened while the phone rang.

"She's not answering. I'm going to go up and check on her."

While Sally threw on clothes, Mim sat absolutely still, deep in thought. Finally, she came to a resolution. She had a plan. She opened up Photoshop.

"I know what to do." Mim announced. She worked quickly, manipulating several photos.

"Now, I'm going to wake some people up," Mim said as she closed the Photoshop program. She waved as Sally left to check on Amy. She removed the flash drive from the USB port, then inserted it again to make sure everything had copied. Perfect. Satisfied, she removed it and turned off the computer.

Mim telephoned Andy Toll who answered on the first ring. In a very few words she explained what she wanted the panel to do. Andy volunteered to contact the other panel members.

Mim had to call Kevin. She checked the clock. Six-fifteen. She would be waking him, but it couldn't be helped. When he answered, she listened to his grumpy and very un-Kevin like "what do you want?" Then Mim outlined briefly to Kevin what they had discovered. Fifteen minutes later, she was dressed and ready to go when a groggy but eager and heartwarmingly repentant Kevin appeared at the door.

Mim made coffee. While they drank it, they discussed what to do.

Mim left a note for Sally—probably unnecessary—saying she would be in the Juniper room. If at all possible, Sally was to bring Amy with her to the breakfast.

Sally took the stairs up to the fifth floor and headed to 515, Amy's room. When she knocked quietly, there was no answer. She knocked again louder. Still no response. Thinking it not a time to be polite, she pounded on the door.

"Amy!" She shouted. There was an answering noise that sounded like a groan. She called again. Then she leaned down and put her ear against the door.

"Can't..." Amy called in a weak voice. "Sick."

"Amy?" Sally called. This time there was no answer. She pounded again and waited.

Amy had said "sick." Obviously, she was too sick to answer. She needed help. Sally turned and raced to the stairwell. She didn't see Marcus Tydings come out of the room next door. She was halfway down to registration before he reached the stairwell.

52

Mim and Kevin took an empty elevator down. When they entered the Juniper Room, they saw that a long table had been set up at the far end of the room. Behind it were six chairs and a large screen. On the table were microphones. Another table held a PowerPoint projector. Everything was in readiness for the panel discussion that was slated to replace JP's program.

Along the right wall was the breakfast buffet. A few Horticultural Writers were already up and helping themselves to breakfast. Kevin went directly to the buffet and heaped his plate.

"How can you eat at a time like this?" Mim called to his back.

"A time like what?" Mim spun around to see Barney Staples.

"It promises to be an exciting morning. You'll be surprised," said Mim. "Please excuse me Barney. I've got to talk to Margaret." Mim hurried across the room to Margaret who was placing handouts on the tables. She snuck a look back at Barney who seemed to be dumbstruck, standing exactly where she had left him.

"Margaret!" Mim called. Margaret stopped and gave Mim a wary look. Her eyes were puffy and red-rimmed as if she were either very tired or had been crying. Or both. "I've got to ask you something." Margaret let out a long, weary sigh

"Can't it wait?"

"Actually no," said Mim. Margaret sighed again, this time a soft puff, and straightened her short, chic jacket.

Marcus Tydings smiled with anticipation. John Bevins, the representative from Perfect Perennials, would be attending this morning's brunch. He was *supposed* to have been at the workshop. Margaret promised that he would be there, but he hadn't shown.

Now, Marcus had a second chance. At the last minute, Margaret had asked him and, presumably others, to choose 'your most promising plant' for a presentation to show at the brunch. This was the chance he was waiting for. Perfect Perennials would jump on 'Sunspot' in a New York minute. They would put it into tissue culture and market it all over the world! It would be the first, but not the last, of the plant introductions that would bring in money and cement his reputation as the premier hellebore breeder in the country—if not the world.

According to the brass nametag pinned to the pocket of his dark purple jacket, it was assistant manager Frank Lowell who opened the door to Amy's room. Inside, they found Amy, her face drained of color, lying on a bedspread on the floor in the bathroom. She had been sick. When her eyes fluttered open, she looked at Sally for a moment uncomprehendingly, then a faint smile curled her lips. She closed her eyes again.

"Thank you," she breathed. "Please. Water."

Lowell turned on the tap and filled a glass of water. Sally held Amy's head while Lowell held the glass to her lips. Then Amy lay back down and closed her eyes.

"I'll call the rescue squad," Lowell said. He was about twenty-five, overweight, with hair and eyes of the same light brown in a complexion that suggested too little time spent in daylight.

"No! Please! Much better," Amy insisted. "I was so sick. Better now," she said hoarsely. "I fainted. I do that sometimes." With Sally's help, she sat up.

"It really would be best if I called…" Lowell began.

"Really! I am *fine*! " Amy voice was small but insistent.

While Frank Lowell paced nervously, Sally squatted on the floor, holding Amy's hand. While she did so, she looked around the room. Amy was neat. Unbelievably neat. Her suitcase rested, closed, square on the baggage stand. Sally wondered if Amy had hung her clothes in the closet and put them into the drawers of the bureau. There were no clothes to be seen. Nothing had been thrown over the second bed or draped over the chairs. In fact, the only sign that the room was occupied, other than the unmade bed, were some crumpled wrappers on the nightstand.

"I think it was the chocolates," Amy said just as Sally spied the wrappers.

"Where did you get them?" asked Sally.

"Housekeeping. They leave them on the pillow when they turn down the bed," said Amy. Her voice was stronger now.

Frank Lowell shook his head as if to dislodge a bird that had landed on it.

"Chocolates! There are no chocolates. I mean leaving chocolates in the rooms is not a practice at the Bentam. And our maids do not turn down the beds."

"You mean housekeeping doesn't leave chocolates?" Amy's eyes were huge.

"Yes. I mean, no, they do not." His eyes followed Sally's to the nightstand. "No," he shook his head decisively. "Leaving chocolates in the rooms is not our practice at the Bentam."

There were still a few stragglers, late-rising Horticultural Writers, filling their plates at the buffet when Margaret Stemple called the meeting to order. She glanced at Andy Toll, who gave her a let's-go nod.

"Good morning everybody!" she beamed at the group. Then her smile faded to an expression of sympathy.

"As you know, JP Chiasson's program this morning had to be cancelled." She shook her head sadly. "We are so sorry for this loss." She paused for a long moment. She made no mention of Amy who had come to the meeting expressly to present JP's program.

"However, we are fortunate to have so many talented and generous members in our group. This morning, a panel of outstanding breeders is going to give us a glimpse of the future of hellebore breeding!" Margaret gestured toward Andy Toll who was standing with Benjy Glover and the Taylors. Joachim Muller and Dennis Cullen approached the stage from opposite corners of the room.

"Please come up, take your seats, and show us the future!" Margaret beamed.

Margaret had also asked several breeders who were not on the panel— including Tydings– to email digitals of their most promising plants. She sighed. Photos of exquisite hellebores flashed on the screen to the oohs and ahs of the audience. Another hour and it would be over. It had been the best Horticultural Writers meeting ever.

She observed that the representative from Perfect Perennials was jotting down information on Marcus Tydings' plant, 'Sunspot.' She would have a word with him directly after the program. Should she have included a photo or two of her own hellebores? No. It was too early. After this, there would be plenty of opportunity.

Joachim Muller spoke up.

"Please," he said, "would the breeder of this plant please give us the background information?"

Tydings rose, flashed his perfect smile.

"That is my Sunspot. It is a cultivar of *Helleborus odorus*," Tydings said. "It is both evergreen," here he gave a slight bow. He looked directly at the representative from Perfect Perennials. "And the flowers are a bright yellow." Muller nodded encouragingly.

"May I ask where you obtained the plants for your Sunspot—that's what you call it?" Muller asked politely.

"I am sorry," said Tydings. "That information is...strictly confidential." Even with the deep tan, his face colored bright red. He sat down abruptly. But Muller wasn't finished.

"You say your Sunspot is evergreen?"

"Yes," snapped Tydings.

"That is very interesting and I will tell you why," said Muller slowly, patiently, and seemingly unaware of the abrupt disinclination of Tyding's response. "In my forty years of studying this genus in the field, I have only once found a *Helleborus odorus* that is completely evergreen. Furthermore, the only ones that I have found that were evergreen had this most exceptional yellow flower—very like your Sunspot," he said, gesturing to the large screen. "So I am very interested in the provenance of your plant." He looked questioningly at Tydings. Tydings looked away.

"May I ask you its provenance?" persisted Muller politely. He was sitting next to Toll who was manning the computer, "The reason I ask is that it is quite similar, perhaps even identical, to these hellebores." He nodded to Toll who clicked on the photo that Muller indicated. It flashed on the screen, showing Tate and JP standing in a field of yellow hellebores.

"I told you. That information is confidential!" Tydings jumped up and strode from the room. Muller looked crestfallen.

"I am so sorry. I did not mean to offend you Mr...." Muller said to Tyding's receding back.

"Tydings," someone offered.

" Please! I never meant to offend Mr. Tydings. My apologies," Muller said, now addressing the assembled company. "I only asked to know the provenance of his plant because its qualities are so very unusual. Very unusual," he said with emphasis. He sat down. Philippa Reed got up and left the room. Kevin watched her go.

Andy Toll forwarded to the next plant, a very double white that was streaked with crimson. It elicited a buzz from the audience. As Darrel Taylor stood up and described the parentage of his plant, Mim met Kevin's eye. She had filled him in on Tate's missing plants. Now, both were thinking the same thing: It was Tydings who had helped himself to them.

Kevin indicated with his eyes the door Tydings and Philippa had just exited. Mim shook her head no. Not necessary right now.

53

The last presenter, Dennis Cullen, was taking questions about his prize apricot double Lenten rose when Sally arrived, one arm supporting Amy whose face was as white as a geisha's. Amy sighed with relief when she sat down next to Mim. Sally found a place next to Kevin.

"And now that we've given you a preview of the future of hellebore breeding," said Andy Toll, the unofficial moderator, "we have a surprise for you!

"Before we do another thing, however, let's give our wonderful director Margaret Stemple a big hand for her tireless and excellent organization skills. This has been a fantastic conference!"

The sustained applause was punctuated by whistles.

"Come up here Margaret! Take a bow!" Toll commanded. Margaret, blushing, walked to the front of the room and bowed her head to applause and chants of "Mar-gret, Mar-gret!"

"Thank you!" Margaret said beaming. She made an awkward cross between a bow and curtsy. As she returned to her seat, the clapping died away. The chanting stopped.

Andy Toll stood to address the Horticultural Writers.

"This has been a great conference. Unbelievable!" He shook his head. "And our terrific director Margaret has given us free range as to how to end it. We were going to have a panel discussion, but we put our heads together and decided to do something else. We have a surprise for you!" He held up a flash drive.

"This is the program that our friend JP Chiasson would have shown you had he been able to attend this meeting. Would you like to see it?"

The assembled company shouted their approval. Some whistled. Others stamped their feet."

"I guess that's a yes," laughed Toll. "Is Amy Tomczyk in the room?" He searched the crowd. "Amy? Are you here?"

At Sally and Mim's urging, Amy stood up, a little shakily.

"Come on up, Amy!" Toll urged. Amy walked slowly and carefully to the front of the room.

"This is Amy Tomszyk," said Toll, putting an arm around Amy's shoulder. "JP's fiancée. We would like very much if Amy would show us JP's program." To Amy, he said, "why don't you sit here." He pulled out a chair. Gratefully, she sat down. Her face was pale and grave and her hand shook as she opened the program and advanced to the title. Again a wallpaper of hellebore foliage gave way to a rosy dot that advanced and became a title, Hunting for Hellebores. A hum of approval set off a round of applause. A smile lit Amy's face.

Mim looked over at Margaret who had tried so hard to keep Amy from speaking. Margaret seemed frozen in place. She shot a glance at Barney who was sat up very straight, eyes glued to the screen. Benjy Glover was nervously looking around. Marcus Tydings had not returned. Mim sat back to enjoy the program.

At the first of the wide angle shots that showed the panorama of mountains, Amy said, "JP wanted to show the kind of place that hellebores grow in." She appeared pale, shy, and uncomfortable, but her voice belied her appearance. She spoke clearly and without hesitation.

"JP said that he used people the way some photographers put coins in their photos to give an idea of the scale." Amy advanced photo after photo through JP's program. The audience was rapt. After the series depicting the development of JP's blue hellebore 'Aimee,' there was spontaneous applause. She forwarded to the next photo. Instead of her collage of hellebore flowers, it was a panorama of mountain.

Amy stared at the photo in surprise. Clearly, this was not in the program she had put together. She looked over quizzically at Mim and Sally. Mim nodded vigorously. Amy opened her mouth in a silent 'oh.' She advanced to the next photo.

Mim stiffened. This was the one that showed Tate on the ledge. Even blown up as it was on the screen, Mim had to use imagination to make out the two people on the ledge. Knowing they were there made it easier to separate them from the textured background. Nobody else seemed to notice anything unusual about the photo. At this scale, the figures blended into the background.

The next shot was the exact same mountain panorama with one addition. In this photo, Mim had used Photoshop to insert a bright red circle around the section of mountain where the two figures were. Horticultural Writers sat up, jarred from comfortable expectation. This was something unanticipated.

In this one, the previous photo had been enlarged to show only the scene within the circle. Two figures were clearly visible against the mountain. Tate Adkins crouched on what looked like a rock ledge. He had one arm raised and seemed to be holding on to something above him. Above and slightly behind him stood another figure. It was almost indistinguishable from the rocky background.

The room was silent for a long moment. Mim watched as members of the panel discussion regarded each other, then turned back to the photo in disbelief.

"That's Tate!" shouted Andy Toll, on his feet. "That's Tate!" Darrel Taylor rose, too, staring bug eyed at the screen. Likewise, Benjy Glover stood up to examine the photo more closely. Most of the Horticultural Writers had heard the story of Tate Adkin's accident while he searched for hellebores high on a mountain—alone. A buzz in the audience rose to a dull roar.

When Amy advanced to the next photo, pandemonium broke out. It was a blow-up of the second figure's head and shoulders. Mim had sharpened the image to make identification easier. Amidst shouts of recognition—some quizzical, some outraged–all eyes turned toward Margaret Stemple—or to the place where she had been sitting.

Margaret Stemple was gone.

Amy sat stunned. Ignoring the audience, the speakers who were to have made up the panel discussion loudly discussed this new development. In the absence of leadership and a program, Horticultural Writers rose from their seats, milled around the room. Some approached the screen. Others stood in groups, loudly discussing what they had just discovered. The noise level was deafening.

Mim and Kevin remained seated, serene in the knowledge that Kevin's Uncle Randy had been waiting in the lobby.

"…In medieval times a victim on the way to the gibbet wore a crown of periwinkle and the Christmas rose."

Penelope Hobhouse, *Plants in Garden History*

54

Over and over, like it is playing on a giant screen in my head, I see Tate's face and that look of comprehension on it as he slipped into infinity. He was quick to understand his mistake. He understood. He had underestimated me.

I heard him call out but it was very, very faint—like it was miles away. After that, just like that, all of my anger vanished. It was so weird! I felt cold from the inside out.

It must have been some time later when I sort of woke up and came back to where I was. I was surprised to find myself sitting down with my back against the mountain. And it was so quiet! The only sound was the wind. It seemed amazing, utterly amazing to me that I was alone. That was the weirdest thing—that, all of a sudden, I was so completely alone.

When my legs stopped shaking enough to stand up and walk, I got up and headed back to the inn. It was hard going. My legs were like rubber. I don't remember anything about the walk back, but when I got there, nobody paid the least bit of attention to me.

I know that I had my backpack with me and must have left his where it was. Without thinking, I carried back the two plants that cost him his life.

I was going to use them in my breeding program in honor of Tate. If I had gotten a really special plant, I would have named it for him. He had a good eye. And he also collected some Helleborus odorus that didn't smell like cat pee. I could have added a little fragrance to the genetic mix.

"An established (Christmas rose) becomes an heirloom, for in all likelihood it will outlive the gardener who plants it."
Elizabeth Lawrence, *A Southern Garden*

EPILOGUE

It was the third Saturday in March. A week ago, Sally had driven down from Connecticut and taken up residence in Mim's guest room, the better to work on their collaboration *Designing with Herbs*. They had spent the morning pouring over photos. Last night, Sally had stayed up to watch a late night rerun of *Sleepless in Seattle*. As a result, she was now upstairs taking a nap.

Mim had gone to bed at her usual ten o'clock. She was feeling downright perky today. She was enthusiastic about the dinner party she was hosting tonight. It would celebrate the publication of Kevin's new book *The Hellebore Murders*.

She went into the kitchen and saw that the bread dough had risen and was ready to bake. After she placed it in the oven, she began assembling the ingredients for seafood chowder.

She was a plain cook. By her lights, seafood chowder was a fussy dish. You had to keep the fish and shellfish from overcooking and make sure the different vegetables were thoroughly cooked, but not overcooked. To do this, she always treated each ingredient separately.

While the fish poached, she chopped onions, garlic, celery, carrots, potatoes. One by one, she steamed each batch. She tested a carrot and, then, a piece of potato. Perfect. Cooked through, but not mushy. She bit into a piece of celery and decided it needed zapping in the microwave.

When the celery was done, she combined all of the ingredients in a creamy fish stock to let the flavors blend. The warm kitchen filled with the intoxicating aromas of chowder and baking bread.

Next, she set the table. Through glass doors that led into the garden, she checked for new life and was rewarded with the deep purple shoots of emerging Virginia bluebells. She loved these ephemeral wildflowers. She had just finished an article about them for the magazine. The new editor loved it.

The garden sported a frosty, brittle crust that glinted in the sunlight and would crunch and buckle underfoot. Nevertheless, she would go outside as soon as the bread was done. She wanted to pick some Lenten roses for the table.

After she put the bread on a rack to cool, she poured the chowder into a tureen and placed it in the fridge. Then she washed and dried the big pot and put it away.

The sun was shining. It was tempting to grab her clippers and nip outside to cut the Lenten roses. She knew better than that. In Maryland, March is the cruelest month. It lures you outside with an inviting appearance of spring that belies its true nature—raw and windy, with the kind of deep, damp cold that penetrates through to the bones.

She slipped into her parka, put on garden clogs over woolen socks, and opened the door. Katie Hiscock, who had driven up from Fredericksburg, was just getting out of her car.

"Hey!" shouted Katie. "You goin' somewhere?"

"Welcome!" called Mim. "Perfect timing! I'm just going out to pick some flowers for the table."

"Can I come with? I need to move!" said Katie, stretching. "Hey, where's Sally?"

As Mim walked through the side garden, memories of the Horticultural Writers conference followed like a ghostly presence. Mim sensed that Katie, too, felt it.

"Have they set a date for Margaret's trial?" Katie blurted as Mim bent to clip a Christmas rose.

"Yes, June," Mim answered with relief at an opening to what they both had been thinking. Why the hesitation? She had organized this dinner as a reunion to celebrate Kevin's book and to commemorate everything that had happened at the conference last December.

She stood up and handed Katie a flower to hold.

"Margaret is in jail. Mrs. Stemple would have nothing to do with her. The old witch sold her house and moved to California. I guess that's where her other daughter lives."

"Harsh! Did you talk to Margaret?"

"No. Kevin told me. He called last week. He keeps in touch with his Uncle Randy. The police have a pretty air tight case against her. They took molds of the tire prints at Amy and JP's place. They were a perfect match to the Garden Center van. She's charged with JP's murder. She admits that she hit him, but she says it was only because she panicked."

"I still can't believe it," Katie said. Mim took a deep breath, then spoke.

"As director of the hort writers conference, Margaret had previewed all of the programs that the speakers submitted. She recognized herself in the photo in JP's program. So she 'lost' that program, but she knew it was only a copy. She knew JP would have the original."

"So she drove up to a meeting at Longwood. It was when they were trying to form a hellebore society. There was a meeting and a dinner. Margaret left during the dinner and drove to Amy and JP's. She wanted to destroy that photo of Tate and her on the mountain."

"She saw JP at the meeting and knew that Amy would be there after work. She went to their house, thinking that neither would be there." Mim stopped and deftly snipped three more blooms. "All she really wanted were their photos, but she emptied out their office to make it look like a burglary."

"JP came back—nobody knows why. He saw the van and came into the house. Randy thinks because JP recognized the van and guessed who it was, he wasn't more careful."

"She hid and hit him from behind—with a heavy brass statue that was on their desk," Mim bent to cut a Christmas rose. "She claims that she was frightened and just reacted out of panic...but, she hit him five times!"

"Oh!" said Katie, grimacing. "Poor JP!" Katie shivered.

"After she took all of their CDs and electronic stuff, she figured she was out of the woods. She told Amy she never received the program and thought that would be the end of it." Katie shook her head.

"It was pure chance that Amy had a copy! She thought she had lost everything in the burglary and then she found the flash drive in the pocket of a jacket. She couldn't remember how it got there. Pure chance!"

"The ironic thing is that Margaret only recognized herself and Tate on the mountain because she is so nearsighted. If she had left it alone, nobody would ever have known. Amy wouldn't have had to make a copy on my computer. Sally wouldn't have recognized Tate on the mountain…."

"You saw what happened at the conference. Nobody noticed a thing in that photo. It wasn't until they saw the section we enlarged that anybody could even make out Tate and Margaret. But she didn't know that. She must have thought that when that photo was blown up on the screen, everybody would see her together with Tate." Katie nodded.

"I'm nearsighted and I wouldn't have noticed anything if you hadn't circled it," Katie said.

"You know what I don't get?" Katie asked. "Why did she dump all of their stuff so close to their house?"

"I wondered about that, too. It turned out she couldn't leave it in the van. She had driven up alone, but she had to pick up Mitch, her boss, on the way home. He was up there buying plants for the Garden Center."

Mim put her Felco pruner into the back pocket of her jeans. It was a practice that had made a hole in the pocket so that the tip of the pruner poked out. All of her jeans had an identical hole in the right back pocket. They turned toward the house.

"Margaret is also charged with attempted murder. Eric Ferris. It appears that she tried to poison him. She took one of Rose Redfern's poisons and poured it in his ear!"

"You're kidding! Why his ear?" Katie asked.

"Well, she was a literature major. She was probably thinking of Socrates. Or Hamlet's uncle."

"Why poison Ferris?" Katie smiled, "I mean we've all considered it…"

"Somehow, Ferris got a hold of a copy of JP's program. It was probably the one that Amy made and put on one of my flash drives. He wore it around his neck to taunt her." Katie's eyes lit up.

"Remember Amy and I found him digging around in the trash?" asked Katie. "Maybe she tossed JP's program and he saw her do it!" Mim nodded.

"Right! Margaret also drugged Amy with chocolates," Mim added.

"How did she manage that?" Katie asked.

"As conference director, she had to order rooms for the speakers. It turned out that she had the room next to Amy's *and* the key to the door that adjoined their two rooms. Just in case she needed it!"

"What about...?" Katie met Mim's eyes and Mim finished the question.

"Tate? Margaret won't budge from her statement that it was an accident, that Tate fell and she was too traumatized to deal with it!" Mim bent down and snipped a Lenten rose briskly. Wordlessly, she handed the stem to Katie. Rapidly, she cut two more, handing each to Katie.

"What do you think?" Katie asked. Mim's look said, 'do you have to ask?'

"She pushed him,"said Mim tersely. "Why else would she murder JP and try to poison Eric and Amy!"

"How are Eric and Amy now?" Katie asked.

"Amy, you'll see tonight!" Mim stood up and smiled. "As for Eric, in a strange way, Margaret did him a favor. Once they got him into the hospital and took care of the immediate problem, they diagnosed porphyria! It's a condition that can make people behave weirdly! Apparently, alcohol exacerbates it."

"Did they cure him? Will he be nice now?" Katie asked.

"I don't know. I hope so for his sake—actually for all of our sakes!" Mim laughed. She looked at the bouquet approvingly. "Let's go inside. You must be freezing!"

"Wow!" Katie shouted. She had stopped walking. She stooped to get a better look at the buds on a hellebore next to the path.

"Those are Tate's!" Mim said proudly. The prominent buds were closed and faint blue veins called to Mim's mind the translucent skin of an infant. But the buds also promised color, gold or perhaps salmon. "These are a little late for Lenten roses. Tate must have crossed them with something that blooms later. I was hoping they'd all be open when you got here."

"Well, take a picture..." Katie choked up. "...when they do!" She stood up and gave Mim a gentle hug, careful not to crush what was now a bouquet.

"Whatever happened to that gorgeous cowboy?" Chase asked. They were assembled in Mim's living room, enjoying a good Cabernet. Mim had just held out a glass to Chase who seized it and took a long draught.

Chase, who never did anything by halves, had come directly from a wedding and reception for which he had done the flowers. He was flat out exhausted, sprawled in an arm chair.

"You mean Marcus Tydings?" Mim asked. Chase nodded in a way that affirmed her question was gratuitous.

"And that gorgeous English woman—the one with the spike heels?" Katie asked.

"Pippa," put in Chase knowingly.

"The word is that Pippa—Philippa–that's her name, was working at Glovers Gardens, but she wasn't happy there nor, it seems, was Benjy happy with her," Mim said. She glanced sideways at Kevin. He caught her glance and smiled affably. Pippa was ancient history.

"She went back to England," put in Sally. "She's working as an *au pair.*"

"As for Tydings," said Mim. "He seems to have dropped off the planet. Nobody has seen or heard from him from the moment he stormed out of the hort writers conference. But even if he did show up, he's *persona non grata.* Nobody will do business with him." Mim held up a finger. "But! Remember the plant Tydings called 'Sunspot'?"

"Yeah!" said Sally. Chase nodded. Kevin smiled.

"Well, Joachim Muller is providing Perfect Perennials with it—it's actually an evergreen *Helleborus odorus.* They're going to put it into tissue culture and market it! And...!" Mim paused to make sure everyone was listening. "The profits are going to finance an annual Adkins-Chiasson Memorial Lecture at Longwood!"

Before anyone could react, the doorbell chimed.

"Good! They're here! They drove down from Philadelphia." To Chase's inquiring look, Mim said, "Amy. And Barney."

An Excerpt from:
Murder House, a Cape Breton Mystery

The Angus MacAskill ferry, named for the Cape Breton giant, can transport up to nine cars across the narrowest part of St.Ann's Bay. The ferry ride saves having to make the longer drive around the bay on the Cabot Trail. The crossing takes only about five minutes. For those waiting to board on the Englishtown or the Jersey Cove side, it is just enough time to catch up on the latest gossip.

On the afternoon of June 13, 1976, both landings were abuzz with talk of David Farquhar, night watchman at Little River. He had been found dead the day before by the lobstermen coming back to the wharf after a morning's fishing. Dave had been young and apparently healthy, though he drank more than was good for him. There was no sign of foul play.

This afternoon, the very lobsterman who had first found Farquhar, Duncan Patterson, was waiting for the ferry, the last in a line of four cars on the Englishtown side. Acutely aware of all eyes upon him, he got out of his Ford pick-up and walked slowly and with dignity to the car in front of him, a white Chevrolet sedan that belonged to Sheila MacDonald, his niece.

She had already rolled down the driver's side window. When he reached her car, he leant into the window and said good morning. He waited for her to ask. Eager for information, she spoke without preamble.

"It was the shock that killed him, wasn't it?"

"For sure," he answered and looked over the bay fringed with apple green marsh grasses. "Ye know it's been three months now since he... ye know."

"Millie Oliver says he hasn't been sober since..." said Sheila

Duncan shook his head, thinking how Dave Farquhar had been found, running down the Cabot Trail, howling and covered in blood and vomit. Duncan shuddered.

"It was too much for his heart."

"Who could know he had a problem with his heart, eh? Him, not yet thirty," Sheila said. Then, lowering her voice, she said, "I heard he was looking at her picture."

"Where'd ye hear that?" Duncan felt exasperated awe at the speed of the Cape Breton grapevine.

"Millie told Ma."

Duncan looked over at the little refreshment stand on the landing. It was run by the Oliver family. Fifteen-year old Millie helped out after school and on vacations. Beyond the stand, he saw the ferry was on its way back from Jersey Cove.

"Hello to your ma," he said, more curtly than he intended, before turning and starting back to his truck.

"It isn't true then?" Sheila called after him. He stopped. She had poked her head out the car window. She was blonde like her ma with big, curious blue eyes.

"It is true," he said kindly. "Was a page from the *Cape Breton Post*. The one that came out day after she...." He found he could not use the word "died." It was so utterly inadequate for the gruesome manner of Marie Campbell's murder.